Praise for Janet Tronstad

JANET TRONSTAD

Sugar Plums for Dry Creek

At Home in Dry Creek

Steeple
Hill®

Published by Steeple Hill Books™

STEEPLE HILL BOOKS

Steeple Hill®

Recycling programs for this product may not exist in your area.

ISBN-13: 978-0-373-65142-9

SUGAR PLUMS FOR DRY CREEK AND
AT HOME IN DRY CREEK

SUGAR PLUMS FOR DRY CREEK
Copyright © 2005 by Janet Tronstad

AT HOME IN DRY CREEK
Copyright © 2006 by Janet Tronstad

CONTENTS

Books by Janet Tronstad

Love Inspired

*An Angel for Dry Creek
*A Gentleman for Dry Creek
*A Bride for Dry Creek
*A Rich Man for Dry Creek
*A Hero for Dry Creek
*A Baby for Dry Creek
*A Dry Creek Christmas
*Sugar Plums for Dry Creek
*At Home in Dry Creek
**The Sisterhood of the
    Dropped Stitches
*A Match Made in Dry Creek
*Shepherds Abiding in Dry Creek
**A Dropped Stitches Christmas
*Dry Creek Sweethearts
**A Heart for the Dropped Stitches
*A Dry Creek Courtship
*Snowbound in Dry Creek
**A Dropped Stitches Wedding
*Small-Town Brides
  "A Dry Creek Wedding"
*Silent Night in Dry Creek
*Wife Wanted in Dry Creek
Doctor Right

Steeple Hill
Love Inspired Historical

*Calico Christmas
    at Dry Creek
*Mistletoe Courtship
  "Christmas Bells
    for Dry Creek"

*Dry Creek
**Dropped Stitches

JANET TRONSTAD

grew up on a small farm in central Montana. One of her favorite things to do was to visit her grandfather's bookshelves, where he had a large collection of Zane Grey novels. She's always loved a good story. Today, Janet lives in Pasadena, California, where she is a full-time writer.

SUGAR PLUMS FOR DRY CREEK

I can do all things through Christ
which strengtheneth me.
—*Philippians* 4:13

This book is dedicated to my grandfather,
Harold Norris, who shared his love of
a good book with me.

Chapter One

Lizette Baker wished her mother had worried less about showing her the perfect way to pirouette and more about teaching her a few practical things, like how to coax more warm air out of her old car's heating system and how to put snow chains on tires so smooth they slipped on every icy patch she found as she drove east on Interstate 94 in southern Montana.

A colder, frostier place Lizette had never seen. Even with a wool scarf wrapped around her neck and mittens on her hands, she couldn't stay warm. It was only mid-November and it was already less than ten degrees Fahrenheit outside. No wonder hers was the only car in sight as she drove along this road hoping to reach Dry Creek, Montana, before her heater gave out completely.

The attendant in the gas station she'd stopped at back in Forsyth had offered to call a mechanic to repair her heater. Another man, with a dirty blond beard and a snake tattooed on his arm, had made a different suggestion.

"Why put out good money for a mechanic?" he'd asked in an artificially friendly voice. Lizette hadn't liked the way he was looking at her. "I'll keep you warm if you give me a ride down the road a bit. I'm looking for my kids." He'd reached into his pocket and pulled out a worn snapshot, which he'd then shoved at her. "Kids need to see their old man. You haven't seen them, have you?"

Lizette would have rather given the snake on the man's arm a ride than the man himself, but she hadn't wanted any trouble, so she'd politely looked at the picture of his two children.

"No, but they're beautiful children." And the children probably would have been beautiful, she thought, if they hadn't looked so skinny and scared. "Sorry about the ride, but I have a car full of boxes. Moving, you know."

Lizette hoped the man hadn't looked at her car too closely. If she'd shifted the boxes around a little, she could have cleared enough room in the front seat for a passenger.

The tattooed man hadn't said anything more, but he'd put the picture back in his pocket.

After a moment's silence, the attendant had finally asked, "So do you want the mechanic to come over to fix that heater? He doesn't keep regular hours, but he can get down here in fifteen minutes flat."

Lizette had shaken her head. "Thanks though."

She barely had enough money left to get her ballet school going; she couldn't afford to fix anything that wasn't actually falling off the car. The heater was spitting out just enough warm air to keep her from freezing to death, so it would have to do for now.

She'd looked out her rearview mirror as she'd pulled away from the gas station and had seen the man with the snake on his arm watching her leave.

It wasn't the first time since she'd left Seattle that Lizette had wondered if she was making a mistake.

Her whole life had changed in the last few months though, and she needed a new beginning. Besides, where else could she get free rent to start her own business? Lizette had learned to be frugal from her mother, Jacqueline. Indeed, it had been Jacqueline who'd found the ad for free space.

Lizette had not known until recently that her mother had saved for years with the hope that they could open their own ballet school someday. When Lizette's father had died, years ago, Jacqueline had given up the fledgling ballet school she and her husband had started and had taken a steady job in a bakery. At the time, Lizette had not realized the sacrifice her mother was making to keep them secure, probably because Jacqueline never complained about giving up the school. When she'd first tied on her bakery apron, she'd even managed to joke. She said she wished her husband could see her. He'd say she was really a Baker at last.

Her mother had made the job sound as though it was exactly what she wanted, and Lizette had believed her back then. Maybe that was because Lizette herself was happy. The bakery was a playground to her. She loved the warm smells and all of the chatter of customers. The bakers even got into the habit of asking Lizette to try out their new recipes. They said she had a taste for what the customers would like.

Giving up that ballet school was only one of the many sacrifices Jacqueline Baker had made for Lizette over the years. Lizette hadn't even known about some of them until her mother had been diagnosed with terminal cancer. That's when she'd started giving instructions to Lizette.

"You'll find fifteen thousand dollars in this safety deposit box," Jacqueline told her as she handed Lizette a key. "I wanted it to be more, but it'll get that school of ours started if we're careful. Then there'll be no need for you to work at the bakery—you'll be free to dance. The money should cover everything for a year. We don't need anything expensive—just something with good floors and lots of room for practice."

Lizette was amazed and touched. So that was why

her mother'd never spent much money on herself, not even after she became the manager of the bakery and started earning a better salary. Lizette could see how important it was to her mother to start what she was calling the Baker School of Ballet.

As the pain increased and Jacqueline went into the hospital, she talked more and more about the school. She worried that Lizette had not been able to find an affordable space to rent even though she'd gone out to look at several places. Jacqueline even asked the hospital chaplain to come and pray about it.

Lizette was surprised her mother was interested in praying. Jacqueline had shown little use for God over the years, saying she could not understand a God who took a man away in his prime. Unspoken was the complaint that He had also robbed her of her beloved ballet school at the same time.

But now, at the end, who did her mother want to talk to? The chaplain.

If they hadn't been in a hospital when her mother asked to speak to a minister, Lizette wouldn't even have known how to find one. She herself had never been to church in her life. Sunday was the one day she could spend with her mother, and Jacqueline made it clear she didn't want to go to church, so Lizette never even suggested it.

Yet on her deathbed Lizette's mother spent hours talking to the chaplain about her hopes for a ballet school. Lizette quietly apologized to the man one afternoon when the two of them had left the room so the nurse could give Jacqueline an injection. Lizette knew the chaplain was a busy man, and she doubted he was interested in ballet schools—especially ones that didn't even exist except in a dying woman's dreams.

The chaplain waved Lizette's apology aside, "Your mother's talking about her life when she talks about that school. That's what I'm here for. It's important."

In the last days, the soft sound of the chaplain's praying was all that quieted Jacqueline. Well, Lizette acknowledged, toward the end it was also those expensive injections that kept her mother comfortable. Lizette never did tell Jacqueline that those injections weren't covered by their insurance plan.

It didn't take much money to open a ballet school, Lizette told herself when her mother kept asking about sites. By then, the extra hospital bills had used up the entire fifteen thousand dollars, and Lizette's small savings account as well. Lizette said a prayer of her own when she promised to open the school in the fall.

"You're right. Fall is the best time of the year to start a ballet school," Jacqueline said as she lay in her hospital bed. "We can start our students right out on our simplified version of the Nutcracker ballet, and they'll be hooked. Every young girl wants to be Clara. Plus we already have all of those costumes we made for you and the other girls when you were in dance school."

Part of the deal in the sale of her parents' ballet school had been that the new owner, Madame Aprele, would give Lizette free lessons. Lizette had studied ballet for years, and even though she didn't have her mother's natural grace, she still did very well.

"And you'll be there to watch." Lizette dreamed a little dream of her own. "You've always loved the Nutcracker."

Her mother smiled. "I can almost see it now. I remember the first time I danced Clara as a five-year-old. And later, the Sugar Plum Fairy. What I wouldn't give to dance it all again!"

Lizette vowed she'd find a way to open a school even without money. Then maybe her mother would get stronger and they could run that school together. With all of the praying the chaplain was doing, Lizette figured they were due a miracle.

Later that week Jacqueline claimed she'd found a miracle—right in the middle of the classified section of *The Seattle Times*. The ad offering free rent for new businesses had been buried in the used furniture section of the paper. Lizette called the phone number from the hospital room so her mother could listen to her end of the conversation.

Free rent would solve all of their problems for the school, and Lizette wanted Jacqueline to share the excitement of the phone call. Lizette hadn't realized until she was halfway through the conversation that the free rent was in a small town in Montana.

Jacqueline kept nodding at her during the conversation, so Lizette found herself agreeing to take the town of Dry Creek up on their offer. She couldn't disappoint her mother by telling her that the free rent wasn't in Seattle.

Of course, Lizette had no intention of actually going to Dry Creek, Montana. She knew nothing about the place. Something about the phone call calmed Jacqueline, however, and she seemed truly satisfied. The chaplain said she made her peace with God the next afternoon. After that, nothing Lizette did could stop her mother from slipping away.

After Jacqueline was gone, Lizette remembered the small town in Montana. Seattle seemed the emptiest city in the world without her mother. Lizette couldn't stay at the bakery, even though she'd worked there for the past six years. Lizette enjoyed the job, but she knew her mother would have scolded her for hiding away there.

Besides baking, the only other skill Lizette had was her expertise in ballet and there were no jobs for young ballet teachers in Seattle. Oh, Madame Aprele offered her a job, but Lizette knew the small school didn't need another teacher, and she wasn't desperate enough to take charity.

No, she had to go somewhere else, and she didn't much care where.

So, here she was—moving to Dry Creek, Montana, and all because of a phone conversation with an old man and an offer of free rent. Lizette wasn't sure the school would work. A small town in eastern Montana wasn't the place she would have chosen to open the Baker School of Ballet.

Not that it was absolutely the worst place to start, Lizette assured herself. So few people appreciated ballet these days, and it gladdened her heart to remember the enthusiasm in the old man's voice when she had called in response to the ad. The man she'd talked to on the phone was gruff, and she couldn't always hear him because of the static, but he seemed excited that she was taking the town up on their offer of six months' free rent. He kept talking about how large the area was that they could set aside for her.

The old man had mentioned tables and chairs and counters, so he might not be too familiar with ballet, but Lizette wouldn't let that discourage her. It was the enthusiasm in his heart that counted. She'd be happy to educate this little town on the finer points of ballet.

Lizette was going to go ahead with a modified Nutcracker ballet. Her mother had been right that it was a great way to start. Lizette decided she would even make Sugar Plum pastries for a little reception after the performance. Stuffed with dried plums and vanilla custard, they were a Christmas favorite with many of the customers at the bakery.

The people of Dry Creek would like them as well.

Yes, Lizette thought to herself. A little music, a little ballet and a cream-filled pastry—the people of Dry Creek would be glad she'd opened her school in their town.

Chapter Two

Judd Bowman was standing at the back of the hardware store in Dry Creek counting nails. He figured he needed about fifty nails, but every time he got to thirty or so, one of the kids would interrupt him because they had to go to the bathroom or they wanted a drink of water or they thought they heard a kitten meowing. Judd sighed. Trying to take care of a six-year-old boy and a five-year-old girl was no picnic. Fortunately, the hardware store had a heater going, and it took the edge off the cold.

"Just sit down until I finish," Judd said when he felt Amanda's arm brush against his leg. He'd gotten to thirty-seven, and he repeated the number to himself. He knew the kids needed reassurance, so he tried to speak two sentences when one would have done him fine. "I won't be long and then we can go over to the café and have some cocoa. You like cocoa, don't you?"

Judd felt Amanda nod against his knee. He looked over to see that Bobby was still drawing a picture on the piece of paper that the man who ran the hardware store had given him earlier.

Amanda seemed to squeeze even closer to his knee, and Judd looked down. She was pale and clutching his pant leg in earnest now as she stared around his leg at the men in the middle of the hardware store.

Judd looked over at them, wondering what had stirred up the old men who sat around the potbellied stove. Usually, when he came into the store, the men were dozing quietly in their chairs around the fire or playing a slow game of chess.

Today, with the cold seeping into the store, the fire was almost out. There was wood in the basket nearby, so there was no excuse for anyone not to put another log in the stove.

But the men weren't paying any attention to the cold or the fire.

Instead, they were all looking out the window of the hardware store and across the street into the window of what had been an old abandoned store that stood next to the café. The store wasn't abandoned any longer. Judd could see the woman as she tried to hang what looked like a sign on the inside of her window.

Judd didn't usually pay much attention to women, but he'd have remembered this one if he'd seen her before. She was tall and graceful, with her black hair twisted into a knot on the top of head. He could see why men would be looking at her.

"They're just talking," Judd said as he rested his hand on Amanda's shoulder.

Judd had little use for idle conversation, but even he had heard a week ago that a new woman was moving to town. Several months ago the town had placed an ad in *The Seattle Times* inviting businesses to move to Dry Creek. The town had sweetened the deal by offering six months of free rent. Even at that, the woman was the only one to actually agree to come, so the town had given her the best of the old buildings they owned.

Judd squeezed Amanda's shoulder as Bobby walked over to stand beside them as well. The boy had become attuned to his sister's moods, and it never took him long to know when Amanda was frightened.

Judd spoke softly. "They're just talking about the new woman who moved here."

"Remember I told you about her?" Bobby added as he leaned down to look his sister in the eye. "She's going to make doughnuts."

"I'm not sure about the doughnuts," Judd said. He worked hard to keep his voice even. Amanda picked up too easily on the emotion in men's voices, and even though Judd was angry at the man who had made her so sensitive and not at *her,* he knew she'd think he was upset with her if he let his voice be anything but neutral.

Getting involved in the problems of Dry Creek was the last thing Judd wanted to do, but if that's what it took to help Amanda realize all anger wasn't directed at her, then that's what he'd have to do. "Let's go see what it's all about."

Judd walked slowly enough so Amanda could keep her fingers wrapped around his leg. She had her other hand in Bobby's small hand.

"How's it going?" Judd asked when they arrived at the group around the stove.

Judd had seen these men a dozen times since he'd rented the Jenkins farm this past spring, but he'd been so busy all summer with farm work and then with the kids that this was the first time he'd done more than nod in their direction.

Fortunately, the men were all too steamed up to wonder why he chose to talk now.

"Charley here is going deaf," Jacob muttered as he leaned back with his fingers in his suspenders.

"I am not," Charley said as he looked up at Judd through his bifocals. "I had a bad connection on that new fangled cell phone. Don't know what's wrong with it. Some of the words don't come through too clear."

"That's when you ask the person to repeat themselves," Jacob said.

The two men had obviously had this conversation before.

"I was being friendly," Charley protested as he stood up and looked straight at Judd. "Everyone kept telling me to be friendly if anyone called. Now, do you think it sounds friendly to keep asking someone to repeat what they've just said?"

"Well, I guess that depends." Judd hesitated. He didn't want to get involved in the argument. He just wanted Amanda to hear that it wasn't about her.

"You know, I got that phone because everybody said people would be calling about the ad at all times of the night and day," Charley complained as he sat back down. "I even carried it to bed with me. And this is the thanks I get."

"So you're all angry because of the phone." Judd nodded. There. That should satisfy Amanda that the argument had nothing to do with her.

"It isn't the phone," Jacob said as he shook his head. "It's what he was supposed to do with the phone. He was supposed to make sure that businesses were suitable for Dry Creek."

"He said she was a baker!" another old man protested.

"I had my mouth all set for a doughnut," Jacob admitted. "One of those long maple ones."

"Well, she kept saying Baker," Charley defended himself. "How was I supposed to know that was just her name? Dry Creek could use a good bakery."

"But she's not a baker. She runs a dance school!" Jacob protested.

"And that's the problem?" Judd tried again. He could feel Amanda's hold on his leg lessen. She was listening to the men.

"Of course that's the problem," Jacob continued. "She doesn't even teach *real* dancing, like the stomp-and-holler stuff they have at the senior center up by Miles City. This here is ballet. Who around here wants to learn ballet? You have to wear tights."

"Or a tutu," another old man added. "Pink fluffy stuff."

"It isn't decent, if you ask me," still another man muttered. "Don't know where she'll buy all that netting around here anyway."

"The store here started carrying bug netting since the mosquitoes were so bad over the summer. They still have some left. Maybe she could use that," the first old man offered.

"She can't use bug netting," Charley said. "Not

for ballet. Besides, she probably wants it to be pink, and that bug netting is black."

"Well, of course it's black," another old man said. "Mosquitoes don't care if it's some fancy color."

"Netting is the least of her worries. She isn't going to have any students, so she won't need any netting," Jacob finally said.

There was a moment's silence.

"Maybe she *will* take up baking—to keep herself busy if she doesn't have any students," Charley offered. "I heard she was trying to make some kind of cookies."

"They burnt," another man said mournfully. "The smoke came clear over here. I went over and asked if maybe a pie would be easier to bake."

"She's not going to be making pies. She's going to go around trying to change the people of Dry Creek into something we're not. It's like trying to turn a pig into a silk purse. I say just let a pig be a pig—the way God intended," Jacob said.

Judd looked down at Amanda. She'd stopped holding on to his pants leg and was listening intently to the men. He was glad she was listening even if she wasn't talking yet. In the three months that Judd had been taking care of the two kids, Amanda occasionally whispered something to her brother, but she never said anything to anyone else, not even Judd.

Amanda leaned over to whisper in Bobby's ear now.

The boy smiled and nodded. "Yeah, she *is* awfully pretty."

Bobby looked up at the men. "Amanda thinks the woman looks like our mama."

Judd's breath caught. Both kids had stopped talking about their mother a month ago. Barbara was his second cousin, but Judd hadn't known her until she showed up on his doorstep one morning. She'd paid an agency to find him because she wanted to ask him to take care of her kids while she got settled in a place. She was on the run from an abusive husband and had the court papers to prove it.

Judd had refused Barbara's request at first. Sheer disbelief had cleared his mind of anything else. Judd had never known his mother, and the uncle who had raised him had been more interested in having a hired hand that he didn't need to pay than in parenting an orphan. The stray dog Judd had taken in earlier in the summer probably knew more about family life than Judd did. Judd wasn't someone anyone had ever thought to leave kids with before this. And one look at the kids showed him that they were still in the napping years.

"You must have taken care of little ones before—" Barbara had said.

"Not unless they had four feet and a tail," Judd

told her firmly. He'd nursed calves and stray dogs and even a pony or two. But kids? Never.

No, Judd wasn't the one his cousin needed. "You'll need to find someone else. Believe me, it's best."

"But—" Barbara said and then swallowed.

Judd didn't like the look of desperation he saw in her eyes.

"You're our only family," she finally finished.

Judd figured she probably had that about right. The Bowman family tree had always been more of a stump than anything. Ever since his uncle had died, Judd had thought he was the last of the line.

Still, he hesitated.

He thought of suggesting she turn to the state for help, but he knew what kind of trouble that could get her into. Once children were in the state system, it wasn't all that easy to get them out again, and he could see by the way she kept looking at the kids that she loved them.

He might not know much about a mother's love himself, but he could at least recognize it when he saw it.

"Maybe you could get a babysitter," Judd finally offered. "Some nice grandmother or something."

"You know someone like that?"

Judd had to admit he didn't. He'd only moved to Dry Creek this past spring. He'd been working long and hard plowing and then seeding the alfalfa and wheat crops. He hadn't taken time to get to know any of his neighbors yet.

He wished now that he had accepted one of the invitations to church he'd received since he'd been here. An older woman, Mrs. Hargrove, had even driven out to the ranch one day and invited him. She'd looked so friendly he'd almost promised to go, but he didn't.

What would a man like him do in church anyway? He wouldn't know when to kneel or when to sing or when to bow his head. No, church wasn't for him.

Now he wished he had gone to church anyway, even if he'd made a fool of himself doing so. Mrs. Hargrove would probably help someone who went to her church. She wasn't likely to help a stranger though. Who would be?

"Maybe we could put an ad in the paper."

Barbara just looked at him. "We don't have time for that."

Judd had to admit she was right.

"Besides, this is something big—the kind of thing family members do to help each other," Barbara said with such conviction that Judd believed her.

Not that he was an expert on what family members did to help each other. He couldn't remember his uncle ever doing him a kindness, and the man was the only family Judd had ever known. His uncle had lost all contact with his cousin who was Barbara's father.

He had to admit he had been excited at first when Barbara had come to his doorstep. It was nice to think he had family somewhere in this world.

He looked over at the kids and saw that they were sitting still as stones. Kids shouldn't be so quiet.

"Are they trained?" he asked.

Barbara looked at him blankly for a moment. "You mean potty-trained?"

He nodded.

"Of course! Amanda here is five years old. And Bobby is six. They practically take care of themselves."

Barbara didn't pause before she continued. "And it might only be for a few days. Just enough time for me to drive down to Denver and check out that women's shelter. I want to be sure they'll take us before I drag the kids all that way."

Barbara had arrived in an old car that had seen better days, but it had gotten her here, so Judd figured it would get her to Denver.

Still, if she had car trouble, he knew it would be hard to take care of the kids while she saw to getting the thing fixed. He supposed—maybe—

"I guess things will be slow for the next few days," Judd said. He'd finished putting up the hay, and he had enough of the fence built so his thirty head of cattle could graze in the pasture by the creek. He meant to spend the next few days working on the inside of the house anyway before he turned back to building the rest of the fence. He supposed two trained kids wouldn't be too much trouble.

Judd didn't exactly say he'd keep the kids, but he guessed Barbara could tell he'd lowered his resistance, because she turned her attention to the kids, telling them they were going to stay with Cousin Judd and she'd be back in a few days. That was at the end of August. It was mid-November now.

Judd still hadn't finished all of the fencing, and it was already starting to snow some. If he waited any longer, the ground would be frozen too far down to dig fence holes. That's why he was at the hardware store today getting nails and talking to the old men by the stove.

Judd watched the old men as they smiled at the kids now.

Jacob nodded slowly as he looked at Amanda. "I saw your mama when she brought you and your brother here. She stopped to ask directions. You're right, she was pretty, too."

"My mama's going to come back and get us real soon," Bobby said.

Jacob nodded. "I expect she will."

Judd gave him a curt nod of thanks. Barbara had asked for a few days, but Judd had figured he'd give her a week. By now, she was at least two months overdue to pick up the kids.

Judd hadn't told the kids he'd contacted the court that had issued the restraining order their mother had flashed in front of him and asked them to help find her. Fortunately Barbara had listed him as her next of kin on some paper they had. The court clerk had called every women's shelter between here and Denver and hadn't located Judd's cousin.

Judd had had to do some persuasive talking to the clerk, because he didn't want to mention the kids. He figured his cousin needed a chance to come back for them on her own.

"She's just hurt her hand so she can't write and tell us when," Bobby added confidently.

"I expect that's right. Mail sometimes takes a while," Jacob agreed, and then added, "but then it only makes the letter more special when you do get it."

The older men shifted in their seats. Judd knew they were all aware of the troubles Amanda and Bobby were having. They might not know the details, but he had told his landlady, Linda, back in the beginning of September that he was watching the children for his cousin for a couple of weeks. By now, everyone in Dry Creek probably knew there was something wrong.

Even if he was a newcomer, he would be foolish

to think they hadn't asked each other why the kids were still here. Of course, the old men were polite and wouldn't ask a direct question, at least not in front of the kids, so they probably didn't know how bad it all was. They probably thought Barbara had called and made arrangements for the kids to stay longer.

"Speaking of letters, maybe we could write a letter to the new woman and tell her we all want a bakery more than a ballet school," Charley finally broke the silence with a suggestion.

"We can't do that," Jacob said with a sigh. "You don't write a letter to someone who's right across the street. No, we need to be neighborly and tell her to her face. It isn't fair that we let her think she'll make a go of it here with that school of hers."

"Well, I can't talk to her," Charley said. "I'm the one who promised her everything would be fine."

"Too bad *she* wasn't the one who was deaf," one of the other men muttered.

"I'm not deaf. I had a bad connection is all," Charley said. "It could happen to anyone."

"Maybe *he* could go talk to her," the other man said, looking up at Judd. "He seems to hear all right."

Judd felt his stomach knot up at the idea. "I got to count me out some nails. I'm building a fence."

He walked back to the shelves that held the boxes of nails. Amanda and Bobby trailed along after him.

Judd looked down at Bobby. "Why don't you take your sister and go across to the café and put your order in for some of that cocoa? Tell Linda I'll be along in a minute."

The Linda who ran the café was also his landlady. She was renting him the Jenkins place, with an option to buy come next spring. Judd had saved the few thousand dollars the state had given him when it settled his uncle's estate and added most of the other money he'd gotten to it for the past six years.

He'd started out working as a ranch hand, but the wages added up too slowly for him, and so he'd spent the next couple of years on the rodeo circuit. He'd earned enough in prize money to set himself up nicely. Right now, he had enough money in the bank to buy the Jenkins place, and he'd already stocked it with some purebred breeding cattle. He could have bought the place outright, but he wanted to take his time and be sure he liked it well enough before he made the final deal. So far, the ground had been fertile and the place quiet enough to suit him.

Judd watched Amanda and Bobby leave the hardware store before he reached into the nail bin and pulled out another nail. Fortunately, the older men had given up on the idea that he should talk to the new woman. They probably realized he'd botch the job.

Outside of talking with Linda at the café and smil-

ing politely when Mrs. Hargrove had delivered the
books the school had sent him when he'd decided to
homeschool the kids, Judd hadn't had a conversation
with a woman since his cousin had left the kids with
him. Well, unless you counted the court clerk he'd
talked to on the phone.

Judd never had been much good at talking to
women, at least not women who weren't rodeo followers. He had no problem with women at rodeos,
probably because *they* did most of the talking and
he always knew what they wanted; they wanted a
rodeo winner to escort them around town for the
evening. That didn't exactly require conversation,
not with the yelling that spilled out of most rodeo
hangouts in the evening.

As long as his boots were polished and his hat on
straight, the rodeo women didn't care if he was quiet.
He was mostly for show anyway—if he was winning.
If he wasn't winning, they weren't that interested
in talking to him, or even interested in being with
him.

The few temporary affairs he'd had with rodeo
followers didn't leave him feeling good about himself,
so eventually he just declined invitations to party. By
then he was counting up his prize money after every
rodeo anyway, with an eye to when he could leave
the circuit and set himself up on his own ranch.

In those years, Judd hadn't known any women outside of rodeo circles, and he thought that was best. Judd never seemed to know what those women were thinking, and he didn't even try to sort it all out. He liked things straightforward and to the point. The other kind of women—the kind that made wives—always seemed to say things in circles and then expect a man to know what they meant. For all Judd knew, they could be speaking Greek.

Judd had a feeling the new woman in Dry Creek was one of that kind of women.

No, he wasn't the one to talk to her about what she was doing here, even though he had to admit he was curious. She sure knew how to hang a sign in that window.

Chapter Three

Lizette shifted the sign with her left hand and took a deep breath. It had taken her the better part of three days to get the practice bar in place along the left side of the room and the floor waxed to a smooth shine. She still had the costumes hanging on a rack near the door waiting to be sorted by size, but she'd decided this morning it was time to put the sign she'd made in her window and start advertising for students.

She could still smell the floor wax, so she'd opened the door to air out the room even though it was cold outside. At least it wasn't snowing today.

Lizette had bought a large piece of metal at the hardware store yesterday and some paint so she could make her sign. The old men sitting around the stove in the store had obviously heard she was setting up a business, because they were full of suggestions on how she should make her sign.

Of course, most of the words centered on the Baker part of the school's name, but she couldn't fault them for that. She was heartened to see they had so much enthusiasm for a ballet school. If this was any indication of the interest of the rest of the people in the community, she just might get enough students to pull off a modified Nutcracker ballet for Christmas after all. She'd even assured the men in the hardware store that no one was too old to learn some ballet steps. In fact, she'd told them that lots of athletes used ballet as a way to exercise.

The old men had looked a little dismayed at her comments, and she wasn't surprised. At their age, they probably didn't want to take up *any* exercise program, especially not one as rigorous as ballet. "You'd want to check with your doctor first, of course," Lizette added. "You should do that before you take up any new exercise program."

The men nodded as she left the hardware store. All in all, they'd been friendly, and she wasn't so sure she wouldn't get a student or two out of the bunch. And if she didn't get any students, at least she'd gotten some good neighbors. One of them had already been over to check on the smoke coming out of the small kitchen off the main room when she'd been baking some cookies earlier and had forgotten they were in the oven. He'd even offered to bring her over some more flour if she was inclined to continue baking. He'd expressed some hope of a cherry pie.

The chair Lizette stood on gave her enough height so she could lift the sign and hook it into the chain she'd put up to hang it with. The sign had a white background with navy script lettering.

Lizette planned to take a picture of the sign later and send it to Madame Aprele. She wasn't sure she'd tell her old teacher that she didn't have any students yet, but she could tell her that the school was almost ready for classes now that the practice bar was in place. Lizette had planned to use a makeshift practice bar at first, because she couldn't afford a real one. Madame Aprele had surprised her by sending her one of her own mahogany bars. Her old teacher had shipped it before Lizette left Seattle, and Linda, next door in the café, had kept it for Lizette until she arrived.

Lizette had called Madame Aprele, thanking her and insisting that she accept payment for the equipment. It would help enough, Lizette explained, if she could just pay for the bar over time. She didn't add that she had no need of charity. Madame Aprele agreed to let Lizette make payments if Lizette promised to call her with weekly updates on her school.

At first Lizette was uncomfortable promising to call Madame Aprele, because she knew her mother would disapprove. But then Lizette decided that whatever problem there had been between her mother and Madame Aprele, there was no need for *her* to continue the coldness.

Twenty years ago when Madame Aprele had bought the school from Lizette's mother, the two women had been friends. But, over the years, Jacqueline spoke less and less to Madame Aprele until, finally, her mother wouldn't even greet the other women when she picked Lizette up after ballet class.

At the time, Lizette didn't understand why. Now she wondered if her mother didn't look at Madame Aprele and wish her own life had turned out like the other woman's.

Not that there was anything in Jacqueline's life to suggest she wished for a different one. Madame Aprele had been born in France in the same village as Lizette's mother. Both women had studied ballet together and had left France together. Lizette's mother had become more Americanized over the years, however, especially after she'd started working in the bakery.

As Lizette's mother became more conservative in her dress, Madame Aprele became more outrageous, until, in the end, Lizette's mother looked almost dowdy and Madame Aprele looked like an old-fashioned movie star with her lavender feather boas and dramatic eye makeup.

* * *

Lizette stepped down from the chair just as she saw two little children cross the street from the hardware store. The sun was shining on the window so Lizette could not see the children clearly, but she could tell from their size that they were both good prospects for ballet.

Lizette didn't know how to advertise in a small town like Dry Creek, but she supposed she could ask about the children at the hardware store, find out who their parents were and send them a flyer.

When the children passed her door, they stopped. The little girl was staring at something, and it didn't take long for Lizette to figure out what it was. The sunlight was streaming in, making the Sugar Plum Fairy costume sparkle even more than usual. Lizette's mother had used both gold and metallic pink on the costume when she'd made it, and many a young girl mistook it for a princess costume.

"If you go ask your mother if it's okay, you can come in and look at the costumes," Lizette said. She doubted things were so casual in Dry Creek that parents wanted their children going into strange stores without their knowledge.

The girl whispered something in the boy's ear. He nodded.

Lizette had walked closer to the children and was starting to feel uneasy. If you added a few pounds and took away the scared look in their eyes, those two kids looked very similar to that snapshot she'd seen several days ago. She looked up and down the snow-covered street. There were the usual cars and pickups parked beside the hardware store and the café, but there were no people outside except for the two children. "Does your mother know where you are?"

Both children solemnly nodded their heads yes.

Lizette was relieved to know the children had a mother. Their father hadn't looked like much of a parent, but hopefully their mother was better.

"Our mother won't mind if we look at the dress," the boy politely said after a moment and pointed inside. "That one."

The rack was very close to the door and Lizette decided she could leave the door open so the children's mother could see them if she looked down the street. Really, if she moved the rack closer, the children could touch the costumes while they stood outside on the sidewalk.

Lizette pushed the costume rack so it was just inside the door. "The pink one is my favorite, too."

Lizette watched as the little girl reached out her hand and gently touched the costume.

"That's the dress for the Sugar Plum Fairy in the Nutcracker ballet," Lizette said.

"What's a ballet?" the boy asked.

Lizette thought a moment. "It's like a play with lots of costumes and people moving."

"So someone wears that dress in a play?" the boy asked.

The boy and Lizette were both seeing the same thing. The little girl's face was starting to glow. One moment she had been pale and quiet, and the next her face started to show traces of pink and her eyes started to sparkle.

For the first time, Lizette decided she had made the right decision to come to Dry Creek to open her school. If there were more little girls and boys like this in the community, she'd have a wonderful time teaching them to love ballet.

Chapter Four

Lizette heard a sound and looked up to see a half-dozen men stomping down the steps of the hardware store and heading straight toward her new school. She wasn't sure, but she thought every one of the men was frowning, especially the one who was at the back of the group. That man had to be forty years younger than the other men, but he looked the most annoyed of them all.

"The children are still just on the sidewalk," Lizette said when the men were close enough to hear. While she hadn't thought anyone would want children to go into a building alone, she certainly hadn't expected there would be a problem with them standing on the sidewalk and looking at something inside. If the citizens of Dry Creek were that protective of their children, she'd never have any young students in her classes.

Lizette braced herself, but when the men reached her, they stood silent. Finally, one of them cleared his throat, "About this—ah—school—"

"The children will all have permission from their parents, of course," Lizette rushed to assure them. "And parents can watch the classes any time they want. They can even attend if they want. I'd love to have some older students."

The younger man, the one who had hung back on the walk over, moved closer to the open door. He seemed intent on the two children and did not stop until he stood beside them protectively. Lizette noticed that the young boy relaxed a little when the man stood beside him, and the girl reached out her hand to touch the man's leg. She knew the man wasn't the children's father because she'd met that man already. Maybe he was their stepfather. That would explain why the father hadn't known where the children lived.

"Well, about the students—" The older man cleared his throat and began again. "You see, there might be a problem with students."

"No one has to audition or anything to be in the performances," Lizette said. She wasn't sure what was bothering the men, but she wanted them to know she was willing to work with the town. "And public performance is good for children, especially if it's not competitive."

"Anyone can be in the play," the boy said softly.

The men had all stopped talking to listen to the boy, so they all heard the next words very clearly.

"I'm going to be a Sugar Plum Fairy," the girl said, and pointed to the costume she'd been admiring.

Judd swallowed. Amanda never talked to anyone but Bobby, and then only in whispers. Who knew all it would take was a sparkly costume to make her want to talk?

"How much is the costume?" Judd asked the woman in the doorway. He didn't care what figure she named—he'd buy it for Amanda.

"Oh, the costumes aren't for sale," the woman said. "I'll need them for the performance, especially if I want to have something ready for Christmas. I won't have time to make many more costumes."

"About this performance—" The older man said, then cleared his throat.

Lizette wondered what was bothering the old man, but she didn't have time to ask him because the younger man was scowling at her.

"So the only way Amanda can wear this costume is if she's in your performance?" he asked.

"I wouldn't say it was *my* performance." Lizette felt her patience starting to grow thin. "All of the students will see it as *their* performance. We work together."

"About the students—" The older man began again

and cleared his throat for what must have been the fourth time.

"I'll sign Amanda up," the younger man said decisively. "If she signs up first, she should get her pick of the parts, shouldn't she?"

"Well, I don't see why she can't be the Sugar Plum Fairy," Lizette agreed. After all, Lizette herself would be choreographing the part for the children's ballet, and could tailor it to Amanda's skills. She'd just gotten her first student. "She'll have to practice, of course. And we'll have to have a few more students to do even a shortened version of the Nutcracker."

The younger man squeezed the boy on his shoulder.

"I'll sign up, too," the boy offered reluctantly.

"There—I have two students!" Lizette announced triumphantly. "And I only just hung up my sign."

The older man cleared his throat again, but this time he had nothing to say. All of the older men were looking a little stunned. Maybe they were as taken aback as she was by the fierce scowl the younger man was giving them.

"You might want to see a doctor about the cold you're getting," Lizette finally said to the man who had been trying to talk. "Usually when you have to clear your throat so often, it means a cold is coming on."

The older man nodded silently.

"And you might ask him about taking up ballet while you're there," Lizette said. "Just to see if the exercise would be all right for you. Now that I have two students, I can begin classes, and you'd be more than welcome."

Lizette decided the older man definitely had a cold coming on. He had just gone pale. He even looked a little dizzy.

"You'll want to wait until you're feeling better before you start though," Lizette said to him. That seemed to make him feel better. At least his color returned.

"I'll think about it," he mumbled.

Lizette nodded. She knew she couldn't manage for long on the income she'd get from two students, but just look how much people wanted to talk about her school. With all of that talk, she'd get more students before long.

Lizette smiled up at the younger man. He might scowl a lot, but she was grateful to him for her first two students. "Your wife must be happy you take such good care of the children."

The young man looked down at her. "I don't have a wife."

Lizette faltered. "Oh, I just thought that because their father showed me their picture that—"

"You know the kids' father, Neal Strong?"

If Lizette thought the men had been quiet before, they were even more silent now.

"No, I don't know him. Some man just showed me their picture in Forsyth when he asked me to give him a ride out this way. He said they were his kids and he was trying to find them. He probably didn't know the address or something."

Judd felt Amanda move closer to his leg, and suddenly he had as great a need to be close to her as she had to be close to him, so he reached down and lifted her up even though he had his heavy farm coat on and it probably had grease on it from when he'd last worked on the tractor.

"Don't worry," Judd whispered into Amanda's hair when she snuggled into his shoulder.

Judd reminded himself that the papers Barbara had shown him when she left the children with him included a court order forbidding the children's father from being within one hundred yards of them.

Judd knew the court clerk well enough now that he could ask for a copy of the court order if he needed one. Of course, that would mean the clerk would guess that the children were with him. No, there had to be another way. Besides, he didn't actually need a copy of the order for the court to enforce it.

"You're sure it was him?" Judd turned to ask the woman. He didn't know how the children's father would even know where they were unless Barbara had told him.

"He had a picture and he said he was their father," Lizette said. "He had a snake on his arm."

Amanda went still in Judd's arm. The kids had told him about the snake.

Judd nodded. He should have figured something like this would happen. He wondered if his cousin had gotten back with her husband, after all. Generally, Judd was a supporter of married folks staying together. But some of the things Bobby had let slip while he was at Judd's place would make anyone advise Barbara to forget her husband.

The one thing Judd knew was that he didn't want that man to come within shouting distance of the children.

"You have a lock on this place, I suppose," Judd said as he looked inside the building the woman was going to use for her school. If he brought the kids to the lessons and then came back to pick them up, they should be safe.

"I could put a lock on," one of the older men spoke up. "It's no trouble. They have some heavy-duty ones over at the hardware store."

"And it wouldn't hurt Charley here to come over and sit while the kids have their lessons," another older man offered. "He always complains that the chairs at the hardware store are too hard anyway. Now that he's got his fancy phone, he can call the sheriff any time, night or day."

Judd nodded. It felt good to have neighbors, even if he hadn't been very neighborly himself. He wasn't sure what he could do to repay them, but he intended to try. "I'll be watching, too."

"Is something wrong?" Lizette looked at the men's faces.

"Their father isn't fit to be near these kids—even the court says so," Judd said quietly. He could see the alarm grow on Lizette's face. "Not that you have to worry about it. We'll take care of the guarding. You won't even know we're here. We can even sit outside."

"In the snow?" Charley protested.

"Of course you can't sit outside in the cold," Lizette said. "I'll put some chairs along the side of the practice area. And I'll be careful about who else I accept as students. I'll check references on any grown man who wants to join the class."

Charley snorted. "Ain't no grown man hereabouts that'll sign up. Not if he wants to keep his boots—"

One of the other older men interrupted him. "I thought you was gonna sign up yourself, Charley. You can't just sit and watch everyone else practice. That wouldn't be right."

"Why, I can't do no ballet," Charley said, and

then looked around at the faces of his friends. "I got me that stiff knee, remember—from the time I was loading that heifer and it pinned me against the corral?"

"The exercises might even help you then," Lizette said. "We do a lot of stretching and bending to warm up."

If Judd hadn't still been thinking about the children's father, he would have laughed at Charley's trapped expression. As it was, he was just glad Charley would be inside with the children. For himself, Judd thought, he'd set up a chair outside the door, so he could keep his eyes on who was driving into Dry Creek.

Judd didn't trust the children's father and was determined to keep the man as far away from Dry Creek as possible. First thing in the morning Judd decided he'd tell Sheriff Wall all about the court order.

Judd had only met the sheriff once, but he trusted the man. Sheriff Wall might not be one of those big-city sheriffs who solved complicated crimes, but he had the persistence and instincts of a guard dog. And the man knew every road coming near Dry Creek, even the ones that were just pasture trails. The kids would be safer with Sheriff Wall on the job.

"I can pay in advance for the lessons," Judd announced. He didn't like the sympathetic look the ballet woman was giving the kids now that Charley had accepted his fate. Judd didn't want the woman to think they couldn't pay their way, especially not when she'd have to give special attention to the security of her classroom.

"There's no need to pay now," the woman protested.

But Judd already had two twenty-dollar bills in his hand and he held them out to her. "Let me know if it costs more."

"That should cover their first couple of lessons," Lizette said as she took the money and turned to a desk in a corner of the large room. "Just let me get a receipt for you."

Judd watched the woman walk over to the desk. He couldn't help but notice that she didn't just walk—she actually glided. He supposed that was what all of that ballet did for a body.

Judd tried not to gawk at the woman. The fact that she moved like poetry in motion was no excuse for staring at her.

Judd heard a soft collective sigh and turned to see all the old men watching the woman as if they'd never seen anyone like her before. Charley had obviously forgotten all about his reluctance to be in the class.

"There's no need for a receipt," Judd said.

The woman looked up from the desk. Even from across the room he could see she was relieved. "But you should have one anyway. Just as soon as I get all my desk things organized, I'll see that you get one. I could mail it to you, if you leave me your address."

"I'm at the Jenkins place south of town. Just write *Jenkins* on the envelope and leave it on the counter in the hardware store."

It had taken Judd two weeks to figure out the mail system in town. The first part was simple. The mail carrier left all of the Dry Creek mail at the hardware store, and the ranchers picked it up when they came into town. The second part still had Judd confused. For some reason, if he wanted to get his mail sooner rather than later, he still had to have it addressed to the Jenkins place even though no one by the name of Jenkins had lived on the ranch for two years now.

When Judd finally bought the Jenkins place, he told himself he'd get the name changed. He'd asked the mail carrier about it, and the man had just looked at him blankly and said that's what everyone called the place.

Judd vowed that once he had the children taken care of and the deed to the place signed, he'd take a one-page ad out in that Billings paper everyone around here read. He'd make sure people knew it wasn't the Jenkins place anymore.

But, in the meantime, he didn't want to have the woman's envelope returned to her, so he'd go along with saying he lived at the Jenkins place.

The woman nodded. "I know about the hardware store. I've been meaning to post an announcement about the school so everyone will know that we're currently taking students."

"About the students—" one of the old men said and then cleared his throat. "You see, the students—well, we're not sure how many students you'll have."

"Of course," Lizette assured him. She knew she needed a few more students to do the ballet, but surely three or four more would come. "No one knows how many people will answer the flyer I put up. But I need to start the classes anyway if we're going to perform the Nutcracker ballet before Christmas."

Lizette figured the students who came later could do the parts that involved less practice.

"Christmas is only five weeks away," Judd said and frowned. He knew when Christmas was coming because he figured his cousin would surely come for the children before Christmas.

Judd had gone ahead and ordered toys for the kids when he'd put in a catalog order last week, but he thought he'd be sending the presents along with them when their mother picked them up. Thanksgiving was next week, and it was likely the only holiday he'd have to worry about. He figured he could cope with a turkey if he could get Linda to give him some more basic instructions. She'd already told him about some cooking bag that practically guaranteed success with a turkey.

"I don't suppose you have a real nutcracker in that ballet?" one of the older men asked hopefully. "I wouldn't say no to some chopped walnuts—especially if they were on some maple doughnuts."

"You know there's no doughnuts, so there's no point in going on about them," Charley said firmly as he frowned at the man who had spoken. "There's more to life than your stomach."

"But you like doughnuts, too," the older man protested. "You were hoping for some, too—just like me."

"Maybe at first," Charley admitted. "But I can't be eating doughnuts if I'm going to learn this here ballet."

Lizette smiled as she looked at the two men. "Well, I do generally make some sort of cookies or something for the students to eat after we practice. I guess I could make doughnuts one of these days."

"You mean you can bake doughnuts?" Charley asked. "I didn't know anyone around here could bake doughnuts."

Lizette nodded. "I'll need to get a large Dutch oven, but I have a fry basket I can use."

"Hallelujah!" Charley beamed.

"And, of course, I'd need to have some spare time," Lizette added.

"And she's not likely to have any time to bake now that she's starting classes," Judd said, frowning. It would be harder to guard the kids if every stray man in the county was lined up at the ballet school eating doughnuts.

Judd told himself that it was only his concern for the safety of the kids that made him worry about who was likely to be visiting the ballet school. He'd been in Dry Creek long enough to know about all the cowboys on the outlying ranches.

A woman like Lizette Baker was bound to attract enough attention just being herself without adding doughnuts to the equation.

Not that, he reminded himself, it should matter to him how many men gawked at the ballet teacher. He certainly wasn't going to cause any awkwardness by being overly friendly himself. He was just hoping to get to know her a little better.

She was, after all, the kids' teacher, and he was, for the time being, their parent. He really was obligated to be somewhat friendly to her, wasn't he? It was his duty. He was as close to a PTA as Dry Creek had, since he was the almost-parent of the only two kids in her class right now. If Bobby and Amanda were still with him in a few months, he'd have to enroll them in the regular school in Miles City instead of homeschooling them. But, until then, it was practically his civic duty to be friendly to their ballet teacher. And he didn't need a doughnut to make him realize it.

Chapter Five

Lizette worried there was something wrong with her. She thought she had been working through the grief of her mother's death, but maybe she was wrong. After all, she hadn't had that much experience with mourning, and the chaplain at the hospital had talked about going through different stages of grief.

Lizette wondered if one of those stages of grief was twitching.

Here she was wrapping up the day's dance lesson, and her mind wasn't concentrated on the three people who were her students or the five more students she needed if she was going to pull off even a modified version of the Nutcracker ballet. Instead, she was all jumpy inside, and her gaze kept going to the window, where she could see Judd sitting on the steps of her school and looking out to the street with a scowl on his face.

If she didn't get a firm hold on herself, she'd be actually twitching when she looked at that man.

Lizette had had three days of lessons now, and for the better part of all of those days Judd had had his back turned toward her and the students. The first day she didn't notice his silence and his scowls. The second day she noticed, but she didn't feel the need to do anything about it. Today, she felt obsessed by the man.

She kept fighting the urge to go out and talk to him—and that was after she'd already been outside five times today to ask him questions. She didn't have much to talk about either, except for the weather, and how many times could she ask if it looked like it was going to snow? He'd think she was dim-witted. There wasn't even a cloud in the sky anymore.

She kept expecting each time she went out and asked the man a question that she would then be able to move on with her lessons with a focused mind.

She was still waiting for that to happen.

The really odd thing was that nothing had changed in those three days.

She didn't need to see his face to know he wore the same scowl he'd worn every day so far. Every time today she'd found an excuse to slip outside and ask him a question, she'd known he'd have the same fierce look on his face even before she opened the door.

Lizette wondered if Judd thought his look would

keep strange cars off the street in front of the school. Actually, he might be right about that one. That scowl of his would stop an army tank from approaching him.

With all of the frowning, Lizette knew there was no sane reason she should feel drawn to go up and talk to him. But she was.

She thought it might be his shoulders. For as hard as his face scowled, his shoulders told a different story. It wasn't anger he was feeling, but worry. Anxiety hung on his shoulders. It was there in the way he angled his head when he heard a sound and the way he stood to take a look down the road every half hour or so.

Judd was taking his duty seriously, and he was worried.

That's it, Lizette thought to herself in relief. She found him compelling because he was protecting the children. She'd just lost her mother, and the man was obviously doing everything he could to guard the children in his care. That made him an unconscious picture to her of her mother, she told herself. She'd be as attracted to a chicken if it sat there guarding its eggs. It had nothing to do with the fact that he was a man. He was simply a concerned parent.

Lizette felt better having figured that out. Not that she would have been opposed to finding the man attractive as a *man,* she just didn't have time for that kind of distraction right now. She only had three students—Amanda, Bobby and Charley. She needed to worry about getting more students instead of thinking about some man's shoulders.

And, yet, she let herself walk over to the doorway. Bobby and Amanda were sitting on the wooden floor untying their dance shoes. Since Charley wore socks instead of dance shoes, he didn't have to worry about ties. Instead, he was pulling in his stomach and admiring himself in the mirror she'd hung behind the exercise bar. None of her students needed her immediate attention.

"They're almost done," Lizette said as she walked out on the porch and crossed her arms in the chill. At least she wasn't asking about snow this time, even though the air felt cold enough for it. She always wore black tights and a black wrap-around dress when she practiced. Unfortunately, the dress was sleeveless. "Aren't you cold out here waiting for the kids?"

Judd looked up at Lizette and forgot to frown. He almost forgot to breathe. She was standing in front of the sun, and although the temperature was low enough outside to make his fingers ache if he didn't keep them in his pockets, the sun was shining brightly and she looked as though she was rimmed with gold. Her black hair was pulled back into a bun, and the smooth lines of her head made him think of an exotic princess. Her face was smooth and, even without lipstick, she looked like a picture he'd once seen of Cleopatra. The flimsy black thing she had draped over her made her look as if she was in constant motion. No wonder there had been so many wars fought back in Cleopatra's day.

Judd was outclassed and he had sense enough to know it. All he asked was that he not embarrass himself around her. "It's not that cold. Forty-six, last I checked."

"Yes, well." Lizette smiled.

"And no snow," Judd added.

He'd already figured out that it wasn't snow she was worried about. The few clouds that had been in the sky this morning were long gone. No, it was the kids' father she was fretting about. She didn't know Judd well enough to know that she didn't have to worry about him leaving his post.

Not that he minded her coming out to check on him. He knew he hadn't been around many women in his life, but he didn't remember women being this naturally beautiful. He almost smiled in return. "So the kids are almost finished? Did they do all right?"

Lizette smiled even wider. "You do make a good mother."

"What?" Judd choked on the smile that didn't happen. Had he heard her right? She thought he made a good *mother?* A mother?

"I mean with all of your concern and all," Lizette continued.

Judd grunted. He'd known he was out of her class, but he hadn't realized he was that far out of it. A man didn't get further away from date material than having a woman think of him as a mother.

"I used to ride rodeo." Judd thought he owed it to himself to speak up. "Won my share of ribbons, too. Bronc riding and steer wrestling. They're not easy events. I placed first in 2003 in bronc riding at the state fair in Great Falls."

"Is that where you got your scar?"

Judd had forgotten he had a scar on the right side of his forehead. The scar hadn't made any difference to his life, and he no longer even really saw it when he shaved. "No, I got that in a fight."

Judd didn't add that it had been a snowball fight when he was eight years old. He'd been dodging a snowball and hadn't seen the low-hanging branch of the tree. He wasn't going to admit he had got the scar playing, however—not when he was talking to a woman who thought of him as a mother.

"I'll bet you're strong," Lizette said, and almost shook herself. That was the most obvious come-hither line a woman had ever uttered, and she felt foolish saying it. Unfortunately, it either wasn't obvious enough for Judd, or he was just not interested. It didn't even make his scowl go away. "I mean, of course you're strong. You'd have to be with the way you swing Amanda around."

Lizette had watched the way Amanda ran to Judd after classes. The little girl would run straight at him, and he'd bend down to scoop her up. While Amanda giggled, he'd gently toss her up in the air.

"You don't need to worry about Amanda and Bobby's father. I can take him in a fight if need be," Judd said. He figured that was what all the talk about how strong he was came from.

Neither one of them heard the two kids come out on the porch.

"He has a gun—my dad does," Bobby said.

"You don't need to worry about your father either," Judd said gently as he put his hand on the boy's head.

It had taken Judd a full month to calm the nightmares that woke Bobby up. The boy still wanted to sleep in a cot at the bottom of Judd's bed. Judd had figured he might as well let him, since Amanda was already sleeping on a cot on the right side of his bed. If he wasn't worried about them rolling out of his bed, Judd would have let the two children share it, and he would have rolled his sleeping bag out on the floor. But the cots were closer to the floor, and the kids seemed to like them.

"But if he has a gun," Lizette said, "shouldn't we let the sheriff know?"

"The sheriff already knows."

Judd had given a complete report. He had even given the sheriff a photo of the kids' father that had been in one of the suitcases Barbara left with them.

That photo had given Judd many an uneasy moment. The photo was a picture of the two children, Barbara and her husband. He knew it had been taken a couple of years ago because a date was handwritten at the bottom of the picture. It had been one of those pictures from a photo booth like the kind you find in an amusement park. Judd had a feeling the family didn't have many photos. The fact that Barbara had left it for the kids might mean she knew she wasn't coming back.

But, right now, the photo was the least of his worries. Judd didn't like the pale look of both of the kids' faces. Of course, that might be because they were outside without their mittens on.

"Where'd you put your mittens?" Judd asked them as he stood up and herded the two children back into the warm room. He'd ordered the mittens from the back of the seed catalog, and he'd since wished he'd gotten three pairs for each of them instead of only two.

"I'm afraid that might be my fault," Lizette said as she followed them inside and closed the door behind herself. "I told them they could have a doughnut after class today."

"We didn't want to get our mittens dirty," Bobby explained. "The doughnuts have sugar on them."

"You don't need to give them doughnuts," Judd said, even though he could smell the doughnuts and didn't blame the kids for leaving their mittens off. The ballet practice room smelled of home. The only smell they usually had in his kitchen was the aroma of his morning coffee. Everything else was canned or microwaved or put between slices of bread in a sandwich. Judd didn't know much about cooking, and he'd never met anyone who actually baked. Even Linda at the café didn't do that kind of baking.

"Of course she needs to give us doughnuts." Charley joined them from his perch on one of the chairs spaced around a work table. "I had to drive up to the Elkton ranch to borrow that Dutch oven. I would have driven further for homemade doughnuts. I mean to have one if it's offered."

"Did anyone see you borrow the Dutch oven?" Jake asked.

"Of course they saw me!" Charley said indignantly. "I didn't steal it."

"I mean, did any of the ranch hands see you borrow it? Or did you just talk to the cook?"

"Pete Denning saw me. He told the cook not to give it to me—said I'd be using the thing to soak my feet! I told him we were using it to make doughnuts."

Jake's worse fears were confirmed. "I don't suppose you told him the doughnuts weren't going to be anything more exciting than flapjacks."

"Now, why would I do that?"

"To avoid a stampede."

"Oh," Charley said as he considered the matter. "I didn't think of that."

Both men looked down the road.

"I don't see anyone though," Charley said. "Maybe Pete forgot."

"Not likely."

"Maybe we should eat our doughnuts now," Bobby said. He'd been standing beside Judd.

"And I'm sure you don't need to worry about someone else coming for doughnuts," Lizette added. "There are plenty of doughnuts to share with a few other people."

Judd grunted. Maybe they were all right. Maybe he didn't need to worry about a stampede of cowboys coming for doughnuts. They probably thought Charley was doing the cooking anyway, and Charley wasn't known for his skills in the kitchen.

Lizette came back with a platter of doughnuts and some white paper napkins. There were powdered doughnuts and maple doughnuts. Twisted cruller doughnuts and apple doughnuts. Even jelly doughnuts.

Lizette tucked a napkin into the neckline of

Amanda's dress and then put one into Bobby's shirt before spreading white napkins on the table in front of each of them.

"You made these?" Judd asked. He felt as wide-eyed as those cowboys he was worried about. He knew Lizette had said she made doughnuts, but he'd never expected that she could make doughnuts like these. He'd expected something more like biscuits. But these doughnuts were so perfect they glistened.

"I used to work in a bakery," Lizette said as she held the platter out to Charley. "Part of that time as a baker."

"There must be two dozen doughnuts here," the older man marveled as he took a jelly doughnut and eyed the rest longingly. "Maybe three dozen."

"Well, if you're making doughnuts, you can't just make a few." Lizette passed the platter to the children next. "The recipes all make about five dozen."

Amanda took an apple doughnut and Bobby took a maple one.

Judd was still standing, but Lizette turned the platter toward him anyway. "I know you're not a student, but you're working, too."

Lizette gave him a small, hopeful smile. Judd would have taken a burnt stick off a platter if she'd offered it to him with that smile. As it was, he picked up the first doughnut he touched—it was a cruller.

"Don't you need a machine or something to make

doughnuts?" Judd said after he ate his first bite of pure heaven. "I didn't know regular people could even make doughnuts like these."

Lizette laughed. "All you really need is something to make the holes. Oh, and a Dutch oven, of course, unless you have a deep fryer."

Charley took a bite out of his doughnut and started to purr. "I could put in an extra practice session this afternoon if you want."

"I don't think that will be necessary," Lizette said. "But if that's a hint that you'd like a second doughnut, you can have one anyway."

"Ah, well, then," Charley said as he took another bite out of his doughnut. "Too bad the boys over at the hardware store don't know you're giving these to your students. They'd be signed up in no time."

Judd stopped eating his doughnut. He'd just looked out the window and had seen several of the ranch hands from the Elkton place go into the hardware store. He supposed it was too optimistic to think they'd come to town to buy nails.

"Well, I could take the tray over to the hardware store," Lizette said as she looked out the window in her studio and into the big window in the hardware store. "We certainly won't be able to eat all of these doughnuts, and we do need a few more dancers to do the Nutcracker."

"Jacob would appreciate a doughnut," Charley

said. "He's been eating his own cooking for weeks now."

"Why don't you go get Jacob and invite him over," Judd suggested. So far the hardware store door was still shut. Maybe the cowboys really had come in for nails. "Just don't tell him there's doughnuts here."

"I know how to keep a secret," Charley said as he slowly stood up. "Although the pastor might want a doughnut, too, and I wouldn't feel right overlooking those two little boys of his if they're there."

"Oh, please invite the children," Lizette said. "I heard the pastor had two boys. I just haven't had a chance to invite them to ballet class yet."

"I'm not sure you'll want them in your class," Charley said doubtfully. "They have a tendency to be hard on the furniture."

"That's perfect then, because I don't have any furniture—at least not in the practice area," Lizette said. So far she had just fixed up the main room in her building. The building had been a grocery store years ago, and it had a nice backroom with a kitchen area that she was using as a small apartment for herself. "And if they're the kind of boys that like to move a lot, I'll just make them be mice."

Amanda giggled. "You can't turn boys into mice."

"Oh, yes, I can," Lizette said as she tousled Amanda's hair. "If I can turn a little girl into the Sugar Plum

Fairy, I can turn little boys into mice or snowflakes or flowers."

"I'd rather be a mouse than a flower," Bobby said.

"Well, we'll see," Lizette said as her hand rested on Bobby's head, too. "Maybe you can even be something more exciting than either one."

Judd wasn't so sure about Lizette's powers to turn little boys into mice, but watching her casual affection with the children sure turned him into something else.

"I'm surprised you don't have children," Judd said. "Of your own, I mean."

Lizette looked up at him. "I do hope to have children some day."

Judd could only nod. He didn't really even have any good reason to feel so disappointed. Of course she wanted children. She had to be ten years younger than him, which would only make her twenty-three or twenty-four. A woman like her would want the whole family thing.

Judd didn't know where the thought had come from in the past few days that maybe he could marry if he just limited himself to a wife and didn't think of children. Children were what made a family anyway. He wouldn't have a clue about how to be a father. Sure, he'd gotten along fine with Bobby and Amanda. But they weren't like other kids. They'd been frightened so badly that they clung to him for safety. If he hadn't been there, they would have clung to that stray dog of his as long as the dog defended them from their nightmares.

Other children would expect more. No, a man like him had no business thinking about raising children. Maybe someday he'd meet a woman who didn't want to have children either, and the two of them could marry.

Suddenly the doughnut Judd was eating didn't taste so good. It was too bad about Lizette.

Chapter Six

Lizette heard the sound of boots crunching in the snow. Lots of boots.

"Better hide those doughnuts," Charley said as he stood and looked out the window. "Another couple of pickups from the Elkton ranch are parked in front of the hardware store. Wonder when they got here."

"It's too late," Judd said. He'd eaten the last of his doughnut, and he pushed his chair away from the table.

The door to the ballet school was closed, and there were a dozen knocks on it all at the same time. Lizette could see, just by looking out the side window, that a lot of men were standing on her porch.

"I don't suppose they want to sign up for class," Lizette said as she stood to go to the door.

"No, I can't imagine they want to be mice," Judd agreed.

Lizette looked over her shoulder at the platter of doughnuts she had on the table. It still had five doughnuts on it. She had the rest of the doughnuts in the back room.

She opened the door and saw a sea of cowboy hats nod at her. "Come in."

"Thank you, ma'am," the man who stepped over the threshold first said.

"My, it does smell like heaven in here," the second man said as he walked into the room.

Each man who stepped into the room craned his neck to see the doughnuts sitting on the platter that was on the table. There was a black mat next to the door, but none of the ranch hands paused to let their wet feet dry there.

"We just stopped by to say a neighborly hello," one of the cowboys said as he craned his neck to look around her at the doughnuts.

"That's nice," Lizette said. She decided that if they didn't notice her standing there, it was futile to point out the black mat. Besides, the mat wouldn't make much difference. If a couple of men stopped to let their boots dry, the others would just keep the door open and the floor would eventually get wet anyway. In addition, the air in the room would be cold.

"The doughnuts are for the ballet students," Charley said before anyone could carry the conversation further. Then he sat back down at the table. "And for the men who have been guarding the school, of course."

Several of the older men stepped forward through the pack of cowboys.

"We're the guards," Jacob said as he stepped forward. Two other older men followed him. "We've been keeping a watch out the windows for strangers."

"That ain't a fair way to decide who gets the doughnuts—they haven't had to do anything but sit where they always sit," one of the cowboys said before he turned to Lizette and swept off his hat. "Begging your pardon, miss. I don't think I've had the pleasure of meeting you. My name's Pete Denning. The boys and I heard you were making doughnuts. What a fine thing to do on such a nice day."

Judd could see that the longer Pete talked to Lizette, the less concerned he'd become about the doughnuts. By the time the man had stopped introducing himself, he had a grin on his face that Judd would wager had nothing to do with baked goods.

"Of course, I'm not asking for any doughnuts for myself," Pete continued, confirming Judd's suspicions. "I just wanted to come over and see if I could do any chores for you—you know, something to welcome you to Dry Creek."

Judd grunted. "She's probably got some dishes to wash now that she's made the doughnuts."

Pete's smile wavered. "I was thinking more along the lines of chopping firewood or something. You know, one of those chores that single women need a man to help them out with."

"I have an electric stove," Lizette said. "And the dishes are all done. All I need is someone to dance for me."

Pete's smile brightened. "I can do that."

"She means the ballet," Charley muttered from where he sat at the table. "She's not talking about line dancing or anything fun."

"She's not?" Pete looked at Lizette. "You're sure? There's a place in Miles City that sets up a mean line dance."

"What place is that?" Jacob asked as he joined Charley at the table. "You're not thinking of the senior center, are you?"

"No, I'm not thinking of the senior center. How romantic would that be? No, I've got my own kind of places," Pete said.

"In Miles City?" Charley asked. "What kind of places are there that we don't all know about?"

There was a moment of tense silence.

"Thanksgiving is almost here, and that's no time for quarreling," Jacob finally said. "It's a time for lighting our candles at church instead." Jacob turned and addressed his words to Lizette. "That's been the tradition here since before the town started. Everyone lights a candle and says why they're grateful. It helps us all be thankful for what we've got."

"What we've got right now is doughnuts," one of the older men said as Lizette started passing the plate of doughnuts to the men who were the regulars in the hardware store. The man who spoke took a maple doughnut off the plate. "And I'm sure enough grateful for having one."

"I have more in back, so there's enough for everyone," Lizette said as the plate made its way around.

By now all of the cowboys were standing with their hats off. Lizette knew she should say something about going back to wipe their wet boots, but she didn't have the heart. They were all gazing at her with hope in their eyes, looking more like little boys than grown men.

Lizette went into the back room and brought out another full tray of doughnuts. She had a row of chocolate frosted ones, a row of powdered doughnuts, a few jelly ones, a row of apple ones and a section of maple bars. She'd even shaken red and green sprinkles over a couple of sugar-glazed doughnuts just to see what they'd look like when Christmas came. She was almost glad the ranch hands had stopped by. What would she have done with all of these doughnuts otherwise?

The men all sighed when Lizette carried the full tray over to where they stood.

"Of course, these doughnuts are to help advertise my ballet classes." Lizette felt she did owe it to herself to say that much as several hands reached for doughnuts. "And, remember, no one is too old for ballet."

One cowboy who was still reaching stopped with his hand midway to the doughnut. "We don't need to do this ballet stuff if we take one, do we?"

Another ranch hand who had already taken a bite of his doughnut sighed. "It would be worth it if we did."

"No, you don't need to sign up," Lizette said. Half of the doughnuts were already gone from the tray. She looked around and saw that everyone had a doughnut. "You could help by spreading the word though. We're hoping to do the Nutcracker ballet before Christmas, and I still need a minimum of five more students."

"The pastor has twin boys that are about six years old," Pete Denning said as he licked his fingers. He'd had a jelly doughnut from the plate earlier and was now eyeing the tray. "I think the pastor went to get them when we heard about the doughnuts."

"Well, we'll have to save some doughnuts for them then," Lizette said as she turned to take the tray out of the room.

"They might not want doughnuts," Pete said as he saw Lizette turn to leave.

Judd snorted. At least *he* knew kids better than that.

Pete heard him. "Well, maybe they'll want a doughnut, but their mother might not let them have one since it's so close to lunchtime and she'll be worried they won't eat their vegetables."

Judd flinched. He probably shouldn't have let Bobby and Amanda have doughnuts, either. This being a parent seemed to have lots of rules that he didn't know. He looked over at the two kids. They both had frosting on their chins and happy gleams in their eyes. It was likely they wouldn't want lunch.

Judd doubted the kids would eat any vegetables either if he put any in front of them at this point. He'd have to be sure they took a vitamin pill when they got home. He'd bought a big jar of children's vitamins when Bobby and Amanda first came. He didn't want his cousin to accuse him of stunting her kids' growth when she came to pick them up.

He wondered if he should take the kids to the dentist, too. When did kids start going to the dentist anyway?

Just then someone knocked on the door.

Lizette started to walk toward the door, but one of the ranch hands opened it before she got there.

Mrs. Hargrove came into the room and looked around with surprise showing on her face. Or at least what Judd could see of her face seemed to show surprise. The older woman had a red wool scarf wrapped around her neck, and she started to unwind it. She was wearing a long pink parka with a green gingham housedress under it. Her gray hair was clipped back with a red barrette. Mrs. Hargrove was always colorful.

"You must have gotten the news then?" Mrs. Hargrove said as she looked around the room. She still stood on the small black mat that was beside the door. "Looks like I'm interrupting the celebration. Sheriff Wall always did say the rumor line beat the phone line in this part of the country any day."

"What news?" Judd asked since she seemed to be looking at him.

"They're just here for the doughnuts," Charley said as he jerked his head at the ranch hands. "They didn't bring anything but their appetites with them."

Mrs. Hargrove looked over at the group of cowboys and frowned. "Don't tell me you came to beg doughnuts off of Lizette when she's hardly even settled in yet? What's she going to think of us?"

"Oh, that's all right," Lizette said. "I'd already made the doughnuts when they came."

"Still, these boys know better than to come in and eat up your food supplies like this. What if you were on short rations yourself?" Mrs. Hargrove looked at the men. "I'll bet each of you have been short a time or two in your lives."

"They're only doughnuts," Lizette said.

"No, she's right, Miss," Pete said as he pulled a dollar bill out of his pocket. "We sure don't expect you to feed us without getting something in return for it."

Pete put the dollar bill on the tray where the powdered doughnuts had been. He hadn't even finished putting the bill there before a dozen other bills joined the one he had placed there. She even saw a five dollar bill sticking out. There must be twenty dollars there.

"You really don't need to—" Lizette protested.

"We're happy to do it, Miss," Pete said. "Those were real fine doughnuts."

"The best I've ever eaten," another man said.

"I'd be willing to buy a whole tray of them if you want to make them," another man said. "It's my turn to bring something to eat when the guys get together on Friday night in the bunkhouse."

"Well, I guess I could make another batch," Lizette said. Now that she had the Dutch oven for the oil, all she would need was a few more eggs.

"I'll pay you a dollar a doughnut," the man said.

"Oh, that's too much," Lizette said. She could use the extra income, but she didn't want to overcharge her new neighbors. "Especially if you buy a few dozen."

"It's worth it to me, Miss," the man said. "Last

time it was my turn to bring the dessert, I tried to make an angel food cake myself."

"It came out flatter than a pancake," another man said as he gave Lizette a pleading look. "You'd be doing us all a favor if you let him buy the doughnuts. We ended up eating crackers the last time he was in charge of refreshments. And even those were stale."

"Well, all right," Lizette said. "But you'll get a bulk discount on the price. How does eight dollars a dozen sound?"

Lizette knew that was somewhere between what a doughnut shop and a bakery would charge for a dozen doughnuts.

"You've got yourself a deal," the man said.

"So you don't know the news?" Mrs. Hargrove said now that she had unwound her scarf and finished scraping her shoes on the black mat. "About the—" Mrs. Hargrove stopped and looked at the children. "Well, the news will keep for a little bit I guess— what with the kids here."

"Are there some more kids who are going to be in the ballet?" Amanda asked Mrs. Hargrove. "We need more kids."

Judd watched as Mrs. Hargrove bent down until she was on the same eye level as Amanda. Judd could see why the older woman was such a popular Sunday-school teacher. She smiled at Amanda.

"I heard you're going to be the Sugar Plum Fairy," Mrs. Hargrove said.

Amanda's eyes shone as she nodded her head. "And I get to wear the fairy-princess dress. Want to see it?"

"Why don't you ask your teacher if you can bring it over and show it to me?" Mrs. Hargrove said.

Amanda ran over to talk to Lizette.

Judd wondered if Mrs. Hargrove was going to invite him to church again. He almost hoped so. He could use an excuse to talk with the older woman some more. She seemed to know all about children and she could probably answer some of his questions—like was Amanda too old to still suck her thumb occasionally and, even if she was, was it better to just let her be or should he try to do something about it?

He wondered what the news was that Mrs. Hargrove had come over to tell. Maybe she'd just heard that they were taking precautions to be sure the children's father didn't come near them. If that was it, he could put her mind at ease. "Jacob and Charley have been keeping the streets of Dry Creek safe. Well, technically, the *street* of Dry Creek."

There was just one main street that ran through the town.

"I understand you have been keeping watch, too," Mrs. Hargrove said with a nod to Judd. She then looked down at Bobby. "And I expect you have a little helper here."

Bobby smiled up at the woman. "We're guarding the ballet."

"So you're in the ballet, too," Mrs. Hargrove said with an approving nod. "What part are you going to play?"

"I don't know yet. I might have to be a snowflake if we can't get any other kids to be in it with us."

"Ah," Mrs. Hargrove murmured. "Snowflakes are wonderful things. Especially at Christmas. Each one is different."

"Yes, ma'am," Bobby said without much enthusiasm.

"Why don't you go help your sister with that costume?" Judd said to Bobby. Judd had a feeling that Mrs. Hargrove wasn't going to tell him the news she had as long as either of the children were around to hear it.

Bobby pushed his chair back from the table and left to follow Amanda.

Mrs. Hargrove sat down in the chair Bobby had left. She didn't waste time but got straight to the point. "Have you heard from the sheriff this morning?"

Judd shook his head. "The kids have had lessons this morning, and I come in with them. I've been here."

"That's what the sheriff thought. That's why he called me. He wanted you to know that they think they've arrested the kids' father over in Miles City. The man won't say who he is, but he had that picture Lizette described with him."

"Did the man have a tattoo of a snake on his arm?"

Mrs. Hargrove nodded. "The sheriff said it was a cobra."

"That sounds like it's him, all right. Did he have a woman with him when he was arrested?"

Mrs. Hargrove shook her head. "No, it was just him. Are you thinking your cousin is hooked back up with him?"

"I don't know what to think," Judd admitted. "She should have been back here weeks ago, even if she'd had car trouble on the way to Denver. Besides, I don't know how he would know where to find the kids if he hadn't gotten the information from my cousin. Though I can't understand why she'd be foolish enough even to talk to the man."

"She must have had her reasons," Mrs. Hargrove said.

"Well, I hope they were good ones."

Mrs. Hargrove nodded. "The sheriff said they caught the man breaking into a gas station in the middle of the night."

"How long will he be in jail?"

"Long enough. They took him to the jail in Miles City for the time being. In a week or so they'll take him to the jail in Billings. If he is the children's father, apparently there's another warrant out for his arrest from the state of Colorado, so when they finish with him here, they're going to ship him down there."

"He's a popular guy."

"I'd say so. The sheriff figures they'll be sending him to Colorado sometime after Christmas."

Judd nodded. "That'll be some Christmas present for the kids."

Amanda and Bobby were starting to walk back toward them with the fairy costume in their hands. Even from here, Judd could see the excitement on Amanda's face.

"Do you think it will upset them to know their father's in jail?"

"I wish I knew," Judd said. "On the one hand, he is their father. But on the other hand, they're afraid of him. Knowing he's in jail might make them more comfortable even coming into town here. They seem a little nervous when they're not at my place."

Mrs. Hargrove nodded. "I wondered if that's why you haven't brought them to Sunday school yet." She didn't leave time for Judd to think of the real reason he hadn't brought the children. "But now that it's cleared up, I'll hope to see you this Sunday. It's the last Sunday before Thanksgiving, and the kids will be decorating candles and thinking about what they're going to say at the service we have the night of Thanksgiving."

"I heard about that—"

"It's a wonderful thing for families to do together," Mrs. Hargrove said as she turned to smile at Bobby and Amanda, who had just reached them.

Amanda was holding the pink costume out for Mrs. Hargrove to see.

"Oh, that's beautiful," Mrs. Hargrove told the little girl.

Watching Amanda talk with the older woman made Judd decide he would take the kids to Sunday school this Sunday. It would do Amanda good to talk to more people, and she certainly seemed to have no trouble chatting with Mrs. Hargrove. It would be good for Bobby, too, to meet some more kids.

The only one it might not be good for, Judd decided, was himself. He would be a fish out of water in church. Maybe he could leave the kids at the church and then walk over to the café and have a cup of coffee. Now that sounded like the way to do this. Although, now that he thought of it, he couldn't remember if the café was open on Sundays. He thought Linda went to the church in Dry Creek, too, so she probably didn't open the café that day.

For the first time, Judd wished Dry Creek were a bigger town. In a place like Billings, or even Miles

City, no one would notice who was going to church and who wasn't. They probably had coffee shops that were open on Sunday mornings as well.

Maybe he'd just have to sit in his pickup for the hour or so that the kids were inside. Yeah, he could do that.

Chapter Seven

Judd still hadn't talked to the sheriff about it all, but it was Saturday, and it had been two days since Judd had learned that the kid's father had been arrested. Hearing that news had surprised Judd enough. But what he was looking at now made that surprise go clear out of his head. He figured pigs were going to start flying down the street of Dry Creek pretty soon. He couldn't believe his eyes. Right there, in the middle of Lizette's practice room, was Pete Denning trying to do a pirouette.

The man's Stetson hat was thrown on the floor, and his boots were next to it. He wore one white sock and one gray sock, but both of his feet were arched up in an effort to hold him on his tiptoes.

"We should start with something simpler," Lizette was saying. She was dressed in her usual black practice leggings and T-shirt and had stopped her stretching on the practice bar to watch Pete.

"No, I saw this on TV and I know I can do it," Pete said as he tried again to stand on his tiptoes.

The man looked like a pretzel that had come out of the machine wrong.

"I see you got another student," Judd said. The kids and Charley were in the other room getting out of their coats and into their dancing slippers. Judd should have positioned himself in his usual chair outside on the porch, but he'd seen Pete, and that had changed everything.

"It's a free country," Pete said.

Judd lifted his hands up in surrender. "I didn't say anything."

"Yeah, but I know what you're thinking."

Judd chanced a quick look at Lizette. She'd paused midway through a stretch, and the curve of her back was the most beautiful thing he'd ever seen. He certainly hoped the cowboy didn't know what he was thinking.

Pete didn't wait for Judd to answer. "You're thinking that a Montana man like me wouldn't know what to do with a little culture."

"I didn't say that."

"But you would be wrong even to think it," Pete continued without listening. Pete was looking at Lizette, too, now. Lizette had stopped bending and was stretching her arm along the practice bar. A faint sheen of perspiration made her face glow, and tiny wisps of black hair had escaped the braid she wore.

Pete sighed. "A true man can appreciate fine art."

Judd didn't like Pete looking at Lizette. The cowboy didn't have fine art on his mind. Judd knew that much at least.

"You might have to wear tights," Judd said. That got the other man's attention away from Lizette, so Judd added, "Pink tights."

Now he had the cowboy's full attention.

Pete wasn't looking at anyone but Judd. He looked horrified. "Nobody said anything about tights."

"I said there would be costumes," Lizette said as she lifted her leg onto the practice bar and made another curve with her body.

"But 'costumes' doesn't mean tights," Pete said as he watched Lizette.

For a moment, neither man spoke.

Pete breathed out slowly. "Well, maybe if they're not *pink* tights."

Lizette finished her ballet move and turned to look at the two men. "Don't discourage him, Judd."

Judd felt that odd sensation in his stomach again. The last day or so Lizette had started calling him Judd, and he liked the sound of his name coming from her lips. Of course, it *was* his name, so it shouldn't be any big deal. It was just that he wasn't used to people saying it all of the time. If he was on the phone with someone, he was usually called "Mr. Bowman." In the rodeo, people had just called him "Bowman." His uncle had called him "You," if he called him anything at all. Judd guessed first names were more of a woman's thing.

"I won't discourage him," Judd finally said. "I'm looking forward to seeing him prance around up on stage." He could see the panic return to the other man's eyes.

"If he backs out, Judd Bowman," Lizette warned. "You're going to have to take his place."

"Me? Up there?"

"It would do you good," Lizette said. "Especially if you scare away any of my students. I don't know what the phobia is about tights anyway. They're really no tighter than football uniforms."

"Yes, but with f-football—" Pete stuttered. "Well, with football, you get to knock people around."

"I'm hoping you're not going to say that that makes you more of a man than ballet does," Lizette said to Pete.

Judd felt a little sorry for the cowboy. The two of them both knew that, of course, football made a man more of a man. And real men wore boots and not ballet slippers. They just couldn't tell any of that to Lizette.

"No, ma'am," Pete finally said. "I'm not going to say that."

"Good, because I'm expecting three more new students today, and with any luck, we can start some serious practicing for the Nutcracker."

Judd almost groaned. He hoped she wasn't expecting three more of Pete's cowboy friends. He couldn't stay out on the porch with all of those cowboys in here practicing their moves. And he didn't know what excuse he would give Lizette for guarding her classroom from inside the room, especially now that they all knew the kids' father was in jail in Miles City.

"This Nutcracker you want me to play," Pete said. "Does the Nutcracker wear tights?"

Lizette smiled at the cowboy. "Usually, he does."

Pete nodded glumly. "The guy sounds like some kind of a nut all right." Another look of alarm crossed Pete's face. "He is a guy, isn't he?"

Lizette laughed. "Yes, he's a guy. He wears a tall red hat with a black band under the chin."

"And tights," Pete said.

"Yes."

Pete shook his head.

"I suppose if you insisted, you could be a snowflake. It's just that I was saving those parts for the little kids."

"Maybe I could be an usher," Pete offered. "They get to wear clothes, don't they?"

"Of course they wear clothes," Lizette said. "Everyone wears clothes. All dancers are fully clothed at all times. What made you think they weren't? I can't afford for that rumor to get around. I won't even keep the students I have if people hear that."

"Maybe you need some help with the scenery," Pete finally offered. "Something with hammering."

Judd watched the disappointment settle on Lizette's face.

"Charley has already offered to build the fireplace that we need. Mrs. Hargrove has offered us her artificial Christmas tree. And we won't have enough dancers to do even a small version of the Nutcracker if you back out now," Lizette said.

Judd was a fool. He just couldn't stand that look on Lizette's face. "I could do something."

"Charley already offered to build the fireplace," Lizette said.

"No, I mean, I could do a dance part."

Judd wished he'd offered sooner. Lizette looked at him like he'd just hung the stars in the sky.

"You would? Dance a part?"

"Now, just wait a minute," Pete said. "I haven't said I *won't* do any dancing. I was just offering some extra help. Besides, I thought the deal was that the first people to sign up got their pick of the parts. Isn't that why your little girl gets to be the Sugar Plum Fairy?"

Judd nodded. He guessed those were the rules.

"So I pick the meanest dancer in the whole thing," Pete said. "Someone who commands respect on the street. Is there a part like that?"

"Well, if you're sure you don't want to be the Nut-cracker, you can be the Mouse King," Lizette said, and then added quickly as Pete started to frown, "he's not a furry little mouse. He's really a rat. He comes charging out of the fireplace and tries to take down the Nutcracker."

"Kind of like in football?" Pete said with a smile. "And I bet he doesn't have to wear tights."

"Well, he does usually wear tights," Lizette admitted. "But the rest of the costume covers them up pretty much."

"So Judd here's going to be the Nut guy?" Pete asked.

Lizette raised a hopeful eyebrow at Judd.

"I guess so," Judd admitted. He only hoped the Nutcracker got to fight back when the Mouse King tackled him. Judd didn't relish going down without a fight.

"Good," Pete said with satisfaction as he looked at Judd. "Let's hope that little black band keeps the hat on your head when I come after you."

Judd hoped the little black band kept his head

on his shoulders when Pete tackled him. "This Nut-cracker guy, he's not a coward or anything, is he?"

Judd had just realized he might be required to run away from Pete. He'd decided to make this little community his home, and he didn't want to get a reputation for running away from trouble.

"Oh, no, the Nutcracker fights him back," Lizette assured them both. "It's a glorious battle. All done in ballet, of course. The audience doesn't know until the last minute who wins."

Judd wondered how he was going to defend himself if he had to do it on tiptoes.

Just then the outside door to the dance classroom opened, and in walked Mrs. Hargrove and the pastor's twin boys.

"Well, we're here to learn to dance," Mrs. Hargrove said as Lizette moved to greet them.

Judd had to admit he was relieved. At least the new students weren't more cowboys.

"Oh, we're going to have such fun," Lizette said as she led Mrs. Hargrove and the twins back to the area where they could take off their coats.

Judd was less enthusiastic. His only consolation was that Pete didn't seem any happier about the arrangements than he was.

"I hope you've got room in those tights for some knee pads," Pete finally said, but he said it like the fight had already gone out of him. "I'd hate to bang up your knees too bad when I bring you down."

"My knees will do just fine," Judd said.

Pete was silent for a moment. "You don't suppose the guys are going to come to see this ballet thing, do you?"

Judd grunted. He figured there was about as much chance of the guys not coming to see this particular ballet production as there was of those pigs deciding to fly down the main street of Dry Creek. No, he and Pete were doomed to be everyone's merry entertainment for the holidays.

"You'd be welcome to come over to my place and hang out for a couple of days after the show if you want," Judd offered. He knew what a bunkhouse could be like when it came to teasing. "You could tell people you'd gone on a trip or something."

"I've been wanting to go to Hawaii."

"Well, maybe you could take that trip then. Winter's a slow time in ranching," Judd said.

"Can't afford to really go," Pete said.

"Well, then I'll just put some Hawaiian music on and turn up the heat in the spare room."

"I appreciate that," Pete said. "That doesn't mean I won't hit you hard when I can, but I do appreciate it."

Judd understood. Pete could no more take it easy on him than Judd could run away when Pete came after him. Even though Lizette had not told them how the fight turned out, Judd figured anyone who was named King, even if it was Mouse King, was the one who won the battle. Judd supposed Pete figured it the same way; the cowboy sure didn't look worried that he'd lose.

When the rest of the dancers came back to begin practice, Judd and Pete were both ready. Judd wondered what kind of nonsense he'd let himself in for. But he was a man of his word, and one thing he knew for sure—Lizette was counting on him to dance a part. His might not be the best part in the whole ballet, but it was the part she needed and he was willing to play it for her.

Judd only hoped Lizette thought he was doing it for the kids. He wouldn't want her to know he'd taken one look at her disappointed face and agreed to make a fool of himself. No, a man had to have some pride, even if he was a nutcracker.

Chapter Eight

Judd ached. It was Sunday morning, and he'd gotten the kids up and dressed for Sunday school like he'd promised them, but his body ached all over. Just a few months ago, he'd loaded two tons of hay bales by hand with nothing more than leather gloves and a metal hook. He hadn't felt a single ache in his body then. He was a man in the prime of his life. He was a rancher. But one day of ballet practice had about done him in.

And they hadn't even started practicing their parts yet. Lizette had just shown them some basic ballet steps. She said she was going to wait to practice the individual steps when she got the costumes she was borrowing from her old teacher and made sure they all fit.

Lizette had taken a moment to tell both Judd and Pete that she was sure both of their costumes would fit. And if not, she said, she'd improvise. Judd figured it was her way of telling them they had no hope of escaping.

After about an hour of ballet practice, Judd had stopped worrying about wearing tights. He didn't care what he wore. He just hoped that the Nutcracker guy stood in one place and let the Mouse King plow into him. His body would hurt less that way than if he had to keep practicing.

"Can you braid my hair?" Amanda stood in front of him after breakfast with a blue ribbon in her hand.

"Oh, but it'll look pretty if we just brush it and tie the ribbon around it," Judd said. He'd never braided hair in his life.

"No, I want it to look like Miss Lizette's," Amanda said. "She's awfully pretty."

"That she is, sweetheart," Judd said as he picked up the ribbon. He supposed he could try to braid hair. He was good at tying knots; he should be able to figure out hair braids.

Judd did a cross between a sailor's knot and a square knot.

"It doesn't look like Miss Lizette's," Amanda said as she stood up to look in the driver's mirror of his pickup. Judd had just pulled into a parking place near the church and was unfastening the seatbelts the children wore.

"The ribbon's pretty," Judd said reassuringly.

Judd looked at the braid again. Amanda was right. It didn't look at all like the one Lizette wore. "Maybe if you keep your head tilted to the right."

Judd wondered how many times he needed to bring the kids to Sunday school before he could throw himself on the mercy of Mrs. Hargrove. If he could just spend an afternoon with her asking questions, he knew he could do a better job with Amanda and Bobby. There should be some kind of a book or something that people could buy when they inherited kids all of a sudden like he had. Something that covered nightmares and braids and the other questions he had.

"You're coming with us, aren't you?" Bobby asked anxiously after he and Amanda had both climbed out of the passenger side of the pickup.

Judd looked over at them. They looked like little refugee children, frightened of a new experience and excited all at the same time. They'd asked so many questions this morning about church and Sunday school that he knew they'd never gone to either in their short lives. They didn't know what to expect any more than he did.

"Sure. I'm coming," Judd said as he opened his door. He hoped this wasn't one of those churches that required ties, because he didn't own one. It had always seemed pointless to have a tie when he didn't have a suit. Judd wished he'd screwed up his courage and visited this little church before the children came. At least then he could tell them what it looked like inside.

"It might have windows with pictures," Judd had said this morning. He couldn't remember actually looking that closely at the church in Dry Creek, but churches had those stained-glass windows, didn't they?

Judd looked down the side of the church now. He didn't see any stained-glass windows showing from the outside. "Even if there's no pictures, Mrs. Hargrove will be there."

The last seemed to reassure Bobby and Amanda. Judd wished he had thought to remind them of that fact earlier.

"She's going to be the Snow Queen," Amanda said. "But her costume won't be as pretty as mine."

"I think you're going to have the prettiest costume of all," Judd agreed as they started walking up the steps of the church. He put his hand on top of Amanda's head.

"There's Miss Lizette," Amanda said when they reached the bottom of the steps.

Judd looked down the street. Sure enough, Lizette was walking toward them. She wore a red wool coat and had a small black hat on her head. She looked more uptown than anything Judd had ever seen in Dry Creek.

"Good morning," Judd said. He couldn't think of one good reason why he'd never bought a suit and a tie in his life. A man should be prepared for days like this.

"Hello," Lizette said as she smiled at them. "Are you going to church, too?"

Amanda nodded. "And we're going to sit in a pew," Amanda leaned over and confided to Lizette. "But that's not a stinky thing. Cousin Judd says it's a long chair and we've got to share it."

Judd figured even a tie wouldn't save him now. "The children were curious about church."

"Of course," Lizette said.

All four of them had come to a stop at the bottom of the church stairs. There were only seven steps to the landing, but Judd didn't feel inclined to step forward and, apparently, neither did anyone else.

"Have you been to church here before?" Lizette finally asked as she stood looking up at the door.

It was a perfectly ordinary door, Judd decided. A good solid-wood double door. It was winter so the door wasn't wide open, but it was open a good six inches or so and he could hear the sounds of people talking inside.

"No, I've never been," Judd admitted.

"Oh," Lizette said, and then looked at him instead

of the door. "But you've been to other churches, right?"

Judd shook his head. "I don't know a thing about them."

"Me neither," Lizette said.

"I thought I should bring the children," Judd finally said.

Both Judd and Lizette looked down at the children and then looked at each other.

Lizette nodded. "Yes, the children should go to church."

Lizette held out her hand to Amanda. Judd held out his hand to Bobby. The four of them walked into church just like they were a family.

Yes, Judd thought. The next time he went to Billings he was definitely going to buy himself a suit and a tie.

Lizette looked around the church the minute she and Amanda stepped through the door. She'd searched through her costume trunk to find the French fedora she wore, and not another man or woman in the church was wearing a hat. She'd tried so hard to blend in that she was sticking out.

"Well, welcome," Mrs. Hargrove said as she walked over from another group of people. She had her hand extended out to Lizette. "I can't tell you how happy I am that you decided to join us this morning."

"I thought the children should come to church," Lizette said, and then blushed. She wasn't the one who was related to the children. It wasn't her place to see that they went to church.

"Oh, we have something for all ages," Mrs. Hargrove said as she extended her hand to Judd as well. "And you made it, too. I'm so glad."

Judd nodded.

"The children are going to decorate candles this morning," Mrs. Hargrove said as she leaned down to the level of Amanda and Bobby. "And you're going to talk about the light of the world."

"Can I make a blue candle?" Amanda asked. "I like blue."

"They have all colors of candles and sequins and all kinds of things to put on them," Mrs. Hargrove said as she motioned for another woman to come over. "Glory Curtis, the pastor's wife, will take you back to the Sunday-school room and get you settled."

Lizette watched the two children walk away with the pastor's wife.

"I can just wait outside until—" Judd began.

"Nonsense," Mrs. Hargrove said as she took them both by the arm. "The pastor has an adult Sunday-school class, and today's topic is how to have a happy marriage."

"Oh, but I'm not—" Lizette began.

"Nonsense," Mrs. Hargrove said as she walked them forward. "What he's going to say will apply to many relationships in life."

Judd decided that Mrs. Hargrove was wrong within five minutes of the pastor starting to talk. Judd had never had a relationship in his life that sounded like what the pastor described. His uncle certainly hadn't acted that way toward him. He'd never had a friend who was like that. Certainly none of the women he'd met on the rodeo circuits had cared about him that way.

He'd never even heard things like the pastor read from the Bible. What kind of person did good things to the people who wanted to do bad things to them? That would be like if the Nutcracker guy just lay down and let the Mouse King dance all over him and then got up and thanked him for it. The world would be all lopsided if that kind of stuff started happening. A man could get all confused about who his enemies really were.

"Inspiring," was all Judd could think of to say when the pastor finished the lesson and came over to greet him and Lizette.

"Very inspiring," Lizette added.

The pastor chuckled. "I'll admit it doesn't make a

whole lot of sense at first. The one thing you'll learn about God though is that He turns things upside down a lot."

Judd nodded. He wasn't sure he wanted to be standing here talking with the pastor about God. What he knew about God wouldn't fill an old lady's thimble, and he didn't want to appear ignorant in front of Lizette, especially not now that she'd taken his arm by the elbow. He doubted she even realized she was leaning into him a little. He liked the faint lilac perfume she was wearing. He wondered if it was okay to notice a woman's perfume in church. He supposed it was a sin. Of course, he couldn't ask. A man should already know something like that.

"We've got coffee out back in the kitchen," the pastor said. "We've got some tables set up, and you're welcome to sit and have a cup while you wait for the kids to finish. We'll be starting church services in about fifteen minutes."

Judd hadn't realized there was more to this church business than what he'd just sat through, but he wasn't about to say anything.

"I could use a cup of coffee," Lizette said.

The church kitchen was painted yellow and smelled like strong coffee. Mugs sat on the counter next to a big urn of coffee. Next to the coffee was another urn that held hot water. A basket of various tea bags sat next to the hot-water urn. Several card tables were set up on the wall opposite the cabinets. Folding chairs rested against the wall.

Judd and Lizette were the first ones in to get coffee. They both moved toward the urn as if they were dying of thirst.

"I don't belong here," Lizette burst out before she even got to the coffee mugs.

"*You* don't belong? I don't even have a tie," Judd muttered as he reached for a mug.

"Nobody here is wearing a tie—or a hat," Lizette said. "There should be a book telling people what to expect in church."

"I guess they just assume most people know those things," Judd said as he held the mug. "Would you like coffee or tea?"

"Tea, please. And how would we know what to expect in church? I've never been to church before."

Judd turned to fill the mug with hot water. "When you say you've never been to church, you just mean recently, don't you? I mean, I know you had a mother and a reasonable family life—I thought all families went to church at some point."

"Not ours."

Judd handed Lizette the mug of hot water. "I'll let you pick the tea you want."

Lizette pulled a lemon spice packet out of the basket and tore the paper wrapping off the tea bag. She put the bag in the hot water. "My mother was always mad at God. I don't think she had ever heard about any of the kinds of things the pastor was talking about back there."

"I wonder if he knows what he's talking about," Judd said as he poured himself a cup of coffee. Then he flushed. He might not know much about church etiquette, but he was pretty sure a visitor wasn't supposed to call the pastor a liar. "I mean, maybe something is translated wrong."

Lizette nodded. "It is pretty odd, isn't it? But I imagine he knows what he's talking about. Mrs. Hargrove seems to trust him, and I noticed she carries a Bible around with her. She must read it and agree with the man."

Judd nodded as they both walked over to one of the card tables. He had a tendency to trust Mrs. Hargrove. "It just must be that church is one of those things people like me don't understand."

They both sat down.

"What do you mean by that?" Lizette had wrapped her hands around her cup of tea, but she was making no move to lift the cup and drink any of it. Her face looked serious.

Judd's heart stopped. Here he had been muttering to himself, never expecting anyone to listen. It looked like Lizette had been listening.

"You keep saying 'people like me' like you were

raised on Mars or something," Lizette said with a smile. "You don't look that different to me."

Judd swallowed. There had to be a lot of clever things to say to that kind of question. Pete would know something brash to say that would turn the moment into a chuckle. But Judd realized he didn't want to avoid the question. "I'm different because I was raised by an uncle who didn't care about me. He never once celebrated my birthday. What am I saying? He never even said 'Good morning' or 'How was your day?' or 'Do you feel all right?' I could have laid down and died and he wouldn't have noticed except for the fact that the chores hadn't gotten done."

"Oh."

Judd plowed on. "I'm not saying that to say I had it worse than everyone else, it's just that I'm different. A lot of things other men know—things like how to be part of a family—those are things I don't know."

There. Judd had made his speech. It wasn't fancy, but it was the first time in his life he'd come out and said why he was so different.

"I do know how to work, though." Judd felt he needed to add something positive. "That's one thing I learned living with my uncle. I learned how to work."

"Oh."

Judd didn't add that he'd also learned not to

trust anyone and not to expect anything from any-one else.

There was a moment of silence.

And then Lizette took a sip of tea. "My mother always wanted me to be a ballet dancer."

"But you *are* a ballet dancer."

"Yes, but don't you wonder what would have hap-pened if I hadn't been able to dance?" Lizette asked. "What would have happened between my mother and me then? I think part of me always wondered about that, but I was afraid to ask her—I was even afraid to ask myself the question."

Judd had never thought that someone who had a family still might have had problems.

"Well," Judd said. He didn't know what else to say, so he just put his hand over Lizette's hand and patted it like he would have patted Amanda's hand if she had been there.

Judd guessed that maybe there was something to this going to church after all. Before he knew it, he wasn't patting Lizette's hand but was holding it instead.

"The tea's kind of hot," Lizette said as she blinked.

"Yeah, so is the coffee," Judd said as he pulled out a handkerchief and gave it to Lizette. He might not have a tie, but he'd started carrying one or two extra handkerchiefs since Amanda and Bobby had come into his life. It seemed like a lot of things were changing since those kids had come into his life.

Chapter Nine

Lizette wasn't ready for her students to come for practice. Oh, she was ready. She'd received the box of costumes and props from Madame Aprele and she had them laid out in the back room. She had the stage book marked for Charley, the narrator, so he could read aloud the abbreviated story of the Nutcracker and direct some of the scenes. What she wasn't ready for was to see Judd.

How did you explain to a man that you aren't crazy? Especially when he's seen your mood swing with his own eyes. She still didn't know what had happened. One minute, she was sitting there drinking tea with Judd and, before she knew it, she was sniffling into his handkerchief and talking about her mother. Lizette hadn't even known all of those questions about whether or not she measured up to her mother's hopes were inside her until they came spilling out to Judd. She was a mess.

It was the pastor's fault, of course. All of the talk about love and family and forgiveness—well, anyone would start to thinking about their life, wouldn't they?

It's just that it couldn't have happened at a worse time. She'd wanted to impress Judd. He was sort of the parent of the first two real students she'd ever had in her life, and she wanted him to see her as a professional.

After listening to her cry yesterday, he probably saw her as someone who *needed* a professional instead of someone who *was* a professional.

And he hadn't even had a choice but to listen to her. He'd patted her hand after her first few tears and told her that it would be all right. She should have stopped then. But she didn't. She'd gone on and on, telling him about this and that, and he'd kept patiently patting her hand. Then he'd held her hand for a bit, and it was the sweetest thing. Most men would have used the whole thing to make a move on a woman, but Judd didn't. Which, when Lizette thought about it, was the most embarrassing thing of all.

She'd been vulnerable and he'd been a gentleman. She'd been around enough to know what that meant—he wasn't interested. Plain and simple. No chemistry.

Not that she cared if he was interested. It was really best that he wasn't. After all, she was the teacher of the children under his care. He certainly wasn't obligated to think of her as anything but a teacher. She didn't *want* him to think of her as anything but a teacher.

And, to make things even worse, when it was all over and she'd cried her fill, he'd taken pity on her and asked her to sit with him and the children in church. Of course, she couldn't say no, because by then other people were coming in behind them for coffee, and she didn't want to turn around and have to face the others. So she had to keep sitting at the table with Judd until she'd blinked away some of the redness in her eyes.

In the meantime, Judd kept enough conversation going with the others so that no one noticed she wasn't turning around and talking. And he'd done it all so naturally, as though he was used to taking care of someone.

Lizette was never going to go to church again.

Judd wouldn't have believed that Lizette had cried in one of his handkerchiefs yesterday morning. Amanda had asked over breakfast if she could invite Lizette over for Thanksgiving dinner, and Judd had actually agreed it was a good idea. He'd thought they'd all had a nice time together yesterday. Now, he wasn't so sure. It was practice time for the ballet, and the woman whose soft hands he'd held yesterday had turned into a drill sergeant today, and she apparently saw him as nothing more than a raw recruit.

"I can march or I can ballet," he finally said. "I can't do both."

Well, Judd admitted, that was an exaggeration. He could march, but he wasn't so sure anyone could call his tortured steps ballet. People couldn't walk like that, could they? Lizette insisted she wasn't trying any advanced moves, but they sure seemed advanced to him.

Mrs. Hargrove and Charley were sitting on two folding chairs at the back of the practice room talking intensely until they both happened to look at him doing his ballet moves. Judd couldn't decide if it was encouragement or astonishment that he saw in their eyes, and he wasn't about to ask. At least they had stopped their conversation and bothered to look at him.

Which was more than he could say for Lizette. She didn't even look at him to see how he was doing when he complained. The only students she looked at this morning were the children. His sole consolation was that Pete looked even more bewildered than he was.

"My toes don't bend backward," Pete said.

"Of course not," Lizette said with some alarm in

her voice as she left the children and went to Pete's side. "You must have your feet placed wrong. Here, let me help you."

Lizette put her arm around Pete and stood at his side. "Now, do this."

Judd grunted. Pete wasn't even looking at Lizette's feet as she showed him how to move his big feet. Instead, the cowboy was grinning triumphantly over at Judd. Well, Judd had to admit that the cowboy knew how to get a lady's attention better than he did even if he was just as bad at ballet.

"Now you try it," Lizette said to Pete.

"Ah." Pete looked around in alarm. "I think I need to see it all again."

"You put your foot like this," Lizette began again.

Judd wondered why she needed to keep her arm around the cowboy when all she was doing was showing him how to stand on his tiptoes. "Shouldn't he be practicing at the bar over there?"

Judd knew the bar was for practicing. He didn't much like looking in the big mirror behind the bar, but he did know what it was for.

"I'm learning just fine here," Pete said. "It's not easy being a rat."

Judd grunted. He thought the other man was doing a particularly fine job of being a rat.

"I think a rat would move his feet like this," Pete said as he danced a little.

Fine, Judd thought, now the cowboy was doing interpretive dance.

"That looks a little like the tango," Lizette said with a frown. "That's good, but it's more like the steps the mice would take. You're the leader. You need more power in your moves. You play a huge king rat."

"Think big and fat," Judd offered. "All of that cholesterol from the cheese."

Pete scowled at him. "I'm sure I'm a very fit rat."

"I don't see you eating any cottage cheese in this role," Judd said. If anyone should have power in their moves, it should be the Nutcracker. Judd had a feeling he was going to need some power.

"At least no one's going to be staring at my legs like they will be at the Nutcracker's," Pete said smugly. "I have a costume that covers my legs."

"Oh, that's right," Lizette said. She moved away from Pete and stood in the middle of the room. "Let's take a break and try on the costumes. Then we'll do a quick read through with the narration so people get familiar with the story. We'll do the actions, but not worry about all of the dance steps yet."

"Good." Judd could do action.

The children and Pete went into the back room

first to look at the costumes. Judd wanted to talk with Mrs. Hargrove.

"Good morning," Judd said as he walked over to her and sat down in the chair that Charley had just vacated. Charley decided to go into the back room to see the costumes, too.

Mrs. Hargrove smiled and nodded. Then she waited.

"I enjoyed church yesterday," Judd lied. It was true that he'd found church very interesting, but he could hardly say that. It made the whole experience sound scientific and cold, and it hadn't been, either. Lizette had been right that there should be some advice book about churchgoing.

"I thought you might think it was a bit too personal," Mrs. Hargrove said.

"Oh, no," Judd lied again. Now that he thought about it, that was exactly what had been wrong with all those things the pastor was saying. Whose business was it anyway how he wanted to treat his enemies? Enemies shouldn't expect nice treatment. Maybe people wouldn't have so many enemies if everyone just stayed with their own business.

"I'm glad you feel that way," Mrs. Hargrove said. "I'll look for you to become a regular at church then."

"Ah," Judd stammered. He didn't want to give that

impression. "I'll certainly come when I can, but I'm building a fence, you know."

Mrs. Hargrove smiled. "Well, I'll pray you finish it quickly then."

"It might be more than one fence."

Judd stopped before the heavens opened and God struck him dead. He'd already told three lies, and it wasn't even noon. He'd better get to the point. "I was wondering if sometime—it doesn't have to be now—if you'd have a few minutes to talk about raising children? I mean, you seem so good at it."

Mrs. Hargrove chuckled. "You haven't talked to my daughter lately if you think that."

"I didn't know you had a daughter."

Mrs. Hargrove nodded. "I do. A more stubborn, opinionated woman you're not likely to meet than Doris June Hargrove."

"Have I met her?" Judd tried to think of the women of Dry Creek. He couldn't remember any of them who were named Doris.

"She doesn't live around here. She insists on staying up in Anchorage even though her heart is back here where the rest of her belongs. And Charley's son knows she belongs here, too. The two of them are just too stubborn to do anything about it."

"Well, some people take longer to get to know each other."

"Humph," Mrs. Hargrove said. "Those two know

each other just fine. Give either one a pencil and paper and they could list every fault of the other in a minute. They'd enjoy doing it, too."

"Well, then, maybe they're happier being apart."

"They're miserable and it's time someone did something about it."

"Well—" Judd started and stopped. He hoped she didn't mean *he* should do anything. He didn't even know either one of them. There hardly seemed anything to say. "Maybe someone will."

Mrs. Hargrove nodded. "That's the first thing you need to learn about being a parent. Sometimes you need to step into your child's business and make it your own."

"Bobby and Amanda are both still a little young for love problems," Judd said. He didn't mention his own problems with the opposite sex. He wasn't sure he'd want Mrs. Hargrove to fix his love life. She looked unstoppable.

"Of course they are. This is information for the future."

"I'm looking more at the next few months," Judd said. "You know, things like nightmares and missing their mother and braids."

"Braids?"

Judd nodded. "I don't know how to braid hair, and Amanda wants her hair to look like Lizette's."

"Oh, of course," Mrs. Hargrove nodded. "It's perfectly obvious that Amanda wants some motherly affection from Lizette."

"It is?"

Mrs. Hargrove nodded. "And it's a good thing. Spending time with Lizette will make her feel better."

"She wants to invite Lizette over for Thanksgiving dinner, but—"

"You're not one of those men who think women are the only ones who should cook, are you?"

Judd shook his head. "I'm not opposed to cooking; I'm just not sure how good I am at it."

"Oh, you'll do fine with cooking a turkey dinner. You just get a bag for the turkey, and I can give you some simple recipes to see you through. You might need to buy a pie though."

"Got a couple in the freezer."

"Well, then, you're all set. I just wish a broken heart was as easy to mend."

Judd looked up in alarm. It was a bit extreme to say his heart was broken. Dented a little maybe, especially after the cool way Lizette was acting toward him today, but not broken. Not at all. "People make too much of broken hearts."

"So you think I shouldn't do anything to make Doris realize she's still in love with Charley's son?" Mrs. Hargrove looked worried.

"Don't listen to me," Judd rushed to say. "I don't know anything about this kind of stuff."

He hadn't even known she was talking about someone else, that's how much he didn't know.

"I'm sure she'll appreciate whatever you do for her," Judd added.

Mrs. Hargrove chuckled. "I wouldn't go that far, but we'll see. In the meantime, why don't I teach you to braid hair after class today?"

Judd nodded in gratitude just as he heard his name being called from the back room.

"Excuse me," he said to Mrs. Hargrove. "That's Amanda calling."

"Look at your hat," Amanda said with a squeal when Judd entered the back room.

Lizette had found an old sofa for the back room and a mound of colorful costumes were spread out on it. It looked as though some of the accessories were sitting on the square table in one corner as well. There was a curtain at one end of the room, and Judd figured the bed was behind it.

He wondered how anyone could make an old room look so inviting. Then he took a good look at the hat Amanda was pointing at.

"It's real red," Judd said. He figured that was an understatement. Some reds could be dignified. This one wasn't. It was bright enough to light up the darkness. "And it's so big."

The hat was two feet tall.

"Well, you are a nutcracker," Lizette said patiently.

"But I didn't know I was a *giant* nutcracker."

Judd didn't need to look over at Pete to know the man was snickering. He could hear the cowboy trying to contain his laughter even if he didn't look at him.

"Remember, the Nutcracker fights back," Judd said as he looked over at Pete.

"What? Are you going to slap me with your top hat?" Pete said as he chuckled.

"Oh, no, you can't damage the costumes," Lizette said. "We're going to need to return them when we finish."

"I'll be careful," Judd said. He wouldn't need a hat anyway to fight back against the cowboy.

"And, Pete, you'll be careful too, won't you?" Lizette asked, turning to the cowboy. "Your tail is a little fragile."

Judd started to grin. "His tail?"

Pete stopped laughing. "My tail?"

"Well, you are a mouse," Lizette said.

Amanda and Bobby both giggled. Judd thought he heard Charley give a snort or two as well.

"Rat," Pete corrected. "You said I was a rat."

"Mouse. Rat. They both have tails," Lizette said as she reached into a bag.

Judd grinned even wider. The tail Lizette pulled

out of the bag had to be five feet long. And it was pink.

"I can't wear pink," Pete said.

Lizette frowned as she looked at the tail. "It's not exactly pink. It's more puce than anything. Your whole costume is puce."

Judd could see that the costume was pink.

"Maybe I could have my tail chopped off," Pete said. "I bet there are rats that've run into trouble and are missing part of their tail. You know, the fighter kind of rats, like I will be."

"But the tail balances out the ears," Lizette said as she pulled two pink ears out of the bag.

Pete was speechless.

Judd decided his hat wasn't such a bad thing. "If you don't like the look of your ears, maybe you should get a hat."

"Well, at least I have to have something to fight with, don't I?" Pete finally said. "I mean, I have to have something to fight with—like a knife or something."

"You have teeth," Lizette said as she also pulled out a rat's head.

Judd had to admit the head looked like a fighter rat. An uglier mask he'd never seen.

"That's more like it," Pete said as he picked up the mask and turned it around.

"Well, everyone try on their hats and heads. I want to be sure everything fits," Lizette said.

Judd looked around him at all of the other dancers. Mrs. Hargrove had come into the room and was fingering a billowing white dress that must be the Snow Queen outfit. Charley was trying on an old tweed bathrobe that was the costume for the narrator. Judd wished *he'd* been the narrator. The bathrobe looked comfortable. Amanda was, of course, eyeing the Sugar Plum Fairy costume that was over in the corner. Even Bobby and the twins looked happy, since they were going to be either mice or toy soldiers in the first part of the ballet and snowflakes at the end.

Judd realized he'd never been in anything like this in his life. His uncle had thought school itself was a waste of time, so Judd had never tried out for any school plays. There were always chores to do. The closest thing to costumes he'd ever seen were the clown costumes at the rodeo and everyone knew those clowns were not for fun.

Judd decided he liked the thought of playing a part in something like this ballet. Especially now that he'd seen the tail Pete had to wear and realized he wasn't going to be the only man who was wearing a ridiculous costume.

Besides, Judd thought as he saw Amanda and

Bobby, he'd never seen the two of them so excited, and it was worth making a fool of himself to see them having such a good time.

Chapter Ten

The first official rehearsal of the Dry Creek Nutcracker ballet was underway. An X was taped to the floor where the artificial tree would be. Charley was sitting on a folding chair next to the fireplace he had built out of cardboard. Mrs. Hargrove was backstage helping the Sugar Plum Fairy adjust her wings. The Curtis twins were being good little mice and sitting in the corner until it was time for them to run across the stage. Bobby was sitting next to the twins in his tin soldier costume. Pete was looking at his new mouse head in the mirror by the practice bars. Judd was holding his hat and frowning at it.

Yes, Lizette thought to herself, they were really going to be able to do this. Even though this was the first time on stage for all of her performers, they already looked like a typical group of ballet students.

The only thing that was missing was for one of the performers to be sick.

Lizette had changed into her Clara costume—with Amanda choosing the Sugar Plum Fairy part and no other young girls clamoring for the role, Lizette had decided to adapt it for herself. For the first time today, she felt as if she was the teacher and had everything under control. Generally, Clara had several different costumes during the performance, but Lizette had decided to keep her costume simple. It was a yellow dress with a short skirt. Clara was a young girl, so Lizette had braided her hair into a single braid down her back and tied the end with a big yellow ribbon.

"Let me get the narrator's book and we'll begin," Lizette said.

Madame Aprele said the book she'd sent was a condensed story of the Nutcracker that she had used for one of her own productions years ago when she was first starting her school. She'd eliminated some of the scenes and changed others. She'd promised Lizette that it was a very simple rendition of the classic ballet. Lizette had briefly reviewed the narration and was ready to begin.

"Everyone take your places," Lizette said as she gave Mrs. Hargrove the audiocassette tape to put into the small stereo system Lizette had set up earlier.

Judd knew ballerinas were supposed to glide, but seeing Lizette dance the first dance left him breathless. She was dipping and bowing and soaring all over the practice floor. And while Lizette was moving, Charley kept reading from the narration about a young girl and her brother who were given special gifts at Christmas time.

The sun was starting to set, and Charley asked Mrs. Hargrove to bring him a lamp that was along the side of the room.

Once the lamp was there, Lizette danced in the circle of light it gave.

Judd was watching Lizette so closely that he didn't notice when his cue came.

"The Nutcracker," Charley cleared his throat and repeated a little louder. "When Clara opened her present, she saw the Nutcracker."

"Just walk into the circle of light," Lizette directed. "You're not alive at this point, so no one will expect you to move."

Judd moved into the circle of light.

"You mean I'm your present?" Judd whispered to Lizette in dismay. "Your Christmas present?"

Judd had gotten Amanda a doll for Christmas with eyes that lit up depending on what kind of eye makeup the girl put on the doll. Judd didn't pretend to know much about little girls, but he was willing to bet that very few of them would be excited about getting a nutcracker for a Christmas present. "Do I at least come with a few walnuts or something?"

"Way to go, Nutcracker," Pete said as he stood by the fireplace holding his rat-king head. "I'd at least bring her some cheese."

"Clara was very excited to open her present and see the Nutcracker," Charley read from the book.

Lizette danced some more, and Judd would swear that the movements of her arms and legs did remind him of an excited little girl. The background music for this part of the ballet was very light and fanciful.

Maybe it wasn't so bad being Lizette's present, Judd thought as he looked over at Pete. The cowboy was still leaning against the wall, only now he was frowning.

"Clara's brother was also given a gift—some toy soldiers," Charley read as Bobby marched forward in a toy soldier costume. "But, even though he liked the toy soldiers, he was jealous of Clara's nutcracker and broke it just when it was time for everyone to go to bed."

Lizette danced into the shadows as the narrator said, "everyone went to bed," leaving the Nutcracker and the toy soldiers in the living room.

"That night after everyone was asleep," Charley kept reading. "Clara and her brother went back downstairs."

"Mice gather over by the fireplace," Lizette whispered, and the Curtis twins hurried over to the fire-place.

"Clara and her brother start playing with the mice," Charley read. Then he reached into the prop bag and pulled out a large wind-up alarm clock. "But then the clock strikes midnight."

Charley pulled a button so the alarm clock would ring.

"When the clock strikes midnight, the mice stop playing. The room becomes darker and is no longer a friendly place. The mice start attacking Clara and her brother. The toy soldiers try to fight back, but they are outnumbered."

The Curtis twins ran up and started flinging their arms around Bobby, who was the toy soldier.

In the middle of the action, Lizette danced around the stage like a wounded bird.

"Seeing that Clara is in trouble, the Nutcrack-er comes to life and starts to defend her from the mice."

"From the mice?" Judd said. "I thought I was going to fight that Rat King."

Judd figured he shouldn't even have worried. The day he wasn't equal to two little kids was the day he'd give up ballet.

Judd spun around on his tiptoes and pulled the cardboard sword out of the sheath on his belt. Then he tried to dance to the music while he fought back the mice. Of course, he was careful not to fight too hard. He didn't want to discourage the Curtis twins in their mice roles.

"Gradually, it looks like the toy soldiers and the nutcracker are pushing back the mice, and then a giant rat comes bursting out of the fireplace."

Pete crawled out of the front of the fireplace. Of course, the cowboy was on his knees and it took a moment for him to stand. It took another second for him to roar.

Judd took a deep breath so he wouldn't laugh. Pete's tail was twisted around his shoulders, and his ears were as lopsided as a rabbit's.

Pete put his rat head down and charged toward Judd.

"Stop," Lizette commanded. "I have to show you how to stage a fight."

Judd figured it was too late to stage anything. So he moved to the side and let Pete catch him on the shoulder.

Charley kept reading. "The giant rat keeps fighting the Nutcracker until the Nutcracker is weary."

Judd didn't feel the least tired. He rather liked the look of concern he saw on Lizette's face. It might take a charging rat for her to worry about his well-being, but it was nice to know that she could do so with the proper encouragement.

"But we need to stage the action," Lizette said. "There shouldn't be any physical contact."

"How am I going to hit him if I can't touch him?" Pete said as he raised his head.

"You pretend. We all pretend," Lizette said.

"It's okay. He can touch me," Judd said.

Pete lowered his head. "Let the story continue—"

Charley cleared his throat. "The Mouse King gets ready for one final attack. The toy soldier is lying on the floor. Only the Nutcracker is left, and he is wounded."

Pete pawed the floor like a bull would do before it charged.

Judd figured this was the final act for him.

"Clara sees the Mouse King get ready to attack and puts herself between the rat and the Nutcracker," Charley reads.

"What?" Judd said.

"What?" the rat echoed.

"I can fight my own battles," Judd said. He'd thought there was nothing worse than dying in this battle. He was wrong. He'd never live it down if the Nutcracker hid behind a woman's skirts.

"I'd never hit a lady," the rat said.

"You don't have to hit me," Lizette hissed. "Remember, there's no physical contact. Everything is staged."

"B-but, still—" Pete stammered.

"Besides, you don't hit me in the story," Lizette whispered. "I hit you."

Charley turned a page in the book and continued. "Clara takes off one of her shoes and throws it at the Mouse King."

Lizette threw her dance slipper at the rat.

"The shoe hits the Mouse King and topples him," Charley continued.

Pete still stood in astonishment.

"Lie down," the Curtis twins whispered to him. They were both already lying on the floor where they had fallen in battle. "You're dead."

"From a shoe?" Pete asked. "I get beat by a shoe?"

Judd shook his head. He supposed he should be happy that the Mouse King was defeated, but he had to wish right along with Pete that it had happened another way. It didn't do Judd's image any good either to be rescued by a woman and her shoe.

Pete reluctantly slid to the floor. "Even if I'm dead, I'm not closing my eyes."

Charley was fumbling in the bag and the music was starting to soar.

"Because of the bravery of Clara and the Nutcracker, the Nutcracker comes to life and becomes a man," Charley read.

Judd liked the sound of that.

The music soared even further.

"When Clara sees that her beloved Nutcracker is alive, she kisses him," Charley read.

"She what?" Lizette said.

"She does?" Judd grinned.

"Well, nobody told *me* that," the Mouse King said, and it looked like he was going to rise again.

Charley looked up. "That's what it says right here."

"Madame Aprele must have changed the text," Lizette said as she walked over to Charley and looked at the book for herself.

"I think a kiss would be nice," Mrs. Hargrove said from the sidelines. "Everybody likes a little romance in a ballet."

"Well, I guess it could be a stage kiss," Lizette said as she walked back to Judd.

"And you need to take his hat off for when he turns into a prince," Charley whispered. "Those are the directions."

Judd forgot all about the room that was around them. He forgot about the dead mice lying on the floor and the live rat looking ready to pounce. He forgot about the Sugar Plum Fairy sitting on the sidelines watching him. All Judd could think about was the green eyes staring straight at him.

Why, she's nervous, Judd thought to himself. The woman who had been treating him all morning like he was a raw recruit and she was the drill sergeant was actually nervous to be this close to him.

"It'll be okay," he said softly.

"It's just a stage kiss," Lizette reminded him.

Judd wasn't even going to ask what a stage kiss was. He figured a raw recruit should be able to plead ignorance.

Judd took the tall hat off his head and set it on the floor beside them. He'd never yet kissed a woman with his hat still on his head, and he wasn't going to start now.

The background music dipped, and the green in Lizette's eyes deepened. She must have guessed his intent, because she gave a soft gasp and her mouth formed a perfect O.

Judd kissed her. He'd meant to satisfy his curiosity with the kiss. He'd been wanting to kiss Lizette since he saw her hanging that sign in her window. When he kissed her, though, he forgot all about the reasons he wanted to kiss her. He just needed to kiss her. That was all there was to it.

Judd finally heard Charley clearing his throat. Judd wasn't sure how long the man had been sitting there doing that, but he figured it must have been for some time. The others were looking at them in astonishment.

Somehow Judd's arms had gotten around Lizette and she was nestled in the curve of his shoulder. She still had her face turned into him, and Judd felt protective of her.

"We were just doing this stage kiss," Judd finally managed to say. His voice sounded a little hoarse, but he was at least able to get the words out.

"Uh-huh," Pete said from where he lay by the fireplace. "You mean the one where there's no actual contact?"

"It's the one the movie stars do," Judd said as he felt Lizette move away from his shoulder a little.

"Sometimes," Lizette said as she took a steadying breath, "actors get very involved in their roles and forget who they really are."

"I'm not getting that involved in being a rat," Pete said as he stood up.

Judd had to admit he wasn't asking himself how a Nutcracker would feel about anything, either. He had enough trouble just knowing how Judd Bowman felt.

Lizette stepped out of his arms and Judd let her go. In that instant, he knew exactly how Judd Bowman felt. He felt as though a truck had run him over, and he wanted to beg it to come back and run him over again. He couldn't breathe.

"I think we've gone far enough in the story for today," Lizette said as she stepped even farther away from Judd. "We'll meet again tomorrow—"

Charley cleared his throat. "But tomorrow is Thanksgiving."

"Oh, yes." Lizette blushed. "I mean on Friday. We'll meet to practice on Friday. And I hope all of you have a nice Thanksgiving."

Judd was starting to breathe normally again.

"But we were going to ask you," Amanda whispered as she came up beside Judd and put her hand in his.

Judd let his fingers curl around the little hand.

"We *were* going to ask her, weren't we?" Amanda asked as she looked up at Judd.

"Yes, pumpkin," Judd said as he tried to get himself to focus. He felt as though he'd been bucked off a stallion and hit his back hard coming down. He looked down to see what Amanda wanted.

But Amanda was no longer there. She'd slipped her hand out of his and gone over to Lizette.

"We want you to come eat Thanksgiving with us," Amanda said loud and clear. "And I'm going to help make the potatoes. Cousin Judd said I could. Bobby gets to help with the vegetables."

"Oh, that's very sweet," Lizette said as she looked over at Judd with a question in her eyes. "But I'm sure you'll be—"

Judd could see the excitement start to dim in Amanda's eyes. If he'd had his wits about him, he'd have given her some excuse about why they couldn't invite Lizette. He knew it did a man like him no good to start dreaming about a woman like Lizette. He could never give her all that she deserved. But he couldn't put his comfort ahead of Amanda's happiness, either.

"Please come," he finally said.

"We're going to have dinner and then go to the candle service at church. Bobby and I get to take the candles we made up front. Cousin Judd said we could," Amanda added.

"I'm sure you both have beautiful candles," Lizette said as she put her hand on Amanda's shoulder.

"I made one for you, too," Amanda said softly.

"Oh," Lizette said, and then she looked at Judd.

Judd figured that was when she decided. He noticed she lifted her chin a little for courage.

"I'd love to join you for dinner," Lizette finally said. "And church, too."

Judd hadn't realized he was holding his breath again until he let it out. So, they were having company for Thanksgiving dinner after all. And then they'd all be going to church.

"I'm doing vegetables," Bobby said as he stood up from the floor. "Mrs. Hargrove told me how."

"Green beans in mushroom soup topped with fried onion rings," Mrs. Hargrove said from the sidelines. "It's the simplest vegetable recipe I know, and it's good."

"I could bring something," Lizette offered.

Judd noticed the color was coming back to her cheeks.

"I think we have everything we need," he said.

"You're sure? I could make a pie," Lizette said.

"You can?" Charley said as he stood up from his narrator chair. "What kind of pies can you make?"

"Well, most kinds," Lizette said.

"If that don't beat everything," Charley said to no one in particular. "She can make pies."

"I like apple," Bobby said. "Can you make apple?"

Lizette smiled. "I'll need to run over to Miles City to get some apples, but I need to go later today anyway to get some flyers printed for the Nutcracker. I want to post them around."

"You use real apples?" Charley asked. "It's not that canned filling?"

"Oh, no," Lizette said. "There's nothing like real apple pie."

"Hallelujah," Charley said.

"I could make one for you while I'm making pies," Lizette offered.

Charley nodded and sighed. "I'd sure be happy if you did."

Judd figured Lizette had already made him happy even if she never made a pie.

"I've heard an apple pie is the way to a man's

heart," Mrs. Hargrove said softly as she stood next to Judd.

Judd remembered Mrs. Hargrove was in a matchmaking mood. He wasn't so sure he wanted the whole countryside to know his heart was taken by Lizette. When the word got out about the pies, Judd figured he'd be one of a long line of broken-hearted men hoping for a kind word from the ballet teacher.

"Lemon's more my pie," Judd said.

"Oh," Mrs. Hargrove said in surprise. "I meant Bobby's heart."

Judd smiled. "Of course."

Judd wondered how he'd made it to adulthood without understanding women.

"Although, now that you mention it," Mrs. Hargrove said thoughtfully. She smiled at Judd. "That was a very unusual stage kiss."

"I'm new to the stage stuff."

Mrs. Hargrove smiled. "You're learning fast."

Judd nodded. He was a marked man and Mrs. Hargrove knew it. His only consolation was that the older woman seemed to be kind. He hoped that she also knew how to keep a secret. Judd wasn't sure he could stand for the state of his heart to become a topic of common gossip around Dry Creek.

Chapter Eleven

Lizette put the lemon pie on the table. She could as well have laid a snake down in front of the man.

"But you made apple pie," Judd said.

They'd already finished their dinner of roasted turkey and mashed potatoes and green been casserole, and it was time to have pie. Lizette had kept the lemon pie in a box in the refrigerator while they ate because it needed to stay cool. She hadn't realized until now that Judd must have thought it was another apple pie in the box.

Lizette had made two apple pies for Bobby. She'd delivered the extra pie wrapped in tin foil so he could freeze it for a later meal. She'd also made an apple pie for Charley. Charley and Bobby had been delighted with their pies. Judd, however, looked horrified.

"You said you liked lemon pie," Lizette reminded him. She tried to keep her voice calm. He was looking at her with questions in his eyes. What could she say? She'd made the man the pie because, well, "I had leftover crust."

There. That should satisfy him that she wasn't attempting to lure him into a relationship. The pie was simply a pie.

Lizette took a knife like the one she'd used to cut the apple pie and cut several small pieces of the lemon pie. "I made three pies with the crust I had, and there wasn't enough dough left to make another apple pie because it takes double the amount of crust, so I made a single-crust pie. Lemon."

"Oh." Judd seemed relieved even though he didn't put his plate forward for more pie like the kids were doing. "I wouldn't want you to go to any extra trouble. I mean, I like apple pie, too."

"Besides, it's really for everyone," Lizette continued. She used a pie lifter to put a piece of pie on Bobby's outstretched plate and then on Amanda's plate. "I'm sure the kids like lemon meringue pie."

Amanda nodded from her side of the table. "And chocolate. We like chocolate pie, too, with the white stuff."

"Maybe next time, sweetie," Lizette said as she put the pie lifter on the plate next to the lemon pie.

Amanda swallowed. "But what if my mother comes back before you make the pie?"

"I'm sure she'll wait long enough for you to eat a

piece of pie," Lizette said, making a mental note to get the ingredients for a chocolate pie the next time she drove into Miles City. It wouldn't hurt to make a crust and keep it in the freezer so she could whip up a pie at a moment's notice.

Actually, while she was making crusts, maybe she should make several crusts. The people of Dry Creek seemed to like their pies. Well, except for Judd, of course. He was still just looking at the lemon pie.

Amanda nodded as she took up her fork. "My mom likes pies, too. She always made us a chocolate pie for Christmas."

Lizette watched as Amanda set her fork back down without taking another bite. The girl's lower lip was beginning to tremble.

"What if my mom doesn't get back in time for Christmas?" Amanda asked.

"Oh, sweetie." Lizette pushed her chair back from the table and stood up so she could go around to Amanda and give her a hug. Judd was already there by the time Amanda reached the little girl's chair.

And that was the way it was supposed to be, Lizette told herself as she stood and watched Amanda reach up to go into Judd's arms. Lizette supposed it was the kitchen table that had confused her. The table was square and had a place for each of them—Judd, Amanda, Bobby, and herself, Lizette. The table had made her feel like she was part of their family.

But Judd was the one the children turned to for comfort. He was the one who was standing in for their mother.

"Don't worry," Judd said softly to Amanda as he held her close. "I've already asked the sheriff to look for your mother, and he said he'll do everything he can to track her down."

"Maybe she's hiding from our dad," Bobby said from his place at the table. "Maybe she doesn't know he's in jail."

"Maybe," Judd agreed.

Lizette admired the way Judd was so honest with the children. He didn't pretend that they were asking questions they had no right to ask. He didn't gloss over the fact that their father was in jail and that their mother hadn't returned when she'd said she would. He didn't promise them things that he couldn't deliver, either.

As a child, Lizette remembered her mother always being so cheerful about their difficulties that she had never really told Lizette what was going on. Lizette had never even known what disease her father had died of until just before her mother was diagnosed with cancer. Lizette had wondered if her mother finally realized all of the things she hadn't told Lizette over the years and was trying to make up for it by telling her everything she could before she died.

Lizette wished her mother had started really talking to her years before she did.

"You must miss your mother very much," Lizette said.

Amanda nodded, her head against Judd's shoulder. "She's not going to be here for her candle."

"Amanda made her a candle," Bobby said quietly from where he still sat at the table. "I told her there was no need to make one. Mom won't be home in time to light it in church tonight."

"We can light it for her," Judd said.

"But she won't be able to say what she's thankful for—" Amanda lifted her head away from Judd's shoulder and protested. "You have to say what you're thankful for when you light the candle. That's what Mrs. Hargrove says."

"I know what your mother's thankful for," Judd said. "The two of you."

"Will you say the words?" Bobby asked. "Amanda and me want to light the candle, but we want someone else to say the words."

Judd nodded. "I'll be happy to say them for your mother."

Amanda had stopped crying by now. "Do you think she'll be able to hear when we say the words? No matter where she is?"

Lizette held her breath. She wondered if Judd would lie to the children.

Judd thought for a minute. "If she doesn't hear them, I'm going to remember them so I can tell her what they were when she gets here."

Amanda nodded. "I'm going to remember them, too."

Lizette vowed she would remember them as well, even though it was absolutely unnecessary. She knew she wouldn't have much of a chance to talk with the children's mother when she came back into town, and if Lizette did get a chance to talk to her, Lizette thought she'd probably have something else to discuss with the woman.

For starters, Lizette knew she'd like to ask Judd's cousin how she could have left her two children for such a long time. Didn't she know they would worry? Lizette knew if *she* was lucky enough to have children like the ones in front of her now, *she* wouldn't be able to leave them with someone else.

"This pie's real good," Bobby said. He'd taken a bite of the lemon pie.

Amanda squirmed to be let down from Judd's arms, and he settled her back in her chair.

"Let me taste it," Amanda said as she took her own bite of the lemon pie.

Lizette couldn't believe that was it. One minute the children had been in tears, and the next they were smiling because of pie. Even Judd was looking happier than he had a few minutes ago.

"Lemon pie has always been my favorite," Judd said as he helped himself to a piece of the pie. "Maybe that's what I'm going to say I'm thankful for tonight in church. Lemon pie."

Amanda giggled. "You can't be thankful for pie. You have to be thankful for people. Mrs. Hargrove says that's the most important thing."

Lizette felt a sudden dart of alarm. People? She was supposed to be thankful for people? "Can't we be thankful for other things, too?"

Amanda thought for a moment and then nodded. "But they have to be big things."

"And you can't be thankful for dragons," Bobby added. "The Curtis twins told me that. One year they told everyone they were thankful for dragons, and everyone said they were cute. Some of the women even pinched their cheeks. I don't want to get my cheeks pinched."

"I could be thankful for my dog," Judd said. "He's turned out to be a fine watchdog for a stray."

Amanda nodded. "A dog would be a good thankful."

Lizette wondered if she could be thankful for a whole town. She was beginning to feel like she had a home among the people of Dry Creek, even though she hadn't expected to feel that way when she moved here.

"I don't know," Judd said as he helped himself to

another small piece of lemon pie. "This is awfully good pie. Maybe I could be thankful for the pie *and* my new dog."

Judd smiled at Lizette before she started to eat the piece of pie on her plate. "I haven't even said a proper thank-you yet for the pie. It's excellent. I don't think I've ever had such good lemon pie."

"Lemon pie's not that hard to make," Lizette said. "You just have to use real lemons."

"Any pie is hard to make in my opinion," Judd said. "I'm not much of a cook."

"I wouldn't say that. The meal today was wonderful."

When Lizette had arrived, Judd had a dish towel wrapped around his waist and he was mashing potatoes with an old-fashioned masher he said he'd found in the pantry. There had been things left in the house, he explained, from when the Jenkins family lived here.

Lizette figured that the curtains had been one of the things left in the house by Mrs. Jenkins. They had to have been hung over the sink by a woman. They were white threadbare cotton, and they had tiny embroidered pansies on the bottom of them. The pansies were lavender, pink and yellow.

The kitchen was a comfortable room that had seen its share of family meals over the years. Lizette had noticed that the doorway from the kitchen to the living room had a series of old cuts in the side of it and two new cuts. The wood of the old cuts was gray, but the color of the newer cuts was golden.

Judd had noticed her looking at the cuts. "Kids' growing marks. I thought I should add Amanda and Bobby. It took me long enough to figure out what the other cuts were there for—I figured some fancy exercise machine or maybe someone just standing there who had a new knife and wanted to try it out. But the marks were too deliberate for either of those."

Lizette had smiled. She knew enough about Judd's childhood to understand how bewildering it must have seemed to mark a child's growth. It was a homey thing that spoke of love and attention.

Lizette wondered if she could list as her grateful the fact that she was a guest in this house today for Thanksgiving dinner. She had expected to have a cup of canned soup in her studio. Of course, some of the other families in Dry Creek had invited her home with them for Thanksgiving dinner. She'd refused all of the other invitations. She didn't want to be with a family that was whole. In a family like that she would be extra. But in this little makeshift family she felt like she had a place, even if it was only for the day.

"I have lots of eggs," Judd said. He'd finished his piece of pie, and he pushed the plate away from him. "If you want any eggs for your baking, just let me know. You're welcome to all you need. I got some chickens after the kids came, so we have lots of eggs."

"Thanks. That's helpful." Lizette figured it was the Montana way to give small gifts like that to your neighbors. "And if you want any baked goods, let me know. Doughnuts. Pies. Anything."

Lizette figured that would be the best gift she could give any of the men around here. After she'd agreed to make doughnuts for the one cowboy, she'd gotten five more orders for closer to Christmastime. It was apparently going to be a merry Christmas in the bunkhouses around here.

"You don't need to pay me with baked goods," Judd said as he stood up from the table. "You're still welcome to the eggs."

"Well, I have to do something for you," Lizette said as she stood up, too. "You've invited me to dinner and offered me eggs and—"

Judd walked over to the kitchen sink. "If you're set on paying me back, you can help with the dishes. I'll wash if you dry."

"Yes, but doing dishes isn't enough."

"You haven't seen how many dishes we have," Judd said as he turned the faucet on and let the water start to run in the sink. "And I'm including the pots and pans."

In the end, Lizette didn't dry many of the dishes. Bobby and Amanda both wanted to help dry dishes, so Lizette found her job involved more reaching the tall shelves to put the dishes away and handing clean towels to the two children and scratching Judd's back.

"Maybe you should see a doctor," Lizette said the second time Judd asked her to scratch between his shoulder blades. "Maybe you have a rash."

"That's the place," Judd said with a sigh as her fingers gave a gentle scratch to the area next to his right shoulder blade.

Lizette let her fingers settle into the lazy circles the man seemed to like. "Maybe there's some cream that would stop the itch."

"No, it'll be fine," Judd said lazily, and then seemed to remember something. "Not that it's a rash. I'm a perfectly healthy specimen. No rashes. No long-term medical problems at all. Good teeth."

"He's got a funny toe," Amanda whispered as she leaned over to Lizette. "Have him show you his funny toe."

Judd figured he might as well give up and declare himself a freak of nature. He sure didn't know much about how to make a woman want to date him. Not that there was much chance that Lizette would want to date a man like him anyway, even if his health was reasonably good. No, she'd go for someone ten years younger, someone more her age. Someone about the age of Pete.

"I think Pete has a rash though," Judd offered. "Nothing serious. Something to do with the cattle."

"It's not mad cow disease, is it?"

Judd groaned. He wanted to scare Lizette away from Pete, not away from the whole town of Dry Creek. "No, I think it was just a little poison ivy he got in one of the cattle pastures on the Elkton ranch."

It was this past summer when Pete had stepped into some poison ivy, but Judd didn't think he needed to be that specific. The hardware store had been buzzing with the news the whole week last summer. Apparently poison ivy was rare in these parts of Montana. But, for all Judd knew, the cowboy still had the occasional itch from the experience.

"I don't have any poison ivy on my place," Judd added just to be on the safe side. "No rashes. No poison ivy. No mad cow disease."

"Yes, but—" Lizette stopped scratching and leaned sideways so she could smile at him. "You do have that funny toe."

Judd didn't know what had possessed him to try to tell the kids the story of the little piggies. He'd seen a woman in a supermarket once playing the game with her baby's toes while they sat on a bench beside the bakery. Judd had been so taken with the singsong way the woman had recited the nursery rhyme that he'd stayed and listened to her for half an hour.

When the kids were so scared that first night they were at his place, Judd had remembered that nursery rhyme. It was the only thing he knew to do to quiet little kids, and Amanda made him tell the rhyme again and again even after she stopped being afraid. Unfortunately, she wanted to use his toes to represent the little piggies, and not her own.

"Amanda thinks my little toe is too big," Judd finally admitted.

Amanda nodded emphatically. "It's not the little-piggy toe at all. It's supposed to go wee-wee all the way home and it's not wee at all."

Lizette smiled. "So it's not broken or anything?"

"Nope, just too big," Judd said.

Lizette smiled at him again, and suddenly Judd felt ten years younger. Maybe he could hope, after all. Maybe she hadn't noticed he was that much older than she was. Maybe she didn't care if he had a big little toe. Maybe she wouldn't even care that he didn't know much about family life and was a poor prospect as a husband and an even poorer prospect as a father.

Maybe—Judd stopped himself. He would have been safer thinking that he could turn his little toe into a squealing pig than that he could turn himself into someone worthy of Lizette.

Judd brought his dreams to a complete halt. He

didn't know much about family life, but he had learned a few things from the kids while they'd been staying with him, and one thing he did know—it didn't pay for a man to have dreams that outreached any realistic hope he had of grabbing hold of those dreams. He'd miss the kids when their mother came back, but he could live with that pain.

What he couldn't live with was getting himself to thinking he could make a home of his own with Lizette. When that dream came crashing down, he'd feel the pain for the rest of his life.

No, it was better to stop the dreaming in the first place.

Chapter Twelve

The steps to the church didn't look as hard to climb at night as they had been on Sunday morning. Maybe it was because Lizette knew there were friendly faces inside. At least she knew what was going to happen this time when she went through those double doors at the top of the stairs.

The kids had given her and Judd complete details on what to expect. They'd mentioned that everyone sat in the pews and different people went up to set their very own candle on the table next to the pulpit. Then the person would light their candle and tell everyone what he or she was thankful for during the past year. Then the person went back to their pew and sat down.

Essentially, Lizette told herself, it was up, candle, thanks and down. She could handle that even in unfamiliar territory like a church.

Lizette had to admit to herself, however, that she no longer felt as much like a stranger as she had expected. The people from the church weren't as critical of her as she had imagined they would be. No one seemed to care if she wore a hat when no one else did or if she had to read the words to the hymns from the songbook when everyone else knew the words by heart.

So, she told herself, she should relax. Besides, tonight there wouldn't be any lessons on how people should treat each other, so there would be nothing that could cause her any awkward tears. She didn't want to risk ending up on Judd's shoulder again. Not after that kiss.

That kiss had been superb acting. She had felt the Nutcracker's passion all the way down to her toes. But it was the mistake of a novice to imagine that the person acting a role next to you onstage actually meant those feelings for you. That's what made a play a play. It was pretend. Lizette thought of all of the actors who had played Romeo and Juliet over the years. Did they get married to each other after the play? No. What happened on stage was pretend.

Lizette must have given herself that speech a dozen times over the last few days, yet she still felt the need to remind herself.

Apart from that kiss, Judd had given absolutely no indication that he was interested in her in any way except as a dinner guest and ballet instructor. In fact, usually he just frowned at her. She didn't know why she was having these fluttery feelings about him, but it had to stop. She didn't want to embarrass herself by making him worry that she was getting romantic ideas just because he'd thrown himself into the part of the Nutcracker with enthusiasm.

And the kiss—well—what man wouldn't be pleased to know he was a prince instead of a wooden kitchen utensil used to break apart nut shells? Didn't she remember that football players kissed their team-mates after winning a particularly important game? Of course, she didn't think they kissed them on the lips, but that was only a matter of location. The principle of the victory kiss was the same.

No, she had no reason to take Judd's kiss personally. She was a professional. She knew how people threw themselves into acting.

Lizette looked over at Judd. They were standing at the bottom of the church stairs as they had before, only this time it was dark and it was hard to read any expression on Judd's face. She did notice that he wasn't frowning though, and that was a good sign with Judd. Now that she thought about it, she didn't think he'd frowned at all today. Except, of course, when he'd first seen the lemon pie she'd made for him.

"You've got your candle?" Judd turned to Lizette and asked.

Lizette nodded. Amanda had already given her the candle she had made for her to use tonight. It was a short pink candle, and Amanda had put glittery sequins all over it, because, she said, it reminded her of the ballet costumes.

"I've got mine, too," Amanda said as she held out her blue candle. She had decorated it with the same kind of sequins and sparkles that she'd used on Lizette's.

"Mine are here," Judd said as he patted the pocket of his coat.

Lizette had already seen the two candles he carried. One was the candle the kids had made for him and the other was the one they had made for their mother.

Lizette had smiled when she had seen the candle the kids had made for Judd. They obviously couldn't agree on what kind of candle Judd would like, so the candle had been dipped in red coloring on one side and green coloring on the other. The two colors mixed in places and made long rivulets of dark purple. The one thing the kids had seemed to agree on was cow stickers, and they had put them all over the candle. The candle they had made for their mother was a tall yellow taper with stickers of two long-stemmed white roses on the side of it.

Bobby hadn't shown any of them his candle. "It's green," was all he would say.

Judd and Lizette seemed to take a deep breath at the same time and they looked over at each other and nodded. Then they each took the hand of a child and started to walk up the steps to the church.

The church was transformed at night. Last Sunday morning the light shining into the sanctuary from the windows had made the place look homey. The light had also clearly shown up the nicks in the back of the pews and the scuff marks on the floor by the entry.

But tonight, there were no nicks or marks showing. There were light sconces on the side walls and a dim glow came from each one. There was also an overhead light that gave a muted light. Instead of the imperfections of the room, the yellow light made everything look richer.

Lizette glanced over at Judd. It also made everyone look more handsome.

"Do they have a ballet here, too?" Amanda whispered in a hushed tone as they stood at the back of the church.

"No, sweetie, those are choir robes," Lizette answered as she followed the direction of Amanda's gaze.

Two women were standing near the piano and they had on long robes made of midnight-blue satin with white collars. They were leaning over to read some music that the pianist was playing. From where they stood, Lizette could hear the soft hum of the women's voices as they sang a song.

"Oh, welcome," Mrs. Hargrove said as she and Charley walked down the aisle toward them. "I'm so glad you came."

"We wouldn't miss it," Judd said as he shook the hand Charley offered. "We have some special candles to light. Besides, I wanted to talk with the sheriff if he's here."

Judd still hadn't talked with the sheriff, and he wanted to know a little more about when the kids' father was coming up for trial. Not that Judd expected to go to the trial. He just thought he should know unless anyone said anything in front of the kids.

"Sheriff Wall had some kind of business that took him out of town," Charley said. "Asked me and my son to give the Billings police a call if anything went wrong around here."

"Does he usually leave someone in charge when he's gone?" Judd hadn't realized how much he'd counted on calling the sheriff if trouble did come up with Amanda and Bobby's father.

"There was never any need for him to leave someone in charge," Charley said. "I think he's just worried because—" Charley glanced at the children and lowered his voice until only Judd could hear "—well, we don't usually have something in town that a criminal wants that much. But now—well, the sheriff said he'd feel easier about leaving the two of us to keep an eye on things, especially until they got the man transferred over to the Billings jail. My son doesn't get into town much except for church, but I'll be around to keep a lookout."

Judd frowned. "Is there a delay with sending him to Billings?"

Charley shrugged. "They needed to wait for an opening. The jail in Billings is full at the moment. So they're keeping him in Miles City."

"There's nothing wrong with the jail in Miles City, is there?"

Charley chuckled. "Nothing some extra heat wouldn't cure. The county doesn't like us to keep folks there in the winter because we can't afford to heat it the way it should be. It tends to be on the cold side."

"But it's secure?" Judd asked.

Charley nodded. "It might not be comfortable, but it's built like a fort."

Judd nodded. He supposed there was no need to worry. The Miles City jail should hold the man, and that was all he cared about.

Mrs. Hargrove smiled down at the children. "Why, look—you've both got your candles."

Judd prepared himself for Amanda to press her face into his leg from shyness, and he had his hand halfway down to reassure her when he realized there was no need. Amanda didn't even look back to see that he was there. She just smiled up at Mrs. Hargrove and started walking down the aisle between the pews.

"We want to get a good pew," Amanda turned around and said to Judd and Lizette.

Judd wondered what made a pew a good pew, but it looked as though Amanda had definite opinions on the matter. If she didn't, Bobby had almost reached her and would no doubt add his advice, as well.

Apparently, going to this church had done something besides make Judd uncomfortable. It had made the children confident in Dry Creek without him.

"I guess they don't need us," Judd said to Lizette now that both children were ahead of them.

Judd looked down to smile at Lizette and was glad he had gotten the words out of his mouth before he did. He'd never seen Lizette in soft light before. He'd seen her in the bright daylight of the ballet studio and the ordinary light of his dinner table. He'd even seen her just minutes ago in the darkness outside as they walked up to the church. But he'd never seen her in soft muted lighting like this.

She was beautiful. Softly beautiful. Stirringly beautiful. She was—

"Whoeee." Pete's voice broke Judd's concentration before he even knew the cowboy had walked up behind them. Not that the cowboy was paying Judd any attention. The man was looking at Lizette like she'd stepped off the pages of a magazine ad for a tropical paradise. "Aren't you something?"

Lizette smiled at the man.

Judd resisted the urge to growl like a guard dog. Well, he tried to resist the urge. No one noticed he didn't quite succeed except for Mrs. Hargrove.

"If you need an antacid, let me know," the older woman said as she looked at him and patted her purse. "I carry a small pharmacy in here. After a big turkey dinner like today, you won't be the only one who needs help digesting it all."

"Thanks, but I'm fine."

Judd told himself he was fine. He was certainly just as fine as Pete.

And Lizette must realize it. She was looking at him now instead of at Pete.

"Maybe Mrs. Hargrove has something in her purse for that rash of yours," Lizette said with a sympathetic tone in her voice.

Judd grimaced. "I don't have a rash." He looked over at Mrs. Hargrove and then at Pete. Their eyes were all bright with curiosity. "I just asked her to scratch my back while I was washing dishes. I just had a little itch. That's all. No rash."

"Hmm," Mrs. Hargrove said with a smile. "Well, I don't think I have anything to treat that with."

"I think I feel an itch working its way up my back right now," Pete said as he stepped closer to Lizette. "Maybe you could scratch it for me?"

"We've got candles to light," Judd said as he took Lizette's arm and steered her down the aisle.

"Here we are," Amanda whispered from the pew she and Bobby had chosen.

Judd almost groaned again. The two of them had chosen the half pew that was off to the right side of the piano. He figured the pew could hold two adults comfortably. But when you added the two children, they would all be very tight.

The kids were geniuses, Judd told himself ten minutes later. The only way he and Lizette could fit in the pew with the children was if he held Amanda on his lap and Bobby sat next to the piano. That meant he and Lizette were in the middle and pressed close together. It was perfect. Judd could watch the light dance around in Lizette's dark hair as she moved her head, and he was also close enough to smell the faint lilac perfume that she wore.

He was a happy man.

"Can I go up with my candle now?" Amanda asked as she squirmed down off of Judd's lap.

Judd looked around. Several people had taken their candles up, but it didn't look like anyone was standing up right this minute. "Sure. Do you want me to come with you?"

Amanda shook her head. "I can do it."

Judd had to blink his eyes when he saw Amanda walk up in front of the whole congregation and put her candle on the table. A few weeks ago she wouldn't even speak to him, and now she was telling everyone why she was grateful.

"I'm glad I get to be the Sugar Plum Fairy," Amanda said after she put her candle on the table. Then she skipped back to the pew where the rest of them sat.

"You did real good, sweetie," Lizette said to the girl as Amanda crawled back up on Judd's lap.

"You sure did," Judd added. It was Lizette who had worked the change in Amanda. Judd had known how to protect the child, but he hadn't known how to make her so excited about something that she needed to talk about it.

Several more people got up to take their candles to the front of the church. Pete was one of them. He had a plain white candle stuck in the bottom of a tin cup, and he said he was thankful he'd gotten to have Thanksgiving dinner with his mother up by Havre.

"Ah, isn't that sweet?" Lizette murmured.

Judd grunted. He'd been unaware that Pete had a mother.

"And I got to bring her a geranium plant that was blooming," Pete continued. The cowboy held his hat in his hands, and Judd couldn't tell if the other man was sincere or just saying what the women wanted to hear. "She appreciated the plant now because her arthritis is bad and she can't be out much."

"Ah," Lizette sighed. "He's good to visit his mother."

Judd didn't point out that for all they knew the cowboy only ever spent one holiday with her. One holiday didn't mean he visited his mother regularly.

Judd was frowning by the time Pete sat down in his pew. Judd knew he was being uncharitable and it made him irritable. The truth was, Pete probably did know more about family life than *he* did.

Mrs. Hargrove stood up next. The older woman carried a candelabra with several candles in it. She said she was lighting candles for those in her family who couldn't be here. "And one of them should be," she added. "And will be by next Thanksgiving if I have anything to say about it."

"Amen," Charley said from his place in the church, and several people nodded.

Judd noticed that the middle-aged man who sat next to Charley didn't nod like everyone else in the church did. He didn't even smile or look the least bit thankful. That must be Charley's son. Judd wondered if the poor man had any idea what his father and Mrs. Hargrove were planning for him. Probably not. But the man looked like someone who could take care of himself, and Judd had enough of his own trouble to worry about.

Bobby went up with his candle after the Curtis twins had finished.

"I'm thankful that my Mom is okay even if I don't know where she is," Bobby said bravely after he added his candle to the table. Judd noticed Bobby had wrapped a yellow ribbon around the candle. It must have been the ribbon his mother accidentally left when she left the children with Judd.

"Shall we go up now?" Judd whispered in Lizette's ear.

Lizette nodded and stood up when he did.

Judd set Amanda down on the floor so she could walk with them.

Sometimes a man had more to be grateful for than he could share with other people. Having Lizette come up front with him and the kids beside him made him feel humble and proud all at the same time. When they were together in church, Judd felt like he belonged somewhere and to someone. He wondered if church did that to other people.

"I'm grateful that the town gave me a place to set

up my ballet studio," Lizette said as she set her pink candle on the table. "It's made my mother's dream come true. I wish she were here to see it."

Judd wished he'd had a chance to meet Lizette's mother. She must have been a special woman to raise someone like Lizette all by herself.

"I have two candles," Judd said as he reached into his pockets. Both Amanda and Bobby were on his right, so he handled their mother's candle to them. "The first candle is for Barbara, Amanda and Bobby's mother. If she were here today, I think she'd tell you that the thing she is most grateful for is her two wonderful children."

Bobby and Amanda carefully set their mother's candle on the table.

Judd pulled the other candle out of his pocket and set it on the table. "As for me, I'm grateful for—" Judd stopped. He meant to say he was grateful for the dog that had wandered onto his farm last spring. And he *was* thankful for the dog. He'd never had a pet before. But he suddenly wanted to be more honest with the people of Dry Creek who were watching him. So he cleared his throat and began again. "I'm most grateful for feeling like I'm part of a family today."

There, Judd told himself. He'd been open and vulnerable and no one had stood up and called him a liar or anything. In fact, what he could see in the dim lighting was that most people were nodding their heads like he was right to be grateful for that. Judd stood with the kids while they waited for Lizette to light her candle.

The rest of the people in the Dry Creek church lit candles. Some of them mentioned being thankful for good health. One or two were thankful for the year's good crops. Still others were grateful that family members were all able to be together for the holiday.

When everyone had finished taking their candles up to the front of the church, the two women in choir robes sang a song about amazing grace. Judd figured they had that about right. He'd never seen much kindness or grace in his life, but he was beginning to think that the people in this church knew something about grace that he didn't. Maybe he should take the kids to church here until their mother came to get them. He'd like for them to know about this amazing grace that was in the song.

He sighed. He guessed if he was going to do this church business, he should do it right. Maybe he could order a tie from the catalog. While he was at it, he'd order a suit, as well.

Judd looked over at Lizette. He wondered if she'd wear that cute little hat to church again if he wore a tie. At least as long as the kids were with him, Judd was pretty sure she'd sit with them in church.

And Sunday was only a couple of days away. Maybe it wouldn't be such a hardship to go to church after all.

Chapter Thirteen

It was the Monday morning after Thanksgiving, and Lizette was making progress on plans for the Nutcracker. She'd seen Mr. Elkton in church yesterday and he'd offered her the use of the barn he owned on the outskirts of Dry Creek for the performance itself. She'd been assured by Mrs. Hargrove that enough people would come to see the Nutcracker performance that they would need to have more space than Lizette had in her dance school.

"Plus, we can set a refreshment table up at one end of the barn for those lovely pastries you mentioned, and we'll need some punch, of course," Mrs. Hargrove said. "Don't you worry about it being a barn. The building hasn't been used as a barn for ten years or more. We keep it clean just for events like this. We'll have our Christmas pageant there on

Christmas Eve, so we'll just get things ready earlier and have the Nutcracker in the barn, too."

Lizette planned to have the ballet this coming Friday evening, December 3. She'd walked over to the barn after church yesterday and checked to see if the floor was smooth enough for ballet movements. It was.

Plus, the barn was charming. There were several windows on each side of the barn, and the sunlight showed off the square features of the structure. There were rafters and square trim around the windows and the large double door. The wood was all golden as if it had been polished.

It was easy to believe that there had been other performances in the building. There was even a small sound system that had been wired around the rafters so that the music she used for the Nutcracker would be easier to hear.

"We're getting to be a regular cultural center here in Dry Creek," Mrs. Hargrove continued. "What with the ballet and then the Christmas pageant. I can take my Christmas tree over to the barn anytime you want and Charley can move the fireplace he made over so we'll be all set for the ballet. And with the hayloft, there's even stairs you can use for when Clara goes up to her bedroom to sleep." Mrs. Hargrove stopped all of a sudden and shook her head. "There I go again. Making everyone's plans for them. I'm working on controlling my organizing spirit this Christmas."

"Don't worry about it with me," Lizette said. "I'm happy to have a little guidance."

Mrs. Hargrove nodded. "Well, I suppose you do need someone to show you the ropes for the first time. It'd be a pity if we didn't have everything ready for our Dry Creek ballet premiere. At least I think we should call it a premiere in our advertising, don't you?"

"Advertising?" Lizette had a sinking feeling. She'd been focused on practicing and getting the costumes ready. "It's probably too late for advertising. I wasn't thinking. Newspapers usually need more notice. The performance is Friday."

"Edna will free up some place in the Miles City section of the paper," Mrs. Hargrove said. "It won't be much, but that's only one way to let people know. We can also put up posters."

"I don't have much money for printing and things like that," Lizette cautioned her. "I thought this would be a small performance since it's our first one."

"Don't you worry about a thing," Mrs. Hargrove said. "And, believe me, we won't have a small turn-out."

Mrs. Hargrove should run for president, Lizette thought a few hours later. And not just of the USA. Mrs. Hargrove could run the world. She had arranged for Edna to do a review of the Nutcracker at a special dress rehearsal the cast would do Wednesday afternoon. That way people in the area would know about the Nutcracker and Lizette wouldn't have to pay for an ad. And, if that wasn't enough, the older woman also talked with Glory Curtis, the pastor's wife, and got an offer from the woman to create full-color posters to hang both at the hardware store and at several locations in Miles City.

"She's an artist, you know," Mrs. Hargrove confided to Lizette when she hung up the telephone. "She used to work as a police sketch artist—that's what she was doing when she first came to Dry Creek— and now she's gaining quite a reputation for her portraits."

"That's an unusual occupation for a pastor's wife. A police sketch artist?"

"Oh, well, she wasn't married to Matthew then," Mrs. Hargrove said. "Although she's always been an independent-minded woman, so it wouldn't make any difference to either of them if she was working for the police still—except for the fact that Matthew didn't like the thought of people shooting at her."

"Well, no, I suppose he wouldn't."

"I tell my daughter, Doris June, that a woman can be and do about anything in Dry Creek these days. She's always so worried about her career, but there's nothing to say she can't have a career right here."

"I hope your daughter does come home soon." Lizette had heard about Mrs. Hargrove's plans to have her daughter come home and marry some local man from Judd. She hated to think that the older woman would be disappointed, but Lizette thought it was likely. "It must be hard when your daughter doesn't do what you want her to do."

"Ah, well," Mrs. Hargrove said. "A mother can hope."

Lizette was glad she was able to make her mother's dream come true even if her mother wasn't here to enjoy the fact with her. Sometimes, when the day was done and the streets of Dry Creek were quiet and dark, Lizette talked to her mother and told her all about what was happening with the Baker School of Ballet.

Sometimes, instead of pretending to talk to her mother, she actually called Madame Aprele and told her about what was happening. The odd thing was, she didn't exactly tell either woman the whole truth.

Lizette didn't want to disappoint them, so she made it sound as if the school was a real school and not just space in an old store. She made her students sound like real students and not just a few people she'd managed to talk into dressing up in costumes. She certainly wouldn't tell either of them that her premiere performance was going to be held in a barn or that both her Mouse King and her Nut-cracker were hopeless at ballet.

One thing she could tell them, though, Lizette thought cheerfully, was that she was having someone from the local paper come to the dress rehearsal to write a review of the performance. That should make them both feel that her school was doing well.

Judd never thought he'd worry about the problems of being a Nutcracker. "If he's wearing a red military coat and black boots, you know he'd never agree to having some little girl stand in front when he's battling a mouse."

"Rat," Pete corrected him. "I'm a rat."

Pete was standing beside the fireplace that they had just moved over to the barn from Lizette's dance studio.

"When he's battling a large rodent," Judd corrected himself. "A Nutcracker just wouldn't do that. He's got more dignity."

Judd had gotten a better picture of the pride a Nutcracker would have when he'd seen the poster Glory Curtis had drawn. The poster showed the Nutcracker standing tall with the little girl, Clara, at his side. Glory had used both Judd and Lizette for models in the poster, and even though the sketch was in pencil, Judd swore it was the best likeness anyone had ever made of him, and the girl looked exactly like Lizette.

Judd figured people would know him as the

Nutcracker for miles around. He didn't want people stopping him in the grocery store and demanding to know what kind of man he was for letting a girl stand between him and danger.

"But Clara owns the Nutcracker," Lizette protested. She was draping an afghan over a wooden rocking chair that Charley would sit in as the narrator. "She's only protecting what is hers."

Judd had nothing to say to that. Actually, he didn't want to say much to that. It made him feel pretty good.

Pete, however, had something to say. "It's only a nutcracker. Who'd be fool enough to risk getting a rat bite just to save a wooden utensil? You could get rabies."

"He's her prince, that's why," Lizette said as she tucked the back of the afghan into the arms of the rocker and then stood back to look at her work. "There. That's straight."

Pete grunted. "It doesn't do any good to have a prince if you're dead because of rabies."

"Don't worry," Lizette said as she moved the rocker closer to the fireplace. "You'll do a good job of fighting him in the beginning and look very impressive."

"I could still switch and be the Nutcracker," Pete suggested.

"Not on your life," Judd said. He knew Pete wasn't

so much dismayed at being a dead rodent as he was envious of Judd for getting to kiss the ballerina. Well, actually, he hadn't kissed the ballerina since that first time, but he figured one of these days Lizette would forget about the stage kiss and go for a real one.

"It's too late to make changes," Lizette said as she put a picture frame on the mantel of the fireplace. "We have the dress rehearsal at two o'clock tomorrow afternoon—I know it's not our usual time, but Edna needs to come then in order to get our review done for the paper."

"She's not going to take pictures, is she?" Pete asked.

Lizette shook her head. "I don't think so. She said there's not much room for the review even."

"Good," Pete said.

"You'll be able to get off work, won't you?" Lizette said to Pete.

Pete nodded.

"I know you don't have to worry," Lizette turned and said to Judd.

"One of the good things about owning your own place," Judd said as he helped Lizette place a small rug in front of the fireplace. "I'm free as a bird when it comes to my schedule."

Judd hoped she appreciated that he was a man with prospects. It didn't seem like she even noticed.

"I'll start with a quick rehearsal of the kids a couple of hours earlier, so I won't take either of you away from your work any longer than necessary," Lizette said as she straightened up after placing the rug.

"I can spare the time. I don't answer to anyone," Judd said as he brushed his hands on his jeans. Lizette wasn't even listening to his declaration of independence, so Judd gave it up. "As long as you've got plans for the kids, that'll give me a chance to run into Miles City without them. I want to check with the courts about their father. I'm wondering if anyone has asked him for more information about Barbara."

"You should have plenty of time to go to Miles City and back," Lizette said. "And if we finish early, I'll just put all of the kids to work cutting up those dried plums for the pastries I'm making."

"Really?" Pete brightened up. "The boys in the bunkhouse have been asking what kind of pastry these sugar-plum things are."

"It's like a cream-filled croissant with raisins, except there's a different kind of cream and the raisins are plums and it's not really croissant dough."

"But you don't need to go to the ballet to get one, do you?" Pete asked.

Lizette laughed. "I'm afraid so. I know you're hoping the others won't come, but that's the only way to get a sugar-plum pastry. Unless there are leftover ones after the ballet."

"There won't be any leftovers," Pete said.

"If you need any last-minute things from the store in Miles City, let me know since I'll be going in there anyway," Judd offered.

"I haven't thought of what to use as a cloth on the table where we'll be serving the pastries and punch," Lizette said. "Maybe you could buy some white silk fabric at the store—some of the washable kind would work best."

"I haven't seen any fabric stores in Miles City," Judd said. He didn't add that he wouldn't know silk if he saw it. He was more of a denim and flannel kind of a guy.

"Oh, I'm sure they must have a store that sells bolts of fabric," Lizette said. "You'll just have to ask around."

Judd decided he would have to take her word for it. She was probably right anyway. It was the kind of thing a woman would know.

Besides, Judd thought to himself, at least buying some silk would give him a good reason for going into Miles City apart from his vague unease. He was beginning to wish that Amanda and Bobby's father was already in the jail in Billings. Maybe there was something Judd could do to speed up the process if he went into Miles City and talked to whoever was in charge at the jail. Surely they could find room in the Billings jail if they put their minds to it.

Judd didn't know why he was feeling nervous. Everyone he had asked said that the jail in Miles City was built like a rock. A body had more chance of freezing to death inside their cell there than of actually making an escape.

Of course, Judd wasn't sure he was worried about the jail.

For all Judd knew, his unease might not even be about the kids' father. It might be about the upcoming ballet. Judd figured he knew his part as well as he was ever going to know it, and he was smart enough to realize that Lizette had organized everything, so he more or less stood still while she went twirling and dancing around him. He was more of a post than a dancer. Still, he was uneasy about the whole thing.

He'd never in his life performed in front of an audience. When he was riding in the rodeo, there had been an audience, but there was nothing required of the performers but to stay on the back of a horse. It was different than the ballet.

In this ballet, he was supposed to be the prince. Him—Judd Bowman. He knew that Lizette didn't have many contenders for the role, but still. He'd never figured he was a prince kind of a guy. He was more like the guy out in the stables who took care of everything while the prince was inside talking to people and impressing the princess.

If Judd had known that the Nutcracker was more than a utensil, he'd have thought twice about volunteering for the role. Even now, if any man but Pete stepped forward and said he wanted to play the role, Judd would be tempted to let him.

A man could just pretend to be something he wasn't for so long in life. Judd figured his limit would be Saturday. He hoped he would get through the ballet with no problems. Then he could go back to counting out his nails so he could finish working on that fence of his like the solitary guy he was meant to be.

There wasn't anything wrong with building fences, he reminded himself. He needed those fences, and that's what he'd started out to do that day he'd come to town with the kids. This whole ballet business had just been a distraction. He needed to get back to business. Besides, the whole world would be a better place if people had more fences.

Chapter Fourteen

It was only six o'clock, but Lizette was wide awake. She was lying in her bed in the back of her dance studio and looking at the hands of the clock on her nightstand. For a moment, she thought her alarm must have gone off, but it hadn't. It wasn't scheduled to go off for another hour.

Lizette had just had a dream about mice escaping into the audience and the Nutcracker's hat falling off his head. The reason she was awake was that she was having performance jitters. She hadn't had those in years. The odd thing was that she wasn't even worried about the dancing. She could dance Clara's role in her sleep, and she'd simplified everyone else's steps so they would look fine even if they forgot everything she'd taught them. Clara did all of the true ballet dancing.

No, she wasn't fretting about the dancing; she was

worried about more basic things—things like the tin soldier dying in the wrong place or the mice giggling in the middle of their fierce attack.

Or the Nutcracker forgetting how to stage a kiss and giving her the real thing. Not that she was worried about thinking the kiss would mean anything. She'd given herself that speech enough times the last time it happened that she didn't think she'd fall for that illusion again. Even if their lips did happen to meet, she would know it was just an acting kiss.

But it could still fluster her so that she would forget some steps in the performance. Since she was really the only one dancing, that could be a problem. She was going to have to remember to tell Judd again that their stage kiss didn't require any physical contact. The audience couldn't see if their lips touched or not. They were supposed to air kiss beside their lips, not on their lips.

Maybe she should draw him a diagram, Lizette thought as she stretched and threw back the covers.

Ohh, it was cold. Lizette had the heat on in her room at the back of the studio, but she had kept it low. Until she knew how much money she would be making each month, she didn't want to spend too much extra on heat. That was an incentive to get more students if nothing else was.

Lizette reached under the quilt that covered her bed and pulled out the sweatpants and sweatshirt that she'd put there last night. Her neighbor Linda, at the café, had taught her that trick. When it was cold out, you took your clothes for the next day to bed with you and they were warm when you got up. Of course, Linda recommended putting them just under the top blanket instead of between the sheets. That way, she assured Lizette, the clothes didn't get wrinkled.

Lizette pulled the sweatpants on.

She then quickly pulled on the sweatshirt, telling herself she should just go over and take another look at the stage they had made in the barn. She wanted to see what everything looked like in the muted light of morning. This lighting would be the closest to the subdued light they'd have on their actual performance and Lizette didn't want to miss any chance to see how the shadows would fall. She wasn't sure how the shadows could help her, but knowledge always made one better prepared.

After all, she told herself as she walked to her stove and turned the tea kettle on, her very first ballet production was going to be reviewed this afternoon. She hadn't realized quite how important that was until she had talked with Madame Aprele a few days ago and told her about the upcoming review.

Of course, she hadn't told Madame Aprele that the review was going to run in a section of the paper called "Dry Creek Tidbits" or that Edna Best, the woman reviewing the ballet, obviously didn't recognize the Nutcracker and was, by her own admission, more comfortable covering the bait and poundage reports during fishing season.

Lizette saw no reason to dismay her former teacher when the basic facts themselves were encouraging. Her ballet performance was scheduled in a large local community center, her dress rehearsal was Wednesday at two o'clock, during which time a reviewer would be present to critique the performance, and the Snow Queen was predicting a good audience turnout for the actual performance.

Madame Aprele was ecstatic with the news, and Lizette told herself she should just focus on the good things that she had told Madame Aprele.

It took Lizette ten more minutes to wash her face and fix her hair. She thought about putting some makeup on just to help keep her face warmer, but decided against it. Then she put her wool coat on and wrapped a knit scarf around her ears and neck. She had put a tea bag in her cup of hot water a few minutes ago, and now she poured the tea into a thermal mug so she could take it with her to the barn.

The air was cold outside. There was no fresh snow, but the snow from yesterday was still on the streets of Dry Creek. It had been tramped down and was starting to be slippery.

The day promised to be gray, and Lizette wondered if she'd gone out too soon. The hardware store

was still closed, as was the café. There was a bathroom light on in the parsonage next to the church,
but there were no other lights in the houses along the
street. Most people had sense enough to stay in bed
until the sun had a chance to warm up the day.

Lizette decided maybe she had the heat too low in
her room. It barely seemed any colder outside than
it had been inside. She would be glad to have the tea
to drink while she looked around the stage.

The windows in the barn were covered with frost,
and thin strips of snow sat on top of the door rim.
The main double door was wide enough for a farmer's
wagon to pass through it. The walls of the barn had
been painted the usual red, and the trim was white.
A wide slab of cement stood in front of the door to
help with the mud.

The place might be humble compared to other performance centers, but it was large, clean and sturdy.
It even had a heating system. Apparently Mr. Elkton
had installed heating in the building after the town
started using it for their meeting center. Of course, it
took a long time to heat up the huge building, so he
had suggested she turn the heat on low several days
before the performance.

Lizette had turned the heat up to fifty degrees
yesterday, and she was looking forward to seeing
what the air was like inside the barn.

"Oh," Lizette muttered as she looked at the barn

door. When she'd turned the heat on yesterday, she'd also locked the front door to the barn. She had brought the trunk over that held the props and costumes and she thought the sight of all those might tempt someone to experiment with them. And maybe it had, because now the door was most decidedly unlocked. It wasn't unlatched, but clearly someone had gone inside since Lizette had been here yesterday.

Of course, Lizette told herself as she opened the door and stepped into the barn, she supposed that half of the adults in Dry Creek had keys to the barn. One of them might have wanted to check to be sure the heat was on.

Lizette turned on the overhead light. She was enough of a city woman to want the lights instead of the shadows until she figured out if anything was missing.

The Christmas tree was there, right in the middle of the area they had decided on as the stage. The cardboard fireplace stood next to the wooden rocking chair. The old Christmas stockings that Mrs. Hargrove had hung on the stairs leading up to the hayloft were still tied in place. Folding chairs lined the edges of the barn and a table was sitting at the far end of the barn where they were going to put the pastries and punch.

No one had moved anything big.

It was the bathrobe, Lizette decided after she looked around. All of the costumes and props were still in the trunk except for the heavy bathrobe that the narrator wore. Maybe Charley had come to get it for some reason. Or Mrs. Hargrove might have decided it needed a good washing and taken it with her. It certainly was nothing someone would steal.

Lizette told herself it really didn't matter as she walked over to the small panel that ran the sound system. A bathrobe was the one costume that she could easily replace. She bet there were a dozen old bathrobes around that the men of Dry Creek would donate if she made the need known. Especially if she promised the bathrobe owner wouldn't have to actually dance in the ballet along with his robe.

Lizette selected the Nutcracker audiocassette, inserted it into the panel, and turned the volume on low.

Pete Denning kept saying that he was willing to do whatever she needed to help with the ballet, and he could probably find a bathrobe in that bunkhouse where he lived that looked as warm and comfortable as the one Charley had been using. Of course, the reason Pete was so helpful was because he was hoping she'd go out with him when the ballet was over.

If Pete had kept the role of the Nutcracker, he would have studied up on the proper way to give a stage kiss.

So far, Lizette had been able to gently refuse his requests for dates, explaining that it was not proper for her to date one of her students. Pete had offered to quit right then if she'd go out with him instead. Fortunately, Lizette had talked him out of that idea, as well. But he was bound to ask her out again after the Nutcracker was finished, and she didn't know what she would say.

The sounds of Tchaikovsky's music filled the old barn. It truly was beautiful, soaring music Lizette thought to herself. Whoever had set up the speaker system had done a professional job. Several speakers hung from the rafters and several more hung either beside the hayloft or on the other side of the barn by where the refreshment table stood.

If the barn were a few degrees warmer, Lizette would be tempted to take her coat off and dance awhile. If nothing else, the sounds of Tchaikovsky would bring enough culture to the people of Dry Creek to reward them for coming to the ballet.

Lizette drank the last swallow of her tea before she walked back to the door and opened it a crack. She looked across the road and saw that a light was now on in Linda's café. Good, Lizette thought, she would forget about the cereal in her cupboard and have a proper breakfast in the café this morning. After all, it was an important day. A critic from the press was going to come and review her performance.

The blinds were half-drawn on the café windows and there were no customers other than Lizette. The floor was a black-and-white pattern and the tables and chairs had a fifties' look about them. A large glass counter filled the back wall. Linda had added a counter recently to sell more baked goods.

There was a phone call just as Linda was bringing Lizette's order out.

Linda set Lizette's plate of food down on the counter and answered the phone.

"Some telemarketer," Linda had said thirty seconds later as she put the phone back on the hook and picked Lizette's plate up again. "Asking about a taxi in Dry Creek. Anyone from here to Wyoming knows there's no taxi in Dry Creek."

"Why would they call the café anyway?"

Linda shrugged as she put Lizette's plate in front of her. "We're the only business in the phone book with Dry Creek in our name. People get confused."

"Well, just as long as it's not Edna Best from the newspaper."

Linda snorted. "Edna was born out this way. She'd be the last to call for a taxi."

Lizette figured it probably was a telemarketer then. In any event, she wasn't going to worry about it. She had a plate of golden-brown French toast in front of her, and it was sprinkled with blueberries and raspberries.

Linda went to the kitchen and came back with a bowl of oatmeal for herself along with an apple and a small glass of orange juice.

"These frozen berries are the best," Lizette said.

"I'm trying out a new brand," Linda said as she sat down across from Lizette.

The two ate in silence for a few minutes. Then Lizette fretted aloud about the newspaper critic. "A review can make or break a production."

"Don't worry. Edna will be positive. She's probably never even been to a ballet."

"Still, it doesn't hurt to be prepared."

"Well, she's liked her coffee strong and black as long as I've known her. Having a full cup will go a long way to giving her a positive impression since it's so cold outside," Linda said as Lizette finished up her French toast. "I'll fix up a big thermal jug for you to come get around one o'clock. And I still have a few of those chocolate chip pecan cookies you made. We'll put those on a plate for her. That should take care of Edna. Did I tell you my afternoon business has picked up since I've started selling cookies to go with the coffee?"

Last week, Linda had offered Lizette meals in exchange for baked goods to sell in the café. So far, Lizette had made individual apple coffeecakes and the cookies.

"I'm thinking I'll try some pies next," Lizette

said as she pushed her plate away. "Maybe cherry and apple with a special order possible for chocolate pecan for the holidays."

Linda sat across the table from Lizette with her glass of orange juice in her hand. "I can sell all the baked goods you give me. You can make money in addition to your meals. We might even make up a batch of fruit cakes."

"The people of Dry Creek sure do like their baked goods."

Linda nodded as she picked up her apple. "They need to eat more fruits and vegetables, but you'll never convince these ranch hands around here. If it's not meat or bread, they think it's not food. I'm surprised you haven't started getting marriage proposals. I guess they're all giving you a month or so to settle in before they start to pester you with their pleading."

Lizette laughed. "If they like good cooking, I would think they'd be stopping at your door instead. I don't know when I've had such good French toast."

"It's the bread," Linda said. "I use sweet bread. Besides, I've refused them all so many times they've stopped asking."

"Don't you want to get married?"

Linda finished chewing her bite of apple. "I was engaged once. That was enough."

Lizette didn't think the other woman could be over twenty-two. "What happened?"

"He decided he wanted to be a music star instead," Linda said as she leaned back in her chair and put the rest of the apple on her plate. "Life here in Dry Creek wasn't good enough for him."

"Oh, I'm sorry."

"Don't be. The funny thing is that he's making it. I've started to hear his songs on the radio. He's even doing some big tour in Europe."

"But he could have taken you with him!"

Linda smiled. "He offered a while back. I just didn't want to go. Who wants to be the wife that keeps him back? And then there are the fans. I didn't want to share my husband with them. No, I'm better off here in the café."

Lizette noticed that the other woman's voice was too bright and brittle to be convincing. "Well, if there's ever anything I can do, let me know."

"Thanks," Linda said as she stood up. "But there's nothing anyone can do. We make our choices in life and then we live with them."

"But have you talked to him since or written him a letter or anything?"

Linda shrugged. "What would I say? Sorry you're becoming a star. I miss the old you. No, he's gone on and I've stayed the same."

"Well," Lizette said as she, too, stood up from the

table. She noticed the sun had fully risen. It was a new day. "Maybe there will be a nice young rancher move into town and you'll come to like him."

"There is Judd Bowman," Linda said as she stopped walking to the back of the café and turned to face Lizette. "He seems nice enough."

Lizette swallowed. "Yes, he does."

"Hmm," Linda said as her eyes started to twinkle. "He does seem a little preoccupied lately, though. I'm not sure I could get his full attention."

"He's just worried about the ballet."

Linda grinned. "Is that what he's worried about?"

"Well, he's probably still worried about his cousin and the kids' father, too."

"I don't know—all I hear him muttering about lately is Pete Denning and how he gets all of the attention in those classes of yours. If I didn't know better, I would say he was jealous."

"I try to give all of my students my full attention," Lizette said. "It's just that some of them are—"

"—more difficult," Linda supplied helpfully. "More independent. More disturbing."

"Yes," Lizette said. She was glad someone understood. "Judd is all of those."

Linda nodded. "Good."

"I don't know if it's good. It does make the ballet more difficult."

"But doesn't it make life more interesting?"

"Maybe," Lizette admitted. "But right now I have a critic to prepare for and plum filling to make."

"The kids can help with the plum filling, and Mrs. Hargrove and I will help you with the custard. I've never made a cream filling, but Mrs. Hargrove will know how."

"You have those kettles with the thick bottoms," Lizette said. "That's the key right there."

"How many pastries do you figure you'll need?"

"Mrs. Hargrove figures we'll need twenty dozen."

"Two hundred and forty!"

Lizette nodded. "She says we're going to bring in crowds from all around."

"I'd better get my salads made for lunch right now then, so I can clear the kitchen for the custard. Mrs. Hargrove will be over any minute."

"Be sure she remembers to come over to the performance area in time to get ready for Edna." Lizette refused to call the place a barn. From today until the night of the ballet, it was a performance center.

"She'll be there. I think she's excited to be the Ice Queen."

Lizette smiled. "She's the Snow Queen. She's in charge of the snowflakes."

"Then you have nothing to worry about," Linda said.

Lizette repeated the words to herself as she left the

café. She had nothing to worry about. The people of Dry Creek would be kind critics. They were looking for entertainment, not perfection. Everything would be just fine.

Chapter Fifteen

Nothing was fine. Lizette's watch was missing. Which meant the schedule was all off. The kids were still at the table cutting up dried plums, and they should be in their costumes if they were going to practice before the dress rehearsal. Plus, Linda had just come over with a message saying that Pete had been out working with the cattle and had run into a bit of a problem, but that Lizette wasn't to worry. He would be there in no time.

It wasn't until Linda mentioned that Pete was late that Lizette looked for her watch. She couldn't believe she hadn't known how much time had passed. She'd been busy diagramming the steps to a stage kiss and it had taken her longer than she had anticipated. That's why she hadn't noticed she didn't have her watch with her. She'd left it on the cardboard fireplace before she'd gone over to the café for breakfast.

"I'm sure it was there," Lizette said as she started walking over to the stage area.

"Maybe the mice took it," Amanda offered. She had followed Lizette over from the table. The little girl had a dish towel wrapped around her neck for an apron and a piece of twine holding her hair in place. She was licking a spoon that had plum mixture on it. "Or maybe the big rat that lives in the fireplace took it. He's scary."

"The mice were over there with us cutting up dried plums and the rat better be in his pickup driving here." Lizette checked to see that the mice really were still at the table before she looked around again. There weren't any cracks big enough for a watch to fall into, and the furniture in the stage area didn't have any pillows or other hidden areas. "Maybe someone came in and borrowed it."

"More likely someone stole it," Linda replied. "You could report it to the Billings police. Charley is probably at the hardware store by now, and I know he's itching to call something in now that Sheriff Wall is out of town and has designated him and his son as the men to watch Dry Creek."

"I don't think anyone would steal it," Lizette said. She'd only paid twenty dollars for the watch. It wouldn't be worth it for anyone to steal it to resell it.

Linda shrugged. "Well, Mrs. Hargrove is making

some bread dough for hamburger buns for me—I'm running low on buns again. But she's going to be here any minute."

Lizette nodded. Judd wasn't back from Miles City, either. He was going to stop at the jail and talk to whoever was in charge there and then he was going to locate four yards of white silk material for her. He should be back any minute, as well. And, when he did get back, she wanted to go over her diagram with him and explain once again that there is no physical contact in a stage kiss.

"So what time is it again?" Lizette asked Linda.

"My watch isn't accurate, either," Linda said. "I was working with it to use it as an oven timer, so I'm not sure if it's twelve forty-five or one forty-five."

"Oh, it can't be one forty-five," Lizette said. "Edna Best is supposed to be here before two and—"

The sound of a car honking came from outside the door.

"That must be Pete," Lizette said hopefully. Or maybe Judd. Or Mrs. Hargrove. Anybody but Edna Best. They weren't at all ready for the reviewer to be here. They weren't even in costume.

"I'll go get that coffee," Linda said as she looked out the window and turned to the door. "And remember, she's one of us. She won't go hard on you, and she's early, anyway. Maybe you should send her over for a cup of coffee."

"Hellooo," a woman's voice called from the outside.

Lizette took a deep breath and put a smile on her face. Then she walked to the door of the barn and opened it up. "Welcome. You must be Edna Best."

The woman nodded. She was a short, plump woman wrapped in a hooded parka. "I wasn't sure where the performance was."

"We have some posters up in the hardware store, and we're making a sign that says 'Nutcracker' to point people to us," Lizette said, realizing she had also forgotten that they needed programs for the evening of the ballet. She hoped that Edna wouldn't ask to see one. That would show her right away that they were amateurs.

"Most folks will know where it is anyway if we say the Elkton barn," Edna said as she stepped inside. "The only question they'll have is about the cost. I didn't see the cost mentioned anywhere in the notes I have so far."

"Cost?" Lizette said. "We weren't planning to charge."

"Of course you've got to charge," Edna said as she looked around inside. "Maybe not much, but enough to pay your expenses. I know props and costumes don't come cheap."

"Most of the costumes are mine, and my former ballet teacher is lending us the props and some more costumes. I'm planning to send her money for postage when I return them to her, but that's not much of an expense."

"Ah," Edna said as she took a small notepad out of her black purse. "That might be a lead. 'Big-city ballet teacher does favor for local teacher.'"

"I don't think Madame Aprele would want to be the feature in your story," Lizette said. "She doesn't like to be written up in the media unless it's for her dancing."

"Madame Aprele?" Edna said as she wrote the name in her book. "That's an interesting name. She's not in the witness protection program or anything, is she? I hear they let you make up your own name. We had a rancher some years ago down by Forsyth that turned out to be in the witness protection program. He never wanted to be in the paper, either. We weren't even sure if we should put his obituary in the paper when he died. We did, of course, but we wondered."

"I don't know if that's her real name," Lizette said as she tried to steer the reviewer toward the folding chairs she had set up earlier around the stage area. "I've always called her that, and I've known her for more than fifteen years."

Edna let herself be led.

"I'm sorry it's not warmer in here," Lizette said.

"Linda's going to bring some coffee and a cookie over for you shortly."

"I heard she's been serving cookies lately. When the guys in the newsroom found out I was coming out here, they all told me to bring back cookies if I could. I hear she's got a baker making cookies for her."

"That's me," Lizette said. "I bake a little in my spare time."

"Now that's the hook for my story," Edna said as she settled herself into a folding chair next to the chair Lizette had been sitting in when she was diagramming the stage kiss. "Baker Turns to Ballet for—" Edna paused. "Why would you say you turned to ballet from baking? For inspiration? For profit?"

"It's been my dream," Lizette said as she tried to figure out a way to get her kissing diagram back before Edna noticed it sitting on the chair next to her.

Maybe the best approach was the most direct, Lizette thought as she reached over to pick up the diagram. "Let me just get this out of your way. It's nothing—just some stage directions."

Lizette willed herself to stop. She always talked too much when she was nervous. "Nothing. It's nothing."

"I had no idea you had stage directions in a ballet," Edna said as she looked up from her notebook and frowned. "I told the guys in the newsroom that I didn't know enough to cover this story."

"Oh, don't worry," Lizette said. "I can tell you anything you want to know."

"They only sent me here because I'm a woman."

"Well, I'm glad you came anyway," Lizette said as she sat down beside Edna. "Just ask me any questions you want. I can tell you everything you need."

Edna's face brightened. "That's kind of you. Not everyone takes the time to explain things. First, tell me about these stage directions. What were you mapping out? The battle with the mice?"

Lizette wished she could lie, but she couldn't. "The kiss."

Edna's face brightened even more. "Who's kissing who?"

"The Nutcracker kisses Clara."

Edna frowned. "Isn't the Nutcracker, well, a nutcracker? And isn't Clara a little girl? I did some research on the Internet just to get the basic plot. I only got the start of the ballet, but—"

"When Clara kills the Mouse King, she turns into a young lady and the Nutcracker turns into a prince. That's when they kiss."

"My, how romantic!" Edna said as she wrote in her notebook. "People around here love a romance. So, tell me, who plays the Nutcracker again?"

"Judd Bowman."

"He's the guy out on the old Jenkins place, isn't he?"

Lizette nodded.

"So the stage directions are for him? On how to kiss?"

"Well, sort of. You see a stage kiss is different than a real kiss—"

Lizette heard another set of tires in the distance. Now, that should be the sound of one of her dancers coming.

The door opened and Linda came inside along with a gust of snowy wind. "There's a regular convention out there."

"Is it Pete or Judd?"

"Neither," Linda said as she brought the thermos of coffee over to Edna. "It's a taxi."

"But there are no taxis here," Lizette said, even as she began to wonder if—

There was the sound of a honking horn and the slamming of a car door outside. Lizette walked to the window. The heat had been on long enough that a small corner of the window was now clear of frost. It was a large enough piece of window that Lizette could see a woman, covered from head to toe in black wool and black scarves. The only color anywhere was a lavender feather boa that the woman had flung around her shoulders.

Madame Aprele was outside.

Lizette hurried to the door even though she wanted to hurry in the other direction and find a place to hide. She opened the door. "Madame. What a surprise! A pleasant surprise!"

"Oh, Lizette." Madame Aprele turned toward Lizette with relief in her voice. Then she started unwinding all of the black scarves and walking toward the open door. "I'm glad I found you. This man was trying to tell me that this barn is the town's performance center. What kind of an old fool does he take me for? I'm so glad you're here so you can show me the way to where you're doing your dress rehearsal for that reviewer. I came to lend my moral support. Newspaper people can be so difficult."

By the time Madame Aprele stopped talking, she had unwound all of the scarves from her head and was fully inside the barn.

"Dear me," was all she said as she looked around.

"Madame Aprele," Lizette said as she held out her arm for the many scarves. "I'm touched that you came all of the way from Seattle. If you'd like me to take your scarves, I can."

Madame Aprele gave Lizette the black scarves. "You're rehearsing here?"

Lizette nodded as she held out her elbow for Madame Aprele to take. "Yes, and I'll take you down for a front-row seat right next to Edna Best, the woman who is going to review us."

"You're rehearsing in a barn?" Madame Aprele asked. "When do you move it to the performance center?"

"The barn *is* the performance center," Lizette said as she started walking Madame Aprele down to the chairs next to the stage.

"But what about the cows?" Madame Aprele said as she sat down in the chair next to Edna Best.

"You have cows in the ballet, too?" Edna asked as she wrote something in her notebook.

"No, there are no cows," Lizette said as she stood beside the two seated women. "Now, if you'll excuse me, I need to get my dancers ready. Madame Aprele, let me introduce you to Edna Best, who's going to review our performance today. Maybe you could answer any questions she has?"

Both women nodded to her and then to each other.

Well, Lizette thought as she stepped away, she'd done all she could. Even if one of her dancers didn't show up, she could deal with it now. All of the things in her nightmare could happen and it wouldn't even faze her now. Madame Aprele had come and seen that she was a fraud.

Her mother's old enemy and her new friend had seen that all of the things Lizette had said about her little dance school were nothing more than the longing in her heart that it be so. The performance center was a barn. Her dance students were over at a table eating a mixture of dried plums and sugar. None of them were in costume. And the only reason any of them were even her students was because they wanted to wear those costumes. The reviewer who was going to write about the ballet, although she was kind, had never even seen a ballet performance before.

There was no way for it to be worse than it was.

Lizette squared her shoulders. She had absolutely nothing to fear now. Let the ballet begin.

Chapter Sixteen

Judd Bowman wished silk had never been invented. Or women. Or both of them. If he hadn't decided to track down some white silk cloth for Lizette before he stopped at the jail to check about Neal Strong, the kids' father, he wouldn't have wasted two hours of valuable time that he could have spent out looking for the escaped prisoner alongside the sheriff's department.

Neal had escaped yesterday afternoon.

Someone had decided that there was room in the Billings jail for Neal and had gone to Miles City to get him in a patrol car. On the way there, Neal complained that he needed to use a restroom. Unfortunately, no one checked to be sure Neal's handcuffs were secure before they escorted him to the restroom. When a backup patrol car came to investigate why there was no response to a radio

message, the officers found one of their own unconscious on the floor of the restroom, and Neal, along
with the officer's gun, nowhere to be found.

Judd demanded to know why no one had called
him last night with the news, only to be told that
they were trying to reach Sheriff Wall in Colorado
to inform him of what had happened.

Judd pressed the gas pedal on his pickup a little
farther down. The police in Billings thought Neal was
more likely to head for a drug dealer or the border
than his children, but Judd wasn't so sure. He wasn't
going to take any chances.

Judd relaxed a little when he saw Pete's pickup in
front of the barn where the ballet rehearsal was going
to happen. The cowboy would see to the kids' safety
if their father was around.

Judd looked at the clock on his dashboard. Speaking of the ballet, he was late. He hoped the extra
yards of white silk he'd bought would be enough to
make Lizette forgive him.

It hadn't been easy to find silk in Miles City. Judd
had had to buy it from a secondhand store owner
who called someone he knew who had some white
silk left from an old customer who had been using
the stuff to make parachutes—or maybe it was bags
for parachutes. Neither store owner could remember.
They did remember it had been extra-strong silk,
guaranteed to hold a hundred pounds, or maybe it

was two hundred pounds. They couldn't remember how much.

Judd assured them the silk only had to be strong enough to hold a punch cup, and that he would take it as soon as the other man could get it there. He only hoped it wasn't nylon instead of silk. No one was really sure on that point, either.

Lizette was still waiting to begin the performance. Linda and Mrs. Hargrove had helped clean the faces of her younger dancers and slipped their costumes over their heads. Charley had fussed about his missing bathrobe so much that Lizette had given him a big towel to wrap around his shoulders. Then Pete had walked in a few minutes ago with a bruise on his cheek, muttering something about a stubborn cow. Lizette had asked him what happened, but he shrugged and said he'd tell her later.

"The show must go on," Pete said with a grin as he took his Mouse King costume off the chair where Lizette had laid it and started toward the stairway leading up to the hay loft. "I'll be right back."

"Oh, you can change down here," Lizette said. She hadn't wanted to send the children up to the cold hay loft to change, so she and Charley had hung a blanket in a corner of the barn.

But Pete was already halfway up the stairs with his tail dragging behind him.

Lizette herself was in her ballet slippers and her yellow dress.

"I can fill in for the Nutcracker," Mrs. Hargrove offered. The older woman had changed into her billowing Snow Queen costume and was chatting with Madame Aprele and Edna Best. "I think I have his lines memorized from watching him practice with you."

Charley was sitting in his rocking chair next to the Christmas tree. "The whole thing?"

Mrs. Hargrove nodded.

"So you'd do the Nutcracker kiss?" Edna Best asked as she pulled her notebook back out of her purse.

"Oh, no," Mrs. Hargrove said, and then chuckled. "I see you're still looking for that headline."

Edna smiled and shrugged. "Nothing ever happens around here. I was hoping maybe I could get a news story in the regular part of the paper as well as a review in the Dry Creek Tidbits section."

"Surely it's news that a ballet is going to take place in a barn," Madame Aprele offered helpfully. The older woman no longer seemed as shocked about everything and was actually giving Edna some valuable pointers on how to review the ballet. "In Seattle, that would be a headline."

"Barns are not news around here," Edna said. "We have so many of them."

"Well, you'll have to wait for Judd to get here to stage the kiss," Mrs. Hargrove said. "Although I must say, he seems to have a mind of his own about how a kiss should go on."

"That's why I drew him a diagram," Lizette said. "He just needs to see how to do it."

Charley snorted. "Whoever heard of a diagram for a kiss?"

There was a thud up in the hayloft that sounded as if Pete was taking off his boots.

Edna was writing notes. "Could you tell me more about what's lacking in the way the Nutcracker kisses?"

"Oh, I didn't say anything was lacking," Lizette said. She hoped the boot thud meant that Pete was almost in his costume. "And I don't really think you should be quoting me on this. I mean, I'm not an expert on kissing or anything. It's just for the ballet scene."

Lizette decided there was really no need to wait for the Nutcracker to arrive before they began the production. "Charley can just read the Nutcracker's lines."

"I can do the Nutcracker's kissing, too," Charley said firmly. "In my day and age, we didn't do any of this stage-kissing stuff. That's just for Hollywood types."

"How do you know? You've never kissed a Hollywood type," Mrs. Hargrove said.

"Now, how do you know who I've kissed and who I haven't kissed?" Charley said with his chin in the air.

"Well, I've known you all your life."

"That doesn't mean you know all about me. I could still surprise you yet."

"Don't think I couldn't surprise you, too," Mrs. Hargrove retorted.

My goodness, Lizette thought, what was wrong with the two of them?

Someone cleared his throat loudly from the sidelines. It must be Pete coming down the stairs, Lizette thought as she looked up.

"Speaking of surprises," Pete said calmly as he stood very still.

Pete hadn't changed into his costume, although he did have another bruise on his face. Still wearing his work jeans and a flannel shirt, he was standing at the top of the stairs with his arms in the air. There were shadows, but there was enough light to see the gun that was being held to the back of Pete's head as well as the man behind him holding the gun.

There was silence for a moment.

"There's my bathrobe," Charley finally said.

Lizette felt two pairs of little arms circle around her legs.

"That's my dad," Bobby whispered as he tightened his grip on Lizette's legs.

"You've been hiding up there all day?" Lizette said. She tried to make her voice sound normal and conversational. She didn't want the children terrified any more than they already were. "No wonder the door to the barn was unlocked. After all that time, you must be hungry."

"I'm not hungry. I have a headache. I've been trying to sleep, except you have that awful music playing and it's making my eyes cross."

The man did look pale, even in the shadows.

"That's Tchaikovsky!" Madame Aprele protested. "He's famous. He's never given anyone a headache!"

"I prefer a fiddle," the man said. "Something with some spirit."

Madame Aprele opened her mouth to say something and then thought better of it and closed it again.

Lizette agreed there was no reason to argue music with a man holding a gun. "I'll be happy to turn the music off, and then maybe you can go back and lie down and have a good rest."

The man snorted. "Nice try, but I think I'll stay right here where I can see everybody. Like you, old man." He pointed at Charley. "I see you reaching inside your coat pocket for something. You got a gun in there?"

Charley held up his open hands. "No gun. I was reaching for an antacid. Stress is killing me."

"Well, you keep your hands out of your pockets." The man nudged Pete to start walking down the stairs. "You all keep your hands where I can see them. We have a situation here."

"We don't need to have a situation," Lizette said as she put her own hands out in full view. "If you just put the gun down, no one needs to get hurt."

"You'd like that, wouldn't you? You always were looking out for yourself first," the man said. "I remember you from the gas station. No room for a poor man like me to ride with you when anyone could see you had enough room. Someone like you thinks they're better than me. Well, you're not better than me now. Not when I've got the gun."

"I don't think I'm better than anyone," Lizette said. "I just want everyone to be safe."

There was an awkward silence as everyone thought about being safe.

"You must be Neal Strong," Edna finally said. She had her hands out in front of her, as well. "I've heard about you. Something about a wrongful arrest."

"You bet it was wrongful!"

"Well, maybe you'd like to put down the gun and tell me about it. I'm a reporter with the newspaper.

If we work at getting your story out there, maybe there's a chance for you."

"The only chance for me is this," Neal said as he nodded toward the gun he held in his hand.

Pete and Neal had reached the bottom of the stairs, but no one started to breathe normally.

Even with no breath left in their lungs, they all gasped when the door to the barn started to open.

Judd held himself perfectly still. He'd come up to the door earlier and heard some of what was happening inside. He'd run over to the café and asked Linda to call the police in Billings and tell them their man was armed and in the big barn in Dry Creek. Then he'd run back to the barn door.

"I know I'm late," Judd said as he stepped into the main area of the barn. He had the white silk under one arm. "I had a hard time finding the silk and—"

Judd broke off his words, hoping he sounded genuinely surprised. "Well, who's this?"

Judd already knew who the man was, but he didn't want to give Neal any reason to be suspicious that Judd had notified the authorities.

"I'm the kids' dad," Neal said as waved his gun around. "You must be that cousin of Barbara's? You look a lot like her."

Judd felt his smile tighten. "You've seen Barbara?"

Neal nodded. "Tracked her down. I told her she had no right to leave the kids off somewhere. I'm their dad. I say where they're supposed to be."

Judd knew he shouldn't argue with the man, but he didn't like the scared look Amanda was giving him.

Judd took a casual step closer to the kids. "Bobby and Amanda are with me for now. They're no trouble. No need to bother yourself with them."

"You and Barbara would like that, wouldn't you?" Neal sneered. "You're two of a kind. Bowmans both of you. You're spoiling the kids."

So that's what family is, Judd thought. Hearing your name coupled with someone else's in a sneer and not even minding it because it meant someone else was in the thick of it with you. What do you know? He did have a family.

"They're good kids." Judd took another step closer to Amanda and Bobby. He figured the gun could go off at any minute, but if it did he had some things to say to some people before he died. "I'm not nearly good enough for those kids of yours, but if they were mine, I'd be proud of it. They're part of my family and I love them both."

Judd half expected the gun to go off when he said he loved the kids. Maybe Neal Strong didn't hear him. The words echoed in Judd's own ears, but that might be because he'd rarely even said he *liked* anyone in his life. He'd certainly never admitted to loving anyone. Love had never been for a man like him. Judd wasn't sure what love was, so he couldn't say for sure that's what he felt when he looked at those two kids holding on to Lizette's legs, but it must be. He was willing to die to protect them. That had to be something close to the love that made a family a family.

All three pairs of eyes—Lizette's and the two kids'—looked up at him.

Judd blinked. He wondered what was happening to the air around here that a man's eyes could tear up just looking at someone.

Judd took the final step that brought him next to Lizette and the kids.

"Now ain't that touching," Neal drawled as Amanda and Bobby left Lizette's legs and wrapped themselves around Judd.

Judd resisted the urge to bend down and lift the children into his arms. Instead, he gently guided both children to the back of his legs so that there would be less of them to be targets if Neal was as unsettled as he looked.

Judd forced himself to shrug. "It's still cold in here. They just like to wrap themselves around something warm. That's all."

Neal snorted. "You don't fool me. I don't let go of what's mine all that easy. Just ask Barbara."

"I've been wanting to talk to Barbara," Judd said casually. "Do you know where I can reach her?"

Neal just laughed. "You ain't getting nothing out of me."

"I'd be willing to pay," Judd said smoothly.

"I've got money."

"I wasn't thinking of cash," Judd said. He hoped the police speculation that Neal had been going through drug withdrawal was correct. "I've got some white stuff out in the pickup that might interest you."

"What is it?" Neal said.

Judd saw the look in Neal's eyes and knew he had him. Hook, line and sinker. "Not something you'd want me to announce right out here in the open."

"Bring it in."

Judd shrugged. "If you were interested in it, I'd throw in the pickup, as well. You might want to get out of here before anyone knows you're here."

Neal took a few steps closer to the door, turning as he walked so that everyone was still in his range of vision.

"I need your keys."

Judd tossed him the keys to his pickup.

"Where's the stuff?"

"In the back of the pickup, alongside the hay bales I have in there. I'm not sure what side it's on."

"What? You can't be too careful with the stuff, man."

"I'm sure you'll take care of it." Judd watched as the man walked even closer to the door.

"Is it good?" Neal asked when he had his back at the door.

"Pure as snow," Judd said as he watched the other man open the door and slide outside.

Judd counted to two. He figured it would take the man that long to get off the steps. "Everybody out the back window."

Pete was already with him on this one and had opened the back window already. The cold air swept across the barn, but no one noticed.

Judd rushed over to the door and locked it from the inside. It would take the man a while to find the key that had let him into the barn in the first place.

"The little ones first," Madame Aprele said as she lifted Amanda into Pete's arms.

Pete lifted the little girl out the window. Then he lifted Bobby.

Charley brought over a chair for the women, and one by one they climbed up to it and then slid out the window with the men's help.

There was a banging on the door to the barn just as Lizette slid over the window's edge.

"What did you have in your pickup?" Pete finally

turned to Judd and asked. "I didn't figure you for a user."

"I'm not. I told him what the white stuff was. It's snow."

"Oh, man, he's going to be mad," Pete said with a grin on his face.

The gunshot echoed throughout the barn.

"Charley, the kids need a guard," Judd said as he and Pete overruled the older man's objection and lifted him out the window. "Get them all someplace safe."

Another gunshot echoed. This one sounded as if it struck metal, which meant Neal had hit the lock.

"Now you," Judd said to Pete.

But the cowboy was already building a barricade of metal chairs. "The others need a few minutes to get away from the window. There's no cover out this way."

Judd moved chairs, too. "I can be as distracting as any two men. No sense in both of us being in here."

Pete flashed him a grin. "I'm the Rat King. I don't run away."

Judd only grunted. He was a family man now. He didn't run away, either.

Something crashed against the barn door, and both Pete and Judd dived behind their shelter of metal chairs.

"Where are you?" Neal demanded as he swung the door wide open and stepped into the barn. "You think you can fool me. I'll show you."

It was silent for a moment. Then Neal said, "I see where you are. Think you can hide behind a pile of old chairs—now who's the fool?"

Judd grabbed one of the chairs. Neal would have to come close to them to actually have any hope of shooting them, and when he did, Judd intended to bash him over the head with one of these chairs. It wasn't much, but with God's help it might work.

Now, where did that thought come from? Judd wondered. It must be all this church he had been going to that gave him this nagging sense that he should be praying.

A loud creak sounded from the middle of the barn floor. Neal was walking this way.

Oh, well, Judd told himself, if he was going to die on his knees anyway, huddled behind a twisted mess of metal, he might as well figure out if God had any interest in him.

"Come out with your hands up!" The sound of the bullhorn made everyone jump.

Judd blinked. For a moment there, he'd thought that was God's voice answering his first feeble attempt at a prayer.

"What's going on?" Neal stood in the middle of the room and demanded.

"Come on out now with your hands up!" the voice on the bullhorn repeated. "We've got you surrounded."

"Ah, man," Neal said as he started walking toward the door. "All I was trying to do was get a good night's sleep."

Judd and Pete waited for the door to the barn to close before they stood up.

"Well," Pete said.

Judd nodded as he held out his hand to the other man.

Pete shook his hand. "Well."

Judd nodded.

Then they turned to walk out of the barn together.

Chapter Seventeen

Lizette wondered how she'd be able to hold the ballet without a Nutcracker. The Friday edition of the Billings newspaper had arrived on the counter in the hardware store, and the men hadn't stopped laughing since. On the first page was Edna Best's lead news story about the shoot-out in the Dry Creek barn. Gossip had circulated that story before the paper could, so the only real news was that the police officer who Neal had hit over the head was doing fine.

No, it was the sidebar to the story that was gathering everyone's interest this morning. The sidebar led to a human interest piece Edna had also written on the ballet that was tucked away on page twelve. The headline read, "Ballet Instructor Teaches Local Rancher, Judd Bowman, How to Kiss Like a Movie Star—Diagram Included."

Lizette's heart had stopped when she read the

headline. Her ballet performance was doomed. Judd would never show up.

Even more important, her friendship with him was doomed. He wouldn't want to be seen with her if people teased him about it, and no doubt some of those ranch hands at the hardware store were already thinking up clever things to say if they saw Judd and her together.

One thing Lizette knew about Judd was that he was a private person. He'd told her he hadn't talked to the people of Dry Creek for the first six months he'd lived here. She figured that was his way of warning her that he wasn't the cozy kind of person most women look for in a male friend. She had received the message and decided to ignore it. She didn't care if he was cozy or not. He was Judd.

She liked Judd and she wanted him to just be who he was. She'd wanted to get to know him better. She'd hoped maybe their friendship could grow into something more—maybe even the kind of love that people get married over.

But those hopes were all gone. Judd was probably home now planning how he could avoid the town of Dry Creek—and her—for the rest of his life.

It was hard to dream of a future with someone who never wanted to see you again.

Lizette couldn't exactly blame him, and she figured if he wasn't going to show up for the rest of her life, then he wasn't going to show up tonight either, so she'd best stop being sentimental and get on with the problem at hand. It was time, she told herself with a mental shake, to go with Plan B. Her heart hadn't been broken. Cracked maybe, but not broken. If she pulled herself together, she could think of a way to salvage the ballet performance tonight. That was what she wanted, wasn't it?

It was funny how the answer to that question was not as clear as it had once been.

In fact, after looking at the gun in Neal Strong's hand two days ago, Lizette had done a lot of thinking about what exactly her dreams were. She'd never been as scared for anyone else as she had been for those two children who were clinging to her legs.

Maybe it was time that ballet wasn't her only dream.

Madame Aprele had been staying in Mrs. Hargrove's spare room and helping with the last-minute preparations for the ballet performance. She could play the Nutcracker part if need be.

Lizette herself, she realized, had more important things to do right now.

There weren't many places in Dry Creek where a person could sit in silence and think. Lizette told herself that was why she headed for the church. It was as good a place as any, she reasoned, to take the things in her life and add them up so she'd know what she had.

Lizette wasn't halfway across the street before she heard the sound of a vehicle starting up behind the church. Somebody had already been there to see the pastor. Lizette wondered if a person was supposed to make an appointment. She'd have to ask.

Glory Curtis, the pastor's wife, was walking down the center aisle when Lizette stepped inside the church.

"Oh, hi," Glory said.

Lizette noticed the other woman didn't seem surprised to see her. "I don't have an appointment or anything."

Glory smiled. "You don't need an appointment. Most folks just know that my husband has office hours from nine to noon every day before he goes over to work the counter at the hardware store."

Lizette had heard the pastor partially supported himself by working in the hardware store. "I don't need to talk to him for long."

"Take your time."

The pastor himself didn't seem to be in any more of a hurry than his wife had been.

"I've never been to see a pastor before," Lizette confessed.

The pastor nodded. "Sometimes when people have been through a traumatic event like having a gun pointed at them, they want to talk to someone. That's what I'm here for."

"I should be able to handle it myself. It's just that it sort of shook me up."

The pastor nodded. "Shook you up in what way?"

It seemed that the gun pointing at her had shaken her up in more ways than Lizette had thought. Her worries and concerns poured out of her. She'd even signed up for more meetings with the pastor. They were going to study the book of John together.

When Lizette left the church an hour later, she realized she'd completely forgotten about the ballet that was happening this evening. Even more amazing, she didn't start worrying when she did think about the ballet. She and the pastor had prayed, and God, she reasoned, would provide a Nutcracker.

The barn smelled like Christmas. Mrs. Hargrove and Charley had spent the afternoon bringing pine boughs down from the mountains and spreading them around the barn. The other scent was the warm smell of the sugar-plum pastries that Linda had baked this afternoon in the café ovens.

Lizette had gone back and forth between the café and the church doing last-minute things and being increasingly grateful for her friends. The Nutcracker performance might not live up to its ballet potential, but it was certainly living up to its friendship potential.

"Here, let me help you with that," Madame Aprele said as she walked alongside Lizette and offered to carry one of the trays Linda was lending them to display the pastries.

Lizette gave her the lightest of the trays. "If nothing else, people will like the pastries tonight."

Madame Aprele chuckled. "It'll all work out fine. You always used to make yourself sick worrying before any of your performances as a child. Remember, I used to say ballet is for fun."

Lizette grimaced. "It wasn't for fun in our house."

"I know," Madame Aprele said as they both stood on the cement area outside the barn. "I blame myself for not thinking of a way to bring your mother back into the ballet herself. Then she might not have demanded you do it for her."

"Oh, but she—" Lizette stopped herself. She'd never thought about the fact that her mother could still have danced. She might not have been able to do it professionally, but she could have danced in the productions at Madame Aprele's. She could have danced the ballet for fun.

Lizette opened the barn door and stood to one side so the other woman could enter.

"With your mother, it was all or nothing," Madame

Aprele said. "If she couldn't be the star of the show, she didn't want to be *in* the show."

Lizette nodded as they walked down to the end of the barn where the refreshment table was. "She used to say the same thing herself. Well, almost the same. She'd say if I wanted to dance, I should dance the main part."

Madame Aprele nodded as she put her tray on the table. "Ballet was never for the joy of it with your mother."

Lizette nodded as she set her tray down, as well. No, ballet was never for the pleasure of it with her mother. She wondered what her mother would do if one of her principal dancers didn't show for a ballet the way Lizette was expecting would happen tonight. Jacqueline would never forgive the dancer who didn't show, Lizette knew that much for sure.

For the first time in her life, Lizette didn't want to be like her mother.

Chapter Eighteen

The first group of people arrived in a noisy caravan of pickups from the Elkton ranch bunkhouse. It was snowing slightly, and the men stomped their feet on the cement outside the barn to knock any loose snow off their boots before they removed their hats and went inside the barn.

The Christmas tree in the stage area was lit with hundreds of tiny lights and all of the ornaments that Mrs. Hargrove generally hung on her tree. There were angels and red birds and golden sleighs. Someone, Lizette thought it had been Charley, had put a small wooden nativity set under the Christmas tree.

Lizette had all of the dancers, except for the Mouse King and the Nutcracker, up in the hayloft so that the audience wouldn't see their costumes until it was time for the ballet to begin. She had hung a blanket in a corner of the loft so they had a changing room, and all of the children were in their costumes. The children had peeked over the edge of the loft and whispered about how many people were in the audience. Even Mrs. Hargrove and Charley were standing near the edge of the loft.

They all saw Pete come in with his friends.

"We're up here," Lizette called, and Pete looked up to where she stood at the top of the stairs leading to the hayloft.

"I'm coming right up," Pete said as he left his friends.

"We still have a few more minutes," Madame Aprele said as she, too, walked to where the others stood and put her hand on Lizette's shoulder. "The children said Judd was coming. That he just had an errand to run in Miles City, and that he'd be back in time."

Lizette supposed she should be grateful that Judd had brought the children into town at least. "We'll have to go on without him if he's not here."

Mrs. Hargrove nodded. "There's still time for him to get here."

Lizette wondered if she could demand that everyone give her their copy of the diagram she'd drawn of how to stage a kiss. In all of the confusion, she'd left hers on the chair next to Edna. The reporter probably didn't even realize Lizette didn't want the diagram published. It had just been an image to go with the text Edna had written. There were now thousands of that image between here and Billings. Some of them were going to be in the barn tonight.

Lizette looked over the rail of the loft and saw at least two ranch hands who had a piece of newsprint in their hands. It had to be the diagram.

There was probably no chance that Judd hadn't seen it, Lizette thought.

"Do you get a newspaper at your house?" Lizette turned and asked Bobby.

The boy shook his head. "Cousin Judd listens to the radio."

Maybe there *was* a chance, Lizette thought. Fortunately, no one on the radio was likely to have heard about the Hollywood Kiss Diagram, which was what Edna had referred to it as.

Fifteen more minutes passed and Judd still hadn't arrived. The barn had filled with a good-size crowd, and everyone seemed to be having a good time.

Lizette had decided she wouldn't sell tickets to the ballet, but Linda had offered to put a bucket near the refreshment table where people could make donations to cover the costs of the production. There was a line now for the coffee, and it looked like most people held a dollar bill in their hand to put in the bucket.

"I'll go down and get the music ready to start," Lizette said. It was five minutes until the time the ballet was scheduled to begin. She looked over at

Madame Aprele and smiled. "You'd best get in the Nutcracker costume. When I come back up, I'll wait a few minutes and then give Linda the signal to dim the lights and push the play button for the music."

Lizette walked down the stairs and onto the barn floor. Half of the chairs were filled with people drinking coffee or punch and waiting for the ballet to begin. The other half of the chairs would comfortably seat the people who were still in line for their beverage.

Linda had suggested they serve the drinks before the ballet and then serve them again after the ballet when they brought out the pastries.

"Hi," Linda said when she saw Lizette walking toward the refreshment table. "We'll be finishing up here in a few minutes."

Lizette nodded. "Judd's not here yet, but he might not make it. When everyone gets settled down here and back to their seats, just dim the lights and then a minute later start the music. The dancers will come down the stairs then and we'll begin."

The chatter in the barn had a warm feeling to it, Lizette thought as she walked back to the stairs. People smiled and greeted her like an old friend instead of a performer, and she liked that.

Lizette climbed the stairs to the hayloft and gathered her dancers around her for a final word of encouragement.

"This is for fun," Lizette said to them all as she nodded to Madame Aprele, who was holding the Nutcracker's hat but still hadn't changed into the entire costume. The older woman had more hope than Lizette did. "I don't want you to worry if you make a mistake. Everything will be fine."

"I'm not going to make any mistakes," Amanda said. She had her costume on, and the wings glittered pink and gold in the light that came into the loft. "I'm a Sugar Plum Fairy, and we don't make mistakes."

"We try not to make mistakes," Lizette agreed. "But sometimes we do."

"Like Cousin Judd," Bobby said. "He's making a mistake because he's late."

Lizette put her hand on the boy's shoulder. "It's all right. It will be okay even if he doesn't get here. We'll all understand."

Lizette hoped that message would get to Judd through the children.

"Uh-uh." Amanda shook her head. "Cousin Judd needs to be here. He's the Nutcracker. Who's going to do the kiss if he's not here?"

Lizette exchanged a glance with Madame Aprele. The older woman would play the part of the Nutcracker. But— "Maybe there won't be a kiss this time around."

"I'd be happy to do the kiss," Pete said as he

stepped out from behind the curtain in his Mouse King costume.

Lizette noticed the ranch hand had not flirted with her since he'd arrived. He wasn't even flirting now.

"On Judd's behalf, of course," Pete added. "As a friend."

"Oh, well—" Lizette stammered. "No one needs to do a kiss."

Pete stepped closer to the edge of the loft and looked over. "I think they're going to demand a kiss."

Lizette stepped closer to the edge of the loft just in time to see the barn door open.

"Well, look who's here," Pete said with relief. "I knew he'd make it."

It was Judd walking through the door, along with a woman who was wrapped in a long black coat with a gray wool scarf wrapped around her face so that none of her hair or skin showed.

Lizette tried not to be jealous of the fact that Judd was walking with his arm around the woman and leading her to one of the chairs in the back of the barn. Who Judd put his arm around was none of her business, Lizette told herself, even though he was carrying a huge bouquet of roses that he gave to the woman when she settled into her chair. Judd called Linda over to the woman before he looked up to the hayloft and saw Lizette and Pete.

The chatter in the barn grew more excited as Judd walked over to the staircase leading up to the hayloft.

"Cousin Judd!" Amanda squealed when she saw Judd coming up the stairs. "You came!"

"Of course," Judd said as he stood at the top of the stairs.

"You need to get into your costume," Pete said as he slapped Judd on the back. "We've got a ballet to do."

Linda dimmed the lights to signal the audience was ready. Judd was already walking over to Madame Aprele, who held out his costume to him. Then he headed for the curtain to change. "If you want to start, I can slip down in a few minutes."

Lizette nodded. "You don't need to be in the first few minutes, anyway. We thought we'd have the family sing a carol in front of the tree to start."

This, Lizette thought, was what a family Christmas felt like even hundreds of years ago when the Nutcracker was written. It was gathering your friends and family together beside a tree and celebrating a wonderful time of gifts and love.

The carol the family sang was "Silent Night." Mrs. Hargrove led everyone in the barn in softly singing the song and the sound filled the whole structure with warmth.

Lizette slowly danced ballet steps to show how a

young girl would see the wonder of that night long ago when Christ was born. The audience was hushed. Lizette had not known until these past few days what it meant to be truly silent on that holy night.

After the carol finished, Charley started to read the story of the Nutcracker.

The Nutcracker came on the stage just when the presents were given to the children, and Lizette realized what she should have done. She should have taken a moment to warn Judd about the kiss. He must not know that everyone had been talking about the kiss he was going to give her tonight.

Lizette danced the part of Clara's excitement over her new gift, hoping to come close enough to whisper in Judd's ear. Unfortunately, none of the steps got her close enough to say a few words to him that all of the others wouldn't also hear.

She'd have to wait for the battle scene, she thought. There would be enough noise with all of the mice attacking that no one would hear her talking to Judd.

What was wrong with the Nutcracker? When they had practiced, Judd had held back as though he wasn't part of the mice attack. He'd let the children attack him, but he hadn't gotten into their play. Now, he attacked with abandon, lifting one mouse up in the air until the mouse giggled and then going after another until even the tin soldier forgot which side of the battle he was on and all of the children swarmed around the Nutcracker.

Lizette didn't have a chance to talk to Judd, so she just kept dancing. She twisted and turned and made it look like the whole stage was alive with ballet.

Then Charley started to read about the attack of the Mouse King, and Pete burst out of the fireplace with a roar that briefly overpowered the music.

Now, Lizette said to herself, as she tried to dance closer to Judd to explain that he didn't need to kiss her. There wasn't a kiss in every Nutcracker production, and there wouldn't be one in this one. The people of Dry Creek would have to get their romance elsewhere this Christmas. Her friendship with Judd was more important than the ballet, even if this ballet affected the future of her ballet school in this little community where she was making her home.

"Psst," Lizette hissed as she danced as close as she could to Pete and Judd.

The Mouse King and the Nutcracker were engaged in a magnificent battle, and the audience was shouting encouragement to them both. There was enough noise that she could deliver her message to Judd if he'd only look her way.

But the Mouse King had the Nutcracker in his grip, and Charley was clearing his throat.

"The shoe." Judd twisted his neck and finally looked at Lizette. "You need to throw your shoe."

Lizette figured she'd have to talk to Judd after she saved his life.

Lizette's shoe hit Pete on the shoulder, and he went down with a groan.

The music swelled up and Charley threw sparkling confetti in the air as if it was a party.

Judd moved closer.

Finally, Lizette thought as she danced closer to him, she'd have a chance to tell him about the kiss.

"You don't need to do the kiss," Lizette whispered as she came close to Judd.

Judd had already taken his hat off, and he wasn't frowning at all. In fact, Lizette thought he looked downright happy. Which meant only one thing. He hadn't heard about the story in the newspaper.

"Oh, yes, I do," Judd said as he moved even closer to her until she had no room left to dance.

"But—" Lizette said before Judd bent down and kissed her. It wasn't a stage kiss, of course. He hadn't taken any of her earlier suggestions. The funny thing was that she didn't care. She had his kiss.

Yes, she thought to herself, this was what Christmas and mistletoe and family were all about.

Lizette was only dimly aware of the applause.

"We're not finished," she murmured as she settled even closer to Judd, if that was possible.

"Not by a long shot," Judd agreed with his lips close to hers.

"We still have the Sugar Plum Fairy."

"That, too," Judd agreed as he smiled into her eyes and then kissed her again.

The applause overpowered the music. Lizette thought there was some stomping, too.

"Oh, yes," Judd said as he slowly pulled himself away from her. "I almost forgot—"

Judd looked to his side where Linda stood with the hugest bouquet of red roses Lizette had ever seen.

"These are for you," Judd said to her as he took the roses from Linda and handed them to Lizette.

She almost cried. Everything was perfect for the moment. But when someone said something about that diagram, she didn't know what he would do.

Judd then turned to the audience and said quite clearly, "And for those of you who are wondering about the secret to a Hollywood kiss, that's it. Bring her roses, boys, that's all there is to it."

The audience loved him. Lizette could see that. Odd that she still had the urge to cry.

"That was a smart move," she said to Judd. She couldn't look him in the eye, but she could look at his chin, which was close enough. "They won't tease you now. It was brilliant."

"Brilliant had nothing to do with it," Judd whispered as he tipped her chin up so her eyes met his. "I'm hoping to kiss you a lot in the days ahead, and I don't want someone stopping to draw a diagram of it every time I do."

"You do? Hope to kiss me?"

Judd nodded. "A man's got to have hope even if he's got no reason to."

Lizette smiled. "You have reason."

Judd grinned and kissed her again.

Lizette danced the next scenes as she had never danced before. Madame Aprele was right about ballet being fun. The Snow Queen must have thought it was fun, too, because she almost frolicked during her scenes.

Then there was the Sugar Plum Fairy. Amanda glowed as she stood at the edge of the stage area and started her dance. Lizette had had more time to teach Amanda dance steps than any of her other students, and the little girl was actually doing ballet.

Lizette had given Amanda a solo part, and so Lizette had danced to the sidelines to wait while Amanda completed it.

Madame Aprele was standing next to Lizette. "She's got promise, that one. She's a natural."

Lizette nodded. It was good to know she had at least one student who was in it for the ballet instead of the doughnuts.

"There will be more," Madame Aprele said with a nod to the audience. "You'll find more students out there."

The applause at the end of Amanda's solo was as loud as the kiss applause, and the little girl glowed under the shower of encouragement until one woman at the back of the seating area stood up to give her a standing ovation.

"Mama," Amanda squealed, and forgot all about being the Sugar Plum Fairy as she ran down the aisle to her mother.

Lizette swore there wasn't a dry eye in the whole barn by the end of the ballet.

Chapter Nineteen

"**W**e're going to need more napkins," Linda announced as Lizette managed to walk through the crowd of well-wishers in order to check with Linda on how things were going. "Next time we should forget asking for contributions for coffee and just sell handkerchiefs. We'll make a fortune. Even I was teary-eyed."

"Who wouldn't cry when Amanda saw her mother?"

"And you and Judd," Linda said as she reached for a napkin. "That sent me over the edge."

"Well—" Lizette wanted to admit that it had sent *her* over the edge, too, but the man was nowhere around and so she wasn't sure she should be thinking what she was thinking, so she didn't want to say anything.

"I mean, when he gave you the second kiss, I

knew—that's the real thing." Linda dabbed at her eyes. "Judd's just so romantic. My boyfriend used to be that way, too."

Lizette couldn't help but think it would be a lot more romantic if Judd had actually hung around to talk to her after a kiss like that. At first she thought he was with the kids and their mother, but she'd looked over there and he wasn't with them, either. She'd heard that Judd's cousin had been in a hospital in Colorado until Sheriff Wall went there to convince her it was safe to come back. Judd had met her in Miles City and brought her out to the performance. After such a long day, maybe Judd was just tired. Maybe he'd just gone home without a word to anyone.

"Ah, there he is," Linda said.

Lizette turned to look in the direction of Linda's gaze.

So there was Judd, coming in the door with Pete right behind him. They were both still in costume although they had put on their hats and their coats, so they looked a little odd.

Lizette could see Judd scanning the crowd and looking for someone until his eyes found hers and the scanning stopped. He started walking toward her.

"If you'll excuse me," Linda said as she started to walk away from Lizette. "I think three might be a crowd right about now."

"Sorry," Judd said as he stopped in front of Lizette. "I had to give Pete a key to my place and I'd left the key in my pickup."

"Pete?"

"Yeah, I told him he could stay at my place for a few days until the teasing dies down about his tail."

Lizette smiled. "I didn't think of that."

"Yeah, this having-a-friend business is a commitment, you know," Judd said as he reached out and touched Lizette on the cheek. "Not that I'm opposed to commitments anymore. I want you to know that. In fact, there's one commitment I'll welcome if I get a chance to make it."

"What's that?" Lizette said.

"This one." Judd bent his head to kiss her.

Epilogue

From the Dry Creek Tidbits column appearing in the March 17 issue of the Billings newspaper:

The bride, Lizette Baker, and the groom, Judd Bowman, were married in the church in Dry Creek last Saturday, March 14, at two o'clock in the afternoon. The groom's little cousin, Amanda Strong, was the flower girl and her brother, Bobby Strong, was the ring bearer.

Both children (who take lessons at the Baker School of Ballet along with eight other children) executed perfect pirouettes on their way down the aisle as a special gift to their ballet teacher.

The bride and groom gave special thanks to the pastor of the church, who had baptized them and received their confession of faith several months prior to their marriage.

Doughnuts were served at the reception along with a five-tiered wedding cake, both made by the bride, who offers her baking services at the Dry Creek Café.

Readers of this column who want to send congratulation cards to Mr. and Mrs. Bowman can send cards to the Bowman Ranch, Dry Creek, Montana (the groom assured me there is no need to refer to their place as the Jenkins place any longer and I believe he's right. It's now the Bowman family's place.)

Readers of this column will also remember that the bride and groom were engaged shortly after demonstrating the Hollywood kiss that was diagrammed in this column. Their kiss after the wedding ceremony rivaled the one many readers saw at the Nutcracker ballet performance before Christmas.

The bride was quoted as saying, "Finally, we have that kiss just right."

The groom offered to keep practicing.

* * * * *

Dear Reader,

I hope you enjoyed reading about Judd and Lizette. When I was telling their story, I thought about what it feels like to go to a church for the first time. Their feelings of awkwardness are repeated many times each Sunday as someone visits a church and isn't sure of what their welcome will be. During the Christmas season, you may see people in your church who do not seem to feel comfortable. Hopefully, you can help them feel like they are among friends.

May you have a blessed Christmas.

Janet Tronstad

AT HOME IN DRY CREEK

Except the Lord build the house,
they labor in vain that build it.
                    —*Psalms* 127:1

This book is dedicated to all of the
Mrs. Hargroves of the world who teach
Sunday school, befriend their neighbors
and do good to others.

Chapter One

It wasn't against the law for her to catch the bridal bouquet, Barbara Strong told herself as she cupped her hands to catch the flowers that had been thrown so expertly at her. Besides, if the bride didn't care that the bouquet went to someone who wouldn't fulfill the prediction of being the next to marry, what did Sheriff Wall care?

The sheriff was standing across the room from Barbara and scowling at her as if she'd just lifted the silverware. There was enough music and chatter all around that Barbara doubted anyone else noticed the sheriff's frown—especially not now that everyone was looking at *her*.

Great, she thought, as she forced herself to smile. The whole town of Dry Creek, Montana; all two hundred people, had seen her catch Lizette's bridal bouquet, and now they had one more story to tell each other about her.

For months, Barbara had thought that the interest people here showed in her and her two young children had been because their arrival was the only thing that had happened in this small town for a long time. The days had been cold and people hadn't been able to make the trip into Billings very often. Some days there had been so much snow on the roads no one went anywhere. Added to that, everyone had complained that the television reception had been worse than usual for some reason this past winter.

People had been bored.

Barbara had understood why they would be looking for something new to entertain them. But she and her children had been here almost five months now. In television terms, they were last year's reruns. Nobody should be watching them with such keen interest, especially not the sheriff.

The chatter increased as people came up to Barbara and congratulated her. It was dark outside, but inside the large community center, strings of tiny white lights glowed along the rustic wood walls. A circle of people stayed around Barbara after the initial flurry of congratulations had died down.

There was a full minute of awkward silence as everyone seemed to stare at their shoes or boots and wait for something. Now that they had her surrounded, Barbara realized, they didn't quite know what to do with her.

Charley, a white-haired man, was the first one to clear his throat.

"I don't expect you've had a chance to meet my nephew. He lives in Billings," Charley said as he stepped closer to Barbara and lowered his voice. Charley was one of the first people Barbara had met when she'd arrived in Dry Creek last fall. "I don't mind saying he's a fine man. Single and he loves kids. Works as a mechanic in a shop, too, so he could provide for a family—even now he might be able to fix you up with a car so you'd have one. Sort of a courting present, you know—like flowers. He's good with cars."

Charley and some other old men spent their days around the woodstove in the hardware store and they seemed to know more than most people about what was going on in this small town. Barbara respected Charley. He had been a rancher all his life and still had a tan line on his forehead that marked where the brim of a straw hat would normally sit. He knew about hard work. He was also one of the leaders of this community. His roots went deep here. That was one reason why Barbara wasn't as annoyed as she could have been with his match-making.

"You know I can't accept a—" Barbara started to

say. She'd begin with the obvious protests and work her way up to all the reasons she wasn't ever going to get married again.

"Oh, it'd be his pleasure, don't worry about that. He'd love to help out a pretty young woman like yourself."

Charley smiled at her. Barbara thought he looked relieved to have his piece said.

Jacob, one of the other old men who regularly sat by the woodstove, shook his head in disgust. Jacob was the one who had invited Lizette, who had just married Barbara's cousin Judd, to come to Dry Creek and open up her dance studio.

"She's young all right!" Jacob protested. "I don't know what you're thinking. That nephew of yours has to be fifty if he's a day. If no one cares about age, I could court her myself. And I'll be seventy-six this July." Jacob's voice rose higher with each word he said and his gray beard quivered with indignation. "Come to think on it, maybe I will do just that—if you can't come up with someone better than your nephew! Besides, what's wrong with that son of yours? He's sitting out there on that ranch of his not more than five miles from here. He could use a wife—and he's young enough." Jacob looked around the room. "Where is he anyway? I don't see him here."

"He doesn't come to weddings," Linda, the young

woman who owned the café, said softly as she stepped closer to Barbara's side. "Besides, Charley's son is already in love with someone else. We need to find Barbara a man who's going to be hers exclusively. That's the only way it can really work."

Barbara was surprised to smell jasmine perfume on Linda. In the five months she had known the café owner, the young woman had seemed to go out of her way to avoid perfume and skirts and anything that would hint that she was an attractive woman. Usually, she just wore a big white chef's apron over her blue jeans and T-shirt.

Linda had spoken of some unrequited love in her life one morning when she and Barbara had sat at a table in the café and shared a pot of tea. Barbara wondered if Linda was thinking of that love now, whoever he was. If she was, it had brought a wistful, fragile look to her eyes.

"I'm sorry, but I'm not—" Barbara tried again. She looked at the faces around her. She liked all of these people. She didn't want to disappoint them. She just wished they could have asked her for something she could give. "Of course, I appreciate it. But you don't need to—"

"Don't you worry none about finding a man who will be yours altogether. My nephew will be faithful," Charley interrupted staunchly. He'd found his second wind, Barbara thought in dismay. "He may be old, but he's a fine man. Committed."

"Well, I'm committed, too, if that's all you need," Jacob replied.

"Should *be* committed is more like it, you old coot," Charley said. "No one here is talking about you."

Barbara saw the vein grow more pronounced on Charley's neck.

"No one needs to be committed," Barbara said as she held up her hands in surrender. A petal or two fell off the bouquet as she lifted it. She made sure she smiled when she talked. She supposed she should be touched that people were worried about finding her a new husband. "It's all been a mistake. I didn't mean to catch the bouquet; it was just reflexes. The thing was coming at me and I just grabbed it so it wouldn't hit me. It doesn't mean anything. I'm not looking for a husband."

She didn't add that now that she'd had a moment to think about it, she wished she'd had enough sense to duck when she'd first seen the bridal bouquet heading her way. Failing that, she should have let it hit her square on. She wasn't sure if she'd live long enough for the story of how she'd caught Lizette's bouquet to fade from the minds of everyone around here.

That was because every story about *her* lasted longer than it should. That was what had finally made Barbara realize something was wrong.

Barbara had been okay with all of the interest at first. She'd moved around enough to know how it was when a new person moved into a small town. The heightened-interest stage came first, but usually it didn't last long, and once it was over, someone would ask the newcomer to serve coffee at a PTA meeting or head up a fund-raiser for the school, and that was an official sign that the person was no longer an outsider but a member of the community.

Barbara was prepared for this cycle. She wasn't sure how many times the person needed to pour coffee before they *really* belonged to the community, but she figured it was probably somewhere around a thousand cups of coffee poured at various functions.

It was the after-coffee place that Barbara wanted to reach—the place where she was a comfortable part of everything just as these people standing around her now were part of it all.

She'd begun to wonder if she'd ever reach that place.

There was a moment of silence as the conversation stopped swirling around Barbara. There was still noise elsewhere in the community center, but the circle around Barbara had grown quiet.

"I suppose we can't blame you for not looking for another husband—you probably still have feelings for the one you have," Charley finally said quietly.

"Of course she has feelings," Linda agreed and then sighed. "Sometimes that's just the way of it. No matter what you do, the feelings stay with you."

"They say even geese mate for life," Jacob added with a grunt. "Doesn't matter what kind of a bird they end up with, they stay hooked to that one. Reckon it's the same with her and him."

Barbara shook her head. Finally, they were at the heart of why the people of Dry Creek were so fascinated with her. If it had only been she and her children who had moved to town, the others wouldn't have been interested for so long. No, the interest was mostly because of *him*.

Her ex-husband was sitting in the jail in Billings awaiting trial for robbing several gas stations. It was obvious that the people of Dry Creek were watching to see what happened with her and Neal before they welcomed her into the fold and asked her to do something as simple as pour coffee for them at some function. Barbara wasn't sure what people expected to learn about her by waiting, but she had a sinking feeling that at least some of them were wondering if she was going to play Bonnie to her ex-husband's Clyde.

Barbara didn't know how to explain to everyone that Neal no longer held any part of her heart or her life. He didn't have the faithfulness of a tomcat, let alone a goose. She wouldn't follow him *anywhere…*

and certainly not into a life of crime. If she had learned anything from Neal, it was that crime ruined lives. She'd never be Bonnie to anyone's Clyde.

She hesitated long enough that a whisper came from somewhere behind her. Barbara knew she wasn't supposed to hear it.

"Poor thing. She's so brave," the woman's voice said, low and filled with pity. "And him sitting there in jail—he's not worth it."

"Hush, now," another woman hissed. "He must be worth something if she married him."

Barbara knew she wasn't the only one who heard the whispers because there was a sudden chorus of throat clearings and foot shuffles. She hoped no one expected her to answer the whispers. Barbara wasn't upset that people wondered about her and her ex-husband—she just didn't know what to say. She wanted these people to truly welcome her into their community, and she doubted anything she said about Neal would make that happen. If they didn't trust her to be an honest citizen, they wouldn't trust her any more because *she* said she would be one.

From the first day Barbara had driven into Dry Creek, she had wanted to belong here. She'd been frantic with worry that day because she was trying to locate her second cousin, Judd Bowman, so she could beg him to take care of her children while she drove to Denver to check out an abused woman's shelter that might take them. Bobby was six at the time, Amanda was five. Now, they were both a year older.

Even in her distress, Barbara had noticed that the town offered its residents the opportunity to put down roots. It had clotheslines that were actually being used and old men who sat around a potbellied stove in the hardware store and talked. It was obvious that people really knew each other here. When Barbara's husband was finally arrested and she was released from the hospital where his beating had put her, she was glad she could come back to a place like Dry Creek.

But becoming rooted here wasn't as easy as she had thought it would be. She and her children had been here since November, and she hadn't poured a single cup of coffee. Even now, although she was a bridesmaid at this wedding for Judd and Lizette, no one had allowed Barbara to do more than walk up the aisle.

People still treated her like a visitor, and she didn't know what to do to change it. At this rate, she wouldn't be accepted into this town until she was lying in the cemetery behind that little church. Even then, they'd probably put a fence around her grave and *Visitor* on her tombstone so that people would know to tiptoe around her in search of the people who *belonged* in Dry Creek.

"Well, it's a beautiful bouquet anyway, with all that baby's breath and green stuff," Linda declared as the others nodded and started to slip away. "And those rosebuds are perfect. You could even take some of them out of the bouquet and press them between the pages of a thick book. They'd look real nice tucked in a big family Bible."

Barbara didn't want to admit that she didn't own a Bible, family or otherwise. She'd moved around so much in the past few years that she didn't even have a cookbook, and she was more likely to use that than a Bible—which was saying something, because most of the hotel rooms where she and Neal had lived hadn't had kitchens and a person didn't need a cookbook to figure out how to heat up a can of soup in a beat-up old coffeemaker.

But a lot of people in Dry Creek valued the Bible and Barbara wanted them to think she belonged here.

"Thanks, that's a good idea," she replied to Linda and smiled a little vaguely. "Maybe I'll do that."

Before long, everyone had left her side. The bad part about the crowd around her thinning was that Barbara could see the sheriff again. He hadn't moved when all of the people had surrounded her, he'd just waited for them to leave. She wondered what his problem was. If his frown was any indication, Sheriff Carl Wall would be the last one to accept a cup of coffee from her even if she *did* manage to pour a cup.

Chapter Two

Sheriff Carl Wall knew he couldn't arrest someone just for their own good, but he was sure tempted. He was standing here watching Barbara Strong, and she had just gotten the attention of every single ranch hand at the wedding reception. Not much escaped the eyes of those mangy fellows, and they had all noticed that she'd caught the bridal bouquet.

Until today, the sheriff had been able to warn everyone off Barbara, saying she was still in shock over what had happened with her ex-husband. After all, it wasn't every day a woman woke up and found out she was married to a thief. The older people in town had agreed with him, and everyone had decided to give Barbara at least a year to catch her breath. No one was going to put any extra strain on her for at least that long. No requests for volunteer help. No urgent need for favors.

The sheriff trusted the older people in town to keep their word.

He didn't trust the ranch hands. One of the older women, Mrs. Hargrove, had added her voice to the sheriff's when he'd talked to the men about giving Barbara a year of peace. Many of the ranch hands had had Mrs. Hargrove as a Sunday-school teacher in their younger days, and they didn't want to cross the older woman, even though it had been many years since they'd sat in her class.

The sheriff made it clear that he felt it would disturb Barbara's peace if she had to brush off countless pleas for dates. The ranch hands had reluctantly agreed that Barbara might need a little time to heal before she had to start figuring out which man among them to marry next. They'd said a year sounded about right—unless, of course, the woman herself seemed unwilling to wait that long.

The sheriff had thought he was doing good to buy her a year. He'd agreed to the terms.

But now Barbara had just destroyed all his efforts when she'd caught the bridal bouquet. She should have just stood up on a chair and announced her intention to start looking for a new husband. She'd probably get a dozen proposals before the night was over.

The sheriff shook his head. He was tempted to tell the ranch hands that the woman they were ogling was being watched by the FBI. *That* would slow them down. Not that it was strictly true. The FBI wasn't watching her; they'd asked *him* to do that for them.

It seemed Barbara's ex-husband, Neal Strong, might not have been content with robbing gas stations. The FBI suspected he might also have joined forces with two other men to rob some bank down in Wyoming. One of the other suspects, Harlow Smith, was in jail in Billings along with Neal, but the third man was unidentified and still free.

The FBI didn't have any real evidence that Neal was in on the bank robbery, but even though the robbers had covered their faces with ski masks, his body had a strong resemblance to a drawing one of the bank tellers had made of the men. The FBI figured that if Neal was in on it, he would give himself away by trying to do something with the $150,000 in cash that was missing. At the very least, they figured he'd lead them to part of the money through his ex-wife.

So far, the sheriff had watched Barbara closely but noticed nothing. He knew how much she earned at her job at the bakery, and she was barely spending that. She sure wasn't spending any extra stolen money. The only thing she had purchased besides groceries was the school supplies she'd bought for her children. He knew because Barbara didn't have a car and Mrs. Hargrove gave her a ride to Miles City to buy groceries. It all checked out.

The sheriff frowned again. The most suspicious thing Barbara had done was what she was doing now. She'd taken that bridal bouquet and was using it as a fan. It wasn't hot inside here, but Barbara's cheeks were all pink and flushed like—

The sheriff followed the direction of Barbara's eyes. He should have known. She was looking directly at Pete Denning. Or Pete was looking at her. The sheriff wasn't sure who had started looking first.

Pete was the worst of the lot when it came to the ranch hands. He flirted. He broke hearts. He would dance with a cactus if that was the only thing he could find to put his arms around. Rumor had it that Pete had been claiming he was ready to get married these days, now that his good friend Judd was tying the knot. The sheriff had known Pete for years. He figured the ready-to-marry line was just Pete's latest pick-up bait.

But Barbara wouldn't know that. Women just couldn't resist a no-good ladies' man who said he was ready to settle down.

Pete had obviously decided to forget about the year of grace for Barbara. He had probably already said his line to her now that he was standing closer to the woman. That must be why she was fanning herself so hard the rose petals were beginning to fall off that bouquet she held. She probably wanted

Pete to know she was listening to his talk about his new-found desire to settle down.

Of course she was listening, the sheriff told himself. Pete was the kind of guy women liked. That was the worst of it. Even when Pete had played a huge mouse in that Nutcracker ballet last Christmas, women had swarmed around him afterward like he was the hero of the piece instead of the villain. Women just naturally thought Pete was exciting.

The sheriff felt himself fade into the background a little bit. He'd long ago made his peace with the fact that women found him dull. They knew he was trustworthy, of course. Women always voted for him for sheriff. But women didn't look at him the way they looked at Pete.

The sheriff knew he didn't understand women. He'd never had much reason to understand them. He couldn't remember his mother. He had grown up in an endless cycle of institutions and foster homes. He'd always been more of a number than a name.

There had never been much demand in adoption circles for a stocky, plain boy who was average in just about everything, so he'd stayed in the state system.

Still, the sheriff was content. He had his job and he was a good sheriff. He understood doing his duty much more than he understood things like being part of a family. Married couples baffled him. Young children made him nervous. But it was okay. He'd found a place for himself in life and it was a fine place.

He'd even made himself a home of sorts on a piece of land outside Dry Creek a couple of years ago. The twenty-acre plot he'd bought had a few trees on it and a creek that ran across the upper northwest corner. The creek wasn't much more than mud in the fall, but in the spring, like now, it ran full and sweet.

The sheriff had bought a used trailer and set it on a foundation close enough to one tree so he'd have shade in the summer. Then he'd built a wooden porch that reached out a good ten feet from the main part of the trailer. The trailer was two bedrooms and, with the porch, felt like a house. Last spring, he'd put a white picket fence around the trailer to keep the deer away from the corn he had planted next to the porch.

Yes, the sheriff thought to himself, he was doing fine.

It's just that he didn't believe in pretending to be something he wasn't. And he wasn't a family man. He could count on one hand the times he had sat down to eat with a group of people when he was growing up and felt like he was eating with a family.

Still, he'd come to peace with who he was. He'd learned some lessons the hard way, but he was a decent, strong man. He might have limitations, but he knew what they were. He wasn't a touchy-feely emotional kind of a man like most women wanted. But that was okay. He knew the importance of duty and he knew how to keep the people in his care safe.

Someday, the sheriff hoped, he'd meet a woman who would appreciate the solid nature of his personality. Of course, she'd probably be a bit dull and colorless herself. He'd figured that out long ago. Whoever she was, she wouldn't be anything like Barbara Strong.

Just look at the woman. She stood there waving that pink-rose bouquet around and looking like a Valentine greeting card doing it. Her dark hair was all curly around her head, and her brown eyes flashed. Her skin was all flushed, and she had a dimple. And it wasn't just her looks that made her seem so feminine—it was the graceful way she fluttered her hands when she talked.

The sheriff could watch her hands talk for hours. He'd noticed long ago that she'd taken off her wedding rings, both the gold band and the diamond engagement ring that went with it. He knew that some women started wearing lots of other rings when they took off their wedding ring, like they were uncomfortable with having the ring gone. But not Barbara. Her fingers stayed bare and her hands moved even more freely with no ring at all.

The sheriff frowned a bit more deeply. Maybe Barbara just didn't have any other rings to wear. That didn't seem right either. A woman like her deserved the best of everything.

She certainly deserved better than to have her heart broken by Pete.

The sheriff sighed. It wasn't always easy looking out for other people. Not that he gave this kind of special attention to everyone who moved to Dry Creek. It was just that he'd started feeling responsible for Barbara when he'd tracked her down to that Colorado hospital after her ex-husband beat her up last fall. He'd sat by her hospital bed for the simple reason that she'd taken one look at him and asked him to stay.

Of course, she might not have been in her right mind when she'd asked him to stay. She'd been drugged with enough pain medication to confuse anyone. For all he knew, she thought he was Elvis or the hospital chaplain or some long-lost purple rabbit from her childhood. But, he'd stayed with her anyway.

When people were drugged, as Barbara had been in the hospital, they tended to mutter to themselves about all kinds of things. While he sat by her bed, the sheriff had heard enough of what was in Barbara Strong's heart to know she dreamed of romance and poetry and knights on white horses. His hopes had sunk with each fanciful dream she shared. She was the kind of woman who would take one look at him and know he didn't have a clue about any of those things she was dreaming about.

The sheriff hoped the day never came when Barbara looked at him too closely. He knew it hadn't come while she was in the hospital, because on the last day of her hospital stay, she'd kissed him. On the cheek like a thank-you kiss. It had been because of the drugs still in her system, he was sure of that. But he'd kissed her back anyway, and not on the cheek. His had been no thank-you kiss, and he hadn't had the excuse of being on any kind of medication.

Barbara had been surprised.

The sheriff had been stunned. He had no excuse for his behavior. He knew he wasn't the kind of man that Barbara dreamed about. He had nothing to offer a woman like Barbara. He didn't even talk about the things women liked to hear. He'd watched Pete flirt with women and realized he didn't have a clue how to go about something like that.

No, he'd always known Barbara would want someone better than him long-term. But that didn't mean he couldn't protect her until she got back on her feet. He meant for her to have her year of peace. He needed it and she needed it, too. She certainly didn't need someone like Pete tormenting her.

The sheriff started moving.

"You got the registration updated on that old pickup of yours?" Sheriff Wall asked as he finished walking over to Pete. When he started asking the question of Pete, the sheriff was standing beside the other man. By the time the question was ended, the sheriff was standing in front of Pete, half-blocking the view the ranch hand had of Barbara.

"Excuse me, ma'am," the sheriff turned and nodded his head toward Barbara. She did look pretty, but he couldn't be distracted. She smelled nice, too. "This will just take a minute."

"That's all right." Barbara smiled at the sheriff. "I need to check on the children anyway."

The sheriff nodded again as Barbara stepped away.

"What'd you do that for?" Pete complained when Barbara was out of earshot. "Now she's going to think I live outside the law like that no-good man she used to be married to! I sent off for the official registration. I told you that when old Charley sold it to me. I've got the temporary permit in my pickup."

By the time Pete had finished explaining himself, both men were standing side-by-side, watching Barbara walk through the crowd of people. Barbara wasn't tall, but she walked tall with her shoulders thrown back and her step confident. She made quite the picture in the lavender bridesmaid's dress she was wearing. The dress had a full shiny skirt that swished and swayed when she walked. If people would only stop talking, the sheriff knew he'd be able to hear the dress.

There, the sheriff thought in satisfaction. A fair number of people had stopped talking. It was almost quiet.

It took a minute for Sheriff Wall to realize what all that silence meant, and he looked around. He didn't have to look far to see a dozen other single men also watching Barbara as she walked across the room to the refreshment table. He scowled at those other men.

"I was just getting ready to ask her out," Pete complained softly.

"That's what I figured," the sheriff said as he gave the ranch hand a friendly pat on the back and turned to walk away.

"Hey, don't you want to see the temporary permit?" Pete called after him.

"Naw, that's fine." The sheriff thought maybe he should get himself a cup of punch from the refreshment table. Just to let the other men know he was keeping an eye on things.

Chapter Three

"Congratulations!" Mrs. Hargrove said as Barbara stopped in front of the refreshment table. Mrs. Hargrove had a long cake knife in one hand and a streak of lemon filling on the white apron she wore over her green gingham dress. The older woman had her gray hair pulled back into a black velvet bun catcher and she wore a pearl necklace.

"Thanks." Barbara thought the older woman looked a little tired despite her finery. She knew Mrs. Hargrove had seen her catch the bouquet, but she didn't want the older woman to have any unrealistic expectations. "Lizette is the one who needs the congratulations though—she's the bride—she was just having some fun throwing her bouquet. She knows I'm not interested in getting married again."

"Oh, you can't give up hope, dear," Mrs. Hargrove said as she sliced another piece of cake and put it on the last clear plastic plate from what had apparently been a stack in front of her. "You're only twenty-nine years old—that's much too young to give up hope."

"Age has nothing to do with it," Barbara said as she caught sight of her children and noted they still seemed to be having a good time playing with the other children. "Marriage just isn't for me."

Not that she was against marriage in general, Barbara thought. She was here celebrating a wedding, after all. And she believed that some people had good marriages. She'd seen couples right here in Dry Creek who seemed very happy. But somehow Barbara doubted that kind of marriage was going to happen for her.

"Not all men turn out to be thieves," Mrs. Hargrove said as she cut another piece of cake and lifted it in the air. Mrs. Hargrove was cutting into the spare overflow sheet cake that Lizette had made because she wanted everyone to have all the cake they wanted. Most people had already eaten a piece of the tiered cake. Mrs. Hargrove looked around to see if there was a plate for the cake she now held on the silver server.

"They don't all turn out to be faithful either." Barbara knew this was at the core of why she didn't believe she would ever have a happy marriage. A happy marriage required a lot of trust, and Barbara had none left. She didn't think she'd ever trust another man with something as important as her heart. But that was okay. A woman could live a fine life without a husband.

Barbara could see there were no plates left for the cake Mrs. Hargrove held. She looked down and saw an open box peeking out from under the white table-cloth. "Here, let me get some more plates for you."

Barbara bent down.

"Oh, no, I'll be fine," Mrs. Hargrove glanced around until she saw the sheriff. "Carl, come here and get these plates so Barbara doesn't have to."

"They're not heavy," Barbara said as her fingers closed around a stack of plastic plates. She knelt down. Unfortunately, the sheriff's fingers closed around the same stack of plates. He didn't look as though he intended to let go.

"Really, I can get them. It's not like they're gold-rimmed china or anything," Barbara protested. Her voice sounded muffled because her head was half-covered by the white tablecloth as she knelt, but she'd thought she made her point.

Apparently she was wrong.

The sheriff knelt down, too and put his head under the tablecloth to look at the plates. He still kept his grip on the stack of plates. "Everything doesn't need to be fancy. Sometimes the plain old ordinary things are best."

"I know. That's what I'm saying," Barbara continued. She wasn't going to give up that easily. "The plates are plastic. Not fine china. They're not worth anything."

No one would steal them, she added to herself silently. You don't need to worry about me taking them.

She wondered if people would talk later about her and the sheriff snapping at each other under the cake table at Judd and Lizette's wedding reception. She hoped not. The one person she had thought would be her friend when she moved to Dry Creek was the sheriff, but it hadn't worked out that way.

She never did know all that she had said to him when he sat beside her hospital bed in Colorado. She knew she was out of it for some of the time. But the rest of the time, she thought they were becoming friends. She'd loved listening to him talk. He'd told her story after story about Dry Creek, some of them from the days when the cattle first came to the area and some as recent as last spring when he'd picked chokecherries for Mrs. Hargrove so she could make jelly to enter in some contest at the state fair.

Barbara had thought at the time that not many men would pick berries so an old woman could win a prize with her jelly. That's when she'd kissed him. It had been impulsive. Sort of a tribute to what a nice man he was. Then he'd kissed her back—really kissed her.

The sheriff was the one who had driven Barbara back to Dry Creek when the hospital said she could go home. She had no home and no car left, since Neal, not content with putting her in the hospital, had taken a sledgehammer to her parked car. Her children had been staying with Judd so she'd been grateful for the ride.

Barbara had no choice but to accept the sheriff's offer of a ride. And she'd decided at the time that it was just as well. She needed to gently explain to him that, as much as she had enjoyed his kiss, she was never going to marry again and she didn't want to lead him on to expect a certain kind of relationship when all she could offer him was friendship.

Barbara had her words all picked out and she had decided, with a man's pride being what it was, that it was best to let the sheriff bring up the subject of the kiss.

She had worried for nothing. The sheriff never mentioned the kiss. Once they were back in Dry Creek, he'd become all official and formal around her. He acted like she was a stranger—an unkissed stranger at that.

At first, she'd thought maybe he had a girlfriend and he'd been worried that she might misinterpret the kiss, but she'd soon learned there was no girlfriend. No, he must have just been concerned she would read too much into that kiss for the simple reason that it didn't mean anything to him.

Well, he hadn't needed to worry. She knew the kiss didn't mean anything. She didn't *want* it to mean anything. Still, she thought he could have at least brought the subject up. No kiss was all that meaningless. She had gotten the message back then and she got it now.

"You're a guest here," the sheriff finally said as he gave another tug at the stack of plates.

Barbara let him have the plates as she moved her head back so she could stand up. "No more than everyone else is a guest."

Mrs. Hargrove smiled at Barbara when she stood. "That's better—you wouldn't want to get frosting on that pretty dress of yours."

Barbara nodded in defeat. A person couldn't force acceptance. She wondered if she'd ever really find a home here. Before she could belong, they needed to trust her at least a little. It was disheartening that they wouldn't even let her touch the plastic plates. She could forget about something as advanced as pouring coffee.

She felt like one of those birds in a gilded cage. It wasn't just that no one let her do anything for the community. She was an outsider in the most basic of ways. No one burdened her with their troubles, even though they all knew hers.

On a day like today, Barbara would have liked a friend to talk to about the wedding, but friendship went both ways. She wouldn't ask a stranger to care about how hard today was for her when no one shared their troubles with her.

She was lonely.

Barbara had known she'd have to listen to Judd and Lizette recite their wedding vows today. She'd been prepared for it to be hard, but she hadn't expected it to be as hard as it was. She hadn't been able to listen to those vows without counting all the times her ex-husband had broken his. Talking to a friend would have made that hurt easier to bear.

"Not all men are like your ex-husband," Mrs. Hargrove said adamantly as she lifted another piece of cake and set it on the plate the sheriff was holding out to her. She then turned her attention back to Barbara. "Carl here's a good boy."

Barbara almost laughed at the startled look on the sheriff's face. She wasn't sure if being called a "boy" was the surprise or if he was shocked anyone would think of him as a husband prospect for a woman whose ex-husband was a criminal.

Barbara wondered if that was why the sheriff had never brought up the subject of the kiss. He was probably dismayed he'd kissed the ex-wife of a thief.

Mrs. Hargrove seemed oblivious to the sheriff's reaction as she kept talking to Barbara. "Just give yourself a year or so and you'll meet someone nice."

Barbara shook her head. There weren't enough years in eternity for that. "I have the kids to think about instead."

She looked over at her children, but she didn't walk away from the refreshment table. She'd give herself a minute to pull her thoughts together. She didn't want the children to sense her unhappiness.

The wedding was bringing it all back to her. It had taken her years to end her marriage to Neal, despite the fact that he had started cheating on her almost from the beginning. When she had tried to talk to him about it, he'd become abusive and accused her of being boring and not open to having any fun.

She'd remembered thinking at the time that it was hard to have fun when they never had the rent money and never stayed in one place long enough to make a home. No, she'd given up on fun. What she hadn't given up on was having a father for her children and a faithful husband for herself. She had kept trying to make Neal into that man, but she'd failed miserably.

"I don't suppose you've heard from your ex-husband?" the sheriff asked Barbara as he passed a plate of cake to someone on his left.

"I've got nothing to say to him."

The sheriff shrugged. "Ever wonder if he has something to say to you?"

So she was right, Barbara decided. It really was her ex-husband that was making the people of Dry Creek hold back on accepting her. Well, there was nothing she could do about it. She'd already divorced the man. That should tell people what she thought of him.

"I should go check on my children." Barbara walked over to where the children were playing a game of hide-the-spoon. She'd initially counted on having her children by her side during the wedding reception today, but when they'd asked to play with some of the other children, she couldn't refuse them. Just because she was uncomfortable at weddings, she didn't want them to miss out on a good time.

Barbara waved at Amanda and Bobby. They both grinned up at her and waved back, but they didn't stop what they were doing.

There was a chair by where the children were playing and Barbara sat down.

What she needed to do was lighten up, she told herself. After all, if she weren't here for a wedding, she would have enjoyed being in the community center again.

The community center was really an old barn that had been donated to the people of Dry Creek. Tonight, it shone with polish. Mrs. Hargrove had organized this reception and, in Barbara's opinion, she'd done a wonderful job. Barbara had offered to help, but everyone had said she should just take it easy. Tables had been scattered across the wooden plank floor, and they were all draped with white tablecloths.

The air smelled like a mixture of coffee and crushed rose petals. There was a hint of lemon too, but Barbara couldn't decide where that aroma was coming from. Maybe it was from the filling in what remained of that five-tiered cake.

The weathered high rafters made the barn look vaguely like a cathedral, especially with the irides-cent white streamers that a couple of high-school boys had strung from them. The night outside was dark, so there was no light coming from the open windows, but rows of small twinkle lights circled the inside walls of the barn. A late-March breeze coming in the windows made the streamers sway a little. Yes, it was all very dignified and very bridal.

The wedding ceremony had taken place earlier in the town's small church, and then people had walked over to the barn for the reception. Lizette and Judd were still shaking hands with people.

Barbara realized she might never have a real home with the people of Dry Creek, but she had no question that she had a family with Judd. When she had tracked Judd down, she was desperate for help. She didn't even know Judd back then, but she had no other family and she'd never lived anywhere long enough to make real friends.

The separation from Neal hadn't been going well. After she'd finally found the courage to leave him, she suspected he would try to find her, and hurt her and she didn't want the children to be with her if that happened. Barbara needed someone to care for the children while she made the trip to find them a shelter.

Barbara knew it was not love that had made Neal angry when she'd told him she was going to divorce him. No, he might not want her to divorce him, but he didn't love her. Neal hadn't just cheated on her once or twice. He'd made it a habit. Barbara hadn't known about the robberies he'd been involved in until later, but she had faced the fact that something in Neal had changed dramatically over the years.

Barbara was only twenty-nine years old, but the day she'd left Neal she'd felt like an old woman. It was as if she'd lived an eternity, and nothing had turned out the way she had hoped it would.

It was odd that it wasn't until she finally found the courage to leave Neal that she found the closest thing to a family that she'd ever had. Judd had invited Barbara and her children to stay with him indefinitely.

Barbara figured it was his new-found religion that made Judd so eager to help them, but she didn't think it was a good thing for him to do. Family did have limits. And life wasn't lived in a church. She hadn't had much experience with God, but she had wondered sometimes if God even knew what went on in the world. He certainly had never paid any attention to what went on in *her* world.

No, Judd and his new wife wouldn't find life as simple as they thought it would be. Marriage never was. Barbara knew all of the things that could go wrong with a marriage and she didn't want to be responsible for any of them happening to Judd.

That's why, now that he was getting married, Barbara had moved off Judd's ranch and into the small town of Dry Creek. Lizette had offered the room at the back of her dance studio as a temporary home for Barbara and the children until they found something more permanent. There weren't any houses for rent in Dry Creek right now, so Barbara knew she'd have to wait. Not that there would be any houses for rent soon.

The only house that wasn't occupied was the old Gossett house, and Mr. Gossett was in prison. Mrs. Hargrove wrote to him regularly, and in her last letter she'd asked him if he'd be willing to rent the house. He wrote back saying he was thinking of giving the house to his nephew, but he'd find out if his nephew was interested in renting it out to her.

Even if the Gossett house did become available,

it would take a lot of repairs before anyone could live in it.

In the meantime, the room in the back of Lizette's dance studio had become the resting place for Barbara and her children. The room wasn't large, but it was bigger than most of the hotel rooms where they'd lived for periods of time over the past few years. Lizette had lived in the back room of her studio before she got married, and there was a kitchen and a bathroom attached to it. It would be fine.

There wasn't much furniture in the studio's back room and Barbara had vowed that, now that she and the children weren't moving so much, she would replace that old folding table with a solid kitchen table, the kind of table children needed for family meals and homework.

They might not have a home yet, but they'd have a table. It was a start.

And, for now, the back room was convenient for Barbara since she was temporarily working in the fledgling bakery that Lizette had started in the front part of the building. Barbara knew she'd eventually need to get a job that was more solid, but she was grateful for the bakery job. It was helping her gain some job experience and it was early-morning work so she was done by the time the school bus came through Dry Creek to drop the children off after school.

Barbara ordinarily kept a close eye on her children,

but she was checking them even more frequently of late. She'd had these funny feelings the past few days that someone was watching her and the children through the storefront windows. Whenever she looked up, however, she didn't see anyone on the street outside the window, so she was probably being foolish.

Besides, even if someone was looking in the window, it didn't mean anything was wrong. People looked in storefront windows all the time, she reminded herself.

Maybe it was just hard for her to get used to their new home, Barbara told herself. It had bigger windows than most places she had stayed. She wasn't used to so much openness.

At least Lizette had hung good, thick curtains on the windows in the back room. There was no chance anyone could look through those windows when Barbara and the children were sleeping.

Barbara shook herself. Now, why was she worrying about this when she was here to celebrate a wedding? Dry Creek wasn't the kind of place where people went around looking into the private windows of other people. They might be very interested in her and the children, but no one would actually spy on them.

There must just be a draft in that old bakery building and a tingle of cold air must blow through now and again and hit her on the back of the neck, she decided. That must be what that tingling sensation was all about.

Or, she thought to herself, maybe the tingling had just been her nerves reminding her of the upcoming wedding. She'd certainly had reason enough to dread the event.

But now that the wedding was over, the nervousness would stop and that would be it. She could get on with earning the acceptance of the people of Dry Creek.

It was too bad that she couldn't begin with the sheriff. Of all of the people there, he suddenly looked like he would be the hardest to win over.

Chapter Four

The wedding reception was still going strong. Laughter and chatter filled the old barn. Barbara watched the sheriff while she sat in a folding chair beside where the children were playing.

The sheriff seemed to be intercepting anyone who was walking toward Barbara. One would think she had a big *C* for "criminal" branded on her forehead. The sheriff took one man by the arm and pointed him in a different direction. He whispered something in the ear of another. She couldn't imagine why he cared if the ranch hands talked to her. They certainly didn't have anything she could steal.

Well, no matter what his reasons were for keeping people away from her, today was supposed to be a happy day and Barbara was determined to keep looking happy even if she had to change her view to do so.

Since no one was going to talk to her inside the

building with the sheriff blocking the way, Barbara decided to go outside. Barbara looked down at the bridal bouquet she still held. Was it just her, or did the flowers look a little wilted?

Sheriff Wall watched Barbara walk back over to Mrs. Hargrove and say something before heading toward the barn door and going outside. Ordinarily, he wouldn't need to follow Barbara everywhere, but if anyone was going to make contact with her, they would do it at some event like this. Strangers stood out in Dry Creek on an ordinary day, but tonight a dozen strangers could wander around and no one would pay much attention to them as long as they held a plastic cup filled with Mrs. Hargrove's special raspberry punch.

Of course, he wasn't worried about Barbara seeking to contact her ex-husband's criminal partners. The sheriff had talked with her enough in the hospital and then later in Dry Creek to know she wasn't likely to turn to crime. She'd seen first-hand what crime did to a person, and she knew it wasn't good.

But that didn't mean Barbara might not unwittingly receive a message from her ex-husband and not realize what it meant. She'd said she hadn't heard from him, but she might be hoping for some message anyway. After all, the two of them had been married for a long time and had children together.

They probably still had business to settle between them.

Yeah, the sheriff told himself, he'd better go outside and stand in the dark with her just to be on hand if anyone came up to her with a message. It could be something as simple as "look in the tool chest for the key to the safety deposit box" or "dig up grandma's favorite rosebush and see what you find."

The sheriff wished again that he had some of Pete's charm with women. At least Pete could go out and stand there without looking like a fool with nothing to say.

Barbara took a deep breath the minute she stepped outside. She looked around and was relieved no one else was close by. It did look as though someone was sitting in one of the pickups parked by the barn, but that was the only sign of life. Most of the cars were over by the church. The moon was out, but it was still dark enough that she couldn't see much beyond the vehicles.

Whoever was in the pickup seemed to be taking a nap, so Barbara felt alone enough to relax.

After living through a cold winter here, she knew she'd never get tired of Montana spring nights. They were such a relief after the snow. It was a warm March, and the sounds from inside the barn were muted enough that she could almost hear the sounds of the outside. Now that spring was here, there was no snow to muffle the night sounds. She heard the sound of a coyote off in the distance. And a dog barking closer to town.

Someone had lined up some folding chairs along the side of the barn, and Barbara stepped over to them and sat down. She set the bouquet down on the chair next to her and slid her shoes halfway off her feet. She wasn't used to wearing high heels any more and they pinched. Barbara leaned back in the chair. Now she almost felt good enough to smile for real.

She heard the sound of a pickup door being opened. Apparently, the man was finished with his nap.

Right then, the door to the barn opened and light spilled out into the darkness.

"Trouble?" Barbara asked when she looked up and saw the sheriff. She'd given it some thought and had almost decided that the reason the sheriff had been frowning so much was because he had official business somewhere. Maybe his mood had nothing to do with her. Maybe she'd just grown so distrustful of men that she saw betrayal and censure everywhere she looked.

Yes, that must be it, Barbara told herself in relief. Someone must be in trouble and the sheriff was passing the word along to others who could help. The sheriff seemed always to be working. Even though he was wearing a regular black suit and not his uniform tonight, he was probably still on duty. She supposed a lot of his social evenings were interrupted like this.

"Trouble? No," the sheriff said as he let the door close behind him. He stood still for a moment. "Unless you've seen something?"

Barbara refused to be disappointed that the sheriff wasn't worried about someone else. "Me? What would I see?"

"Oh, you never know when someone sees something out of the ordinary." The sheriff walked over to the folding chairs where Barbara sat and stretched out on the chair closest to the barn door. It was six chairs away from Barbara.

"No, nothing out of the ordinary here."

Maybe the sheriff was just worried from habit, Barbara decided. She was glad she had nothing to worry him further. She had noticed that whoever was getting out of the pickup had changed his mind and settled back into the seat. But there was nothing unusual about one of the men around here deciding to take a bit longer with his nap. A lot of them worked hard and were tired. The only thing that was unusual lately was that strange tingling sensation she'd had at the back of her neck. "Has anybody thought of getting a big streetlight around here?"

"A streetlight? We only have the one street."

"I know, but it's a very dark street—especially at night."

"People like it that way. If they get a streetlight, they worry they won't be able to see the stars."

"It could be a small light."

The sheriff shrugged. "The county is voting next month on all the business. Bring it up at the town hall meeting we have. See what people think."

"Me? Would I go to the meeting?"

"I don't see why not. This is where you live, isn't it?"

"Yes, but—" Barbara had never voted in a local election before. She'd never been in one place long enough to qualify for anything like that. She'd gotten a library card once, but that was all.

"There'll be a vote for sheriff coming up," he added. "If you're interested in voting, that is."

Barbara was relieved. Whatever was troubling the sheriff, he must not suspect her of anything. He was asking her for something that implied she was almost one of the citizens of Dry Creek. "Well, you can count on my vote—I mean, if I don't need to own property or anything."

"Nope. No property. Just show up at the barn here and vote."

Was it really that simple? It wasn't pouring coffee, but voting had to count for something. Maybe becoming part of life in Dry Creek was possible after all. Barbara felt a rush of enthusiasm at the thought. "I suppose you have a campaign team already lined up?"

She knew the sheriff was reliable and did a good job. He'd saved a life or two and he'd even tracked her down last fall. She'd heard enough talk around to know he was well thought of in Dry Creek.

"Campaign?" the sheriff looked startled.

"Yeah, you know, your campaign to get peoples' votes. I'm just wondering if you have anyone working on the campaign. I could help pass out flyers or something if you need someone else to help. Just let me know who to talk to about it."

There, Barbara thought. It was the perfect place to start. A flyer was worth less than even a plastic plate, so no one needed to trust her with anything. Unless, of course, the sheriff thought she wasn't good enough to hand out his flyers. Maybe since she'd been married to a criminal, he was afraid that she would taint his campaign.

Barbara held herself still. "That is, if you want me to work with you?"

The sheriff felt his collar get tight and he swallowed. He should have worn his uniform instead of this suit. He'd never given any thought to a campaign. People around Dry Creek didn't need a campaign to know to vote for him for sheriff. For one thing, there was no one running against him. But Barbara didn't know that, and if she was working on a campaign with him, she'd have to spend time with him. That would keep her away from guys like Pete.

It would also be easier for him and the FBI to keep an eye on her. Now that he thought about it, it was almost his duty to spend as much time as possible with Barbara Strong.

The sheriff took a deep breath. "Sure. We could get together for dinner tomorrow night at the café and work out a campaign strategy." His voice sounded a little strained, but he hoped Barbara wouldn't notice. He seldom asked a woman out on a date. Not that this was a date. At least, he didn't think it was. "I'd buy, of course."

"Oh, no, I couldn't let you buy—"

"No, it would be official campaign business."

Barbara pinked up for a moment and then she nodded. "Well, then, yes—I'll ask Mrs. Hargrove to sit with the children while I step over to the café. But she might not be able to since it's Saturday night and she needs to get ready to teach Sunday school the next morning."

The sheriff couldn't help but notice how pleased Barbara looked. He could hardly keep his mind on Mrs. Hargrove. He sure wondered if this was going to be a date. But in any case, Barbara was right. They needed someone to watch the children.

"I'll talk to Mrs. Hargrove," the sheriff said.

"That's right—I forgot you know her pretty well. She said you fixed her roof a couple of weeks ago."

"Just a few shingles. Nothing much," the sheriff said. He didn't want to derail the conversation by talking about Mrs. Hargrove's chores. He knew there had to be a chore on her list that was worth a night's babysitting even if it was a Saturday night. "Linda has a great steak special going on Saturday nights."

"She might agree to let us put some of your flyers in the café, too," Barbara said.

The sheriff swallowed. "We sort of need to make a flyer before we can pass it out."

Barbara brightened even more at that. "You mean no one's done a flyer yet? Would it be okay if I worked on that, too? We'll need a slogan. Something catchy. Something that sets you apart from your competition."

The sheriff felt his mouth go dry. He couldn't not tell her. Not when her face was getting so excited. "About my competition…so far I don't have any."

The sheriff closed his eyes.

"Well, surely someone will run against you," Barbara said. She frowned a little. "They probably just haven't put in their name yet."

The sheriff sat up straighter. She was right. Someone could decide to run against him. It wasn't likely, but it could happen. Maybe there'd even be a write-in campaign. One or two people usually wrote in a name on the ballot instead of voting for him. The name was usually Daffy Duck or Santa Claus, but legally it was a vote for another candidate. That had to mean something. He moved a couple of chairs closer to Barbara without even thinking about it. "It's a good thing we're going to do a campaign then."

Barbara smiled. "It's always good to get out the vote. It helps the whole community. We need to think of things that would rhyme with Sheriff Wall."

"There's *all*," the sheriff said, noticing that Barbara had picked up the bouquet she'd caught and was holding it in her lap. He slipped over onto the chair next to her.

"And a button, we'll need a button," she said. "Something in blue. People trust blue. Or maybe red. Red is power."

The sheriff nodded. He didn't care if Barbara decided to dress him up in a clown suit and have him pass out suckers in front of the café. She was sitting next to him and talking and her hands were going a mile a minute.

Saturday night was definitely going to be a date if the sheriff had anything to say about it. He smiled his best smile. "I appreciate anything you can do—for the campaign, that is."

"I'm handling the bakery while Lizette and

Judd are gone on their honeymoon, but I can think about the slogan while I work." Barbara held up the rose bouquet as though she was seeing it for the first time. "And, another good thing about this campaign is that it will help people forget I caught this thing."

The sheriff couldn't ask what the first good thing was. He had a bad enough feeling in his stomach about the second good thing. "Why is that?"

"Everyone talks during a political campaign. There'll be issues and answers. People will forget I caught the bouquet and that I'm supposed to be the next one to marry. People think Lizette knows I'm hoping to get married again and that's why she tossed me this bouquet. But I've told Lizette it's just the opposite. I'm never going to get married again."

"Oh."

Barbara stood up. "I'm going to be a good citizen though."

"You can be a good citizen and married at the same time." The sheriff thought he should point that out.

It was too late. Barbara was already opening the door to go back inside the barn.

Barbara looked around when she stepped back inside. She felt better than she had since she'd come to Dry Creek. This was the perfect solution to her problem. If she campaigned for the sheriff, people would surely see that she took a firm stand in favor of law and order.

Granted, it wasn't like being asked to do a fund-raiser for the school or anything that involved money, but it was a start. The next thing she knew, she'd be asked to join the Parent-Teacher Association. Then maybe they'd ask her to pour coffee for the town at some event.

She was so excited. She really was going to make a home for herself and the children here in Dry Creek. And, maybe while she campaigned for the sheriff, she'd mention to people that the town needed a street-light. That showed even more civic spirit. Eventually, she'd have a normal life with a house of her own.

And, just so she'd know the real house was coming, she'd work on getting herself that kitchen table for her and the children. It was time she learned to cook something besides sandwiches, and time they started having Sunday dinners at their own table. Fried chicken would be good. Or maybe a pot roast. Having Sunday dinners together was something Dry Creek families did, just like they hung their sheets on the clotheslines in the summer to dry.

Barbara had noticed a clothesline behind Mr. Gossett's old house. It had fallen down, of course, just like most of the things around the house. The good thing about the Gossett house, though, was that it had a picket fence around it. The boards weren't white any longer and they weren't all standing straight, but a coat of paint and a few well-placed nails would change that. She didn't know what she'd do if Mr. Gossett wrote and said his nephew wanted the house so he couldn't rent it out.

No, that wasn't true. She did know what she'd do. She'd just keep looking. She was going to make a home here or, at least have the satisfaction of knowing she'd done everything possible to make it happen.

Chapter Five

Meanwhile, in the pickup truck parked in the night shadows outside the barn, Floyd Spencer had been watching Barbara and the sheriff and muttering to himself. His timing had been lousy ever since he'd robbed that bank with Neal and Harlow.

It'd been his first robbery and he'd since decided that he just didn't have the stomach for crime. Everything had turned out badly. His two partners were behind bars and they were likely to turn informant on him next week if he couldn't get a message to them and let them know that he needed more time to get their money into those off-shore accounts.

He had buried his own money in his backyard so deep that even his dog couldn't find it. He was too nervous to move it inside under his bed. He didn't know when he'd ever have the courage to dig it up.

But it was the other men's money he had to worry about first.

Floyd had been watching Neal's wife off and on over the past two weeks to see if she ever went to the prison to see Neal. If she did, Floyd would try to get her to take a message to her ex-husband about the additional time he needed to open those off-shore accounts. The message couldn't be anything obvious, of course, or the people at the jail would stop it from getting to Neal.

Floyd couldn't spend too much time watching the ex-wife, however, because he didn't dare call in sick to his job at the bank. He hadn't planned on the whole thing taking so much time.

It had all sounded so simple when Harlow had planned it. But, these days, Floyd couldn't even take a long lunch at the bank. It hadn't been *his* bank that had been robbed; Floyd wasn't that stupid. But it had been the bank in a nearby town, and the jittery nerves had spilled over to his bank. He hadn't thought about that happening.

Everyone was watching everyone these days, and Floyd sure didn't want to make anyone suspicious enough to remember that he'd called in sick on the day the other bank had been robbed. He had thought it would be easy to do everything Harlow had asked. But it wasn't as easy as Floyd had thought it would be to transfer money into those accounts without anyone knowing about it. He'd found the instructions to make the transfer, but he didn't see how it could be done secretly. Harlow and Neal had each set the accounts up in partnership with another person so, even in jail, they said they would be alerted when the money was in the accounts.

Floyd didn't know how all of that was to happen. He was a bank cashier, not a thief—well, until now, that is. All he knew was that Harlow was clever enough to do whatever he said he was going to do and Neal followed the other man's directions. Harlow had been the one who'd talked Floyd into helping them rob the bank. He would never forgive Harlow for that. Robbing that bank had been the worst mistake of Floyd's life.

But there was nothing to do about it now except to go forward and try to find some time alone with Neal's wife. If she wouldn't help him, Floyd thought he'd take a day off work and try to impersonate a clergyman going to visit Neal. It was a long shot, but who else would care about Neal except someone who was paid to care, like a minister?

Floyd didn't know what he'd do if he couldn't take time off work. Maybe he should leave some money for Barbara Stone at the bakery just in case he needed to go to his back-up plan.

Floyd vowed that if he got out of this mess, he'd never break any laws ever again. He wouldn't even cross the street against the light. He'd come to the conclusion that his nerves just weren't good enough for a life of crime. He couldn't sleep. He'd barely eaten since he'd helped rob that bank. Once he got the money into those offshore accounts, he planned to go to a hypnotist and try to get the memory of what he'd done wiped out of his mind.

Chapter Six

Barbara's alarm clock went off at five o'clock in the morning and she groaned as she reached over to turn it off. It was dark and her children were still asleep. Fortunately, it wasn't cold inside the room she now called home. Not that it was warm either. She sat up on her cot and pulled a blanket around her shoulders.

Her alarm clock gave off a green hazy light so Barbara could see the two lumps in the bed next to her cot. Both Amanda and Bobby were curled in on themselves as they slept. They'd been tired enough last night that they would sleep another few hours.

Barbara yawned as she remembered last night.

The wedding reception had become more enjoyable after she had asked to work on the sheriff's re-election campaign and she'd spent more time talking with Mrs. Hargrove about local politics. Mrs.

Hargrove had gotten so involved in the conversation, she hadn't seemed to notice that Barbara was helping clean up the refreshment table.

The two of them had cleared off the cake crumbs and picked up empty punch cups while they talked. Barbara had learned enough about local politics to know that she probably didn't need to campaign for the sheriff to win the election.

Of course, Mrs. Hargrove encouraged her to work on the sheriff's campaign anyway.

"Campaigning is more like fun than work, isn't it?" Mrs. Hargrove had anxiously asked her for the second time as she looked over to where the sheriff stood.

Barbara had nodded.

"Well, then I guess it's okay—it's a great way for you to meet people. Besides, it never hurts to remind people to vote," Mrs. Hargrove said as she turned her attention back to the table and scraped some white frosting off the cake knife before wrapping the knife in a wet paper towel.

"I'd enjoy it," Barbara said. "Really I would. I want to do something for the community."

Mrs. Hargrove nodded. "We've become a little lazy around here when it comes to voting for the sheriff. And it's an important job—we can't have just anyone as our sheriff. I've known Carl Wall since he was a teenager, and he's a good man."

Mrs. Hargrove finished her wrapping and stood to face Barbara. "You know, now that I'm thinking about it, I'm not sure we give the man enough recognition for the job he does. And here he is risking his life day after day to see that we're all safe. Why, he could take a bullet any time and here we sit, not even having the courtesy to go vote for the man."

Barbara had lain awake last night trying to wrap those words of Mrs. Hargrove's into a snappy campaign slogan—something like "Vote for Carl Wall. He'd take a Bullet for Us All." Last night she'd thought that slogan had possibilities. This morning she wasn't so sure.

Oh, well, she thought as she stood up. Even if it was Saturday morning and Amanda and Bobby wouldn't be getting up quite yet, she certainly needed to get moving. The first thing she needed to do was to make three dozen donuts for the display case at the Dry Creek café. Then she needed to make six dozen maple donuts for the Martin ranch, six assorted fruit pies for the café in Miles City, and—well, she'd need to check her list for the other two orders. She knew one of them was a dozen corn muffins for someone and the other was a sour cream raisin coffeecake.

The bakery business was booming in Dry Creek.

Lizette was starting out small. She was only taking direct orders and she advertised that they'd fill any order as long as it met the minimum order amount of fifteen dollars. Delivery was an extra charge, but it was small enough to encourage business.

All of the items were made fresh every day. The only things a person could buy without a pre-order were the donuts that Linda stocked in the café. Every morning, the bakery sent three dozen donuts over to the café. Lately, if they had time, they'd added a pie or two as well.

The bakery was building up a steady stream of regular customers, and Barbara was pleased that Lizette had felt comfortable leaving the business in Barbara's hands during Lizette's honeymoon. When she returned from her honeymoon, she had said she planned to devote most of her time to her small dance studio and turn most of the bakery duties over to Barbara.

As Barbara wrapped herself in her robe and walked to the bathroom, she planned her day. If she started now, she should have the bakery orders done by nine-thirty this morning. Mrs. Hargrove had volunteered to go with her as she delivered the orders since Barbara didn't know her way around some of the back roads yet and didn't have a car to drive anyway. Neal had seen to that.

Barbara told herself she wasn't going to think about Neal today. She'd enjoy the drive with Mrs. Hargrove.

Amanda and Bobby would both enjoy a ride out to some of the ranches as much as Barbara would.

If she got a minute, Barbara decided she'd even take a few of the flowers from that bouquet she'd caught and press them between two boxes of sugar. It wasn't a book, but the boxes should give enough weight so the roses would press down good.

The sheriff always checked Mrs. Hargrove's house as he drove into Dry Creek in the early morning. He didn't have to go out of his way, because Dry Creek only had the one main gravel road that went through the little town and he went straight down it. Mrs. Hargrove's house was on the left, a few houses down from the café. The sheriff checked to see that her kitchen light was on when he looked at her house.

The sheriff knew the older woman would be indignant if she knew about his daily checks, but he'd started to worry a few years ago about her living alone. Seeing a light on in the kitchen eased his worries. He figured that if Mrs. Hargrove could get downstairs to the kitchen, she was doing all right. If the light wasn't on when he drove by at seven o'clock, he'd make a swing back around nine o'clock. If it wasn't on then, he'd call her on the telephone with some question or another.

It wasn't often that Mrs. Hargrove's light didn't come on before nine. This morning, though, there wasn't a light on anywhere in her house when he drove by at nine. The sheriff figured she was just tired from the wedding reception last night, so he decided to wait another half hour before he called her. This time he even had a good excuse. He needed to ask her what chore he could do in exchange for a Saturday-night babysitter.

In the meantime, he should call and check in with the FBI.

Not that there was ever anything new with the FBI. He'd report that there'd been no suspicious activity from Barbara Strong and they'd report that Neal and Harlow were still in jail and looking more hopeful than they had any right to be. Neal had even asked for a calendar yesterday. There'd been some debate about whether or not having access to the correct date was a constitutional right, but, in the end, it had seemed harmless to give him a calendar.

The sheriff shook his head. He knew about people's rights and he was all in favor of respecting them, but he wasn't inclined to do any favors for a man like Neal Strong. A man that would hurt a good woman like Barbara and the two little ones…well, a man like that didn't need to know what day of the month it was.

Barbara had the maple bars all boxed up and the pies cooling on the table next to the triple batch of chocolate chip cookies the Elkton Ranch had ordered. It was nine-thirty in the morning and she was ready to start her deliveries. She'd thought Mrs. Hargrove had said she would drive by the bakery and pick her up at nine o'clock. Barbara took another look at the street in front of the bakery. There was still no sign of the older woman.

"Can I take my bear with me?" Amanda asked as she came out of the back room.

Amanda had already asked to take her Raggedy Ann doll and her princess doll.

"You can only take one toy with you, but it can be any one you want," Barbara said.

"Bobby's taking a book to read," Amanda offered. "A big one. One he can read all by himself."

Barbara recognized the hint of jealousy in her daughter's voice. "You'll be able to read those big books right alongside him pretty soon."

One of the reasons Barbara wanted to make a home for the children here was that they needed more stability in their lives. She wished Dry Creek was large enough to have its own school, but the one in Miles City was good and the children were happy there. Since today was Saturday, they had the whole weekend to be with her. They would enjoy their weekend, but they wouldn't fuss on Monday when they got ready for the school bus.

Barbara heard the phone ring and thought it must be Mrs. Hargrove calling. Maybe her car wouldn't start or something.

"Hello, Dry Creek Bakery," Barbara answered the phone. The phone was for bakery business, so she always answered it that way even if it was after hours and she knew it was a personal call. "Can I help you?"

"I'd like to order a cake," a man's voice said.

The voice sounded muffled, as though the man didn't want anyone to overhear him. Calls like that had come to the bakery before, for surprise birthday parties, so the voice did not alarm Barbara.

"We can do a special design for you—or a special cake. What kind of cake would you like?"

"A patience cake."

Barbara frowned. "I don't think I've heard of that."

Barbara could hear what sounded like office noise in the background.

The man's voice got even smaller. "I looked on the Internet. It's got coconut filling inside and yellow cake outside."

"Well, I can certainly make a yellow cake with coconut filling for you."

The man's voice was down to a whisper. "It needs to say it's a patience cake."

"We could put a card with the cake that says it's a patience cake." Barbara figured the cake was to remind some usually cranky boss somewhere to be patient on his birthday. It occurred to her that there weren't many offices within their delivery area. She should probably check. "Our usual delivery only goes into Miles City."

"I'll pay extra if you take it to Billings."

Barbara hesitated. "We'd have to charge an extra forty dollars to cover the gas. I'm not sure it's worth that to you. I can give you the name of a bakery in Billings if you want."

"Last night I left two hundred dollars for you under that wooden planter on your porch."

"Here?" Barbara was starting to get that tingling feeling on her neck again. Why would anyone be leaving things on her porch at night?

Barbara took the phone with her as she walked over to the door and opened it. There was only one planter on the porch and it was empty. The geranium had died during the winter. Barbara lifted up the planter.

"There's three one-hundred-dollar bills here."

"Yeah, that's like I said. I must have given you an extra big one without thinking. Is that enough?"

Barbara was silent. No one around here paid three hundred dollars for a cake even if it was very special. Or very big.

"How many people does this cake need to feed?"

"Just one."

Barbara was silent. People around here also

didn't mistakenly leave an extra hundred-dollar bill anywhere. Most of them didn't even carry hundred-dollar bills. "You've paid too much money. Even with delivery to Billings, the whole thing won't be more than eighty dollars."

"You can keep the change."

"Oh, that wouldn't be fair—"

"I want to send a message, too, so it's not just the cake," the voice continued. "Do you have a pen to write it down? It's important that the words go just the way I say them."

Barbara walked over to the counter where the phone message pad was. "Do you want a singing telegram or someone to deliver your message in a costume or something?"

She was still trying to figure out why so much money had been left on her doorstep.

The man cleared his throat. "No, it's just the message. Here it is. 'Be patient. God's preparing riches in glory for you next week. This cake comes from your spiritual brother—who, but for the grace of God, would be where you are now.'"

Barbara wrote down the man's message with a frown. "You don't want to say 'Happy Birthday' or anything?"

"Should I?" the man whispered.

If Barbara hadn't been holding three hundred

dollars in her hand, she would think this was a joke. Not a funny joke, but a joke of some kind.

"Where do you want the cake delivered?"

"I don't know the exact address," the man hesitated. "But I know who. He's in jail in Billings. Name of Neal Strong."

"What?" Barbara held her breath. This had gone beyond weird. The only sensible explanation was that someone was playing one of those cruel jokes on her. It had to be one of her Dry Creek neighbors. No one else knew who she was. "Who are you?"

"Please, just take him the cake." The man hung up the phone.

A minute went by before Barbara heard the sound of a car outside. She looked out the window, expecting to see Mrs. Hargrove's old car.

Instead, she saw the sheriff's car. He drove a white sedan with the county insignia on the door and a siren on top.

She'd never been so glad to see the man, and that included the time when she was in the hospital and he was the one to remind the nurses that she was due another shot for her pain.

"Look at this," Barbara said, holding out the pad of paper. The sheriff was standing in the open door to the bakery. She'd been so rattled she hadn't even closed the door when she'd come in from the porch earlier.

* * *

Sheriff Wall looked at the words Barbara had scrawled on the notepad. The first thing he saw was *Neal Strong* at the bottom.

"Someone said they wanted to send Neal a—a cake," Barbara stuttered. Her face was white. "A patience cake with coconut filling."

"I see." The sheriff didn't know how much to tell Barbara. She might be better off not knowing that this was probably the contact the FBI had been expecting.

"He made it sound like he was some kind of religious person. Called himself a brother. But he's not. I mean, I don't know much about religious people, but this guy is creepy. Nothing like Pastor Matthew over at the church."

"Oh, no, I don't suppose he is anything like Matthew." The sheriff wasn't a regular churchgoer, but he knew he would be sitting there this Sunday, right after he finished helping Mrs. Hargrove with her Sunday-school class. Mrs. Hargrove drove a hard bargain. She had agreed to babysit so he could take Barbara to dinner tonight, but she had named her price.

The sheriff was to help Mrs. Hargrove with her class of first- and second-graders and then sit through the church service that followed. He'd rather have reroofed her whole house than help her with her Sunday-school class. He'd even offered the roof. She'd said no.

Then he had pleaded ignorance. He'd mentioned his childhood with all the foster homes and never a Sunday-school class. He didn't have a clue about how to help her. He couldn't even remember ever hearing about Sunday school. He didn't even know what they did there.

Mrs. Hargrove had a hard heart. She didn't bend with his panic. She said that if he didn't know what went on in Sunday school, it was high time that he learned. Then she said he'd have the whole church service after the class to recover from Sunday school anyway.

The sheriff was glad he'd gotten to know Pastor Matthew over the years. At least a man like that might have something worth listening to during the church service.

"I don't think anyone has any business ordering a cake for Neal." Barbara folded her arms, then looked at the back of the room. "Oh, the children—"

Barbara stepped away from the sheriff and smiled at the children who had slid soundlessly into the room, dragging blankets and toys with them. They both stood still, looking at their mother with big eyes.

"There's nothing to worry about. Someone just wanted to order a cake. Go in the back and get your jackets on for when Mrs. Hargrove comes to drive us on the deliveries."

The sheriff cleared his throat. "Mrs. Hargrove slept late this morning. I'm going to help with the deliveries."

Barbara nodded. "It'll just take me a few minutes to put together a cake. Lizette keeps some sheet cakes in the freezer, and we have some coconut filling in the cupboard."

The sheriff noticed that Barbara kept the smile on her face until the children had gone into the back room.

"You're actually making a cake for this guy?" the sheriff asked.

Barbara nodded. She held out the three one-hundred-dollar bills. "I don't know if these are real and I don't know who ordered the cake. Even if it's just some sick joke, I can't have people saying the bakery isn't filling the orders they take over the telephone, especially when—if these bills are real—someone left money for it. I told Lizette I'd take good care of the bakery while she's gone. I won't let her down. I'll just put the man's change back under the planter where he left these."

The sheriff took the bills from Barbara and looked at them closely. "They look real to me." He looked up. "I don't suppose he left the bills in an envelope, did he?"

Barbara shook her head. "Why?"

"We might be able to trace an envelope—you know, fingerprints and all."

Barbara shook her head again. "You could try to get fingerprints off the bills."

"Too many prints. It'd drive our guys crazy trying to pick them all out."

"Well, he didn't do anything illegal by ordering the cake," Barbara said. "It's not very nice, but that's about it. It has to be a joke—I mean, I can figure that out. Although I thought everyone here liked me well enough…"

The sheriff hesitated. The FBI had made it clear that the decision about whether to tell Barbara Strong that she might receive a message for or from her ex-husband was the sheriff's to make. If he felt Barbara needed to know for her own safety, he could tell her.

The sheriff didn't think Barbara was in any physical danger, but he hated to see that stricken look on her face.

"I mean, I know people are probably talking about me a little bit because of Neal, but—" Barbara's voice sank so low the sheriff could barely hear her. "Well, Neal's not the best person and I know I did marry him and I suppose it might seem like a funny joke to play on me to have me deliver a cake to him when he's in jail."

Barbara was looking down at the floor. She had that expression on her face that the sheriff remembered from when she was in the hospital.

"It's not a joke," the sheriff said as he put out his hand and lifted Barbara's chin until he could see her eyes. He tried not to be distracted by the soft feel of her skin or the tears that were gathering in the corners of her brown eyes. Why did brown eyes always make him feel so protective? He didn't remember that he used to feel that way.

The sheriff let go of her chin. He needed to. "Don't worry about it."

"Well, it might be more of a prank than a joke," Barbara mumbled. "And I know newcomers can expect some of that kind of thing. I just didn't think that in Dry Creek—"

"It's not anyone from Dry Creek," the sheriff said. The woman didn't know how to stop fretting, and he couldn't stand to see her cry. He hoped he was doing the right thing to tell her. "It's probably a message from one of your husband's friends."

"My husband doesn't have any friends," Barbara said and then she swallowed. Her eyes got big. "Oh, you mean—"

The sheriff nodded. "He apparently didn't work alone all of the time."

"But why would they send a message through me? I don't even visit Neal."

The sheriff nodded. He knew that. "Maybe that's why they're paying you to make the cake and take it."

"Well, I won't do it now. I'll just put all of the money back under that empty planter with a note that we can't make the cake. No one would expect the bakery to bake a cake for a criminal."

The sheriff hesitated. If Barbara delivered the message, whoever it was who had been working with her husband would most likely leave her alone. But, if she didn't deliver the message, the man might not be so happy with her. "I think its best just to do what he asks. At least, until we find out who he is."

"Neal doesn't even like coconut," Barbara said as she took the hundred-dollar bills back from the sheriff. "I don't suppose you have five twenties?"

The sheriff shook his head.

"Well, if I'm going to make the cake, I'm going to charge for it. Lizette can use the business. I quoted the man eighty dollars, including delivery, so that's what I'll charge. I'll need to get some change from the café." Barbara started walking toward the porch.

"Is there anything I can do to help?" the sheriff said. He was relieved to see that Barbara's tears had gone.

"Watch the children while I go over to the café and get change."

"Me?" the sheriff asked, but Barbara had already left the room.

When the sheriff had asked if he could help, he'd thought more along the lines of—well, when he thought about it, he realized he hadn't had any specific actions in mind. But, if he had, they wouldn't have anything to do with watching little children. The sheriff knew about juvenile delinquents—he'd lived with some until he turned eighteen—but he didn't know anything about the crop of sweet little kids that was springing up around Dry Creek these days.

Fortunately, the children didn't know he was unprepared to deal with them. Bobby and Amanda had both come out into the main room carrying their jackets and looking at him cautiously.

The sheriff forced himself to smile. The children didn't smile back. They just stared at him.

The sheriff reminded himself that the children were going to be adults someday. There couldn't be that much difference in the conversation of a child and an adult. He just needed to pretend they were a little older.

"Doesn't look like it's going to rain today like the weatherman said," he remarked. "You'd think that the weatherman would get it right more often than he does."

Bobby and Amanda continued to stare at him. He could have been speaking a foreign language.

"Makes you wonder if there's some sort of weatherman's school," the sheriff finally continued. "Of course, a weatherman's school wouldn't be like the one you go to—how is school going anyway?"

The sheriff could kick himself. He did know that no child liked to be asked about school. He'd hated that question himself. "Not that it's any of my business," the sheriff added. "I'm not checking to see if you've done your homework or anything. It makes no difference to me. Now, whether or not you go to school, that's my business. I can arrest you if you're truant. But homework—"

The sheriff could see Bobby's eyes grow large.

"Can you put people in jail if they don't do their homework?" Bobby swallowed. "I was going to do it. Honest. But I forgot."

"I don't want to go to jail," Amanda added. Her lower lip started to tremble and she wailed. "I can't even read the big books—not like Bobby can."

"I'm not here to arrest anyone," the sheriff assured them both. He needed to stop the conversation before he had them both in tears.

"My princess doll doesn't want to go to jail either," Amanda said with a sniffle as she dropped the jacket that had been over her arms and showed him the doll that had been hidden under the jacket. "Only bad people go to jail. Bad people like my daddy."

The sheriff swallowed. He wondered if it was too

late to make another comment about the weather. If he'd been talking to an adult, he might have done just that. But Amanda and Bobby were children, and all children deserved to think the best they could of their fathers.

"Your daddy did something bad. That's why he's in jail. He's not necessarily a bad person," the sheriff explained. "People sometimes do things that they shouldn't—or don't do things that they should. Then they're sorry for it."

"I promise I'm going to do my homework. It's just that I don't understand the math questions," Bobby said as he looked up at the sheriff. "They talk about peaches."

"Don't worry about your homework," the sheriff said as he put his hand on the boy's shoulder. That seemed to calm Bobby. "It's okay if you don't do it."

The sheriff realized he should have kept an eye on the open door.

"No, it is not okay," Barbara said as she came back into the room with some twenty-dollar bills in her hand. "He has to do his homework. Don't tell him he doesn't need to finish his homework."

"I didn't mean—" the sheriff mumbled. "Of course, he needs to do his homework, it's just that it's not a crime if he doesn't."

"It's a crime around here."

The sheriff surrendered. He'd never be able to explain. "Yes, ma'am."

"I'm not a 'ma'am,'" Barbara protested. "A 'ma'am' is someone like Mrs. Hargrove. And she's in her seventies."

The sheriff was beginning to wish he was in jail himself. Except then he would have missed the picture Barbara made with her dark eyes flashing and indignation making her cheeks rosy. He smiled and ducked his head. "Well, you're not like Mrs. Hargrove, that's for sure."

The sheriff thought of adding that he'd never had the urge to kiss Mrs. Hargrove on the lips, but he thought he'd better not say that.

Barbara's eyes stopped flashing, but her cheeks stayed rosy. The sheriff couldn't stop staring at her. She was a picture.

Everyone was quiet for a minute.

"I still don't understand about the peaches," Bobby finally said.

"I could—that is, well, if it's the peaches that are the problem, I could help you with them," the sheriff offered. He forced himself to turn his eyes to Bobby. "Just to be sure you get your homework done."

The boy smiled. "It's subtracting."

The sheriff nodded. "We'll figure it out—why don't you bring it along while we deliver the bakery stuff? You can ask me questions on the road."

The sheriff figured a few questions would keep his mind off the boy's mother.

Bobby nodded.

"I don't have any peaches," Amanda said. She moved a step closer to the sheriff. "But I have a princess. See?"

The sheriff nodded. The girl looked just like her mother must have at that age. He wanted to pat her on the head.

"You can't see from way up there," Amanda said.

The sheriff knelt down so he could admire the princess doll. "Well, you're right, she's very pretty, isn't she?"

Amanda nodded. "And she's going to learn to read big books, too. It won't be hard for her 'cause she's a princess."

"I'm sure she's going to learn to read all kinds of books just fine," the sheriff agreed. "Just like you will."

"You'll learn to read better next year," Barbara said as she walked toward the back room. Amanda had not gone to kindergarten so she was behind some of the kids in the first grade class, but the teachers assured her she would catch up. "I'll just be a minute with that cake."

"Take your time, ma'—" the sheriff floundered. "I mean, Mrs.—that is, Barbara."

The sheriff couldn't help but remember the days in the hospital when he'd called Barbara "dear." Of course, she was so confused from all the pain medication at the time that she'd never even reprimanded him. She probably hadn't even heard him.

There was nothing wrong with her hearing now. Barbara turned around and frowned as she walked through the doorway leading to the back of the building. "I'm not a Mrs. anymore. Barbara is fine."

The sheriff watched her go into the other room. The woman was more than fine. "Yes, Barbara."

The sheriff wondered if Barbara had any idea of how very perfect she was. Probably not. Unless, of course, someone like Pete Denning had already begun to tell her. The sheriff wondered if the thought of Pete sweet-talking Barbara should trouble him as much as it did.

He sure hoped he wasn't falling for Barbara Strong in a serious way. He had a feeling it would take a long time to get her out of his system once she married someone else.

And, of course, that's what she would do. A woman like her could have her choice of the single men around here. One of them was bound to strike her fancy. The sheriff would be a fool to hope otherwise. His days of calling Barbara "dear" were long gone. He'd be calling her "Mrs. This" or "Mrs. That" before he knew it, so he'd best not think of her as anything but "Barbara."

The sheriff sighed. He sure wished he could go back to calling her "dear."

But the sheriff never was one to grieve over what couldn't be helped. He just needed to do something to meet more women. There was bound to be someone sensible whom he could date. Maybe he'd meet someone in Miles City. As he recalled, Charley had a niece somewhere in Miles City who was single. Maybe he should ask the older man to set up a blind date for him.

The sheriff sighed again. That's what he should do all right. But maybe he'd wait until he got this stuff finished with Barbara and her children first. Then he'd be able to concentrate on dating someone.

Chapter Seven

The sheriff had never been on his knees around children. Apparently, Amanda and Bobby got under his skin as much as their mother did. "Maybe we should talk about some of those peaches about now."

The sheriff needed to get back to something familiar, and homework about peaches would do as well as anything, especially if it was math homework. Math was clean and reasonable. A man knew when he had the right answer. There was no guessing at what something meant or wondering if there was a better way to say something.

The sheriff felt like he didn't know anything. Knowing the answer and helping a boy with his homework were two different things. The sheriff knew he shouldn't just give Bobby the answer to the question, so it took him twenty minutes to help Bobby think through how many peaches Howard would have left to enter in the best peach contest at the state fair if he started with eighteen, then sold four before he got there, ate three himself and gave one to each of five friends he met on his way to the fair.

Bobby had a question about whether Howard was supposed to give a peach to everyone he met along the way or only his friends. The sheriff didn't know a thing about friends, but he couldn't say that to the boy, not when Bobby was looking at him as though he knew how the sun and stars were hung in the sky. So the sheriff did his best to answer the question the way he thought Barbara would want it answered.

The sheriff acknowledged that if Howard had given a peach to everyone he passed on the way he would have none left to enter in the contest at the fair. So, it couldn't be right to give everyone a peach.

Together the sheriff and Bobby decided that a peach only really needed to be given to someone who was very hungry. That was duty, the sheriff explained and it was important to do one's duty. Giving the peaches to his friends, well, the sheriff reasoned that was something Howard had done because he wanted to do it. It wasn't related to the job. A wise man, the sheriff counseled Bobby, would look in his basket and count how many peaches were left before he gave them all away.

"But I want to have lots of friends," Bobby said.

"Somebody would sure be my friend if I gave them a peach."

The sheriff was exhausted. He felt as if he'd interrogated a dozen prisoners instead of figuring out the fate of a basket of peaches. There was more to homework than the sheriff had expected. And it didn't end with Bobby's peaches.

It took the sheriff another ten minutes to reassure Amanda that she was a smart girl and would learn to read better at the right time and, when she did, that she'd be able to do the kind of homework that Bobby had in front of him right now. And, yes, Bobby would, of course, give one of the peaches to her. Sisters came before friends in the peach line.

The sheriff half expected to feel sweat on his forehead when he rubbed his hand over his face. He wasn't used to talking to children at all. He certainly had never been called upon to help in questions like this.

"I'm ready," Barbara called out from the back room just before she came back out with a triple-layer cake in a square box with a cellophane window.

The sheriff wondered how the woman did it. She was obviously doing a great job of raising her kids. She probably handled a dozen peach questions every day. And she made it all look so easy.

The sheriff rose to his feet when Barbara came into the room. Not only did she raise the kids, she also made one great-looking cake. No wonder Pete was flirting with her. The sheriff could see through the cellophane to the flaky coconut topping of the cake inside. She'd even tied a blue ribbon around the box to make it look festive.

"That's very nice," the sheriff said. He noticed that a long strand of dark hair had escaped the clip that Barbara had used to pull her hair back and away from her face. She was wearing a pressed white blouse and jeans. If she hadn't been carrying the cake box, he was sure her hands would have been gesturing all around. She still didn't wear any rings on her fingers.

"I've got the note right here," Barbara said as she used her chin to point to the card that was slipped under the ribbon. She sounded triumphant. "I copied it word for word. If it contains some secret message for Neal, he'll get it."

"That's good," the sheriff said. The sheriff looked down at Bobby and Amanda. The two children had moved closer to him as he helped them with their homework and they had stood up shortly after he had. Amanda was leaning against his leg and Bobby was standing just inches away from him. The sheriff put a hand on each of their heads. "I guess we're ready to go then."

The sun had risen several hours ago, but it hadn't brought any heat with it. The sky was overcast and the sheriff figured spring would take its sweet time in coming to Dry Creek. It sure wasn't making an appearance today. The air was cool and a breeze was coming from the north.

Barbara and her two children were gathered with him around his car as it stood parked beside the front steps of Lizette's place. The road came close to the building, but there was a lane left bare for parking and the dried ruts of car tires from previous rains had turned the ground uneven. Everyone was wearing a sweater and the baked goods were packed in the trunk of his car.

The sheriff decided the odds were good that it would rain before the day ended and that was fine with him. If the day got cooler, it would only make the inside of his car feel cozier.

He was glad he had the use of the full-size official sedan. There were no bucket seats in the car and, if Barbara were so inclined, she could slide a little closer to him on the ride back later today after they'd made all of the deliveries.

Something about thinking about all of those peach friends of Bobby's made the sheriff want to draw a little closer to someone. Maybe life wasn't always about having enough peaches to enter the contest. Barbara's children had slid closer to him this morning when they did their homework, the sheriff reasoned. Maybe it was just a sliding kind of a day since it was cold and gray. Speaking of the children, they would probably be napping in the car by the time they were all driving back from Billings, especially if it was still drizzling outside.

If the afternoon was cold, the sheriff told himself that maybe he'd put on some slow-moving music in his cassette player to make the inside of the car feel warmer. It wasn't poetry, but a man couldn't go wrong with music. Maybe Barbara would slide over and not even realize it. They might even have one of those comfortable conversations they'd had by her hospital bed, those long talks that had been about nothing and everything all at the same time. If they talked like that for awhile, maybe Barbara would forget all about trying to find a husband like Pete Denning.

Yes, a rainy day would be good.

If the sheriff hadn't been dreaming of impossible things, he'd have noticed sooner that they had a problem right here and now that had nothing to do with the weather or peaches or music. It was Barbara who pointed out the problem. There was nothing for the children to sit on when they rode in his car.

"I have handcuffs," the sheriff offered after a few seconds as he bent down to peer into the backseat of his car, hoping to find more than he knew was there. "Of course, they don't lend themselves to much height, but they would keep the kids in place if we cuffed them to the seat straps—"

"You can't put handcuffs on my kids!"

"Well, it wouldn't be for criminal purposes, it would be for their safety in the car."

"I can't believe the county doesn't supply you with booster seats."

"So far we haven't had any prisoners so short they need extra seats," the sheriff said. "If we do start to arrest them, I guess then we'll get the seats."

"I did my homework," Bobby said softly.

"I know you did, son," the sheriff said as he reached over to put his hand on the young boy's shoulders. The sheriff smiled down in the most reassuring way he could. "Like I said before though, it's not an official crime with the state if you don't do your homework some days."

Barbara looked at him a little strangely, but she didn't say anything.

For the first time in his life, the sheriff wished he had a way with children. He knew some men were just natural Pied Pipers. Children followed them anywhere, giggling and smiling. The sheriff wasn't the kind of man whom children considered fun. Look how nervous he'd made Bobby even before they'd talked about peaches. The boy had thought he might be arrested at any minute for failing to do something as simple as his homework.

Of course, the sheriff knew some other things were more important to a child than fun. And he knew he was some of those things. He was reliable and children could count on him. He'd protect a child with his life. That might not be fun, but it was certainly useful if a child was ever in trouble.

The sheriff moved his hand from Bobby's shoulder to his back. He felt Bobby lean into his hand slightly.

Barbara was right, the sheriff knew. Even if it was for safety, he wouldn't stand for someone putting handcuffs on this young boy or his sister either.

The sheriff took off his hat and rubbed his forehead. Barbara and the children were all standing next to him on the left side of the car. The morning air smelled of wet grass. The sheriff felt the crunch of gravel under his boots as he moved around slightly and he heard the sound of a pickup in the distance. He could tell it was an old pickup because of the grinding sound of the engine. The sheriff thought it was too bad he didn't have engine trouble with his own car. That would at least buy him some time.

The sheriff didn't relish explaining his predicament to the entire town of Dry Creek. He was the sheriff; he was supposed to think ahead and be prepared. Now that Barbara had caught that bouquet, he knew people in this town would be measuring the men around her to see who was the best candidate to be a new husband. Pete Denning would probably have thought of booster seats and arrived at Barbara's door with a bouquet of flowers this morning in addition to the seats. The sheriff was more used to solving crimes than anticipating the needs of a family.

The hardware store was directly across the street from where they all stood and the sheriff could see one or two of the older men stand up so they could see them better out the window.

The sheriff ignored the urge to wave to the men. He didn't want them to take a wave as an invitation to come over. The older men inside the hardware store were always helpful to anyone in town who had car trouble, and the sheriff suspected the men thought it was mechanical trouble that was keeping him, Barbara, and the children outside in the chilly air, looking at the car instead of just climbing in and driving it down the road.

"It's just that Amanda is small for her age and really needs one. Bobby is on the edge so he can get by. But we at least need one for Amanda," Barbara finally said. Her cheeks were pink from the cold and her hair was mussed from the slight wind that had started to blow. "I'll have to get the seats that Mrs. Hargrove uses in her car when she takes us someplace."

The sheriff heard the sounds of the hardware door slamming shut. He hoped that meant one of the men was going to go out to his pickup so he could drive home.

"She'll lend them to you, but don't be surprised if she asks a return favor," the sheriff said. He might not be good at anticipating all of a family's needs, but he did know Mrs. Hargrove. "She's recruiting people to help her with her Sunday-school class tomorrow."

Barbara turned white. Mrs. Hargrove had asked her to bring the children to Sunday school before, but the older woman had never pressed her when Barbara gave an excuse not to accept the invitation. And some of her excuses had been pretty thin. "Maybe instead of helping, I could make her a pie with some of the tart apples Lizette bought before she left. I'm sure Mrs. Hargrove would like an old-fashioned apple pie. Charley said it's the best he's ever tasted."

Barbara had watched the older man as he marched across the paved road from the hardware store to where she stood with her children. He'd obviously been listening to her talk as he walked.

"That's a fact," Charley said as he stepped within easy talking distance. The old man was wearing a red-and-black-checkered wool jacket. The jacket swung open and showed a pale-blue cotton shirt underneath. Charley took another step and was close enough to Barbara so he didn't have to raise his voice to be heard. "I keep saying it was some of the best pie

I've ever eaten. Reminds me of the pies folks make around here at Thanksgiving time when the apples are more tart than sweet."

The older man paused for a moment, whether out of respect for the apples or because he was caught up in the memory of a long-ago pie.

Then he gave Barbara a look and started again, "Just for the record, my nephew likes apple pie, too. I wouldn't be surprised if it was a family weakness. If some woman were to make him an apple pie, I reckon he'd propose on the spot. If she threw in a basketful of fresh-fried chicken, he'd even set the wedding date."

"I'm not looking for a proposal—or a wedding date," Barbara said. She smiled at the older man to show there were no hard feelings. "I'm just looking for car seats."

"Well, my nephew could get you the whole car, seats and all. Who has a car without car seats anyway?"

"She means car seats for the kids—booster seats," the sheriff said. He took some comfort in the fact that car seats seemed as bewildering to Charley as they were to him. Maybe Pete wouldn't have thought of them, after all. At least the sheriff seemed to know more than Charley about them. "Mrs. Hargrove has some—we're just thinking about asking her to lend them to us."

Barbara seemed not to have heard anything the

sheriff was saying. He heard her continue to mutter to herself.

"I could throw in a batch of donuts. She likes maple donuts," Barbara murmured under her breath.

The sheriff grunted. "I offered to reroof her house so she'd babysit while we have dinner tonight and she didn't agree. That's a thousand-dollar job if she has to hire it out. But she didn't bite. She said she needs extra help with those kids in Sunday school. That was her only trading offer."

Charley chuckled. "She's always looking for help with those kids."

Barbara shook her head. "How bad can they be? They're in Sunday school! I wouldn't think they would dare give anyone much trouble no matter how bored they were."

Charley laughed. "I've never heard any of the kids complain about being bored in Mrs. Hargrove's class. She keeps it all lively."

The sheriff grunted again. "Let's go over to her place. We'll see what she says."

Barbara looked down the street. "I'll have to walk with the children."

The sheriff nodded. "That's what I figured. I'll walk with you then, too. I can carry the seats back here if you agree to her terms."

"I don't think there will be terms," Barbara said. "I'm going to offer to give her a pie."

The sheriff nodded. He didn't want to discourage her, but he had known Mrs. Hargrove a lot longer than Barbara had.

Charley turned to go back into the hardware store. Barbara held out her hands to Amanda and Bobby and started walking. The main street of Dry Creek was made of hard-packed gravel. She felt the stones through the soles of her shoes. She looked over her shoulder at the sheriff. "I don't think she's going to ask me for any favors. I think you're teasing me."

The sheriff caught up with her and smiled. He wished he did know how to tease her. "Yes, ma'am."

"Barbara." She kept her eye on the sheriff as she kept walking. He was enjoying this. She hadn't seen him smile this much at her since she was lying in that hospital bed. The pain medicine she'd taken had made everything vague in those days so she didn't remember many exact conversations that she'd had with the sheriff. But she did remember the feeling she'd had. She'd dreamt he called her "dear" and tucked her in at night. She'd felt safe for the first time in years with him in her hospital room. The fact that he was smiling so much now made her uneasy. It was a dead giveaway that he believed she'd be on the losing end of her deal with Mrs. Hargrove.

Barbara lifted her chin. She'd surprise the sheriff.

Mrs. Hargrove looked as if she was delighted to have the children use the booster seats she kept on a shelf in her garage. "Of course they can use them. That's what neighbors are for—I'm glad you came to me."

Barbara was breathing easier. She and the sheriff were standing in Mrs. Hargrove's yellow kitchen, just inside her back door and next to the bench where people sat to take off their muddy shoes. So far the older woman hadn't mentioned anything about Sunday at all. Of course, Mrs. Hargrove had her hair in curlers so she might still be a little sleepy, but she didn't look as if she was even going to try to bargain.

Barbara decided Mrs. Hargrove probably had all the help she needed with her Sunday-school class since she had Sheriff Wall to help her. What child would be disobedient when the sheriff was there? "I appreciate you letting us use the seats very much."

Barbara glanced over at the sheriff and added, "We have to use them. It's the law."

Mrs. Hargrove nodded. "You'd use the seats anyway. You're a good mother."

"I try to be," Barbara said as she turned to look through the screen door. Amanda and Bobby were both sitting on the back steps of Mrs. Hargrove's house playing with a calico kitten.

Mrs. Hargrove nodded. "That's why I figured you were just waiting to settle in a bit before you started Amanda and Bobby in Sunday school. I'm sure they will love to come once they start."

"Oh." Barbara didn't know what to say. Mrs. Hargrove hadn't exactly asked her anything so it seemed safest to not answer anything.

"Bobby was asking me about the Red Sea just the other day." Mrs. Hargrove didn't wait for an answer. Her voice was conversational, as though she was just chatting away on a fine spring morning. "One of the other kids had told him about it—you know, the story about when Moses parted the sea and everyone walked through on dry ground. Bobby couldn't figure it out."

"Yes, well—" Barbara cleared her throat and looked over at the sheriff. "He's never seen much water. We went to Devil's Lake in North Dakota once, passed through a town named Whitman, but that's all."

"He was probably just thinking about how much water there is in a lake," the sheriff said. "You know, if ten people poured a gallon into the lake and five people took a cup out, how much lake do you have left?"

Barbara looked over at the sheriff and smiled in gratitude. "Yes, it's probably just something like that."

Mrs. Hargrove nodded. "The boy's a thinker all right. But it wasn't math that was concerning him. It was more along the lines of whether miracles actually can happen."

"I wouldn't want him to be disappointed," Barbara said. She knew all she needed to know about miracles. She knew they weren't for the likes of her. She doubted her children were destined to encounter any either.

"A child needs to know there is Someone who is bigger than their problems," Mrs. Hargrove said softly. "Bobby would like Sunday school. It's the perfect place to look for answers to all the big questions."

"He's too young to have big questions."

Barbara knew she was wrong the minute she heard the words come out of her mouth. Bobby was a seven-year-old boy with a father in prison. He had to have questions. He would probably also want a miracle.

"No one's too young for big questions," Mrs. Hargrove said, as if the matter were settled. "Of course, you'll want to come with him—and bring Amanda, too. And, since you'll be there anyway, you might want to watch the children as they draw a picture of the Bible lesson." Mrs. Hargrove looked over at the sheriff. "Watching the children draw is complete pleasure. It's not work at all."

The sheriff made a funny strangling sound.

"I'm not sure I could be much help," Barbara said.

"I don't know what any of the Bible lessons would look like."

Mrs. Hargrove shrugged. "There's usually some camels and sheep. The kids put them in any scene whether they are mentioned or not. It's okay. As long as nobody puts in a car or a flying carpet, that's all we bother correcting. You'll be perfect. Besides, Carl here is going to tell the story, so you'll be able to figure out what the pictures are supposed to look like."

"I am?" The sheriff seemed surprised. "I'm telling the story?"

"I was going to make you an apple pie—" Barbara tried again. She could swear the sheriff looked as if he'd swallowed something sour. That couldn't bode well for Sunday school. "Lizette got some tart green apples from that produce stand just outside Miles City."

"Oh, an apple pie would be wonderful," Mrs. Hargrove said. "And you could take a picture of it with Carl, here, for your campaign. There's something about apple pie that makes folks want to vote. Besides, if you're both there in the Sunday-school class, you'll be able to take more pictures to use in Carl's campaign. It's not exactly kissing babies, but it's pretty close if you take a picture of him with the children. You might even do a press release about it."

"They'll let someone take pictures in church?" Barbara asked. It didn't sound proper to her.

"Sure," Mrs. Hargrove shrugged. "Although this is Sunday school and not church, so it's even less formal. There will be graham crackers and crayons all around."

"I don't know about taking pictures." The sheriff frowned. "Isn't that a little—well, I wouldn't want to seem self-serving."

"This is a political campaign, Carl Wall. You need to be self-serving," Mrs. Hargrove said bracingly. "Besides, people love to see their children in the paper. We might even be able to talk the Miles City paper into doing a feature on your campaign if you offer the Sunday-school pictures."

"People want to know I can fight crime, not that I can pass out crayons to six-year-olds."

"People want to know that you have this community's best interests at heart," Mrs. Hargrove declared. "There's no better place to prove that than in my Sunday-school class."

Mrs. Hargrove sent both Barbara and the sheriff a look.

Barbara nodded meekly. She doubted Mrs. Hargrove needed the sheriff in her class to maintain order.

Barbara looked out the screen door at Amanda and Bobby. Had she misjudged their need for answers to the questions in their lives? They were so young, she had a hard time thinking that they might have questions about good and evil.

"And the pie will be lovely, too," Mrs. Hargrove said as she opened the screen door to lead the way to her garage and the car seats. "I do like an apple pie for Sunday dinner. Maybe you'll have a chance to make it before next Sunday."

Barbara nodded. She'd planned to make a pie for Mrs. Hargrove anyway. The older woman had helped her with many things since Barbara had come to Dry Creek. "I'll make one next Friday or so."

"That's plenty of time. Just don't work on it today. I don't want it to interfere with getting ready for your date tonight," Mrs. Hargrove said cheerfully.

The sheriff's face went white.

"What date?" Barbara asked in confusion. "You must mean our dinner tonight. That's not a date. It's a meeting about the sheriff's campaign."

"Well, whatever it is, I hope you have fun," Mrs. Hargrove waved her hands at them. "And don't worry about rushing through dinner. It's not good for a body's digestion to eat fast."

"We won't hurry," the sheriff said.

Barbara thought the sheriff looked a little grim. He didn't need to look so worried. She knew it wasn't a date.

"I'll go pick up those booster seats," the sheriff added as he stepped outside.

The children followed the sheriff when he went down the steps.

Mrs. Hargrove watched them all walk toward her garage. "Yes, Carl Wall is a fine man." The older woman looked back at Barbara. "He'd make someone a fine—" Mrs. Hargrove paused a moment and studied Barbara's face. "Sheriff. He'd make a fine sheriff."

Barbara didn't know why she was disappointed. She had planned to point out to Mrs. Hargrove just why she, Barbara Stone, didn't care if the sheriff would make a fine husband to some woman or not. Or a fine date either. She had been so sure that was what the older woman was going to say.

And why shouldn't Mrs. Hargrove say it? Barbara asked herself glumly. The older woman was right. The sheriff *would* make some woman a fine husband. He couldn't spend his whole life driving divorced women and their children around in his car. He probably was doing it because it was his duty, anyway, especially now that she'd received the note to pass on to Neal.

"I need to buy a used car before long," Barbara said.

Mrs. Hargrove nodded. "In time. Everything will happen in its time."

Barbara wasn't so sure about that. But she wasn't

about to tell the older woman her doubts. Mrs. Hargrove would make her go to Sunday school for more than just this Sunday if she thought Barbara was asking big questions. Barbara's only consolation was that the sheriff didn't seem any more enthused about teaching Sunday school than she was.

Chapter Eight

Floyd reached into his pocket for an antacid pill. He had been standing behind a tree next to this old deserted house, watching Barbara Strong and those kids of hers for the past hour, and they'd spent more time in the company of the sheriff than Floyd thought was necessary. He wondered what they were talking about during all that time. He'd seen that big box with the blue ribbon that Barbara had loaded into the trunk of the sheriff's car. That had to be the cake. At least she had made it.

Floyd put the antacid pill in his mouth to let it dissolve.

And he tried to relax. Fortunately, no one knew he was the one who had ordered that cake for Neal Strong. Even if Barbara told the sheriff about the cake, no one could trace anything to him.

Floyd wondered what he was thinking: he

shouldn't be worried about the cake. He should be worried about what would happen to him if the word didn't get through to Neal and Harlow that he needed more time to get their money deposited in those bank accounts.

Even though his two partners were locked up in jail, Floyd had no doubt that Harlow had the connections to see that Floyd was hurt if Harlow thought he'd been double-crossed. Harlow wouldn't leave a bone unbroken in Floyd's body. Harlow had said as much before they committed the robbery. At that time, Floyd had wondered what could go wrong.

Now Floyd knew everything that could go wrong, and he wished he could go back in time and tell Harlow that he, Floyd Spencer, was not the man Harlow needed for the job.

Floyd watched as Barbara Strong, her two children, and the sheriff all left the yard of that old woman's house. Floyd wished he could talk to Neal and Harlow directly and assure them that he was doing all he could.

He didn't like pinning his hopes on a cake.

Floyd looked more closely at the children walking beside Barbara and the sheriff. He could tell by the way Barbara put her hands on the boy's shoulders that she loved him. He supposed even Neal loved the boy.

Floyd thought a minute. He sure hoped Neal loved

his son. If the message didn't get to Neal with the cake, Floyd would have to think of some other way to get the attention of his partners. The son was Floyd's best bet. Neal would make sure nothing happened to Floyd if Floyd had his son.

Floyd took a deep sigh. He just hoped everything went okay with that cake. He'd have to go to the jail and see if anyone took that cake inside. If the cake was inside, Neal would get the message. At least, Floyd hoped so.

Floyd took another look at the boy. The kid was kind of skinny, so he shouldn't be much of a problem if Floyd needed some extra insurance. And the girl was small, too, which was good if he had to take them both.

Floyd gave another sigh. He didn't like any of this. He reached for another antacid. If this kept up, he was going to have to get another packet of them. He'd bought this one at a little grocery store next to the motel where he'd been staying in Miles City. At this rate, he'd need to buy another packet tonight.

Chapter Nine

The sheriff was walking down the street away from Mrs. Hargrove's place when he got a bad feeling that this cold gray morning was going to bring him more trouble than it already had. It was about ten o'clock and both booster seats were slung over his back, one resting on each shoulder. Bobby was holding onto the left edge of the sheriff's jacket.

Barbara was walking on the sheriff's other side and she held Amanda's hand in hers. Earlier, the sheriff had tried to balance both booster seats on one shoulder so he'd have one arm to swing in unison with Barbara's just in case she could be convinced to hold his hand to keep her fingers warm. He'd almost dropped both seats before he decided any hand-holding would have to wait for another chilly spring day. It was March, so another day like today would come along soon enough so that wasn't what was troubling him.

No, the bad feeling he had wasn't about the weather. The sheriff wondered if it was nothing more than a sense of being fenced in. He was surrounded by a woman and her children. It was an unusual place for him. Maybe he felt trapped. No, he realized, as he tried the idea on in his mind to see if it fit. It wasn't that way at all.

In fact, he kind of liked this feeling he had, and if this was what trapped felt like, then it was okay with him. A man could get used to being pulled in all directions and having little voices fire off questions at him while he kept his eyes on the ruts in the road just to be sure he didn't lead one of the children to make a misstep that would cause them to take a tumble.

No, it definitely wasn't feeling trapped that was the problem, the sheriff thought as he looked up from the ruts. When he raised his eyes, he saw where the danger really was. It was coming straight at them and moving fast.

Pete Denning was stomping down the street, swinging his arms and muttering things that were probably curses, although the sheriff couldn't hear the actual words so he didn't know for sure. Even from a distance, the sheriff could feel Pete's eyes glare at him. Something was wrong. And, whatever was wrong, the sheriff figured Pete thought the sheriff was it.

A wind was blowing around a few things that rustled and a dog was barking somewhere, but the sheriff still thought he caught the sound of a soft growl coming from Pete's throat—which was odd, since Pete was wearing a white shirt that was so well pressed that it had creases down the long sleeves. It wasn't the kind of shirt that a man would normally wear if he was planning to make trouble. Added to that, the ranch hand's boots were polished until they looked like they'd just come out of the store's box.

Unless the sheriff was mistaken, Pete was even wearing that belt buckle he had won in the rodeo in Miles City last year. That buckle was Pete's pride and joy. He kept it dangling from the mirror in his old pickup, vowing it was too good to wear.

Pete was dressed like he was going to a funeral, but the sheriff was never wrong about the fighting look in a man's eyes, and Pete had that look all over him.

Pete stopped a few yards away from the sheriff and braced his legs.

The sheriff didn't have room to get into a good fighting stance, not with Barbara on one side of him and Bobby on the other. Even if he could get ready to fight, he wasn't about to fight a Dry Creek citizen without knowing what the other man was so agitated about anyway.

"Is there a problem?" the sheriff asked in what he hoped was a friendly tone. Until the sheriff knew Pete's intentions, he wasn't going a step closer to the man. And before he moved, he would see that Barbara and the children were out of harm's way and he'd put down those booster seats on some dry patch of ground so they wouldn't be damaged.

After that, if Pete was still determined to brawl, the sheriff wouldn't back down

"Is it about the permit for your pickup?" the sheriff prodded when Pete was silent.

"You know it's not about the pickup," Pete ground out and then spat on the ground. "It's about you making fools out of all of the rest of us guys. You just wanted a head start. You and your phony year of peace."

"Oh, goodness, what's that?" Barbara asked as she moved up until she was even with the sheriff. She was still holding Amanda's hand. "Is the sheriff's department sponsoring some campaign for non-violence or something? I could make a flyer."

The sheriff had a sinking feeling that he knew what year Pete was referring to. "The sheriff's department always sponsors non-violence."

There was a moment of silence.

"Well, it's only Pete," Barbara finally said as she

took a step closer to the man and smiled at him. "How's everything today?"

Pete ground his teeth into a smile. "Good morning, ma'am. Everything's just fine."

"Please, call me Barbara. Everyone does."

Pete nodded at Barbara without taking his eyes off the sheriff. "I'm just wondering if some folks standing here don't call you something a little more affectionate than Barbara."

Barbara gasped. "Why—"

The sheriff lowered the booster seats to the ground and took a step closer to Pete. He motioned for Barbara and the children to step back. Pete looked determined to fight and the sheriff wasn't feeling as opposed to it as he had at first.

Then he heard a boy's thin voice coming from behind him.

"I call her Mommy sometimes," Bobby confessed in a rush. "I know I'm not supposed to—I'm going to start calling her Mom. The other boys call their mommys Mom instead of—well, you know. Now that I'm seven, I'm too old for a Mommy. The other boys told me so."

Pete's eyes softened as he looked past the sheriff and down at the boy. "I wasn't worried about you. I think it's great that you call her Mommy."

"I call her ma'am," the sheriff said. He knew

it wasn't always true, but usually it was. "Or Mrs. Strong if it's an official matter."

The sheriff might wish he called her something more affectionate, at least when she was able to hear him, but the truth was that he didn't have the nerve. The only times he had called her "dear," she'd been in the hospital so doped up with pain medication that she wouldn't have heard a drum if it was beating nearby. A "dear" like that didn't count for anything but dreaming.

The sheriff would fight a man if he had to, but he drew the line at fighting anyone over something that hadn't even happened.

"I'm not really Mrs. Strong any more," Barbara offered.

"Well, I'll call you Mrs. or Miss whatever you want," the sheriff said.

It occurred to the sheriff that he'd been a little disrespectful here. He hadn't even asked Barbara if she objected to being called Mrs. Strong. That's what the FBI called her, and he had gotten into the habit of referring to her by the same name. He'd change that though. "Are you going back to your real name? The one you had before you got married? You should let the post office know."

"Forget about names. Can we get back to our problem?" Pete said from where he stood. "I haven't got all day."

The sheriff could tell the ranch hand was weakening in his anger. Confusion would do that to a man. "I don't have all day either."

"We have to finish delivering the bakery orders so we can meet for dinner to work on the sheriff's campaign," Barbara informed Pete.

Pete frowned. "You're going to dinner together to work?"

Barbara nodded. "I'm helping with a flyer for the campaign."

"So, it's not a date like Charley said?" Pete asked.

"Why would he think that?" Now Barbara frowned. "It's a working dinner. To get the vote out. I thought the men in Dry Creek saw women as equals. You wouldn't object to a man having dinner with the sheriff to discuss the campaign, but the minute a woman does it, you question her integrity!"

The sheriff was a little distracted by the pink flush that anger brought to Barbara's face. He didn't suppose that now was the time to remark on how cute she looked though. "No one's questioning your integrity."

Barbara turned on the sheriff. "He thinks we're going on a date!"

For the life of him, the sheriff couldn't think why that was such a bad idea.

"So, it's not a date?" Pete asked again more cautiously. The ranch hand shifted his weight. He didn't look ready to fight anymore. He did have a grin growing on his face though.

The sheriff wondered how a grin could annoy him so much. "It could be a date."

Pete chuckled. "Not if it's just to get the vote out."

The sheriff grunted. "Nobody votes around here anyway."

"I voted last election," Pete said. His smile grew even wider. "Of course, I voted for Santa Claus."

"Well, you need to vote for the sheriff," Barbara scolded him.

"Why?" Pete said with a shrug. "He's going to get the job anyway. I didn't want to waste my vote."

"Do you know Santa Claus?" Amanda's small voice interrupted.

Pete shifted his feet and knelt down so he was eye level with the girl. "Well, now, I've been known to write the old fellow a letter or two in my day. I reckon he still remembers me. Did you want me to send him a message?"

Amanda nodded. "Bobby says I'm too old for Santa Claus."

"It's only March. Christmas is more than half a year away," the sheriff said. He didn't like that Bobby had slid away from his side and was now leaning against the ranch hand too. "There's no need to send a message now."

"I don't know," Pete drawled as he winked at Bobby and Amanda. "Like they say, the early bird gets the worm."

"Yuck, I don't want a worm," Amanda said. "Unless it's a princess worm. But it would have to have a crown."

Pete nodded thoughtfully. "With diamonds? I think all princesses wear diamond tiaras. I don't know about worm princesses though. Diamonds would be too heavy for their heads. And they're expensive. Where would a worm get enough money to buy a diamond?"

Amanda giggled. "You're silly."

The sheriff knew before he turned his head that Barbara was smiling at the ranch hand the same as her children. What was it about Pete, the sheriff wondered, that made women and children like him so much?

The sheriff was beginning to regret that there wasn't going to be a fight. Taking a swing at the ranch hand would make the sheriff feel a lot better about now.

Barbara hadn't heard Amanda giggle very often lately. Pete was right about diamonds. They were expensive. She remembered the diamond engagement and wedding ring set that she had tucked away in her things in the back room of the bakery. She and Neal had bought a matching set of three expensive rings. She wondered how much the two she had would be worth if she sold them. She should get enough money to buy a nice dining room table and chairs.

Barbara would get more if she had Neal's ring to add to it though, because then she'd have all three rings. Maybe she could buy carpet for the floor, too. She wondered what Neal had done with his ring and if he'd give it to her to buy carpet.

After Amanda's giggle faded, Pete stood up again.

"We'd best get going," the sheriff announced.

Barbara nodded. Since she'd probably see Neal today, she'd just flat out ask him for his ring. That was the best thing to do. He certainly didn't need it as a souvenir.

Three hours later, the sheriff sat with his hat in his hands and watched the children. Amanda and Bobby were sitting in a corner of the visitors' area at the Billings prison. Bobby was reading to Amanda from his book.

For the first time all day, the sheriff wished there was someone else to watch the children so he could pay more attention to Barbara as she talked to her ex-husband through the Plexiglas. The sheriff wondered how, since he was sitting so far away from both of them, he was supposed to know that her ex-husband didn't pass her any messages.

Of course, the janitor sweeping back and forth near Barbara and her ex-husband was an FBI man, so the sheriff figured he'd find out soon enough if any messages had been passed. He just wasn't sure he liked the fact that Barbara's voice was low and he couldn't hear what she was saying. He could see that Neal Strong was smiling, and he hadn't even opened the card that went with the cake. No, it sure looked to the sheriff that Neal was smiling just because Barbara was there talking to him.

Barbara bit her lip. She could see Neal's face clearly through the Plexiglas and could tell he was trying to be pleasant. He obviously knew, as she did, that they were being closely watched.

The visitors' room in the jail had tall ceilings and a faint echo. A row of chairs on her side matched the openings in a long counter with Plexiglas windows. It all smelled of cigarette smoke. There were two other visits going on at the same time that Barbara sat there.

"I thought the children would do better with their homework if they had a table to sit at," Barbara said in a low voice. She'd just asked Neal if she could have his wedding ring.

Neal shrugged. His eyes were rimmed with weariness and his face was unshaven. "Sure. Sell it. I had it on when I came in here. They have it up front someplace."

Barbara nodded. "I'll tell the kids that you wanted to help with the table."

"Yeah, well. Whatever."

Barbara thought she saw guilt in Neal's eyes.

"I didn't exactly plan for it all to end this way," Neal finally said. "They're good kids."

Barbara nodded. "Yes, they are."

"I'm glad you came so I could tell you that," Neal said.

Neal looked over her shoulder and Barbara knew he was watching the children where they sat in the corner.

"I wouldn't have except for the cake," Barbara said. She didn't want Neal to think everything was forgiven and forgotten. She'd never forget.

Barbara had given the cake to the guard when she first arrived for the visit. The sheriff had told everyone about the card so Neal was allowed to have the cake and card. Barbara assumed the FBI was hoping Neal would respond to the card and give them some kind of a tip. But Neal didn't. He didn't even seem to notice the cake.

"The cake has some coconut, but I kept it light," Barbara said. "I know you don't like coconut."

Neal nodded. "Thanks."

"Well, I'm going to be going then," Barbara said. She thought of all of the angry things she had thought she'd like to say to Neal if she saw him again, but now she didn't want to say any of them. He looked so defeated.

Barbara looked around and signaled for the guard.

"Ask him if I need to sign something so you can have what was in my pockets when I came here," Neal said.

Barbara nodded. "Goodbye, Neal."

The sheriff opened the car door for Barbara. The visit with her ex-husband had been fruitless. The guard had reported that Neal had signed over his belongings to Barbara and that she had taken them, but the FBI had already examined everything he had in great detail so there were no new clues there.

"Keep your eyes open for any new purchases though," one of the FBI men had told the sheriff as they whispered outside the jail while Barbara started walking the children back to the car. "That's the only way we're going to know if she's in on any of this."

"Don't you think the fact that she told me about the cake pretty well clears her?" the sheriff asked.

The FBI man had shrugged. "Telling you about the cake got the cake to him, didn't it?"

The sheriff shook his head as he walked away from that discussion. Those FBI men saw too much crime. They'd be suspicious of their own mothers. As far as the sheriff was concerned, Barbara was in the clear.

"Let's get out of here," the sheriff said as they finished walking to the car. Barbara already had the children settled in the backseat and was opening the door on the passenger side of his car for herself.

Barbara nodded as she sat down in the seat. "I feel chilly."

"I'll turn the heater on in the car," the sheriff said as he sat in the driver's seat. He didn't like the whiteness in Barbara's face.

The sheriff noted that the sky was overcast. He was right about it being a cold afternoon. With the heater going nicely, the children would probably doze off in the backseat before they were ten miles down the road. He didn't have much hope that Barbara would want to slide closer to him and snuggle, though. He only hoped she wasn't going to cry.

Chapter Ten

It was five-thirty in the afternoon when they arrived back at Barbara's place in Dry Creek. All of the bakery items were delivered. Now that they were back, the sheriff offered to carry a sleeping Bobby inside to a bed. Barbara didn't usually have visitors in this back room where she slept with the children, but Bobby was too heavy for her to lift, so she nodded her agreement.

Barbara was the first one through the outer studio and stopped at the doorway of the back room. She winced as she looked around. She wished she'd at least taken the time to paint the room before she'd moved into it several weeks ago. The walls were drab and made everything look worse than it was. Not that drabness was the room's only problem.

"This is only temporary," Barbara told the sheriff as she stepped into the room so he could also enter.

She switched on the overhead light, hoping it would make things look cozier. It was late afternoon and dusk seemed to be creeping in earlier than usual, probably because the day was still overcast. The extra light didn't do much for the room in Barbara's opinion. Maybe it would have been better to leave everything in shadows instead of turning on the light in the ceiling. "I plan to find us a real home soon."

The sheriff laid Bobby on the bed. "And what makes a real home?"

Barbara shrugged. "A yard with a white picket fence, I guess. Something solid where the kids can feel secure." Barbara looked at the sheriff and smiled. "At least something with more than one room. They need that."

The sheriff nodded, but his eyes didn't leave her face to look around the room. "That'd be good for all of you."

"I can do it, too," Barbara said. She looked closely at the sheriff so she could judge his reaction. Her ex-husband had never thought she was serious about wanting a home. He had never thought she could do much about it either so it wasn't surprising that she'd given up on even talking with him about her dreams. She wondered if the sheriff knew what a real home would mean to her children.

The sheriff nodded. "You can do anything. You just need a little time."

The sheriff's eyes were a mossy green with golden flecks and Barbara could see that they were serious. He believed she meant what she said. She'd do it, too. "I'll have to work hard. Maybe get a second job."

The sheriff frowned and the green of his eyes darkened. "You don't want to work too much, not with the kids needing you."

Barbara nodded. "That's what has stopped me from taking a second job so far."

The sheriff looked like he was going to say something else, but he didn't. He just ran his hands over his head like he was trying to straighten out his hair. "I need to get Amanda," he finally said as he left the room.

Barbara realized she'd never noticed before what a fine head of hair the sheriff had. First his eyes and now his hair. She wondered why it had taken her so long to see his finer points His hair was an ordinary kind of light brown, but it was thick and looked like it had a nice texture to it. He should really leave his hat off more often, especially in the spring when a hat wasn't needed for warmth or shade. Then people would see his fine eyes and hair.

Barbara would have to mention the hat to him some day when he was more likely to take her advice. No one seeing this room right now would want to take her advice on anything related to looks and fashion. Maybe it was that realization that made her look at the sheriff more closely. For months, she'd thought of him as plain, but maybe he really wasn't. Maybe he was like this room and just needed to make a few changes to bring out his positive points.

Barbara went to the counter that ran along one side of the room and wiped it with a dish towel even though there was no need. The counter was stained, but nothing had spilled on it. The room was clean. It was just also—well, *used up* were the only words that came to mind.

She was wrong in thinking that the sheriff was like this room. There wasn't a positive point to this room, and the sheriff had his share of pluses.

Barbara sat down in a folding chair and rested her arms on the folding table. The table felt as though it could collapse at any time. Everything in the room was old or stained or temporary. None of the dishes matched. The silverware was mostly plastic. Even the lamp by the bed was missing a shade and looked ready for the trash.

A footstep sounded in the outer studio and Barbara looked up as the sheriff entered the room and then carried Amanda to the bed. Barbara wondered when the children had grown too heavy for her to lift. They were changing, just as Mrs. Hargrove had indicated. They were old enough to notice things like not having a proper home.

"I'll be back in an hour," the sheriff said as he

pulled a blanket up over the children and looked over at Barbara. "Don't let them sleep too much or Mrs. Hargrove won't have a chance at getting them to bed at a reasonable hour later. By the way, I'll pick up Mrs. Hargrove on my way."

Barbara stood up. "Don't worry. They adore her. They'll probably pretend to go to sleep if nothing else just to please her."

The sheriff smiled and nodded. "I'll be back soon then."

"I'll be ready."

Barbara watched the sheriff walk out of the building. He didn't appear to have noticed how worn everything was, but maybe he was too polite to remark on it. Just as she was too polite to mention that he should stop wearing a hat. She walked over to the stove and turned on the heat under the teakettle.

Barbara shook her head. She needed to forget about the sheriff's hat and do something about a better home for herself and the children. Listening to Mrs. Hargrove talk this morning had made her realize just how much her children thought about everything. She wondered how all of this temporariness was affecting them. They had lived hand-to-mouth all of their lives with their father. She wanted them to know they could trust her to take care of them and give them a normal life.

Barbara longed with all her heart to be deeply rooted in Dry Creek, but she had never asked herself if her children also felt like outsiders and wanted to belong. People seemed to have friendships that lasted a lifetime in this little town. Even people who grew up here and then moved away stayed connected. Barbara wanted that for herself and her children.

Barbara wondered what her children thought it would take to belong. She knew her signal was something as simple as being invited to pour coffee for those in the community. Her children might be longing for a real home to make them feel part of this small town. All of the other children here had regular houses. It was a normal expectation for a child.

She and the children might still have to wait for the people of Dry Creek to fully accept them as their own, but Barbara vowed she would do something now to let her children know it would happen soon.

It would probably be months before she could actually rent a place, and that included the old house Mr. Gossett's nephew was supposed to decide if he wanted to rent to her. The house was across the street from where they were living now and down a little. Barbara could see its yard when she looked out the windows of the studio in front.

Often, during the day, she'd stop what she was doing and look across the street at that house. The fence around it was half falling down and the house itself had ceased being white a long time ago. Now, it looked mostly gray where the paint had been worn down by the winters around here. No grass grew in the yard. There were a few pine trees that had managed to survive around the house. Anything else that had once been planted had died, either because of the winter cold or the summer heat.

Barbara saw all of the house's shortcomings, but for her, that old place was a dream she wanted to come true. She could almost see what the place would look like if it had someone to care for it.

So far, Mrs. Hargrove hadn't received another letter saying the Gossetts had made the decision to rent the house to someone. And Mrs. Hargrove might not get such a letter for months.

Barbara decided her children couldn't wait much longer without hope that things would change. A sturdy table was a beginning, and she wanted to be able to give them that much now. It would signal that a change was going to happen.

Barbara knew she could afford a table if she sold the rings. She almost reached for the phone to ask Mrs. Hargrove to advise her on how to sell the three-ring set, but then she pulled back. She didn't want to have to run to Mrs. Hargrove for advice on everything.

There had to be a pawnshop in Miles City, Barbara reasoned. Maybe whoever ran it would give her a few hundred dollars for the rings. That was a quick and easy way to get money. She'd ask about catching a ride into town on Monday with Mrs. Hargrove. The older woman had said earlier that she was going to a dentist appointment then.

The whistle of the teakettle distracted Barbara, and before long she was holding a cup of hot tea. The steam from her cup warmed her face. The smell of cinnamon in the tea also made the room seem more welcoming. She wished she'd had tea steeping when she and the sheriff first got back here. She'd have to leave a pot steeping when he came back later to go to dinner. Mrs. Hargrove would probably like some tea while she watched the children anyway.

Forty-five minutes later, Barbara looked at herself in the old mirror that hung above the sink in the small bathroom next to the main room. The mirror had grown a little warped over the years, but it gave back a pretty accurate image even if it did make her face look yellow.

Barbara had washed and curled her hair until it flew around her face. She had brought out her makeup bag and put on a foundation cream and a little blush powder. She debated about putting on her eye liner and some green eye shadow before deciding that a little makeup couldn't define a dinner as a date. It was only natural that she wanted to look her best for the meal.

Barbara used the same logic as she pulled out

one of the four dresses she owned. She'd picked the
dress by elimination. Her oldest dress was a sleeveless
cotton summer dress, and she didn't even consider
that for tonight because it was too cold outside to
wear it. Another dress was more of a navy suit, and
Barbara had already decided she would keep that back
for Sunday school and church tomorrow morning.

The third dress was that lavender bridesmaid's
dress and Barbara knew she'd cause a huge amount
of gossip if she wore that to dinner with the sheriff.
She smiled to herself just thinking about it. Several
of the younger couples in the area made it a habit to
come to the café for the Saturday-night specials, so
there'd be plenty of witnesses to her dinner with the
sheriff. The story about her wearing a bridesmaid's
dress to dinner with someone would last even longer
than the story of her catching that bridal bouquet.

The remaining dress was her only choice, and
that was the one Barbara was wearing. When she'd
been married to Neal, this had been her "reconcil-
iation dress." In the early days, when they'd had a
fight, Neal would take her out someplace to dinner
later and she would wear this dress. The dress was
a deep violet that was so close to being black that it
shimmered back and forth between the two colors,
looking like one or the other depending on the way
the light shone. The dress was fitted and long enough
that it looked elegant. And it had a deep neckline that

made it look even more as though it belonged in a supper club, especially when Barbara added a string of pearls around her neck.

Barbara always felt like a lady when she wore this dress.

She knew the dress was too elegant for her dinner with the sheriff, but Barbara had decided to wear it anyway. After the sheriff had gotten a good look at the room where she lived, it wouldn't hurt to try and impress him. She at least wanted him to know she had some nice clothes.

Barbara heard the car drive up to the steps leading into the outer studio room and come to a stop. She had left one of the overhead lights on in this room and she could see the shadows of two figures through the curtained window on the door. She listened for a knock.

The sheriff adjusted his tie. He hadn't fussed about what to wear some place in years. He knew he should probably have just put on a clean uniform and been done with it. That's what he would normally wear to a dinner business meeting. But he knew that this dinner wasn't about business; at least, it wasn't for him. So, he'd put on his one suit, the same black one he'd worn to the wedding and the same one he'd wear to church in the morning. At least he had a new white shirt to wear with it tonight. He had even borrowed Mrs. Hargrove's iron so he could press it.

"You look fine," Mrs. Hargrove said as she stepped up until she was even with him at the door. "Do you want me to knock?"

"No, I should knock." The sheriff rapped on the door with his knuckles. He wondered if Mrs. Hargrove knew how nervous he was.

"You're a handsome man, Carl Wall, and don't you be forgetting it," Mrs. Hargrove said staunchly as they listened to the footsteps coming toward the door.

"Thanks," the sheriff said, resisting the urge to smooth down his hair. He knew Mrs. Hargrove was just being supportive, but he did appreciate her telling him he looked fine. And everything would go fine, too; he just needed to take a deep breath and relax. The sheriff got his breath out, but he never got it back in again.

The door opened instead and he saw a movie star. Or one of those fancy magazine models. Whoever it was, she was dressed to go somewhere on the arm of a millionaire instead of a poor man who was going to pass out any minute now if he didn't take a deep breath.

The sheriff gulped.

Mrs. Hargrove slapped him on the back at the same time as she said hello to Barbara.

"Is he okay?" Barbara asked Mrs. Hargrove.

"More than okay," the older woman said. "I think he's going to do just fine."

The sheriff breathed again. At least, he thought he must be breathing, because he hadn't passed out.

"I'll just go on back to where the children are," Mrs. Hargrove said as she walked through the doorway and headed toward the back room. "You two have fun now."

The sheriff noticed that that thought seemed to alarm Barbara.

"We're going to work on a slogan," Barbara turned to say the older woman.

Mrs. Hargrove didn't even break her stride as she walked across the floor toward the back room. "You'll come up with a good one, too."

Mrs. Hargrove entered the back room, and the sheriff heard the excited shrieks of the children.

"I see they woke up," he said, wishing for the tenth time today that he'd been born with the gift of gab. He'd never seen the use of chitchat before tonight. But now he was coming to appreciate the skill of making small talk, even though he didn't have any of it.

Barbara nodded. "I fed them a sandwich earlier."

The sheriff nodded. "Do you need to do anything else before we go? Because I can wait if you need. That's no problem."

The sheriff paused for breath. He sure wondered what Pete Denning would say to a woman in this same situation. "You did something different with your hair. It's nice." The sheriff wondered if that was adequate. "Real nice."

Barbara smiled as she lifted one of her hands to her hair. "Thanks. And I guess I'm ready. Just let me go get my shawl. It looks cold outside."

The sheriff nodded. "It is a little chilly."

The sheriff watched Barbara walk across the floor to the doorway of the back room. He hoped he could catch his breath while she was back there. He didn't want to give the impression that he couldn't walk a few steps without being winded. Especially now, because he planned to offer his arm to Barbara for the walk down the street to the café. He'd decided when he put the suit on earlier that it would be the proper thing to do.

If he didn't get his wind back though, she might think he was offering his arm so that she could steady him. That wasn't the impression he wanted to give. Not at all. He took another deep breath. This one sat easier inside. Mrs. Hargrove was right. He'd do fine.

Chapter Eleven

Barbara hadn't stepped completely through the door into the café before she knew something was wrong. She'd walked into this same café hundreds of times in the past five months, and she'd never seen it look like this.

Usually on Saturday evenings, Linda added a candle to each table. But she also had fluorescent tube lighting in the ceiling that streamed down and gave everything a homey appearance. The candles were only an accent. No one actually ate by candle-light.

The Dry Creek Café wasn't a romantic place. It had a black-and-white-checked linoleum floor, and even with the white tablecloths Linda used on Saturday nights, it looked like a place where one would go to order a hamburger with friends instead of a gourmet meal with a date. In fact, the usual Saturday-night specials were bacon cheeseburgers and T-bone steaks.

But tonight was different. The lighting was so low no one could see the person in front of them, let alone the color of the floor at their feet. Soft instrumental music was playing on the stereo Linda kept in the kitchen. Even Linda herself was transformed. Instead of wearing her usual T-shirt and jeans, she was wearing a black dress with a white collar and a white bib apron. Linda's hair was drawn back into a bun and clipped with a gold barrette.

"Isn't anyone else having dinner?" Barbara whispered when she and the sheriff walked past Linda. Usually, the café had a half dozen people in it at this hour. In the past month or so, Linda had even been talking about hiring extra help. Saturday was the big night for people in Dry Creek to go out to dinner. The place shouldn't be empty.

"The Redferns were in earlier and ate," Linda said calmly as she closed the door behind Barbara and the sheriff. "Oh, and the Curtis family were here, too. And the Martins."

"But it's not even dinnertime yet, and they're all finished," Barbara said. She couldn't believe it. "What about the Elktons? They always come in around this time on Saturday night. They're like clockwork."

"They ordered takeout tonight. I just gave them their bag not five minutes ago."

"Takeout? No one ever orders takeout here."

Linda shrugged and gestured for Barbara and the sheriff to sit at the one table that had been moved to the center of the room. It was clearly a table for two, its size small enough for close conversation. Usually, large group tables sat in the middle of the café floor. Barbara knew the smaller table had been placed there especially for her and the sheriff. Someone had even stuck a long red rose in a silver vase and put it in the center of the table. For good measure, there was a doily under the vase.

"My best table," Linda said as she pulled back one of the straight-back chairs.

The sheriff stayed standing until Barbara sat down and then he moved closer to settle her chair under the table.

When the sheriff finished pushing in her chair, he went back and sat in the other chair.

"Our specials tonight are garlic-roasted pork loin or grilled Atlantic salmon. Both are served with cream of asparagus soup and a nice rice pilaf," Linda announced.

"Cream of asparagus soup," Barbara repeated. What had happened to the chili burgers and tuna melts? Even the steaks Linda offered on Saturday nights were usually served with fries. People in Dry Creek didn't eat much rice pilaf. She was sure they didn't eat asparagus soup. "That sounds good."

"Which would you like?" the sheriff asked.

"I'll take the salmon," Barbara answered.

"Make that two," the sheriff said.

Linda nodded and walked back to the kitchen area.

Barbara waited until she and the sheriff were alone before she whispered, "Did you make some kind of special reservations for dinner tonight?"

The sheriff shook his head. "I didn't make any reservations at all—no one has ever needed reservations here before. I did mention to Mrs. Hargrove what time we were planning to eat, but that was only because she needed to know so she could watch the children."

"I'd guess that more people than Mrs. Hargrove know that we're having dinner here tonight at six-thirty," Barbara said.

The sheriff nodded. "I'm glad I wore my suit." He looked at Barbara and smiled. "I would hate to waste all of this on my uniform. Linda's gone to a lot of work."

"Pork loin and salmon? I guess we should feel honored," Barbara said.

Barbara knew there was a general misunderstanding being spread around Dry Creek. No one else had private dining in the café. Either she or the sheriff had the measles, or there was some other reason they were being left alone tonight.

"They think we're on a date," Barbara stated the obvious.

"Maybe we are," the sheriff said.

"I don't think—"

"We're both dressed up and eating together by candlelight at a table with a fresh rose on it," the sheriff declared. "And people are worried about our privacy. Oh, yeah, we're on a date."

"Well, maybe—but it's a business date. To figure out a campaign slogan."

The sheriff shrugged. "We can do that, too. It shouldn't take long. How about Vote for the Sheriff?"

"You at least need to have your name with it," Barbara protested. "People might vote for your competition instead if you're not clear."

"I don't have any competition. Besides, people always call me the sheriff. Mrs. Hargrove is the only one who uses my name."

"Oh." Barbara blinked. That didn't seem quite right to her somehow. "Everyone should have a name that people use."

"Folks around here just know me as the sheriff."

Barbara smiled. "But what if you weren't the sheriff, what then?"

The sheriff looked at her as though she'd suggested the unthinkable. "I've been the sheriff here for fifteen years—ever since I was twenty-one."

A loud noise interrupted them. It sounded as if several pots and pans had fallen on the floor in the kitchen. Barbara's suspicions were confirmed when she saw Linda poke her head out of the kitchen door. Linda's black dress was still neat, but her hair looked like she'd been through a whirlwind. The bun was gone and strands of dark hair fluttered around her face.

"I'm sorry for the racket," Linda said, a little breathlessly. "I'll have your soup out in a minute. I just need to whip up some more—if I can find some more asparagus back there. I thought I bought more."

"Don't worry about the soup," the sheriff said.

"But we wanted the dinner to be special for you," Linda fretted. "Especially since it's your first date and all."

The sheriff put his hand over the one Barbara had on the table as though to stop the words he knew were ready to come out of her mouth. She supposed he was right. No one believed her when she said it wasn't a date anyway.

"We're doing just fine here," the sheriff said.

Barbara nodded. "We'd be fine with hamburgers and fries too, if that's easier for you."

"You would?" Linda said. She looked relieved.

"I've always liked the hamburgers here," the sheriff

said. "Some of the best in the state—especially the ones with the pepper jack cheese on them."

Barbara wondered how long the sheriff expected to keep his hand over hers. He'd probably forgotten that he even had it there, and she knew he had only put it there as a request that she be silent, but she still thought he should move it. It was causing her to feel, well, warm for one thing. Plus, it was also causing her to remember that kiss the sheriff had given her when she was in the hospital. He'd never even mentioned it since. The man must make a habit of making gestures that he never acknowledged.

"You're a flirt," Barbara said when Linda had gone back into the kitchen. The sheriff's hand still cradled hers.

"What?" The sheriff seemed astonished.

Barbara nodded. "You could move your hand. I got your message. But you just leave it there like you don't even know that it's there. Conveniently forgotten. It's just like that kiss you gave me in the hospital. You do it and then you don't even bother to acknowledge it."

"I—" The sheriff cleared his throat.

Barbara nodded again for emphasis. "I suppose you're worried that I'll mistake them for something they are not, so you don't even mention them. But it's only polite to at least acknowledge that something happened—"

"I—" The sheriff looked a little short of breath again.

Maybe that's why he still hadn't moved his hand.

"You should know that I am not foolish enough to read anything into a kiss—no matter how good it was—or to make something over a little hand-holding, even if it is in public," Barbara stated.

The sheriff's hand moved, only not in the direction Barbara had anticipated. Instead of moving away, his hand moved around until he had hers firmly in his grasp. "You thought the kiss was good, huh?"

The sheriff didn't look at all as though he had trouble breathing now. He even grinned.

Barbara wondered if she was the one who needed some air. "You were very good to me when I was in the hospital—I'm grateful for that."

Barbara remembered how close she'd felt to the sheriff then. She'd told him all her secrets. She'd never told Neal things like that, not even in the early days when she'd still loved him. The sheriff had heard all her dreams and her fears. She'd thought later that it was the pain medication that had loosened her tongue. She usually didn't trust men with her inner thoughts. But maybe it had been something more. It was odd that sitting across the table from him now in this darkened café, she was starting to feel close again.

"I don't need your gratitude," the sheriff said as

he moved his hand away. His grin was gone. "It's my job to help people."

Barbara wondered when it had gotten so cold in the room. Then someone opened the outside door and enough wind blew in to lower the temperature even more.

"Who turned the lights off?" a man's voice said from where he stood by the open door.

The room was so dark that it was hard to see the man clearly. Barbara thought she recognized Pete Denning, but she wasn't sure until she saw the reflection from that gold-plated belt buckle of his.

"We're closed," Linda said as she walked out from the kitchen and into the main café area.

"How can you be closed when they're here?" Pete said as he took a step into the café. "Besides, they're the ones I wanted to see."

"Is there trouble somewhere?" the sheriff asked, as he began to rise from the table.

"Probably," Pete said as he walked over to their table. "But I'm not here about trouble. I'm here to do my civic duty."

The sheriff sat back down and asked cautiously, "What civic duty would that be?"

"You never do your civic duty, Peter Denning, and don't you pretend otherwise," Linda said as she walked further into the room. She had a spatula in one hand and she waved it around for emphasis. "Why, you don't even vote."

"I voted last election," Pete protested.

Barbara thought he sounded a little self-righteous.

Linda snorted. "I heard. You voted for Santa Claus. All the slots—even the school board members."

Pete grinned. "Well, I figure Santa's been good to me, and it's the least I can do for him. The old man seems to have an image problem around here."

"That's because he's not a real person," Linda said as she pointed at Pete with the spatula. "No one votes for someone who isn't real."

Pete grinned even wider. "Half of the politicians in the world aren't real either. They're just images created by their public relations staff. At least Santa Claus is around from year to year and doesn't take a dive on the voters."

"Well, I don't care who you vote for, you just can't do it tonight. Not here. We have an exclusive party here." Linda said as she marched up to Pete and took his elbow in her hand so that he had to rise up from the chair he'd pulled close to the table. "If you drive around to the alley in back, I can give you a take-out hamburger through the back window."

"Like a drive-in?" Pete said in amazement. He

stopped walking. "Since when do you do a drive-in business?"

"Since we have a date in the front dining room—" Linda ground out the words.

Barbara didn't even think about protesting. She was having too much fun watching Linda and Pete grimace at each other. She was going to have to ask Linda if Pete was the man who had left her broken-hearted some years ago. There certainly seemed to be something between the two of them. Maybe it wasn't as hopeless as Linda thought.

"They aren't on a date," Pete said as he shook his arm free from Linda's hand. "It's a business meeting to set up a slogan for the sheriff's political campaign. Barbara told me that herself."

Pete looked at Barbara, and she felt she had to nod in confirmation even though by now she was confused as to what this evening was.

"It's both a date and a campaign meeting," the sheriff finally said as he ran his finger under his collar and loosened his tie. "The one thing it sure isn't, however, is dinner." The sheriff smiled toward Linda before turning to Pete. "Not that it won't be dinner just as soon as you let the cook get back to her cooking."

"Well, I guess I could settle for a hamburger to go," Pete said grudgingly. "I'm just trying to figure out what's what around here."

Barbara could sympathize with the ranch hand.

"I'll throw in a batch of fries if you wait out back," Linda offered Pete as she gestured toward the door.

Pete lifted an eyebrow, but he did begin to walk toward the door. "With some of that barbecue sauce on the side?"

"I know how you like your fries," Linda said.

Barbara couldn't help but notice that the ranch hand turned around to watch Linda as she walked back into the kitchen. And when he did, he had a vulnerable look on his face that made Barbara wonder.

"Well, that was interesting," Barbara said when Pete finally left the café. "How long ago was it that he and Linda dated?"

"Pete and Linda?" the sheriff asked in surprise. "Why there's nothing between the two of them. Linda's been waiting for that boyfriend of hers, Jazz, to give up on that band of his and come home. She's been waiting a good three years now. They started this café together before he left Dry Creek to try and become a rock star. What a waste of a man's future."

"Three years is a long time to wait for someone," Barbara said slowly. She could already smell the hamburgers cooking on the grill in back. She also heard the sound of a pickup driving around behind the café.

"How long are you planning to wait?" the sheriff said quietly. "Before you marry again, that is."

"Oh." Barbara flushed. "I'm not going to marry again."

The sheriff didn't say anything.

"I'm just not very good at it," Barbara finally confessed, partly because she felt uncomfortable not giving any reason at all. Plus, there was nothing else to fill the silence.

The sheriff shook his head. "I don't believe it. Now me, I'm the one who wouldn't know how to go about this family business. But you? You have it down pat already."

Maybe it was the fact that the café was still dark and she only saw flashes of the sheriff's face. It was like being in a confessional. Whatever it was, Barbara went ahead and told him everything. "It's not about family life. I can do that. It's just that I'm not any good at picking men. You know, like some women aren't any good at picking watermelons. I don't seem to do very well with picking men. I doubt Neal ever loved me, not even at first when I thought he did. I should have known better."

They sat in silence for a moment.

"I figure a woman can learn to pick out a good watermelon," the sheriff finally said. "And, if she can't, she gets a neighbor to help her pick one out."

Barbara smiled at that. "I don't know of too many neighbors who want to pick out a husband for someone."

The sheriff snorted. "You could've fooled me on that one. It seems everyone around here has an opinion on who should marry who."

Barbara frowned. Now that she thought about it, that was true. "Especially who should marry me."

She remembered the night of the wedding reception when Charley had offered his nephew and Jacob had offered himself.

"But it's not the same," Barbara said. "No one should pick out a partner for someone else. It should be something special that just happens between the two people."

"I wouldn't know about that," the sheriff said.

Love was a whole lot different than picking out a watermelon, Barbara thought. Love made a woman lose the sense she was born with. Picking out a ripe piece of fruit never did that.

She didn't get a chance to tell the sheriff that though, because the door to the kitchen opened and Linda came out with a small plastic basket in her hands. "I thought I'd bring you some fries to get you started. Your hamburgers will be out in a minute. What kind of cheese do you want?"

"I'll stick with the pepper jack," the sheriff said.

"I'll have mine plain," Barbara said. "With lots of catsup."

"And some mustard for me," the sheriff added.

Linda set the basket of fries down on the table and went back into the kitchen.

Barbara and the sheriff were silent for a minute.

"I'm not planning to get married again anyway," Barbara finally said. She thought she should tell him that. After all, he had been kind enough to understand her watermelon theory.

The sheriff nodded as he picked up the basket. "You've made your feeling on that subject clear. Want some fries?"

Barbara reached into the basket and pulled out a hot French fry. "I think Linda should get married though. I can't help thinking about Pete and her."

The sheriff grinned. "See what I mean about picking out watermelons for your neighbors? Everybody wants to do it."

"Who would you pick?"

"For you?" the sheriff said. His grin was gone and he looked serious.

Barbara shook her head. "No, for Linda."

"I'd pick Pete," the sheriff said promptly. "Just to keep him away from you."

"That's not a very good reason."

"It is to me," the sheriff said with a nod. "He's not good enough for you. Not by a long shot. You need to marry a man with—" the sheriff seemed at a momentary loss for words "—well, with lots of money, I guess."

Barbara gasped. "I'd never marry a man for his money."

"Of course, you wouldn't," the sheriff agreed and wiggled his eyebrows. "That's why you need to let a neighbor like me do the picking for you."

Barbara laughed. She had forgotten about the sheriff's eyebrows. He'd told some of the best stories when she was in the hospital and, as often as not, they'd ended with that wiggle of his eyebrows. She didn't even pay any attention to the sounds of the kitchen door opening.

When the sheriff saw she was laughing, he wiggled his ears, too. And then his nose.

"You need to read a bedtime story to the children some night," she said when she got her breath back from laughing. "You'd do a great three little pigs."

Barbara gradually became aware that Linda was walking toward them.

"I brought your hamburgers," Linda said cautiously as she sat two platters down on the table. "I'll be back with the catsup and mustard."

Barbara wiped a tear away that she'd gotten from laughing. "Thank you, we're really not crazy. We're just—"

Linda held up her hand. "You don't need to explain. Tonight I'm an anonymous waitress. Your date is private."

"Well, it's not so much a date as it is—" Barbara stopped to think a minute. "Well, really, it's just two old friends having dinner together."

The sheriff nodded. "I can live with that. As long as it's not just business."

Linda smiled and turned her back to walk toward the kitchen. "There'll be blueberry pie for dessert if you want some."

"Blueberry is my favorite," the sheriff said. "We'll sit here a bit after we eat our hamburgers and have some."

"And we do need to think of a slogan for you," Barbara said.

"We've got time," the sheriff said. "I'm not fussy and I don't mind lingering over dessert."

Barbara felt the sheriff's hand cover the hand she had on the table again and give it a squeeze before letting it go.

"Right now you're probably hungry for these hamburgers though," the sheriff said as he unfolded the cloth napkin by his plate and put it on his lap.

Barbara couldn't remember when she'd tasted a better hamburger.

"Uhmmm, that's good," the sheriff said as he took a bite of his own hamburger.

Barbara smiled. She liked watching the sheriff enjoy his meal. She liked the way the evening had slipped into friendship as well. She took another bite of her hamburger.

After a minute, Barbara sat her hamburger down on the plate. "Now isn't this better than being on a date? Just two friends eating together. No pressure. No—you know—"

The sheriff lifted his eyebrow as he put down his own hamburger. "'No—you know'? What's that?"

Barbara shrugged. "Holding hands. Kissing. That sort of thing."

The sheriff smiled. "Oh, I intend for there to be kissing."

"But—"

"It wouldn't be fair to have Linda go to all this work for us and us not even to kiss after," the sheriff said. "It might discourage her from doing this sort of thing for others."

Barbara knew she should protest. But somehow she didn't really want to argue about it. It seemed churlish to argue when the stereo in the kitchen was playing old love songs now. She could afford to kiss the man again. In fact, she'd begun to wonder what it would be like to kiss the sheriff again now that she was free of pain and not sedated at all. She'd probably find out that a kiss now wasn't the same as the one had been back then anyway. It would actually be good for her to kiss the sheriff. It'd be an experiment of sorts.

If the sheriff had expected an argument, he didn't say. He just kept eating his hamburger as though everything were normal. But Barbara knew that things were far from normal. For one thing, the temperature in the café had shot up as though someone had turned the furnace on. For another, the hamburger that had tasted so good a moment ago now tasted like sawdust.

Barbara had finished her hamburger before she convinced herself that the sheriff had been teasing her about the kiss. He must have been teasing, because he looked as if he'd completely forgotten about any kiss. Between bites, he kept humming along with the tunes on the stereo. When he did talk, it was about the weather. A man didn't do that if he had kissing on his mind. Yes, he must have been just teasing her.

Barbara and the sheriff had both finished their hamburgers and folded their napkins when Barbara realized how wrong she had been. The sheriff hadn't forgotten and he hadn't been teasing.

The sheriff stood up and offered his hand to Barbara. "Would you like to take a stroll before dessert?"

Barbara didn't even have to answer him; he just put her hand in the curve of his elbow and escorted her out of the café and onto the front steps. Together they stepped down onto the ground.

"Let's step out a few feet," the sheriff said as he

led her away from the building. "We can see the stars better then."

On the walk over to the café, Barbara hadn't paid any attention to the sky. Now she was surprised anyone could walk beneath it and not notice the spattering of jewels up there.

"The clouds left at least," the sheriff said as he looked up. "I was hoping they would."

So that's why he was wondering about the weather during dinner, Barbara realized. He wanted to be sure they could see the stars.

"It's beautiful," Barbara said softly.

They were silent for a moment, just looking upward.

"I guess this makes it a date officially," Barbara said with a little laugh. "We're out looking at the moon and the stars."

"No, that doesn't make it official. This does."

Barbara felt the sheriff turn toward her and she lifted her face to his. She told herself it was not a real kiss. It was just a kiss to knock the memory of that other kiss out of her mind.

The next thought she had was that looking at the sky wasn't the only way to see stars. She felt the sheriff's kiss all the way down to her stomach. Or was it her toes?

"Oh, my." Barbara breathed when she could.

The sheriff took his own deep breath. "—dear."

Barbara looked up in panic. The sheriff was going too fast.

The sheriff looked at her for a moment before smiling a little ruefully. "That's the way it all goes. It's 'oh, my dear.'"

"Oh," Barbara said in relief. "That's right."

Trust the sheriff to think about things like completing a phrase at a time like this, Barbara thought to herself as they walked back into the café. But it was good that one of them was thinking of something sensible. She didn't quite seem able to at this time.

Chapter Twelve

It seemed like a long walk to Sunday school the next morning even though the church was only two doors down and across the street from the place where Barbara and the children lived. Barbara could see that the children were much more excited about going there than she was.

"They have a birthday bank," Bobby had confided to her this morning over a breakfast of toast and cereal. "On your birthday, you get to go up and put a penny in the bank for every year old you are. Then they sing Happy Birthday to you and give you a pencil."

Barbara had no idea that Bobby knew so much about what happened in the Sunday school at the Dry Creek Church. The other kids had obviously told him all about it.

"And they sing songs," Amanda had added solemnly as she carefully poured milk on her second bowl of cereal. "But nobody has to sing all by themselves so it's not scary."

"I'm sure none of it will be scary," Barbara had told the children.

And, even now that they were walking toward the church on this fine spring morning, she was sure that what she had said was true for the children. She, on the other hand, had every right to be terrified about going to Sunday school.

People expected adults to have at least a nodding acquaintance with what went on in a church. Barbara didn't. She knew about the Golden Rule and the Lord's Prayer, but she didn't know anything about what actually went on in a church. She didn't know if you bowed to the minister or stood when the choir sang. She knew the Christmas story, but that's all she knew about the Bible.

Yet, even though she had told Mrs. Hargrove that she didn't know anything, the older woman had still wanted her to help with her first- and second-grade Sunday-school class. Amanda and Bobby would both normally be in that class, so she had agreed. She didn't make her children go to the dentist alone; she wouldn't make them go to Sunday school alone either.

Besides, Barbara didn't plan on making Sunday school a habit, so she didn't suppose it mattered what class any of them attended. At least Mrs. Hargrove had a class of younger children instead of junior-high kids. Barbara hoped the class would be easy.

Barbara adjusted the jacket of her suit and then took both of her children's hands in hers before she started up the steps to the church. Even though they'd never had a steady home, she had taken the children to the dentist at least once a year. It was just one of those things a parent had to do for their child. Church was probably like that, too. They could do this, she told herself.

Fifteen minutes later, Barbara decided she was wrong. She, for one, couldn't do this. She should have known better. They didn't even have Novocain.

It had been easy enough to get directions to the room where Mrs. Hargrove held her Sunday-school class and the stairs down to the basement were clearly marked. The basement had been painted bright colors and there were high windows along all of the walls. The basement was marked off into several areas for different Sunday-school classes and each area had a long kid-sized table with a dozen chairs around it. Mrs. Hargrove had a chalkboard in her area with her name on it so Barbara would have known which space belonged to the older woman's class even if Mrs. Hargrove hadn't been there.

Finding the right place seemed to go pretty well, Barbara thought. After that though, things stopped being easy.

Five minutes after Barbara and the children settled into chairs around the table, Mrs. Hargrove led the children in a game called a sword drill. The older woman gave Bibles to both Bobby and Amanda so they could play with the other children.

Barbara was glad that Mrs. Hargrove hadn't offered her a Bible. She didn't know where anything was located in the Bible, and it was quickly obvious that this was the skill required to solve puzzles in the game. Mrs. Hargrove called out a man's name with a number behind it—like John 3:16—and the children tried to be the first to find where those words were written in their Bibles. Barbara was dumbfounded that the little kids could find things so quickly. She wouldn't have even known that the children weren't using the full Bible if Mrs. Hargrove hadn't told her.

Fortunately, the sword drill didn't last long and then it was time for the sheriff to tell the story. Correction, Barbara reminded herself, it was time for Carl Wall to tell the story. She had decided some time during the night that she was Carl's friend and friends called each other by their name and not their job title.

By the look on Carl's face, he could use a friend about now, so Barbara nodded encouragingly to him as he stood up. He'd been sitting in a folding chair in the back corner of the room until he stood. Barbara thought he looked a little uneasy until one of the boys rolled a piece of paper into a wad the size of a marble and threw it at the girl across the table from him.

Carl straightened right up then. "That's not allowed in here."

The sheriff saw the look of panic on the boy's face and glanced at Mrs. Hargrove. He didn't want the older woman to have a heart attack because he'd frightened one of her precious students. Besides, the boy was probably only six years old, and right now he was stiffer than some men had been when he'd called out, "Drop it."

The sheriff thought the boy was a Campbell—Sam or Danny or something like that. He knew the boy's father was Frank Campbell. Frank worked for a gas station between here and Miles City.

"No spit wads," the sheriff said in what he hoped was friendlier voice than he'd used initially. To make sure he was nice enough, he added a smile. "We're here to learn, not throw things at each other."

At least that's why the kids were here, the sheriff told himself. He was here because he'd bartered his Sunday morning in exchange for his Saturday night and, as uncomfortable as he was now, he still thought he'd gotten the better of the deal.

"She started it first," the boy said with an indignant protest. "She kicked me under the table."

The sheriff looked at the girl that the Campbell boy was scowling at and, sure enough, she wouldn't meet the sheriff's eyes. The boy's trouble with women was starting early. The sheriff knew the girl's name. It was Suzy Holmquist. The family lived out by the Elkton place.

"Well, there's better ways to handle things," the sheriff finally told the boy.

"Are you going to arrest me?" the boy asked, looking defiantly up at the sheriff. "Bobby told me you might arrest him if he didn't do his homework."

Where did the kids come up with these ideas? the sheriff wondered. "I'm not arresting anybody today."

"Not even if a bad man shows up?" Suzy asked, finally deciding it was okay to look the sheriff in the eye. "You'd have to arrest a bad man. You're the sheriff. It's your job to protect everyone in Dry Creek."

"I'm off on Sundays," the sheriff said.

"Oh." Suzy looked surprised. "Well, who protects us on Sundays?"

The sheriff looked over at Mrs. Hargrove. He was out of his league with these kids, and he had the good sense to know it. "You're sure you don't want a new roof instead?"

Mrs. Hargrove smiled as she shook her head. She did, however, stand up, which to the sheriff's dismay seemed to make the children pay a little more attention to what was going on. He doubted anyone kicked anyone else under the table while Mrs. Hargrove was on duty.

"Suzy is asking a good question, class," Mrs. Hargrove said. "Who protects us if the sheriff isn't around?"

There was a moment of silence.

"My dog," one boy said hesitantly. "He's good at scaring people away."

Mrs. Hargrove nodded. "Is there anyone else who is even more powerful than your dog?"

"She means God," a redheaded girl said. "He's around to help us out if we meet up with trouble."

There was another moment of silence.

"God would have a hard time beating up a bad guy," another boy said. "I'd rather have the sheriff working on Sundays."

The sheriff knew he shouldn't let that make him feel good, but it did. Though, at least he had the sense to know that it wasn't what Mrs. Hargrove wanted to hear.

"Can the sheriff protect you from twenty lions

even if he doesn't have a gun?" Mrs. Hargrove asked the class.

The sheriff was gratified to see that the children seemed to be debating the question instead of just saying no.

"Does he have pepper spray?" Suzy finally asked.

Mrs. Hargrove shook her head. "He has absolutely nothing."

Several of the children shook their heads.

"The sheriff is going to tell you what happened to a man who had to face more than twenty lions and didn't have a gun or pepper spray or anything," Mrs. Hargrove said and then paused. "Well, he did have one secret weapon. Listen to the story and see what it was."

The sheriff had to admit that Mrs. Hargrove did know how to get the attention of these kids. They were all caught up in the story of Daniel in the lion's den even though the sheriff just read it to them from the book Mrs. Hargrove had given him. He showed them the pictures from time to time, but the children seemed content just to listen to the words being read.

"And so, what was the man's secret weapon?" Mrs. Hargrove asked when the story was finished.

"God," the children answered together.

"And what did he do when he was in trouble?"

"He asked God to help him," Suzy said.

Mrs. Hargrove nodded. "That's what we do when we pray. We ask God to help us. And then we trust Him to do what He has promised."

Barbara felt as if she'd run a marathon. She'd watched the expressions on the faces of Amanda and Bobby as they listened to the story, and she could see the longing in each of them. She was clearly not all that her children needed to feel safe and protected. If she were, they wouldn't be looking so hungry for more words to the story.

She had to admit she felt a certain wistfulness herself. She would sleep better at night if she believed someone was watching out for her, listening to her prayers or cries. She supposed though that one had to have the trust of a child to believe such a thing. She'd long since given up on being that trusting of anyone.

"Thank you, Carl," Mrs. Hargrove said as the sheriff went back to the chair he had sat in earlier.

Somewhere a bell rang.

"That leaves us five minutes," Mrs. Hargrove said. "Just enough time to say a few prayers. Who wants to go first?"

Barbara watched her children bow their heads along with the other children. One of the boys prayed that his brother would get over the flu. A girl prayed for the children in Africa.

And then Barbara's heart stopped because her daughter prayed. Amanda's voice was clear and steady as she made her request. "Dear God, my mommy wants a house for us to live in."

"Amen," Mrs. Hargrove said just as she'd said at the end of each child's prayer.

Barbara just sat in her seat until the children finished praying and scrambled out of their seats to go upstairs. Before long, Amanda and Bobby were the only children left around the table.

"Thank you," Mrs. Hargrove said as she looked from Barbara to the sheriff. "You've been a blessing."

"Carl told a good story, didn't he?" Barbara said.

The sheriff looked surprised. "No one except Mrs. Hargrove calls me Carl."

"They do now," Mrs. Hargrove said with an approving nod at Barbara. "And it's about time."

Barbara liked seeing someone as flustered as she felt. Both she and Carl were in foreign territory here. Neither one of them had even intended to come to church. Mrs. Hargrove had just been so compelling. "We forgot to take some pictures."

Barbara had a disposable camera in her purse and she had been all set to take a few shots.

"We can try again next Sunday," Mrs. Hargrove said serenely.

"Next Sunday?" Carl said with a gulp. "The deal was for *this* Sunday."

Mrs. Hargrove smiled slightly. "I understand you both had a good time last night. I thought you might want to repeat the deal next weekend."

"Does everybody know about our d—" Barbara stopped herself from saying *date*. "About our dinner?"

"Oh, I expect so, dear," Mrs. Hargrove said, just as though it weren't anything unusual.

Carl grunted. "Maybe next Saturday we should drive into Miles City."

Barbara smiled. So there was going to be a next Saturday.

"There's a coffee time before church," Mrs. Hargrove said as she picked up her books. "Next to the kitchen in the area at the top of the stairs."

"Do you need anyone to pour the coffee?" Barbara asked. It was starting to be a rather nice day. It wouldn't hurt to ask.

"Oh, no, dear," Mrs. Hargrove said as she started walking toward the stairs that led up to the main part of the church. "We couldn't ask you to do that. You're a guest."

"Oh," Barbara said.

"They have cookies, too," Bobby said as he and

Amanda walked over to Barbara. "Some guys told me. He said to take the ones that have chocolate chips in them."

Barbara could see her children would want to come to Sunday school again.

"Well, I guess we wouldn't want to miss out on the cookies," the sheriff said as he put his hand on Bobby's shoulder and the two of them started walking toward the stairs.

Barbara put her hand on Amanda's shoulder and started walking too. She supposed they would all sit together during church. She almost hoped so. Her worry about doing the wrong thing in church would be easier with someone beside her who could arrest people for harassment if things went bad.

Chapter Thirteen

Floyd Spencer looked at the church building and swore. He hadn't planned to drive back to Dry Creek this morning. He'd seen that the cake was delivered yesterday, and he thought that would be enough for the time being.

But last night someone had come into his house while he was sleeping and left a note taped to his bathroom mirror. The note said he had three more days. There was no signature to the note, but he knew who it was from. Harlow Smith was letting him know that the cake wasn't enough.

Floyd didn't know what to do. The door to his house had been double-locked. The windows had been locked, too. Whoever had come inside hadn't even had to break into his house, and he'd even changed the locks a few weeks ago. Someone had picked the lock. That was the only explanation. And if Harlow had someone working for him who could pick locks, Floyd wasn't safe anywhere.

Floyd knew it was probably foolish of him to come to Dry Creek. He'd spent the past hour hiding behind those pine trees in back of the deserted house. He didn't want anyone to see him. But he was a desperate man. If he could find a way to take that boy of Neal's as a hostage, that's what he was going to do. He'd already nosed around that place where Neal's wife and the kids stayed, but they weren't there this morning. It looked like the only place they could be was in that church there.

He'd hoped to catch the boy alone, but it didn't look like that was going to happen today.

Floyd patted his pocket. He needed one of those antacid pills. He'd bought another packet this morning at the same grocery store next to the motel where he stayed in Miles City. At this rate, he'd spend all of the money he'd gotten from the robbery on gas driving out to Dry Creek and on antacid pills to keep his stomach settled down.

Chapter Fourteen

The next morning, for the first time in fifteen years, the sheriff stood in front of his bedroom mirror and debated about whether or not to put on his uniform. Of course, he knew he had to put it on. Monday was a working day for him, and people needed to know that he was on duty.

It was just this business of Barbara calling him Carl that made him feel unsettled inside. He'd always liked people calling him Sheriff instead of Carl. It said who he was, and that was enough. People needed a sheriff.

It should be enough for a man, shouldn't it? The sheriff shook his head. He wished he knew. It had certainly been enough for him for all these years.

He'd never had a family and he'd never expected to have any friends. He didn't need to be more than the sheriff to anyone. Or did he?

He wasn't sure what had changed things for him. Maybe it was Barbara using his first name all morning yesterday or maybe it was sitting with her and her two children during church. Whatever it was, he found himself having dreams of something he'd never known—a family. At least, he thought it was dreams of having a family. He didn't even know what a family felt like. He'd never come close to anything like it in all those places where he'd lived growing up. He hadn't even missed it. Everyone had limitations. He'd been content with his life. Until now.

The sheriff reached for his shirt and started putting it on.

Church had been a surprising thing for him, too. He'd never thought someone like him belonged in a place like that. Church was mostly for families and children.

He had always been more comfortable with the ranch hands, his boots hitched up on a corral when the rodeo hit Miles City. He hadn't thought he would like sitting in church, but he had. People came up and shook his hand after the whole thing was over and he knew he was welcome. The church at Dry Creek didn't have any of the fancy frills he'd feared, either. The building was a place where people could just be themselves.

The sheriff reached for his pants.

He'd been able to follow the talk Matthew Curtis

had given, the sheriff thought with satisfaction. It was mostly about a person trusting God when they were in trouble. The sheriff had no problem with people doing that. He knew he couldn't be everywhere. It was good for people to ask God for help sometimes, too.

Of course, the sheriff hoped no one was foolish enough to ask God for help when they really needed a sheriff instead. After all, a lawman carried a gun.

The sheriff reached for his belt that looped onto his gun holster.

Yes, the sheriff told himself, he needed to be ready to do his job. Today was a day just like any other work day.

When he had finished dressing, the sheriff walked over to his dresser and opened the top drawer. Somewhere in there he had a brass name badge that he'd been issued with his uniform years ago. He shoved aside some socks and found it. It wouldn't hurt to wear the badge, he told himself as he pinned it on to his shirt—just in case other people wanted to call him by name, too.

Barbara started baking early so she'd get the donuts and the pies ready this morning before nine. It was a fairly light day for bakery orders; Monday always was, probably because people ordered so much for Saturday that by Monday they were thinking they needed to eat a little more fruit instead of baked goods.

She was fine with having a quick morning today though because Mrs. Hargrove had happily agreed to take her into Miles City at ten o'clock when she went for her dental appointment. The children had both caught the school bus at seven-thirty and it was a good day for Barbara to go to Miles City. Mrs. Hargrove had even offered Barbara the use of her car while she was in the dental office so that Barbara could do her errands.

Barbara was determined to find a pawnshop in Miles City so she could ask about selling the ring set she had. Ever since Amanda had voiced her prayer for a house, Barbara had been determined she'd do what she could to let the children know that a house was coming soon. She didn't want them to worry. Barbara didn't want just to give them a promise, either. They'd both heard too many promises in their lives from their father, and none of them had come true. No, she wanted to show the children that she was serious.

Barbara walked over to the oven and pulled a coffee cake out of the oven. That was the last of the baked goods. Everything needed to cool for a minute and then she'd be ready to go. In the meantime, she'd go see how the weather looked outside.

Barbara didn't even bother to lie to herself as she stood in the open doorway to the outside. She was looking down the road to see if Carl was driving by anytime soon. There were several pickups parked in front of the hardware store, but there was nothing else coming down the road into town. The sheriff must have driven by earlier.

Oh, well, Barbara told herself, she had better things to do today than keep an eye out for the sheriff.

She needed to change clothes before Mrs. Hargrove picked her up in fifteen minutes, and Barbara didn't know whether to dress poor or rich. If she dressed poor, she might get more from a pawnbroker for the rings she was willing to sell. But if she dressed too poor, the pawnbroker might think the rings were stolen.

In the end, Barbara settled for wearing jeans and a sweater. She looked just like what she was, a young divorced woman who was trying to do something better for her children.

The sheriff had to go out to the Elkton ranch the first thing this morning to take a report on a fight in the bunkhouse. The two ranch hands had both been tight-lipped about the fight and the sheriff didn't see much reason to do a report when he could see the two men would be at each other when he left anyway. But the foreman insisted.

"See that you keep it to fists," the sheriff told the two men after he'd written down the notes for his report. "Remember, any knives or broken bottles— anything like that and it becomes assault with a deadly weapon."

Both men gave him a curt nod and the sheriff told himself he'd done all he could.

"I hope this isn't over a woman," the sheriff gave a guess before he walked to the bunkhouse door.

"How'd you—?" one of the ranch hands said in surprise.

The sheriff shrugged. "It's usually either money or women. I figure you both get paid about the same, so it had to be a woman."

The sheriff turned and walked back to the men. "The pity of it is that she's going to pick the loser in the fight instead of the winner anyway."

The men looked up at him in astonishment.

"Well, think about it," the sheriff said. "How do you figure it's going to go?"

The men stopped being so closemouthed soon enough as they thought about just who would end up with the woman if they kept fighting. The sheriff felt he'd done his job and he left.

All of the way back into Dry Creek, the sheriff wished he knew an easy answer to the questions about the woman who was troubling him. He wasn't worried any more that she might be breaking the law by hiding some of her ex-husband's stolen money. But he was worried that he'd be setting himself up for a deep disappointment if he kept on dreaming the way he was.

It was almost eleven o'clock before the sheriff drove into Dry Creek for the second time that morning. He'd swung by earlier around seven o'clock and checked that Mrs. Hargrove's kitchen light was on. Then he'd gotten the call to go to the Elkton ranch and had ended up there. The sheriff knew that Barbara was going into Miles City with Mrs. Hargrove, so he didn't really expect her to answer the door when he knocked on the outside of the building that housed the dance studio and bakery.

The sheriff didn't get an answer to his knock, but he decided to walk around the building anyway. The fact that someone had left that money for the cake on the porch here without anyone hearing or seeing anything made him realize how vulnerable Barbara and the children were. It wouldn't hurt to be sure all of the windows closed securely and the door at the back was sturdy.

Once he finished looking around this building, he might even step over to the old Gossett place and have a good look at that house. Mr. Gossett had asked him to keep an eye on the place for him, and it had been a couple of months since the sheriff had made an inspection of the house to be sure everything was still locked up tight. Unless he was wrong, he thought the Gossett house would be a much sturdier building. It needed some paint, but that didn't weaken the house any.

The sheriff had finished his inspection of the building Barbara was living in and found it was in the same condition it had been in the last time he looked. It would do for the time being, but not for long.

The sheriff looked down the street a little at the Gossett house.

Mrs. Hargrove had told the sheriff that Barbara was interested in renting that house, but he hadn't given it much thought until lately. He was sure old man Gossett would want to rent the house. Why would he pass up some good income?

The sheriff left his car parked where it was and walked down the street to the Gossett house. When he came to the wooden fence surrounding the house, he reached for the lock on the inside of the gate. That was odd, he thought, as he saw that the lock was undone. The sheriff frowned; he didn't like the thought of someone nosing around the old Gossett place. It was probably just kids, but still—

The sheriff walked around the house carefully and checked that none of the windows were unlocked. No one had tampered with the two doors either. The sheriff decided he had been right and that it had been curious kids who had unlocked the gate when he noticed the papers behind one of the pine trees.

These weren't left by kids, the sheriff told himself, as he picked up the wrappers for several rolls of antacid tablets.

The sheriff thought a moment and decided that whoever had been standing here hadn't been interested in vandalism because nothing had been disturbed. There was something about an unpainted place that just attracted trouble, he finally decided. It wouldn't hurt for him to put a coat of white paint on that fence. Maybe that would stop anyone from making themselves at home in the backyard.

Barbara stood at the counter of the pawnshop and opened up the envelope that held the three rings she was selling. She was surprised that she didn't have some feelings of sadness as she rolled the rings out onto the counter of the pawn shop so that the man could look at them more closely.

Maybe she wasn't more upset about giving up the rings because she had had such a hard time finding a pawnshop. When she'd told Mrs. Hargrove that she wanted to go to a pawnshop when they got to Miles City, the older woman had said she didn't think Miles City had any pawnshops. Then Mrs. Hargrove had offered Barbara the use of her car so she could drive to Billings.

Barbara was reluctant to drive Mrs. Hargrove's

car, but the older woman had finally convinced her to borrow it.

"There's some kind of a pawnshop just this side of Billings," the older woman had said. "You can be there and back before I'm through with my appointment. It's a long one today."

Barbara hadn't told Mrs. Hargrove that she was selling the rings. She wasn't altogether sure that the older woman would approve. There seemed to be something cold about selling wedding rings. Maybe it just reminded Barbara of all that she had lost, she thought. It wasn't just the years that she had used up being married to Neal; it was also the reluctance she felt now to trust any man with her well-being or, even more important, the well-being of her children.

She might date again, Barbara admitted. But it would have to be a casual friendly thing with no expectations by her or anyone else that it would deepen into a real romantic relationship.

And, she thought, smiling to herself a little as the man in front of her kept looking at the rings, the only reason she was even willing to date a little was because she was hoping Carl would want to have dinner with her every so often. That would be nice.

"I'll give you five hundred dollars for all of them," the man behind the counter finally announced. "And

I've got to be a fool to go that high. If you were a man, I'd give you four."

"I don't think that the fact that I'm—" Barbara started and then shut her mouth. Instead, she smiled. "Thank you. That sounds fair."

Barbara was grateful to get that much for the rings. She would have to pick up a newspaper and look at the classified ads. Someone surely had a sturdy dining table for sale. Maybe she would even have enough to buy some dishes and silverware as well. And a small rug for the bathroom.

Oh, Barbara thought as she took the stack of twenty-dollar bills that the man handed to her, there were so many things that she and the children could use. If she had time today, she'd try to buy a few of them.

Floyd Spencer didn't feel too good. He was sitting at his desk at the bank, but he wished with all his heart that he was home in his bed.

"How are you doing there, Floyd?"

Floyd looked up to see his manager standing beside his desk. "I'll get those reports soon."

Fortunately, he'd kept no records of the times he had tried to transfer that money to the offshore accounts for Harlow and Neal, so he had nothing on his desk he needed to hide.

His manager was frowning at Floyd anyway. "How are you feeling these days?"

"Ah, fine," Floyd mumbled. He hadn't slept for six days straight, but he didn't want to look like he was falling down on his job. He needed this job.

The manager nodded. "The Human Resources division at corporate is worried that the staff here has been suffering from stress related to that bank robbery. Even though it didn't happen here, it was close."

Floyd was worried that he might stop breathing. Was this a clue that someone suspected something? "I'm not stressed."

"It's nothing to be ashamed of." His manager sat on a corner of Floyd's desk. "I've noticed you seem a little more tired than usual. Have you been sleeping okay?"

"Ahhh." Floyd sat there like a deer in the headlights. He didn't know which way to turn.

"If you need to take a couple of days off to get some rest, don't be shy about asking. Just fill out the form," the manager finally suggested as he stood up. "You haven't taken much sick time this year."

Floyd waited for his manager to leave before he started to breathe again. He sure could use a couple of days off. Maybe he could even get his stomach to settle down.

Chapter Fifteen

When Barbara arrived at the dentist's office to meet Mrs. Hargrove, the older woman's jaw was still frozen, and she nodded in relief when Barbara offered to continue driving the car through to Dry Creek.

"'Hank 'ou," Mrs. Hargrove mumbled.

Barbara stopped at the grocery store before leaving Miles City and bought a bag of frozen peas so that Mrs. Hargrove could hold their coldness to her cheek.

"I always got frozen peas for the kids when they had dental work done," Barbara said as she came back from the store, carrying a bag with the vegetables and a few other items. She handed the peas to the older woman through the open window in the car.

"'Onderful," Mrs. Hargrove said as she gratefully took the peas.

At least Mrs. Hargrove let her help some, Barbara reflected as she walked around to the driver's side of the car, stopping to put the rest of the grocery bags in the backseat. Barbara was glad she could do some small service for Mrs. Hargrove. Maybe a person needed to work up to coffee-pouring around here, she reflected. Maybe it would start with a bag of frozen peas.

When Barbara slid into the driver's seat, Mrs. Hargrove reached for her purse and pulled out a five-dollar bill. "'Et me 'ay 'ou."

"You don't need to pay me for a bag of peas," Barbara said. "Neighbors borrow things like that. It's like a cup of sugar."

Mrs. Hargrove shook her head and offered the bill to Barbara again. "'Or the children."

Barbara shook her head, too. "The children and I are fine." Barbara reached into her jacket pocket and pulled out the stack of twenties. "See? We're fine."

"Ah," Mrs. Hargrove said as she lowered her five-dollar bill into her lap.

Mrs. Hargrove slept on the way back to Dry Creek, with the bag of peas pressed between the side window and her cheek. The ride was peaceful for Barbara. One thing she never got used to was all the space that there was here in southern Montana. She liked looking at these empty vistas filled with browns and grays and the blue of the sky. There wasn't much traffic on Interstate 94, so she watched the gray cloud formations in the sky as she drove. It was restful.

It was three o'clock before Barbara drove the car into Mrs. Hargrove's driveway. The sky had grown increasingly full of gray clouds as the hours passed. It felt like it should rain, but no drops had fallen.

Barbara was glad she'd sent the children to school with jackets today. It was still another hour before they'd get here on the school bus, and it might be raining by then.

One would think, she told herself, with all the rain they had had lately that some grass would be starting to grow beside the road and in the spaces between the houses around here. The ground still looked like gray and brown mud though. There weren't any leaves on the few oak trees around, either. Only the sturdy pine trees held their green needles.

Barbara helped Mrs. Hargrove into her house. Ordinarily the older woman wouldn't need any help getting anywhere, but today she seemed a little wobbly after her dental appointment.

The house was cold and Mrs. Hargrove asked Barbara to turn on the heat, so she did. The thermostat was located in the dining room.

Mrs. Hargrove's house wasn't anything special. It had a big lived-in kitchen on the first floor, along with a small living room and dining area. Upstairs, Barbara guessed, there were two large or three small bedrooms and a bathroom. Many of the walls had floral wallpaper on them, and the paper didn't always match the curtains at the windows or the rugs on the floor, but together everything looked cozy.

Barbara dreamed of having a house like this. She'd never demanded a fancy place with designer furniture. What she wanted instead was a house that had more artwork on the refrigerator than on the walls. A place where everyone felt at home and guests didn't have to take off their shoes to walk on the kitchen linoleum. A place like that would be a happy place for her children.

Maybe, she decided, she should walk past the building where she lived and go down a few houses to take another look at the old Gossett house. She needed to do something to make her dream seem as if it could happen.

The sheriff hoped the rain would hold off enough for him to finish painting at least the front of this fence. He'd bought a gallon of white outdoor paint and a couple of brushes from the hardware store an hour or so ago. He always had some old clothes in the trunk of his car for the days when he needed to do a quick chore for Mrs. Hargrove. Once he'd slipped an old sweatshirt over his uniform, he'd started painting up and down along the spikes of the old picket fence.

Surprisingly, the wood seemed to be in good shape, except for the places where a nail had come loose and the board was swinging. The sheriff would fix those later. Maybe with a coat of paint and some nails, it would stand up for another year or so until old man Gossett's nephew decided what to do with the house.

For the time being, the sheriff hoped Barbara would be able to rent the place. It wasn't the house he figured she wanted eventually, but it would be good for the children to have something now. They needed a place to run and scream and be kids.

The sheriff had never thought much about houses until the last few days. Mostly, a house to him was just some place to sleep and keep his things. The trailer had suited him fine. Oh, a year or two ago, he had bought plans for a three-bedroom log cabin from some ad he'd seen in a magazine. He'd thought about building that log house and tucking it next to those trees on his place so the huge porch it showed in the picture would have lots of shade in the summer.

He had enough in his savings account for a down payment on the kit they sold to build the house. It included all of the materials; all he'd have to supply was the work. He already had a well and septic system on the property. Electricity, too. It wouldn't take much to actually make that log house a reality.

But something held him back. Maybe it was just

that since it was only him, he'd rather rattle around in a tin box instead of setting himself up in a house that was meant to be shared. A man could get awfully lonesome sitting on that big porch all by himself.

The sheriff wondered if that was why old man Gossett hadn't kept up his house. Maybe it had become depressing to the man when he was living all alone in it. Some things were just meant to be shared and a house was one of them. The sheriff thought about the old man as he kept painting the fence boards. Too bad Mr.Gossett hadn't started going to church, the sheriff finally decided. That would have made him feel better.

The sheriff had to admit there was something that drew a person to the church two doors down from where he stood. For the life of him, he didn't know what it was. He knew that Matthew gave some good advice in his sermons. Even if he hadn't gone there yesterday to hear one for himself, the sheriff had talked with Matthew enough over the years to know that the man had a good head on his shoulders. But just good advice didn't seem like it covered the reason why so many people seemed so content to be there.

The sheriff put his brush down on the rim of the paint can as he stood to stretch his back. He might just have to go back to that church next Sunday. Not that he wanted to help Mrs. Hargrove with her class again. Those little ones would cause him grief soon enough when they were teenagers. He wondered what the town would think if he deputized Mrs. Hargrove to keep them in line when the time came. She'd do it, too, he thought with a smile.

The sheriff heard the sounds of footsteps coming down the gravel road and turned to see Barbara walking toward him.

"Well, look who's here. I was just thinking about you," the sheriff said.

The afternoon was developing quite a chill and Barbara's cheeks were rosy from the cold. She hugged her jacket to her, her arms crossed in the wool sleeves.

She was pretty as a picture, the sheriff thought as he took a moment to enjoy the sight of her.

"Hello, Carl," Barbara said. "Are you the one who has been doing all this painting?"

Barbara had smelled the paint when she passed the hardware store. It was the smell that had made her look up to see that someone had been painting the fence around the old Gossett house.

"Want to help paint?" the sheriff asked. "I've got an extra brush and an old sweatshirt in the trunk of my car."

Barbara took a deep breath. "I've thought about painting this fence myself—just in case Mr. Gossett ever decides he can rent the house to me."

"I've been thinking the house would suit you," the

sheriff said. "The inside would need some painting, too, but the rooms are sound and the ceiling is tight. No leaks that I've seen."

"You've seen inside?" Barbara asked. "I've been tempted to look in the windows, but the gate was locked and—"

The sheriff frowned. "I think someone broke the lock on the gate to get back in the trees."

"I hope it's not someone else like me who wants to rent the place," Barbara said. "I know I've been tempted to tamper with the gate."

"I don't know of anyone else who's thinking of renting it," the sheriff said.

"But as long as the gate is open," Barbara said, "I don't suppose it would be trespassing just to take a little look in the window?"

The sheriff grinned. "I'm supposed to be checking out the place now and again, so I think we can look through a few windows."

Barbara couldn't help herself. When the sheriff used a handkerchief to wipe away a spot on the window so she could see inside the kitchen of the Gossett house, she knew right where she wanted to put the table.

The kitchen was a square room, with an old refrigerator and stove pushed to one wall. The window she was looking in was over the sink. A light blue linoleum covered the floor and what looked like yellow paint covered the walls. There were no curtains on the window and only a bare bulb hanging down in the center of the room

"I want a round table for the middle right there." Barbara pointed to the place directly under the light bulb. "Maybe one of those old oak ones—you know, the ones that have leaves that you put in when you have company? I bought the classified ads so I can look and see if anyone has one to sell. It'd be perfect for Sunday dinners."

"Tables like that are hard to find," the sheriff said. "Even used they're a pretty penny."

Barbara nodded. "They're worth it though. There's a place to put a Tiffany-style lamp right over it. I can just see Bobby sitting there and doing his math homework. I should check the classifieds for a Tiffany-style lamp, too, although that's not likely to be listed."

"No, no, it's not," the sheriff said.

Barbara finally pulled herself away from the window. "Can we look in the living-room window too? I want to know what kind of a sofa to look for—it'll have to be used, of course, but there's still a pretty good selection."

The sheriff used his handkerchief to clean a circle on the next window too.

"Oh, there's still a rocking chair in there," Barbara said.

The living room was also square-shaped, but it

had a nice wood floor that Barbara thought would clean up nicely. With a little wax, it would even shine. The walls in this room were such a dirty mauve that she knew it had been a long time since anyone had painted or even cleaned the walls.

"There's two fair-sized bedrooms in the back and a third one that's pretty small off the dining room," the sheriff said. "One of them has a bed in it. That was the room old man Gossett slept in. I don't think there's much in the other rooms. Maybe some old dressers."

"I can get furniture," Barbara said. She was filled with confidence. She had the money from the pawnshop in her pocket and she'd make every penny count. If she was buying used, she should be able to furnish the whole house with the money she had.

Barbara would have kept looking in the windows even longer, except she wanted to help finish painting the fence before the children came home from school. She was full of excitement herself, but she didn't want to get the children's hopes up. She didn't know, after all, if the Gossett house would ever be available for her to rent.

After they walked back to where the sheriff had left the paint and brushes, he went to his car and opened the trunk. He held up two old sweatshirts. "The black one or the purple one?"

"Purple," Barbara said as she walked over to take the sweatshirt. "It's too nice a day to wear black."

"It's going to rain."

Barbara smiled as she took off her jacket. "All the more reason to wear purple. Now, can I leave this in your trunk?"

Barbara held out her jacket to the sheriff. He took it.

"You don't want to lose anything," the sheriff said as he carefully laid her jacket in the trunk. "Jackets like this should have zip pockets."

The sheriff put his hand right over the wad of twenty-dollar bills Barbara had in her pocket, but she wasn't sure if he saw them peeking out of the fold. He must not have, she decided, because he didn't say anything.

Not that there was any reason he shouldn't see the money, she told herself. She just didn't want people to know she had sold her wedding rings. There was something so sad about it, even though, she had to admit, she'd felt pretty good since she'd sold them. Thinking of all the furniture she could buy when she moved into a house with the children made her feel as though everything was possible.

Chapter Sixteen

Floyd stopped once he arrived in Miles City, and went to the grocery store to buy graham crackers. He had seen the boy eating graham crackers one day. Floyd hoped the boy would be reasonable and understand Floyd's need to keep him for a while.

He wouldn't hurt the boy any, Floyd told himself. Some boys would even like a little holiday away from school and their mothers. The room Floyd stayed at in the motel had a video player; maybe he should rent some cartoons for the boy or something.

It wouldn't be so bad. Especially if Floyd didn't need to take the girl, too.

Of course, it'd be easier if he took both children. He'd gotten a second note taped to his bathroom mirror last night. Again, all of Floyd's windows were secure and the new lock he had on his door had not been forced open. Whoever Harlow had working for him, the man was a professional.

Floyd didn't mind admitting he was scared.

But it would all be okay soon. Just as soon as the ex-wife got word to Neal that someone had his children, Neal would find a way to talk to Harlow. Neither of the men were in solitary confinement. They must talk. Harlow would listen to Neal, Floyd felt certain of that.

It would all work out just fine.

The sheriff wanted the night to turn to its blackest before he got up from the chair in his trailer. He'd been sitting here ever since he'd come home, trying to keep his suspicions from running around in his head. He'd seen that wad of twenties Barbara had in the pocket of her jacket.

Maybe Barbara had gotten the money someplace legitimately, but the sheriff knew she hadn't had that kind of money a couple of days ago. She'd had to walk over to the café to get change for the hundred-dollar bills that were under that geranium planter.

It looked as if Barbara had five or six hundred dollars in her pocket now. The bills had been crisp new bills, too—just the kind of bills a bank usually had.

Barbara didn't have a bank account, and she usually took her salary in cash. Since Lizette wasn't back from her honeymoon, no one had been around to pay Barbara.

The sheriff hated being suspicious, but he was. He'd almost forgotten that the FBI had asked him to watch Barbara Strong for this very reason. Those bills reminded him of his duty.

The sheriff put a jacket over his uniform before he walked to the door of his trailer and stepped outside. He didn't have a light on the outside of his trailer, so he always had to stand a bit when he first opened the door so his eyes could adjust to the dark. He shivered a little. The night air was cold and even damper than it had been earlier today. It still hadn't rained, but the air was heavy with it.

The sheriff looked over at the trees on his left. He could see the black shapes of their branches silhouetted against the night sky. Yesterday, when he'd come back to the trailer, he'd gone over there and stood on the spot where he'd thought about building that log house. Ever since then, his eyes had been drawn to that spot when he stepped out of his trailer. He shook his head. He supposed there was just no stopping a fool from dreaming.

The sheriff could not remember a time when he'd disliked his job—until now. Even so, that wouldn't stop him from doing it.

The first thing he needed to do was check under that planter on Barbara's porch. He'd been thinking that maybe she'd just borrowed those hundred dollar bills and taken them somewhere to get them changed into twenties. He couldn't fault her for that; in fact, he was hoping that was what had happened. If those bills were gone, he could just go home and go to sleep.

It wasn't more than twenty minutes later that the sheriff stood in the dark on the gravel road that ran through Dry Creek. There were no lights showing from any of the houses. He'd parked his car along the side of the road a little before he got to the buildings. Now, he would walk the rest of the way into town.

The town of Dry Creek wasn't much more than a dozen or so buildings, half on one side of the gravel road and half on the other. Not one of the buildings was anything to brag about. None of the houses had swimming pools in their backyards, in fact, they barely had backyards. Spring had not fully come to Dry Creek and there were no green lawns sprouting anywhere.

The sheriff knew Dry Creek wouldn't make it onto most maps. But it was his town and his responsibility. He had sworn to keep it safe.

The sheriff stepped off the gravel road when he came close to the building where Barbara lived. She and the children were in the back room and should be asleep by now, but he didn't want to make any unnecessary noise. The hardware store was across the street, but no one was there. The sheriff had never noticed how black the night could be in Dry Creek.

Barbara was right about them needing a street-light, the sheriff thought as he finished walking to the steps. The planter was close to the edge of the small porch. He lifted it easily while standing on the dirt beside the porch. The night dew had already made the wood planter cold and damp.

The sheriff had good eyes. He couldn't miss the bills lying there on the porch. He saw the two hundred-dollar bills on the bottom and a couple of twenties on top. He put the planter back down.

There was nothing he could do tonight, the sheriff told himself as he started to walk back to his car. He wasn't going to wake those two kids up just so he could question their mother about laundering stolen money. Not that he'd get any sleep tonight himself.

The sheriff had to walk past the church to get to his car and he had a sudden urge to sit for a while on the steps of the church. He lowered himself until he was doing just that. Then he put his head in his hands. He figured it was as close to praying as he knew how to get. He hoped that God knew what he was so stirred up about, even if he couldn't seem to put it into words himself. The sheriff sat there for a good half hour before standing up and walking to his car. It was going to be a long night, he thought, as he slid into the driver's side of his car and turned on the heater.

* * *

Barbara woke up early. It was five o'clock in the morning and she couldn't lie in bed any longer, so she hugged her robe around her and pulled one of the folding chairs up to the folding table. She didn't want to turn a light on and wake up the children, so she reached for the classified ads section of the newspaper she had bought yesterday.

There wasn't enough light filtering in through the curtains for her to actually read the classifieds, but Barbara liked holding the pages anyway. She was as excited as the children were at Christmas, maybe more so. After she got the bakery orders out, Barbara planned to sit down with the telephone and make a few calls on items in those ads.

The children wouldn't get back from school until four o'clock this afternoon. A person could set their watch by the school bus and Barbara knew she'd be able to make a lot of calls before then. If everything went her way, she might even be able to arrange for delivery of some of the things she was buying.

Barbara smiled just thinking of the squeals the children would make when they saw real furniture in this place.

Barbara went to the stove and turned on a burner under the teakettle. She'd boil some water for tea and instant oatmeal for breakfast. Maybe she'd even make some French toast as well. It was, after all, a special morning. Who knew what delights the day could bring?

Unfortunately, after breakfast it took an extra long time for the children to get dressed because Bobby had lost a button on the shirt he wanted to wear. Barbara knew she had a needle and thread in a small tin box, but it took her a while to find the box. When they had a real house, she told herself, she'd have everything in its appointed place so she'd always know where to find anything at any time. That alone would be a luxury.

In the meantime, she was fortunate to have found the sewing tin in the suitcase with the winter coats. She'd packed up those coats a week ago when spring seemed so close. The weather now was overcast, though, and Barbara wondered if she shouldn't bring the heavy coats back out for another week or two.

She pulled Bobby's coat out of the suitcase. "Maybe you should take this coat today."

She gave Amanda her coat as well. "It's a cold day today."

Twenty minutes later, Barbara stood on the porch and watched the children climb into the school bus. The bus held about thirty passengers, and all of the children from Dry Creek rode it to go to school in Miles City. At first, Barbara had been doubtful about leaving her children with the bus driver, but she soon saw that Bobby and Amanda made friends with the other children on the bus. Sometimes, she thought riding the bus was the best part of the day for them.

Barbara watched the school bus as it drove down the road out of Dry Creek and then she turned to go back into the building that was as much dance studio as it was bakery. Lizette had opened the dance studio before she had the bakery, so Barbara always thought of the space as a studio first and foremost.

The counter in the back room helped with the bakery operations and Barbara had three final pies in the oven. Linda said the café could use two pies regularly now that business was growing. Barbara had made an apple and a blueberry.

She smiled a little bit to herself, wondering if the sheriff would have a piece of the blueberry pie when it was at the café later. The man sure did enjoy his food.

The telephone call came just as Barbara picked up her classified ads again. She'd sat down at the folding table not two minutes earlier. It was almost eight o'clock, and the work of the day was already done.

"Hello," Barbara said as she pulled the telephone over to the table.

Barbara heard the man's breathing before he began to speak. She knew then that it was the same man who had called about the cake. She was going to hang up when the man spoke.

"I have your kids." The man's voice was low and thick, as if he was trying to disguise it.

"Amanda and Bobby!"

"Called them over, right off the bus stop. Said I had word from their father."

"That's impossible," Barbara said. Whoever that man was, he was a sick, sick individual.

"Listen," the man said.

"Mommy?"

Barbara would know Bobby's voice anywhere. "Where are you?"

"He doesn't know," the man said with a chuckle. "But don't worry about it. You'll have them both back soon enough if you do what I say."

"I'll do anything," Barbara whispered. She knew that wasn't a good negotiating tactic, but she wanted the man to know she would do whatever he asked. "I have a few hundred dollars—"

The man laughed louder. "That's nothing."

"I could borrow—"

"Lady, I'm not asking for money. All I want is for you to go to your ex-husband and tell him he's got to get Harlow to give me more time. Tell him to stop whoever is leaving those notes for me. But first call the school and tell them your kids are out sick."

The man was crazy, Barbara thought, but at least he asked for something she could do. "I can take that message to Neal."

"Oh, and don't tell anyone. You understand me? No cops. And call the school."

Barbara nodded. "Yes, of course."

"Just tell Neal I've got his kids."

The man hung up before Barbara could say anything else.

Barbara sat at the table, frozen with the telephone in her hand. Please, don't let her children's fate rest with Neal, she thought to herself. She had no idea if Neal would care enough to do anything for the children.

Maybe the man would call back later and she could tell him to ask for something else. No, she realized, she couldn't wait for the man to call. She would have to get a message to Neal.

Barbara was already dressed in blue jeans and a cotton blouse, so she just pulled her own winter jacket out of the suitcase and put it on. At least she'd given the kids their winter jackets this morning. She'd hate to think they were cold wherever they were.

There was only one way for her to get a message to Neal, Barbara knew. She had to go to the prison in Billings and ask to see him the way she'd done on Saturday. She could only hope that Mrs. Hargrove would let her borrow the car again today.

Barbara was almost to the door when she remembered the money in her other jacket. She went back and pulled it out of the pocket. She might need it.

* * *

The sheriff had gotten a phone call from an old rancher north of Dry Creek around seven o'clock in the morning. The man wasn't technically in the sheriff's territory, but he wanted help and the sheriff never turned anyone away. The man thought someone might be stealing cattle from him, and he wanted the sheriff to come and look around.

Since he hadn't been able to sleep, the sheriff was happy to have an excuse to drive up into that country. Some of the winter frost still clung to the ground there. Later, green would start spreading along the hills, but until then the dead grass of last year lay flattened to the ground, giving the hills their dried brown look.

It didn't take the sheriff long to find a break in the fence, and the man found his cattle not too far from there. By then, the sheriff realized that the man was just lonely so he accepted the rancher's offer to have a cup of coffee with him after they'd chased the cattle back into his pasture.

It was a gloomy day, and the sheriff didn't mind sharing part of it with another lonesome soul.

When he'd procrastinated as much as he could, the sheriff headed into Dry Creek. He had to question Barbara Strong, and he'd just as soon do it while the children were in school. The thought of what he had to do made the air feel cold, and the sheriff put his heater on for the drive into town.

The sheriff pulled into town at the same time that Barbara was walking down the street toward Mrs. Hargrove's house. Actually, the sheriff noticed, it would be more accurate to say Barbara was running.

Although the sheriff didn't want the children around when he talked to Barbara, he didn't mind talking to the woman in front of Mrs. Hargrove. The older woman could pick a liar out better than anyone he'd seen, including himself. She probably got it from all of her years teaching Sunday school. Not that it mattered much where Mrs. Hargrove got her skill. The sheriff could use another set of eyes. He didn't trust himself on this one.

Chapter Seventeen

Barbara was breathing hard when she knocked on the front door of Mrs. Hargrove's house. She usually went to the older woman's back door, but today Barbara didn't want to take the extra time to walk around the house when the front door was right there. The middle section of the door had a glass panel with a lace curtain hanging over it.

Barbara knew her face was red from walking in the cold, and she hoped that would explain the tears that kept slipping from her eyes. She needed to appear normal enough to ask Mrs. Hargrove about borrowing her car without raising the older woman's suspicions that anything was wrong. If Mrs. Hargrove thought something was wrong, she wouldn't let up until she knew what it was. Barbara knew she couldn't tell anyone.

The man on the phone hadn't specifically said she

couldn't tell Mrs. Hargrove about the danger to her children, but Barbara didn't want to take any chances. *Oh, Bobby and Amanda,* she thought, *hang on.*

Barbara heard the sounds of Mrs. Hargrove walking across her wooden floor toward the door at the same time that she heard a car pull in front of Mrs. Hargrove's house. Barbara didn't even turn around to see who had come to visit Mrs. Hargrove. She just hoped that whoever it was would distract the older woman so she didn't look too carefully at Barbara's face.

"Well, hello, dear," Mrs. Hargrove said when she opened the door. "Come in out of the cold."

Mrs. Hargrove was wearing a pink gingham dress with a zipper up the front. She wore a navy cardigan sweater over the dress and a white apron around her waist. Her gray hair was wrapped around soft green curlers and her feet were in tennis shoes.

"I have hot water on the stove, dear, if you'd like a cup of tea," the older woman said as she stepped back into the house so Barbara could enter.

Barbara knew Mrs. Hargrove had seen the distress on her face. She shook her head and stayed where she was. "I'm in a hurry, but I do have a favor to ask."

Mrs. Hargrove nodded. "What can I do?"

Barbara heard the footsteps behind her. Whoever had stopped to visit would be at the top of the steps soon. Barbara knew she needed to get her request out there quickly. Maybe then the other person could distract Mrs. Hargrove.

"I'd like to borrow your car." Barbara tried to keep the desperation out of her voice. "I need to drive into Billings."

Barbara knew someone stood on the step beside her. She didn't even need to turn her head to know it was the sheriff. She could see the brim of his hat out of the side of her eye. She felt a sudden gladness that he was there, until she realized that she couldn't tell him anything about what was wrong. That man had said he would hurt her children if she told a cop. The sheriff was the last person she could tell.

"I can take you to Billings," the sheriff offered.

He must not like her asking to use Mrs. Hargrove's car, Barbara thought. She couldn't think of any other reason for the cold edge in his voice.

"I'm planning to pay for the gas, of course," Barbara added. She'd filled the gas tank before for Mrs. Hargrove. "And give her maybe twenty or so extra for—" Barbara spread her hands "—wear on the tires and all."

"Oh, but you don't—" Mrs. Hargrove began.

"You're sure free with your money these days," the sheriff said. He drew the words out, and there wasn't a friendly sound in any of them. "Did you get a raise or something?"

"Carl!" Mrs. Hargrove sounded startled.

Barbara blushed even more at the tone in the sheriff's voice. She stepped farther away from him so she could turn and look at his face fully.

"I don't have time to stand here and talk about my salary," Barbara said. She needed to focus on the children. She used to be good at putting a mask on to hide her feelings when Neal started yelling at her. She'd never thought she'd have to use it with the sheriff.

"Of course, you don't, dear," Mrs. Hargrove said as she reached out a hand toward Barbara. "Just give me a minute to get the keys to my car."

Mrs. Hargrove stepped farther back into her house. Barbara wished the sheriff would go inside with her neighbor. Or turn around and leave. She didn't see any need for him to keep standing with her in front of Mrs. Hargrove's door. They looked like salespeople.

"I never did ask you how Neal was doing the other day," the sheriff finally said.

"You might not have, but your friends did," Barbara said wearily. She hadn't really minded all of the questions the staff at the prison had asked about Neal. She was open to telling them anything she knew.

The sheriff nodded. "I don't suppose he had a message for the children or anything. Something you forgot to tell the others."

"I didn't forget anything."

Ten minutes ago, Barbara had believed she was

building a life here. But she had been wrong. Everything was slipping away. She'd thought she and the children were safe in Dry Creek. She'd been wrong about that. She'd thought she would make friends here; she was beginning to wonder if that would ever happen.

She'd even started to think the sheriff was different from other men she'd known. It looked like she'd been wrong about that, too.

Barbara kept looking straight ahead until Mrs. Hargrove came back with the keys.

"Here it is dear." The older woman held out the key ring to Barbara.

"Is there anything you'd like to tell me before you go?" the sheriff asked stiffly.

Barbara shook her head as she took the keys from Mrs. Hargrove.

"Is there trouble?" Mrs. Hargrove asked as her eyes went back and forth from the sheriff to Barbara.

"Everything's fine," Barbara said. "I just need to go into Billings."

"I'm asking again if I can drive you," the sheriff said.

Barbara shook her head. She kept her hand curled around those keys. She didn't know what she would do if Mrs. Hargrove asked for them back.

"You're not sick, are you, dear?" Mrs. Hargrove asked anxiously. "If you've got some bad news from a doctor or something, you shouldn't be by yourself. I could go with you."

"I'm fine alone," Barbara said. She did smile at the older woman, however. At least Mrs. Hargrove was being kind, unlike the other person standing here. "I haven't heard from any doctor. My health is good."

Unless you counted the fact that her heart was being squeezed by fear, Barbara thought to herself.

"But you don't need to be alone," Mrs. Hargrove insisted as she reached behind the door. "I've got my purse right here. I think it's best if I come with you."

"Oh, no, I couldn't—that is, I'll be fine without—" Barbara stammered.

Mrs. Hargrove was already stepping out onto her porch and pulling her door shut behind her. "It's no problem. I could use some more peppermints anyway. I like to keep them on hand for guests."

"I thought you had water boiling for tea," Barbara said. There had to be some sane reason why Mrs. Hargrove couldn't go.

"I turned it off when I got the keys," Mrs. Hargrove said as she walked between Barbara and the sheriff to head down her steps. "I like to be ready for what the day holds. Sometimes God just gives me a feeling that tells me to go, and that's when I head out. Like now."

Mrs. Hargrove turned around to grin at Barbara

and the sheriff. Barbara felt something shift in the sheriff's manner, and she looked him in the face again. He gave her a wry smile.

At least, Barbara thought, the sheriff was looking her in the eye again.

"I thought that was just your arthritis talking," the sheriff said as he turned to Mrs. Hargrove. "It does look like rain out."

"Don't you be doubting the Lord's leading, Carl Wall. You'll see for yourself what I'm talking about someday." Mrs. Hargrove clucked as she made her way down her steps and then looked back up the stairs. "Well, is anyone else coming or not?"

Barbara figured there had to be some way to be in the same car with Mrs. Hargrove for the long drive into Billings without telling the older woman what was happening. She might even find it comforting just to have someone sitting beside her as she worried about Bobby and Amanda.

The sheriff decided he should just deputize Mrs. Hargrove one of these days and be done with it. He watched as the two women drove off in Mrs. Hargrove's old rattletrap of a car. The muffler was blowing a little smoke, but he was sure that wouldn't stop the women. If he ever needed backup, he should remember Mrs. Hargrove did a fine job of picking up the slack.

* * *

Barbara wasn't a mile out of Dry Creek before she saw that there was a car following her. It was the sheriff's car, of course. At first, she thought she was just being paranoid, and that he was just going in the same direction as she was. There was, after all, only one road between Dry Creek and the interstate. Barbara deliberately slowed down so the sheriff could pass. He didn't pass her. She sped up and he went faster.

"He's following us," Barbara said indignantly.

Mrs. Hargrove nodded brightly. "I thought he might. Carl's a man of strong emotions."

Barbara didn't want to argue with Mrs. Hargrove, especially not when she was sitting in the woman's car, but she couldn't let the older woman weave any fantasies either. "I don't think this is about his emotions."

Barbara didn't want to press her foot to the gas pedal too hard. She'd noticed that the muffler was making a little noise. The whole car shook some, but she supposed that was only to be expected given the car's age.

"You never did tell me how you got this car," Barbara said. That should give Mrs. Hargrove something to talk about. It was a safe topic.

"It used to belong to Mr. Gossett," the older woman said. "He gave it to me one year for Christmas. He said it was to pay me back for all the loaves of plum bread I'd given to him over the years."

The older woman smiled. "Of course, I refused, even though the car wasn't worth much back then either. It's a 1971, you know."

"What changed your mind?" Barbara looked in the rearview mirror. The sheriff was still there.

"He started trying to bake *me* loaves of plum bread," the older woman said and then chuckled. "He was determined to pay me back, and I feared he'd burn his house down if he kept trying to bake."

Even the thought of Mr. Gossett's house couldn't get Barbara's mind to relax. She felt as if someone had come along and twisted her whole body into knots. "Do you really think it's going to rain?"

Barbara didn't know if Bobby and Amanda were being kept outdoors or not. They could catch pneumonia if it rained. The nights were still so cold around here.

"Is rain what's bothering you?"

Barbara shook her head. "Just curious."

"I see," Mrs. Hargrove said as she looked straight ahead.

The older woman was silent for a while. "The windshield wipers don't work very well. I don't think I told you that. I was going to have Carl fix them when he fixes the muffler."

Barbara nodded. She had refused to look in

the rearview mirror for the past five minutes, and her neck was beginning to ache from the tension of keeping her head from doing what it wanted to do. Oh, well. She looked up to steal a glance at the mirror. The sheriff was still there.

"If the sheriff isn't coming along because of his emotions, is it because it's his duty?" Mrs. Hargrove quietly asked.

Barbara didn't move a muscle.

Mrs. Hargrove waited a minute. "Sometimes people think that if they've done something against the law there's no hope, but the law is there as much to help as to hurt. It gives a person a chance to make a new beginning."

"I can't tell you what's wrong," Barbara finally said. If she didn't admit that much, Mrs. Hargrove would be digging away at her until they got to Billings.

The older woman nodded. "Well, if it comes the time when you can tell me, I'm here to listen."

"Thank you," Barbara said.

"I know how hard it is to trust again when someone has betrayed you," Mrs. Hargrove said.

Barbara swallowed. "It's not that I don't trust—"

Barbara stopped. She couldn't even finish that sentence. Of course she didn't trust anyone. The man on the phone had told her not to tell the cops, but Barbara acknowledged to herself that she wouldn't have told anyone anyway. She was used to solving her own problems. Or trying to, at least. For the first time in a long time, she wished it weren't so. She'd give anything to have a friend who could share this burden. She was afraid to even mention Bobby's or Amanda's names for fear she'd start to cry and it would all spill out.

"Trust was one of the hardest things I had to learn, too," Mrs. Hargrove said as she opened the purse she held on her lap and rummaged around inside it. Finally, she pulled out a roll of butterscotch candy. She held the roll out to Barbara. "Want one?"

Barbara shook her head.

Mrs. Hargrove nodded and then unwrapped one of the candies and put it in her mouth. "Took me a long time to trust God. I finally realized I couldn't do it until I learned to trust people some first. So, I started with my husband." Mrs. Hargrove smiled. "But you don't want to hear an old woman's story."

"Yes, I do," Barbara said before she saw the gleam in the older woman's eyes and realized she'd fallen for the bait.

Mrs. Hargrove began to talk, and Barbara let the words flow over her. It was soothing. The older woman talked about her days as a newly married woman who'd just moved to the small town of Dry Creek. Mrs. Hargrove was an undemanding story-teller and was content with Barbara's occasional comments. It gave Barbara time to worry about Bobby and Amanda in peace. And to think about trust. The more the older woman talked, the more Barbara wanted to tell someone that a bad man had her children and it was all up to Barbara to save them.

She just felt so inadequate, Barbara admitted to herself. The reason she didn't trust others was not because she thought she didn't need anyone or that she should do it all by herself. She just did not have any faith that anyone would help.

There was a flash of red, and Barbara looked in the rearview mirror.

"What's—" Barbara started to say.

The sheriff had just turned on his siren.

Barbara pulled over. She drummed her fingers on the steering wheel as she waited for the sheriff to walk up beside the car and motion for her to roll down her window.

"I wasn't speeding," Barbara said when she rolled down the window. "You can ask Mrs. Hargrove here."

"Hi, Carl," the older woman said as she looked over to see the sheriff, who had bent down so his face could be seen in the driver's-side window.

"I know you weren't speeding," the sheriff said. "I just thought I should get that muffler hooked on a little better or you're going to be blowing black smoke here soon. Then I'd have to give you a ticket for polluting the air."

"We don't have time," Barbara said.

"It'll only take fifteen minutes," the sheriff said. "The thing needs to cool off a little before I do anything. Why don't you pull off on that road up ahead? There's a couple of trees down in that coulee. You and Mrs. Hargrove could take a little walk."

"I have a can of peaches in the trunk," Mrs. Hargrove said. "We could have a picnic."

The older woman was already reaching up and unwrapping the curlers she'd worn all morning.

"That's the spirit," the sheriff said as he stood back up. "I'll meet you there."

Barbara rolled her window back up. "The muffler's not that bad. He didn't have to stop us now."

"Oh, I agree," the older woman said as she took out her last curler. "Like I say. It's his emotions."

"Well, if you count emotions as being stubborn, nosy, and hard to understand, then I guess it is."

Mrs. Hargrove chuckled. "My husband and I went on a picnic with nothing but peaches back when we were courting." The older woman looked sideways at Barbara. "Of course, that was before I'd learned to trust him."

Barbara nodded. She hoped that man on the phone would understand about a lunch break. She supposed she should be glad that it was only going to take fifteen minutes.

Before long, the sheriff slid out from under Mrs. Hargrove's car, stood up and wiped his hands on a rag he kept in his trunk for such purposes. They didn't have a highway patrol near Dry Creek and the sheriff had found it useful to learn a fair amount about fixing cars. Sometimes there just wasn't a tow truck around that could come and the sheriff was the only official who was there to help.

Of course, he always worked on Mrs. Hargrove's car anyway. He figured it would be good experience if he ever wanted to work for a museum. The mustard-colored car had been around for over thirty years, and its outside was starting to fade to a dirty yellow. The car's inside, under the hood, didn't bear thinking about.

Anyway, fixing a car always steadied him some, and he wanted to see how Mrs. Hargrove and Barbara were coming along. He looked down the slight incline where the two women had walked. Mrs. Hargrove had found a small blanket in her trunk and Barbara was spreading it on the ground now.

The sheriff figured that, unless it was something illegal, Mrs. Hargrove would get Barbara to talk about what was wrong. So far, that hadn't happened. He didn't have a good feeling about the situation at all. Barbara wasn't the kind of person to panic over nothing. And he could see that she was just about as rattled as a person could be without spilling any secrets. He knew he should be pressing her to talk, but he just couldn't do it.

And that was why, the sheriff told himself as he started to climb down the shallow incline to where the women were, a sheriff needed to forget about having any friends.

Chapter Eighteen

Barbara could still taste the peach juice on her lips when they got into Billings. The sheriff was still following them and Mrs. Hargrove was still being so nice that Barbara wanted to cry. It was all too much.

Barbara parked the car on a side street next to the prison. The sheriff parked his car right behind her.

"Will you stay with Mrs. Hargrove?" Barbara asked as she opened the car door and saw the sheriff already walking toward their car.

Barbara noticed that the coldness had left the sheriff's face. Now, he looked more weary and sad than anything else.

"I'm the sheriff. You can tell me what's wrong."

Barbara shook her head. "I can't be seen with you. Don't follow me inside."

The sheriff nodded. "You have your rights. I can't stop you from trying to see your ex-husband."

"*Trying* to see him?" Barbara looked up. She'd never thought about being refused admittance. "They can't stop me, can they?"

"He is in jail," the sheriff said. "They let you talk to him the other day because they were hoping he would tell you something."

"But I need to talk to him—I—"

Barbara couldn't stand there any longer. She turned her back and started walking down the street to the prison.

"I'll call and ask them to let you talk to him," the sheriff said.

Barbara turned around when the sheriff spoke. "Thank you."

The sheriff nodded.

Once Barbara was inside the prison's main office, she knew she wouldn't have been allowed to see her ex-husband if the sheriff hadn't called. It wasn't the right time of day, and Neal wasn't scheduled for visitors anyway. They told her she'd have to wait almost a half hour, but they did agree to let her see him.

Neal looked surprised to see her. "I wondered who was here."

Barbara waited for Neal to be seated at the Plexiglas division and for the guard to walk away before she began to speak. "I need to talk to you. A man called on the phone. He has Bobby and Amanda and he says you have to talk to Harlow somebody and ask Harlow for more time. And to stop sending the notes. The notes were important."

Neal's surprise deepened and then turned to caution. "Who told you I know any Harlow?"

"Please, Neal, you need to help. The children are in trouble."

"Is this some kind of a trap?" Neal looked over his shoulder at the guard.

"Please, Neal, these are your children. They could be cold or worse."

Barbara had never begged Neal for anything in their years of marriage. But she didn't care any longer. She couldn't afford her pride when her children needed her. "Please, please—I'm so afraid of what will happen."

Neal snorted. "You don't even know that some man has the kids."

"I heard Bobby's voice on the phone. Please— I—"

Neal stood up and turned to the guard. "I need to go back now."

Barbara watched as her ex-husband walked away from the partition. She'd never felt so much despair in all her days of knowing Neal. How could a father abandon his children this way?

Finally, Neal disappeared behind the prison door, and Barbara was the only one left at the Plexiglas divider. She slowly got up and started to walk to the door. For the first time, she was glad that Mrs. Hargrove had come with her into Billings. Barbara didn't know if she'd have the strength to drive the car back alone.

The prison didn't clank as much as she expected, Barbara thought to herself as she walked down the hall to the main office. But the floor was squeaky, and it did smell. She would never forget what hopelessness smelled like.

The air outside the prison was as chilly as it had been when Barbara had entered the place almost an hour ago. She hoped the children remembered to zip up their jackets so they wouldn't be cold.

The sidewalk led Barbara down toward where she had parked Mrs. Hargrove's car. There was no grass anywhere.

When Barbara could see Mrs. Hargrove's car, she saw a man standing outside it with his back facing her. The man was leaning in the window and talking to Mrs. Hargrove. It looked like the sheriff, only Barbara knew it couldn't be. The man wasn't wearing a uniform.

As Barbara walked closer, she saw that the man was wearing a light denim shirt and darker denim jeans. A leather belt curled around his waist. One of the ranch hands from Dry Creek must be in Billings, Barbara thought.

It wasn't until she got closer and the man stood up and saw her that she recognized him.

It was the sheriff.

Barbara had hoped to be able to get into the car without having an argument with him. Maybe she still could, she thought. The sheriff must be planning to stay in Billings and socialize or something. He was certainly never without his uniform in Dry Creek.

The sheriff didn't say anything as she walked closer. He just watched her.

Finally, when she was only a few feet away he spoke. "How did it go?"

Barbara nodded. "Fine."

There was a silence. Barbara looked at the ground.

"I figure you don't want to talk to me because I'm the sheriff."

Barbara looked up when he said that.

"But I was wondering if you could talk to me if I was your friend, Carl."

Barbara blinked back a tear only to have another one fight to fall.

"I know you're in trouble, and I'd like to help. As your friend."

Barbara hiccupped.

"I even went to a store and bought new clothes so I wouldn't scare you with the uniform."

Barbara nodded. "They're nice."

Finally, Carl opened his arms wide.

Barbara couldn't help herself. She threw herself into his arms. "Someone has my children and I don't know what to do."

The tears were all over her face by now, Barbara noticed as she tried to wipe them away. She no longer felt chilled once Carl wrapped his arms around her. When she talked, she talked into his shoulder.

Carl rocked her a little as he stood there. "We'll find them. I promise."

"You can't promise," Barbara said as she attempted to raise her head from his shoulder. "No one can promise."

"I can," he whispered. "I'll find them."

Barbara was too exhausted to make any decisions. But that was okay, because Carl was doing everything that was needed. He called another sheriff he knew and arranged for the man to drive the county car back to Dry Creek. At the same time, he told the man that there had been a kidnapping, but that he didn't want a lot of uniformed officers walking around Dry Creek as that could endanger the children who were missing. They made arrangements for one officer, who was already near Dry Creek on some other business, to go there now, and others would come later.

Then Carl insisted on driving Mrs. Hargrove's car back home.

"Barbara can't be seen in my car," he told the older woman, and she nodded as though that explained everything.

"If your legs would fit in the backseat, I'd offer to drive so the two of you could sit together back there," Mrs. Hargrove said.

"I don't mind a muscle cramp or two," Carl said. "But I thought Barbara would need to rest."

Mrs. Hargrove shrugged. "Seems to me she could rest just fine on one of those big shoulders of yours."

Barbara wondered when they would stop talking about her as if she weren't there. She didn't protest too much though, especially not when Carl settled her in the backseat with his arm around her and her head on his shoulder.

"Now, tell me everything you can think of that might help the kids," Carl said as Mrs. Hargrove started the car.

Barbara told Carl everything she could think of, from the eerie feeling she'd had that they were being watched to the color of the socks that Bobby and Amanda had each worn to school today.

"Did you think to call the pastor while you were

making your calls?" Mrs. Hargrove asked as she stopped at a traffic light. "Tell him we have a request for the prayer chain and that some little children need help urgently. The pastor will understand when you say we can't name names. But he'll get the calls going."

"What's a prayer chain?" Barbara asked.

"It's a telephone list we use when we have an emergency prayer request. Each person on the list calls the person below them on the list until everyone knows they need to be praying."

"They would all pray for Amanda and Bobby?"

Mrs. Hargrove snorted as the light changed and she started the car forward. "They prayed for Charley's bunions; they'll pray for Amanda and Bobby."

Barbara couldn't imagine a whole town that would care about someone's feet enough to spend two minutes thinking about them, let alone praying about them.

"Does it work?"

Mrs. Hargrove was out on the open road now. "Well, we're still waiting on the bunions. The doctor says that Charley needs to give up his boots to get rid of the bunions. So now we're praying about the boots. Giving up his boots would be a big change for Charley."

Carl made the call to the pastor. "A couple of other sheriffs—undercover—are coming to help me for a bit. The first one will be there in ten minutes. I'm going to ask him to go look in the pine trees on the old Gossett place. There's some wrappers for antacid tablets there. I'd appreciate it if you'd point out to him where the Gossett place is. Then see if anyone knows where a person can buy that brand of antacid tablets around here. Sorry I can't tell you more. But I appreciate it."

Once the call was made, there was silence in the car.

Barbara kept searching her mind for anything she could remember that would help her children. "They're just so little."

Carl nodded. "We'll find them."

Barbara raised her head from Carl's shoulder long enough to wipe at the damp place that had absorbed her tears. "Sorry about getting you all wet."

Carl's arm tightened around her. "Denim dries."

That made Barbara want to cry some more.

The town of Dry Creek came into view as the sun had almost set. Barbara realized she'd never driven into town at quite this hour. The sky was deep pink from what was left of the sunset. The whole town was lit up; it looked as though a light was turned on brightly in every room of every store and house in town.

"What's happening?" Barbara asked as they saw the lights.

Even the church was lit up. Barbara looked more closely. Maybe it was lit up even brighter than the other buildings. And cars were parked everywhere around the church. "Is there a meeting at the church?"

"Not that I know of," Mrs. Hargrove said as she drove the car past her house and stopped outside the church. "Let's see what it is."

Barbara nodded. She wondered if something else bad had happened in Dry Creek. Maybe someone was sick or something.

The three of them went into the church together. It was Mrs. Hargrove though who asked Jacob what was happening. Jacob was standing beside the door with his hat in his hands.

"There's some little kids in trouble," Jacob whispered. "Some of the women are praying. We think they might be lost somewhere. So we lit all the lights in town so they can see us if they come close, and the men and the women who are up to riding are out on horses looking for any strays."

"They're not lost," Barbara said and couldn't speak anymore. She had never known anyone to care about her and the children this much. They didn't even know it was Amanda and Bobby who were missing. They were ready to help any little children who needed them.

"They're not?" Jacob scratched his head. "We thought that when that other sheriff came asking about those wrappers for antacid pills that the children had left them in some kind of a trail. That sheriff wouldn't tell us nothing about what was going on."

Jacob looked at Carl indignantly. "You might speak to him about that."

Carl nodded. "I might. Did he find out anything about those wrappers?"

"Marlene Olson said they sold that brand at the grocery store where her cousin works in Miles City. Not every store carries them, she said. Seemed proud of the fact, like it was some big deal," Jacob said.

"Is that the Country Market?" the sheriff asked.

Jacob nodded. "That's the one all right."

Barbara felt Carl pull away from her. "I've got to go change and do a few things," he said. "I'll leave you here with Mrs. Hargrove."

"You don't need to worry about me," Barbara said.

"I know." Carl smiled. "Maybe I want to though."

Barbara didn't have an answer to that. Maybe she didn't need one, she thought, as she watched Carl walk away.

"How long did it take you to trust your husband?" Barbara asked, turning to Mrs. Hargrove.

The older woman smiled. "About as long as it will take you to trust Carl."

Barbara sat in a church pew until the night was deep. Mrs. Hargrove and several of the other women still sat in the church, sometimes praying and sometimes singing a song. Barbara wondered how she could feel such contentment and such anxiety all at the same time.

"I've made some more tea," Mrs. Hargrove whispered as she came over and sat beside Barbara. "Are you sure you won't have some? Linda brought over some pie, too."

"Oh, the bakery stuff," Barbara suddenly remembered. "I never made any of the deliveries this morning."

"Don't worry," Mrs. Hargrove said. "You can have a day-old sale tomorrow."

"Today, you mean," Barbara said. The last time she had looked at her watch it had been one o'clock in the morning. Carl had been gone for over six hours now. "I wonder if Bobby and Amanda are sleeping."

Mrs. Hargrove put her hand on Barbara's arm and squeezed it.

The phone rang somewhere in the distance.

"That'll be in the pastor's study," Mrs. Hargrove said as she stood up. "I'll go answer it."

"It could be Carl," Barbara said as she rose, too.

The two women walked to the back room.

The phone call was from one of the men working at the Elkton ranch. He'd been trying to call his sister in Miles City. It was a wrong number.

"Tonight of all nights," Mrs. Hargrove muttered sympathetically as she put her arm around Barbara and they walked back toward the main part of the church.

The church had long windows that rose above the pews on both sides. They were frosted so no one could see through them clearly. In the front of the church there was a large cross.

Barbara felt she'd found a home here tonight in this church. Even if she didn't find all of the answers she needed, she'd found a comfort within these walls. She didn't walk reluctantly back to the main room. Mrs. Hargrove had told her they called the room the sanctuary and she thought it was a fitting name.

The pastor's study was joined to the sanctuary by a hall, and the two women had almost finished walking the length of the hallway when the door at the back of the sanctuary opened. Barbara didn't see the door open because she was still in the hallway, but she heard it.

"Mommy," she heard Bobby's voice call out softly.

"Oh," Barbara said as she ran through the doorway and into the sanctuary. At the back of the room Bobby stood with his hand in Carl's. Amanda was curled up asleep in Carl's other arm.

"Oh," Barbara said again as she raced down the aisle to meet them.

Bobby let go of Carl's hand and flung himself into Barbara's arms as she knelt down to hug him.

Barbara breathed in the smell of her boy and ran her hands over his back and his arms to be sure he was okay. By then Amanda had awakened and was reaching for her mother as well.

"Thank you." Barbara looked up to Carl as she held her arms out for Amanda. "Thank you so much."

Carl nodded. "We arrested the man who had them, and I still have some paperwork to do that will require me talking to them, but, for tonight, you can take them home and put them to bed. They've had a long day."

"Thank you." Barbara repeated herself. She wished she knew something clever to say to thank Carl, but she didn't. "Thank you so much."

Barbara spent the rest of the night just watching Bobby and Amanda sleep. She had such a sense of gratitude for their well-being. It didn't seem sufficient just to thank the sheriff. She knew that part of tonight's rescue was due to the prayers and concern of the people of Dry Creek as well. She didn't even know how to thank the sheriff adequately; she had no idea whatsoever about how to thank God. For now, she'd just have to be content with the feeling she had that He knew. Tomorrow, she'd ask Mrs. Hargrove to help her say a prayer of thanks.

The next morning dawned slowly. A pink blush swept the sky before gray clouds pushed it away. Barbara had baked goods she needed to prepare for today and the children had school. Perhaps, though, she thought, they all needed a day of rest. Barbara would do the standing orders for the bakery, but she would keep the children home from school. In fact, until she found out more about how they had disappeared from school, she wasn't sure she was comfortable with sending them back anyway.

Bobby was the one who told Barbara how it all happened. The bus had gotten to school a little earlier than usual and Bobby had followed Amanda off the bus. Amanda was the one who first heard the man in the car saying he had a message for them from their father. Amanda started to walk over and Bobby followed her.

"I was like Daniel," Bobby informed Barbara proudly when she served him some scrambled eggs at breakfast. "I just trusted God that no lion would get me and Amanda."

"There's no lions around here, silly," Amanda giggled.

Barbara was glad Amanda didn't seem to realize the dangers they had faced.

Barbara had already hugged her children so many times last night and this morning that Bobby was becoming indignant about it. Instead of giving him another hug, she smiled at him. "I trusted Him, too."

Barbara wondered if trust always came from desperation.

"I trusted the sheriff too," Bobby added, his eyes shining. "And his gun. He had that gun aimed right at the man who took me."

"I'm sure the sheriff is very careful with his gun," Barbara said. "Guns are not toys."

Bobby nodded. "And he let me run the siren on the way home."

Barbara smiled. It was good to have her children back.

Chapter Nineteen

Several days later, the sheriff stood at his closet door
and wondered what to wear. He was worse than some
debutante at her first ball. He'd pulled his suit out
and it was lying on his bed. It didn't seem the right
thing to wear for what he had in mind. He'd already
passed on wearing his uniform.

He had an old T-shirt from a Miles City bowling
league he'd joined once. He supposed that made him
look like a man who had interests, but he'd only
bowled a few games before he realized he didn't
really like rolling a ball down a lane.

He had a few white cotton shirts that he wore with
his suit, but they seemed a little boring when all was
said and done.

That left the denim shirt and jeans. He was wishing
now he'd bought the shirt with the pearl snaps instead
of the ordinary buttons. He hadn't realized until he

started to get dressed tonight that he had such an unexciting wardrobe. Oh, well, the denim would do, even with the buttons. It would be getting dark before long anyway.

It was Saturday night, and the sheriff was taking Barbara to dinner again. He was more nervous than he had any right to be when she'd already decided she only saw him as a friend. But, the night was clear and full of promise. It was warm enough that everyone knew spring was really here. And women sometimes changed their minds.

He'd seen Barbara every day this week, and each time she'd thanked him for what he'd done to bring her children back. The sheriff tried to tell her he'd only been doing his job. It hadn't even been difficult really. The tip on the antacid wrapper had led him to the Country Market, which had led him to the motel next door. The motel clerk had said the man in unit 314 had brought two children with him on this trip. All the sheriff had needed to do was go knock on the door.

The day after the children came home, the sheriff and Barbara had both sat with Bobby and Amanda while the sheriff asked questions for the report he needed to file. When the sheriff had mentioned his suspicions about the money she had, Barbara had willingly told him about selling her wedding rings. She'd even shown him the receipt the pawnshop had given her before telling him once again how very grateful she was.

"You don't need to keep thanking me," the sheriff had said for the third time that day. "It's my job to arrest kidnappers."

"It wasn't your job to let Amanda wear your hat on the way back," she'd said. "Or to tell Bobby what a brave boy he'd been."

"Well, they are brave kids," the sheriff protested. "I wouldn't lie to them."

"I know," Barbara said with another smile. "That's why I'm thanking you."

The sheriff had waited all week for the thank-you's to die down. He didn't want Barbara to feel so grateful to him that she stopped being herself.

The sheriff looked at himself in the mirror. The denim shirt did look a little plain, he thought, as he reached for the brass name tag that the department had issued him. This might dress it up a bit.

Before he left the trailer, the sheriff picked up a manila envelope that was on the bookcase by his door. He also picked up the long-stemmed red rose he'd bought earlier today in Miles City. The rose had one of those little tubes on the end of it and the clerk had told him the rose would stay fresh for hours with no other water. It's amazing what nature could do, the sheriff thought as he closed and locked his door with one hand.

As always, he paused on the steps of his trailer and his eyes strayed to that spot in the trees where he planned to build. Before long, the grass would be growing there. He might even plant a rosebush over there now so it'd be mature when he got around to building the log house.

Barbara sat down at the oak table that she had bought to replace the folding one. She'd bought four chairs to go with it as well. Sometimes she sat down at the table just for the sheer pleasure of running her hands over the wood top and feeling how sturdy it was. Mrs. Hargrove had given her four placemats for the table and Barbara kept one under the vase she'd bought and kept in the center of the table.

Spring had started to warm up Dry Creek. Barbara had seen a few stalks of grass in the past few days. Before long, there would be flowers around and she'd bought the vase so she'd be ready to pick some wildflowers.

Thoughts of spring had flooded Barbara's mind since Bobby and Amanda had been returned to her. She felt as though her heart was shooting up a few stalks of grass just like the ground in Dry Creek was. The ground had been frozen all winter, but now, when the sun was shining, it sent up a couple of stalks to see if the season was really changing.

Barbara knew that, for her, one of those stalks

was her hope that maybe she'd been wrong about God. She'd seen the concrete love and concern of the people in the church here and she couldn't help but wonder if what they believed was true. How else could these people care so much about each other?

Barbara looked at the clock. Mrs. Hargrove had invited Bobby and Amanda to spend the night at her house so Barbara had the rare luxury of getting dressed without needing to worry about the children. She still had twenty minutes before Carl was due to pick her up for dinner.

Maybe she needed to do something different with her hair, she thought as she stood up. Earlier she'd thought that she should just leave it down. But maybe it would be better to put it up in a twist. And she needed to change her earrings, too. She'd gone from silver dangles to gold posts.

By the time she heard a knock at the outer door, Barbara was wearing black bead earrings and her hair was pulled back with a black clip.

The sheriff noticed right away that Barbara had done something different with her hair. "It looks sophisticated."

Barbara smiled. "Thanks."

The sheriff fretted all the time he and Barbara walked over to the restaurant. He should have worn the suit. Barbara looked too well-dressed for his denim. Women were sensitive to things like that. If he wasn't so worried about his clothes, he would have noticed the activity in the café sooner.

"Oh," Barbara said when the sheriff opened the door to the café for her.

The sheriff grimaced. He hadn't exactly expected the solitude they'd been granted on their last date, but he hadn't expected a convention either. It felt as though every person in Dry Creek was eating in the café tonight.

"It's busy," Barbara said.

The sheriff nodded. Neither one of them had even stepped inside the café yet. "I suppose we should close the door."

The conversation from the tables was a loud rumble. Linda was writing on a small tablet as someone called out an order for chili fries.

"Come on in," the pastor called out from the table where he sat with his wife, Glory, and their twin boys. They were all eating platters of hamburgers and fries.

Once the pastor had greeted the two newcomers, no one else bothered.

The sheriff and Barbara stepped inside and closed the door.

"Is the café running a special?" Barbara asked.

"They always have a Saturday-night special," the sheriff muttered. "I thought it was to encourage couples to date a little."

One of the pastor's twins threw a plastic catsup bottle to a boy at the next table. Somebody somewhere turned up the music. It was a children's song.

"Maybe it's family night," Barbara said.

The sheriff looked around. There wasn't even a free table for them to sit at. He felt like a fool carrying this rose in his hand. Were people so blind they didn't see that here was a couple on a date?

"You're welcome to sit here," Jacob called out from one side of the room. "I can fit you in."

Jacob was sitting at a small table like the one the sheriff and Barbara had had the last time they'd had dinner here.

"Thanks, but we'll wait for a table," the sheriff said. The sheriff decided maybe people hadn't seen the rose. He held it up a little higher. He figured he could live with the teasing he'd take tomorrow morning in church if it would get him a little privacy tonight.

"Suit yourself," Jacob said. He didn't even look at the rose. "But there's plenty of room."

"You're welcome over here," Pete Denning called from his table.

The sheriff couldn't help but notice that Pete had a big table all to himself right next to the kitchen. It looked as if Linda had draped her apron over the other chair at the table.

"Ah, come on." Pete waved them over. "I've got

an idea for that campaign slogan you've been working on."

"We have a slogan already," Barbara said.

"We do?" the sheriff whispered. They hadn't worked on the campaign any more. He thought maybe Barbara had forgotten about it. He knew he had.

"Yes," Barbara nodded. "It's Vote for Carl Wall for Sheriff." She turned to the sheriff. "We'll put *Carl Wall* in big letters. These people need to learn your name and start using it."

The sheriff grinned. He couldn't argue with that.

The sheriff figured no one was ever going to notice the rose he held.

"It's a nice night," the sheriff whispered to Barbara. "And there are stars out. We could just get some hamburgers to go and sit outside."

Barbara nodded. "At least it will be quiet enough to talk."

Barbara couldn't help but notice that even though she'd said she wanted it to be quiet enough for talking, she couldn't think of anything to say once she and Carl were outside with their bag of burgers and fries. They were sitting at the top of the church steps and there was quiet all around them. The church had a small light outside its double doors, and someone had turned it on tonight. The light was small enough that they could still look up and see the stars.

Carl had brought a rug out of his trunk that he said he used if he needed to slide under someone's car to repair it.

"It's clean," he assured her as he spread it on the landing at the top of the steps. "I have another one I use if the job is going to involve grease."

Barbara nodded. "You're too kind."

Carl had asked for an extra plastic cup and he'd set the rose up in the center of a napkin that he'd spread for them like a tablecloth. The rose was the perfect touch. Barbara wondered what he had in the envelope he carried.

They ate in silence.

"The hamburgers are good," Barbara finally said.

"It's the cheese," Carl agreed.

There was more silence.

"I haven't thanked you yet for dinner," Barbara said. "It's delicious."

"You don't need to thank me," Carl said with a grimace. "I wanted to talk to you."

"About the campaign?"

"No." Carl frowned. "Actually, the only reason I agreed to a campaign anyway was to spend time with you."

"Oh."

Carl nodded. "I would have campaigned for my competition if I had to in order to spend time with you."

"Oh."

"Of course, I don't have any competition." Carl was quiet for a moment. "In the campaign, that is."

"Well, it's a good thing," Barbara said with a smile. "You'd lose for sure if people saw you campaigning for someone else."

"You're not upset?"

"No, I think I'm flattered."

Carl was quiet for another minute. "There are some things about me you don't know."

"Do you want to tell me?"

Carl nodded. "I was raised in foster homes. A whole bunch of them. One after another. I don't think I'm very good at family stuff. Don't know how it's done."

Barbara smiled. "There are days when I'm not sure I know either. But, if you're asking my opinion, I have to say that you've been wonderful with both Amanda and Bobby. Bobby practically idolizes you."

"He's grateful," Carl said. "He was scared, and I'm the one who got him out of it."

Barbara shrugged. "That's most of what parenting is."

Carl was silent for a moment as he took another

bite of his hamburger. "Have you heard any more about old man Gossett renting you his place?"

"Mrs. Hargrove says his nephew is real sick, and Mr. Gossett is thinking the nephew and his family might want to move here. Good air for the children and all that."

"I'm sorry it's not for rent."

Barbara nodded. "I expect they'll wonder why that fence is painted so nice and white when the house is all weathered."

Carl grunted. "Never heard of anyone complaining about a free paint job."

Barbara sighed. "I think it was the fence I liked so much about the place."

"I have a fence." Carl's face paled. "I mean, I don't have a house like you'd want, but I have a fence."

Barbara got very still.

Carl was silent for a minute. "I told you I wasn't very good at this kind of thing. I had it all thought out in my mind, and now I got ahead of myself with the fence so I may as well just spit it out."

Carl swallowed hard. "I live in a trailer, so it's nothing fancy. It suits me fine, but I know it's no house. The thing is, though, that I've got plans all drawn up for a log house that could be built on my place. I brought the plans to show you later. The house would be right back in the trees and it'd be no trouble at all to put a fence around it. I know you're real set on a good house."

"I—" Barbara started.

Carl took a quick breath and kept going. "Let me finish. I know you don't see us as being anything more than friends. But things can change."

"I—" Barbara began again.

"I'm not asking anything right now, so if that's what you're thinking, you can rest easy," Carl said. "I figure you need a full year of grieving before you're over your ex-husband, and I got time to wait."

"I—" Barbara began again and was surprised when he let her keep talking. "Well, I—let me see. First, I know that a house is just a house. It is the people who make the home. Second, yes, things can change. And, third, I'm grieving for my lost dreams, but not my ex-husband. The man doesn't even care about our children."

"So things can change?" the sheriff asked.

Barbara couldn't help but notice that the sheriff's face wasn't pale anymore. In fact, it was looking, well, certainly more healthy than before. "Slowly, things can change slowly."

"We've got time," Carl said. His face was beaming now. "I figure we're due to drive into Miles City for dinner next time."

"And miss out on this?"

Carl slid a little closer to her. "Well, we can see the stars from here."

Barbara slid a little closer to him as well. She remembered that there was more than one way to see stars when Carl was around.

Maybe things wouldn't need to go all that slowly, she thought, as Carl bent to kiss her. No, she thought, they might not need to go slowly at all.

Epilogue

The wedding was to be in the fall. Barbara and Carl had both gone through premarital counseling with the pastor of the Dry Creek Church and decided to add a confession of faith to their wedding vows.

They were working on the wording of their confession of faith with Mrs. Hargrove and her Sunday-school class. The children were excited that they could play a part and, under Mrs. Hargrove's guidance, were coming up with some good suggestions. The children's favorite suggestion was to work in the story of Daniel in the lion's den.

"You could say that you realize it is important to trust God when the beasts of life are coming at you," Mrs. Hargrove suggested.

"Lions—they need to say lions," Bobby said. "When the lions are coming at them."

Barbara and Carl were regular helpers in Mrs.

Hargrove's class now, so they were there for the discussion.

"We could say lions," Carl said.

It was going to be a unique wedding anyway. The bride had decided she wanted to pour the coffee for her reception. She'd ordered a cream-colored gown that was frothy with lace and had the added value of having a veil that was short enough so that it wouldn't get in the way when she poured that coffee.

The bride was debating sending into Billings for a rental silver urn for the coffee just so the ceremony would have a little extra polish.

Then, a few weeks before the wedding, the bride noticed that a shy young woman had just moved into town. The woman sat in the back pew of the Dry Creek Church and never stayed long to talk with anyone. The Sunday before the wedding, the bride asked the woman if she'd be willing to pour coffee for her wedding reception.

"You don't know what this means to me," the young woman said. She was wearing a modest cotton dress that had seen many washings. Her shoes were a little scuffed, as if they had been polished and re-polished until the leather refused to take any more black polish.

The bride just smiled. "I'm glad you will enjoy it. Welcome to Dry Creek."

The groom was holding the bride's hand and, when the young woman left, he whispered to his wife-to-be. "That was generous of you."

The bride had told him about the coffee. "Mrs. Hargrove already asked me to pour coffee on election day."

"Won't that prejudice people to vote for me?"

The bride grinned. "I hope so. We never did get around to making that sign."

"Who needs a sign when I have you?" the sheriff said as he bent down to give the bride a quick kiss.

There were half a dozen people still in the church and no one even looked up at the kiss. The sight of Carl kissing Barbara didn't even make a good story any longer. It happened all the time.

* * * * *

Dear Reader,

I wish for all of you many days of pouring coffee and sharing fellowship at your church. Our lives are meant to be lived in community and, as often as not, that means taking time to serve each other.

I thoroughly enjoy writing about the church in Dry Creek, primarily because it is a focal point of the community. It is the place where troubles and joys are shared with the whole town.

I'd like to give a nod of thanks to people like Mrs. Hargrove who help such local communities run. I've known many women—and men—like her in the churches I have attended. You'll usually find such people in the kitchens or in the Sunday school rooms or serving communion on certain Sundays. Without them, our shared communities wouldn't be nearly as rich as they are.

Sincerely,

Janet Tronstad

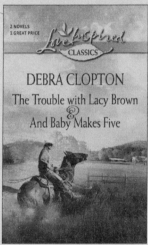

REQUEST YOUR FREE BOOKS!

2 FREE INSPIRATIONAL NOVELS
PLUS 2
FREE
MYSTERY GIFTS

YES! Please send me 2 FREE Love Inspired® novels and my 2 FREE mystery gifts (gifts are worth about $10). After receiving them, if I don't wish to receive any more books, I can return the shipping statement marked "cancel." If I don't cancel, I will receive 6 brand-new novels every month and be billed just $4.24 per book in the U.S. or $4.74 per book in Canada. That's a saving of over 20% off the cover price. it's quite a bargain! Shipping and handling is just 50¢ per book.* I understand that accepting the 2 free books and gifts places me under no obligation to buy anything. I can always return a shipment and cancel at any time. Even if I never buy another book, the two free books and gifts are mine to keep forever.

105/305 IDN E7PP

Name   (PLEASE PRINT)

Address   Apt. #

City   State/Prov.   Zip/Postal Code

Signature (if under 18, a parent or guardian must sign)

Mail to Steeple Hill Reader Service:
IN U.S.A.: P.O. Box 1867, Buffalo, NY 14240-1867
IN CANADA: P.O. Box 609, Fort Erie, Ontario L2A 5X3

Not valid for current subscribers to Love Inspired books.

Want to try two free books from another series?
Call 1-800-873-8635 or visit www.morefreebooks.com.

* Terms and prices subject to change without notice. Prices do not include applicable taxes. N.Y. residents add applicable sales tax. Canadian residents will be charged applicable provincial taxes and GST. Offer not valid in Quebec. This offer is limited to one order per household. All orders subject to approval. Credit or debit balances in a customer's account(s) may be offset by any other outstanding balance owed by or to the customer. Please allow 4 to 6 weeks for delivery. Offer available while quantities last.

Your Privacy: Steeple Hill Books is committed to protecting your privacy. Our Privacy Policy is available online at www.SteepleHill.com or upon request from the Reader Service. From time to time we make our lists of customers available to reputable third parties who may have a product or service of interest to you. If you would prefer we not share your name and address, please check here. ☐

Help us get it right—We strive for accurate, respectful and relevant communications. To clarify or modify your communication preferences, visit us at www.ReaderService.com/consumerschoice.

LIREG10R

*When Texas Ranger Benjamin Fritz arrives at his captain's
house after receiving an urgent message, he finds him
murdered and the man's daughter in shock.*

*Read on for a sneak peek at DAUGHTER OF TEXAS
by Terri Reed, the first book in the exciting new
TEXAS RANGER JUSTICE series, available
January 2011 from Love Inspired Suspense.*

Corinna's dark hair had loosened from her normally severe
bun. And her dark eyes were glassy as she stared off into
space. Taking her shoulders in his hands, Ben pulled her to
her feet. She didn't resist. He figured shock was setting in.

When she turned to face him, his heart contracted pain-
fully in his chest. "You're hurt!"

She didn't seem to hear him.

Blood seeped from a scrape on her right upper biceps.
He inspected the wound. Looked as if a bullet had grazed
her. Whoever had killed her father had tried to kill her. With
aching ferocity, rage roared through Ben. The heat of the
bullet cauterized the flesh. It would probably heal quickly
enough.

But Ben had a feeling that her heart wouldn't heal anytime soon. She'd adored her father. That had been appar-
ent from the moment Ben set foot in the Pike world. She'd
barely tolerated Ben from the get-go, with her icy stares
and brusque manner, making it clear she thought him not
good enough to be in her world. But when it came to her
father...

Greg had known that if anything happened to him, she'd
need help coping with the loss.

*Ben, I need you to promise me if anything ever happens
to me, you'll watch out for Corinna. She'll need an anchor.*

I fear she's too fragile to suffer another death.

Of course Ben had promised. Though he'd refused to even allow the thought to form that any harm would befall his mentor and friend. He'd wanted to believe Greg was indestructible. But he wasn't. None of them were.

The Rangers were human and very mortal, performing a risky job that put their lives on the line every day.

Never before had Ben been so acutely aware of that fact.

Now his captain was gone. It was up to him not only to bring Greg's murderer to justice, but to protect and help Corinna Pike.

*For more of this story, look for DAUGHTER OF TEXAS
by Terri Reed, available in January 2011
from Love Inspired Suspense.*

Love Inspired

Bestselling author

JILLIAN HART

brings readers another heartwarming story
from

the
GRANGER
FAMILY
RANCH

To fulfill a sick boy's wish, rodeo star Tucker Granger surprises
little Owen in the hospital. And no one is more surprised than
single mother Sierra Baker. But somehow Tucker ropes her heart
and fills it with hope. Hope that this country girl and her son
can lasso the roaming bronc rider into their family forever.

Look for

His Country Girl

*Available January
wherever books are sold.*

www.SteepleHill.com

Steeple
Hill®

LI87643